Three thousand  orate patterns on the ski rron, granting them acces orld.

Twelve dragonm with the powers granted by the dragonmarks, their chosen few bearers have wrought many wonders in the world, forging a society like none ever seen before.

But tales survive of a thirteenth dragonmark, lost for thousands of years—the feared Mark of Death. For generations, it has been lost, its power finally gone from the world. . . .

Until now.

THE LOST MARK

Book One
MARKED FOR DEATH

Book Two
THE ROAD TO DEATH
January 2006

Book Three
THE QUEEN OF DEATH
December 2006

MARKED FOR DEATH

THE LOST MARK BOOK 1

MATT FORBECK

MARKED FOR DEATH

The Lost Mark · Book One

Cover art by Adam Rex
Map by Dennis Kauth
First Printing: March 2005
Library of Congress Catalog Card Number: 2004114220

9 8 7 6 5 4 3 2 1

US ISBN: 0-7869-3610-X
ISBN-13: 978-0-7869-3610-6
620-17676-001-EN

U.S., CANADA,
ASIA, PACIFIC, & LATIN AMERICA
Wizards of the Coast, Inc.
P.O. Box 7071702
Renton, WA 98057-0707
+1-800-324-6496

EUROPEAN HEADQUARTERS
Wizards of the Coast, Belgium
T Hofveld 6d
Groot-Bijgaarden
Belgium
+322 467 3360

Visit our web site at www.wizards.com

FOR MY HERO, ANN.

Special thanks to Mark Sehestedt, Peter Archer,
Christopher Perkins, and Keith Baker

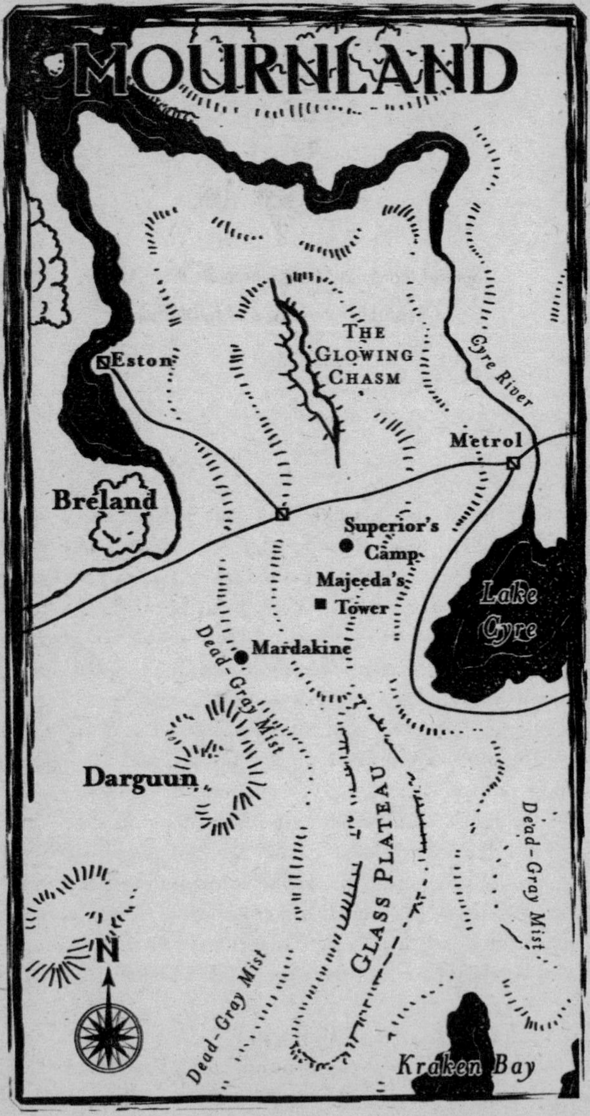
MOURNLAND
The Glowing Chasm
Eston
Cyre River
Metrol
Breland
Superior's Camp
Majeeda's Tower
Lake Cyre
Mardakine
Dead-Gray Mist
Darguun
Glass Plateau
Dead-Gray Mist
N
Dead-Gray Mist
Kraken Bay

CHAPTER

1

Boss!"

Kandler snapped awake and grabbed the hand on his shoulder. Head still half in his dreams, he looked up. Bright wolf-yellow eyes set wide across a dark face stared back at him over a large, flat nose. Thick black fur clung to the figure's forearms and lower legs, and a coarse mane fell across his shoulders. Long sideburns nearly covered his pointed ears, and sharp teeth bared at Kandler's sudden movement.

"Damn it, Burch!" Kandler said. "Don't do that."

"We got a body on the east ridge," Burch said. He pulled his hand from Kandler's grasp and stepped back into a crouch.

Late as it was—or was it early? Kandler wondered—Burch was fully dressed. He wore a short tunic of rough, steely links over a wool shirt and leggings the color of long-dead coals. A long knife rode his hip, and a crossbow lay slung across his back, next to a full quiver. His feet were bare, exposing the dark, clawlike nails on his toes, which matched those on his thin fingers.

"You sleep too deep," Burch said.

"That's why I keep you around." Kandler groaned as he swept a hand through his brown, wavy hair. He kept it cropped

1

short, not because of the few strands of gray that were starting to show but out of pragmatism. Sitting up, he felt far older than his thirty-five years. The ghosts of his old war wounds tugged at his back. He rubbed his eyes with a hilt-callused hand. "What time is it?" he asked.

"Two hours past midnight. Sun-up in three. Temmah's up there with the body, waiting."

Kandler sighed. "Esprë still sleeping?"

Burch nodded, the light from the everbright lantern in his hand glinting in his wide, yellow eyes. "No nightmares tonight. Norra's my next stop."

"Tell her it's an emergency."

Burch put the lantern on the windowsill next to Kandler's bed and loped out of the room. He closed the front door to the little house behind him as he left.

By the time Burch came back with Norra, Kandler was dressed in clean clothes, standing in his house's main room and buckling on his long sword. It was curved and sharp as a sliver of the moon, but the scabbard was simple worn leather.

Burch didn't knock before leading the girl inside. Still dressed in her nightclothes, Norra stifled a yawn as she entered and pulled her dark hair back from her pale face, exposing her soft, brown eyes.

"What's the matter?" Norra whispered with a frown, worry furrowing her brow. "Is someone else missing?"

Kandler picked up the lantern from his dining table and looked down at the girl. "That's what I need to find out. Can you stay with Esprë?"

"Of course," Norra said. "I'll just crawl into bed next to her. She won't miss you till morning."

Kandler nodded his thanks, grabbed his cloak from its hook beside the door, then stepped out into the night, Burch dogging his heels. Using the hand signals they'd employed together during the Last War, Kandler motioned for the shifter to lead the way.

Burch sprang ahead, ranging back and forth across the path

toward the eastern rim of the deep crater in which the little town of Mardakine lay. He moved with an easy gait and grace that betrayed his race's heritage. Although dozens of generations or more separated the shifters from the werebeasts from which they descended, the animal in them was impossible to deny.

The night sky, starkly clear, formed an unbroken dome from one towering wall of the crater to the other. Stars twinkled overhead—distant, silent, and cold—and among them, watching like a court of indifferent judges, nine of the moons sat in their places in the night sky. Stars and moons were so bright that the Rings of Siberys seemed no more than a glow dusting the southern sky.

Kandler wrapped his cloak about him to ward off the chill. Mardakine slept undisturbed but for the walking pair. The air smelled faintly of the woodsmoke escaping from the chimneys of the houses that Kandler and Burch passed as they trudged along the lane toward the crater's eastern rim. Burning wood reminded Kandler of one of the many stenches of the battlefield—the cooking pit, the campfire, the sentries' torch, or the funeral pyre. Best not to think of that now.

"Who found it?" Kandler asked as they left the easternmost of the houses behind.

"Pradak and Rissa."

"Mardak's son?"

"And Rislinto's daughter."

"The rumors were true, I see."

"Two frightened youngsters," Burch said, "came out to watch the sky and kiss. Found a body instead."

"Who is it?" Kandler had put off the question long enough.

At first Burch remained silent, but after a few dozen paces he said, "Not far now."

The land grew steeper as the pair moved forward. Burch hung closer to the ground and switched naturally from walking on two feet to climbing on all fours. Kandler followed his friend's example a few minutes later when crater floor became a leaning wall. There was a switchback trail a few hundred yards to the south, but it would be slower and wouldn't let out at the right place.

"Where are Pradak and Rissa?"

"Temmah sent them home. They looked too scared to ever kiss again."

Kandler laughed. "You underestimate two sixteen-year-olds."

"Maybe." Burch shrugged.

As they reached the crest of the crater's ridge, Kandler looked beyond and grimaced. A wall of menacing gray wisps reached thick, swirling tendrils out over the ridge in a perpetual attempt to swallow the crater whole, town and all. This was the edge of the Mournland, a place where not even death rested peacefully. The wall of dead-gray mist towered over Kandler and Burch as they approached it. It stood more than a mile high and stretched north as far as the eye could see. To the south, it disappeared around the eastern edge of distant Point Mountain, the last of the Seawall Mountain chain that ran from the Thunder Sea at the southern shore of the continent of Khorvaire, right up to within a hard day's ride of Mardakine. Craning his neck, Kandler could see the first hint of dawn stabbing its way over the Mournland's permanent shroud.

"You wanna wait for daylight?" Burch asked, his broad nose twitching as he sniffed at the air. His lip curled into a hesitant snarl.

"It's only one body, right?" Kandler paused a moment. "Right?"

"One body." Burch nodded. "In many places."

Kandler breathed a soft curse. "That's something new. Where's the head?"

Burch pointed off to his left and right.

Kandler swallowed. "Show me the face—or the biggest part of it."

Burch bounced forward along the crater's crest, his shorter

legs moving fast to keep ahead of Kandler's pace. When he reached a scrappy bush squatting just on the crater's inside edge, he stopped and pointed to something lying beneath it.

Kandler knelt and shone the lantern on the thing. A pair of dead eyes stared back at him, the blue orbs frozen in their final moment of terror. The back of the head was missing, but the face was mostly intact. The skin was tanned and wrinkled. A small scar ran across the left eyebrow. Smile lines still stretched at the corners of the mouth.

"Shawda," Kandler said. He closed her eyes, wincing at their cold stiffness. After a long moment, he turned to Burch. "Where's Temmah?"

"With her chest. Pradak and Rissa found that part first." Burch pointed further north along the ridge, and Kandler motioned for him to take the lead once again.

Kandler heard the dwarf before he saw him. As Kandler and Burch approached, they found the stout, squat Temmah sitting on a flat-topped rock and weeping into wadded fistfuls of his long, blond beard. Kandler smelled fresh vomit, along with scent of meat. He came up behind Temmah and put a hand on his shoulder. The dwarf stood and looked up at Kandler and Burch with his red-rimmed, crystal-blue eyes.

"We finally found her," the dwarf said, his voice thick with grief.

"Good work," Kandler said, patting Temmah on the back.

"She's dead, Kandler. Dead."

"I know."

Temmah used the end of his beard to dry his face. He shook his head as his wide cheeks flushed with shame. "I saw plenty of death in the War."

"That was in battle."

Temmah nodded. "This . . . this is nothing like that." He steeled himself as he wiped his eyes again, then he pointed to a spot a dozen yards away. "The young ones found her over there," he said. "Some of her anyhow."

Kandler leaned over and whispered to Temmah, "If I

wasn't the town's justicar, I wouldn't be here either, my friend. It's a matter of duty."

Temmah grimaced. "Duty," he said. The word wrapped oddly around his tongue, but he held on to it tight.

Kandler patted Temmah on the back again and then walked over to the spot, Burch right behind him. Temmah stayed behind and sat back down on the rock to collect himself.

The rising sun turned the morning sky as gray as the mists of the Mournland towering over them. Almost it seemed the entire world could be a part of the Mournland and the two friends would be condemned to wander through its endless mists forever. Kandler shuddered and looked down.

A large portion of a female human's torso lay on the ground before him. It was on its front, still wrapped in what was left of a bloodstained blouse and a sliced-up cloak. Kandler motioned for Burch to turn it over.

The chest had been split open like an overripe melon. The contents were still there, but as the torso turned over, they spilled out. They were as gray as the dawn's light.

Kandler heard Temmah coming up behind him. "Some animal just tore her apart," the dwarf said. As he did, he shivered and looked over his shoulder at the swirling mists.

"I don't think so," Kandler said as he knelt down over the body. He pointed at the severed neck. "The cut is too clean. This was done with a blade."

Burch crouched down across from Kandler, his knees spread wide as he stared at the body. "What are you saying, boss? None of the other bodies had a mark on them."

Kandler hunched down to examine the torso closer. "This cut is spotless. The others are too. Blades that sharp don't wander around by themselves.

"A Darguul raiding party maybe?"

"Goblins don't have anything like this. Orcs neither."

"Think someone in Mardakine did it?"

Kandler rubbed the day's growth on his chin. "I doubt it. There's only one blade in town that could make such a cut"—he gripped the pommel of the sword hanging from his hip—"and I'm wearing it."

"Maybe something out of the Mournland?" Burch said.

Kandler felt the ground under the torso. "Probably. It's a long way to another town from here."

"Uh, Kandler?" Temmah cleared his throat and looked sidelong at Burch. "Could it have been a warforged? Rumors say they've been rallying around this so-called 'Lord of Blades.' Perhaps this is their work."

Kandler shook his head. "I suppose it could be, but the warforged don't tear a body to pieces like this. It's something else. Something different."

He stood up and looked around. The cloudless expanse above and to the west filled with a hint of blue. It was going to be a warm day.

"How far apart is she spread?" Kandler asked.

"I . . . um, I haven't found all of her yet," Temmah said, "but there's at least a fifty-yard split between her head and her . . . well, I found a thigh over there."

"Have you found any blood?"

Temmah paused. "Now that you mention it, no. I mean, I hadn't thought about it. You would think there would be plenty of blood from someone killed like that."

Kandler nodded. "She wasn't killed here. She was dead before she got here."

"Why?" asked Burch.

Kandler stared into the shifter's wide, yellow eyes. "That I don't know," he said, "but I aim to find out."

CHAPTER

2

Kandler, Burch, and Temmah set to gathering Shawda's remains. They picked through the scattered ground cover, hunting for the dull flash of a piece of gray skin against the crater's darker floor. Whenever one found a piece, he alerted the others and then reverently carried the part back to them.

Kandler had taken off his cloak to use as a litter, and the trio laid the pieces gingerly atop the thick wool, reassembling Shawda like a macabre puzzle made of flesh. As they worked, the growing light made the job easier. Soon, they had collected most of the body.

After they found all they could, Kandler carefully wrapped the bits up in his cloak and led the others down from the crater's rim and back into Mardakine. By this time, the sun had cleared the mist and was climbing into the sky, burning the dew from the grayish-green grass that grew in patches all around the town but nowhere else in the crater.

As the three walked into town, Temmah cleared his throat, his voice still hoarse from his tears. "Kandler?"

"Yes?"

"Who will tell her?"

Just then, they turned a corner in the lane. The town's

main square lay directly ahead of them. A crowd already milled about there. A shout went up as someone saw the three approaching.

"Me," Kandler said.

He heard the dwarf sigh with relief, but the sound caught in Temmah's throat as he saw the people gathered before them.

"How could they already know?" Temmah asked.

"Pradak and Rissa," Burch said as he bounded along at Kandler's side. "They've been back here for hours."

The trio continued on in silence. Kandler saw faces peeking out of windows and open doors, the people too frightened to ask what he cradled in his arms and too curious to look away. As he walked on, some of the watchers left their houses and fell into step behind him. By the time he reached the main square, the people of Mardakine surrounded him.

Pradak and Rissa and their parents stood in the center of the square, the rest of the town arranged around them. Pradak's father Mardak, a tall, hard man with a face like a hawk, stepped forward as Kandler neared. "Justicar, is what my son tells me true?" he asked.

Kandler raised the bundle in his arms just a hair. It seemed heavier than before. "We have a body."

The rest of the color drained from Mardak's already pallid face as he looked down at the too-small bundle. "Who?" he asked.

Kandler looked around at the crowd. "I'd rather not say here."

"Justicar," Mardak said, a tremble in his voice, "we have lost a dozen souls in the past two weeks. These good people have waited long enough for an answer. As founder of this town I order you to give it to them."

Kandler stared back at Mardak, as impassive as the shifter beside him. Temmah whimpered softly, once, and then fell silent.

"Now," Mardak said.

"Don't you think—"

9

"Now!"

"It's Shawda!" Temmah blurted. He began to weep again and buried his face in his beard.

A wail erupted from the rear of the crowd. The people parted, revealing Norra, who had collapsed to her knees, her face buried in her hands. Kandler's stepdaughter Esprë, a slim girl with long, blonde hair and pointed ears, stepped forward and wrapped her arms around Norra to comfort her.

Kandler nearly dropped his bundle to run over and comfort the girls. Instead, he looked to Burch. The shifter, barely taller than Esprë, bounded over and took the girl's hand. Others leaped to Norra's aid. Nearly mad with despair, she thrashed and hurled herself about, and her wails followed Kandler all the way to the Mardak's house.

"Had I known . . ." Mardak said to Kandler, then trailed off. He turned away from the bundle in Kandler's hands to address the crowd. His voice shook as he spoke.

"I will hold conference with Justicar Kandler," Mardak said. "I hope to have a plan before nightfall. Until then, go back to your lives."

"For as long as you can," Kandler heard Temmah murmur.

The crowd dispersed, and the people walked away with their heads held low. Many of them wept. Those holding Norra carried her to her home.

Burch signaled that he would take Esprë home and wait with her. Kandler nodded his approval.

"Shall we?" Mardak asked.

Kandler led the way, Shawda's remains still wrapped tightly in his cloak. Mardak followed close on his heels, with Rislinto—a burly man with a bushy, red beard and a blacksmith's arms—right behind. Temmah lagged along at the end, rubbing his eyes as he trotted to keep up.

When they arrived at Mardak's house, Kandler waited for Mardak to open the door. "You wish to bring the body into my house?" the older man asked, his hand on the door's handle.

"You'd rather I unwrap her out here?"

Mardak hesitated a moment more, then opened the door.

Inside, Kandler strode over to the dining room table and lay his burden down. He unwrapped the cloak and arranged the pieces of Shawda's body on the table.

"Do you have to do this here?" Mardak asked, wrinkling his nose.

"Your children are grown," Kandler replied. "Your boy has already seen her—at least one part—and my table isn't nearly big enough."

"But my wife—"

"Doesn't have a problem with it," a feminine voice from the other room finished. "We must do everything we can to help catch the villain behind this." The men looked at each other for a moment before Priscinta continued. "But I hope you'll forgive me if I don't bother to come in for a look."

Mardak smiled softly. Temmah's eyes stopped tearing.

Kandler waited for a moment, then spoke. "Shawda was the third of our people to go missing. Her husband reported her gone eight days ago. She was there next to him when he lay down that night. The next morning she was gone."

"You questioned him thoroughly?" Mardak asked.

Kandler ignored the implication that he didn't know his job. He knew Mardak was looking for someone to blame for all this, and he was determined not to get into another row about it. "She'd been having trouble sleeping. She was disturbed by the other two people missing at that point. It's possible she went out for a walk, despite the warnings."

"How long has she been dead?" Rislinto asked.

"It's impossible to tell. If she was killed in the Mournland . . . well, bodies don't decay in there."

"But we're not in the Mournland," Mardak said. "How do you know she was killed there?"

"I don't."

"What *do* you know, justicar?"

"Let's not start this again, lads," Rislinto said. "We've more important matters to consider."

Kandler nodded. After a moment, Mardak shrugged and looked away.

Kandler continued, "Given the number of insects I found under Shawda's body parts, I'd guess she's been lying along the ridge for less than a day."

Kandler reached over and brushed the hair off the dead woman's face. Although she looked peaceful now, he could hear her soul crying out to him for justice. "There wasn't any blood there. She was probably killed someplace else and dumped along the ridge. Whether she was killed yesterday or days ago, I don't know."

"That's not much help," said Mardak.

"What does this mean for the others?" Rislinto asked, interrupting Mardak's attempt to get a rise out of Kandler.

"They're dead for sure," Temmah said, his voice but a whisper. "All of them."

"Not for sure," Kandler said as he rewrapped Shawda's remains. "But I wouldn't expect them home soon."

"So what do we do?" Rislinto asked.

"The same," said Kandler. "We warn everyone to stay inside at night. We keep the round-the-clock watch on the perimeter of town. And while it's still daylight, we should start searching the rim." He turned to look down at Temmah.

The dwarf turned a pale shade of green but steeled himself to the task. "I'm on it," he said as he thrust his long-bearded jaw forward. "I'll draw off some of the extra guards, and we'll scour the east ridge from end to end."

"What else can we do?" asked Mardak, having mastered his frustration for the moment.

Kandler looked up at the rail of a man. "Tell people to stay indoors as much as possible. You two," he said, glancing at both of them, "you're lucky your children aren't missing too. What kind of fools go out near the mists at night?"

"They're teenagers," Rislinto said with half a grin. "There's no controlling them."

"If your daughter hadn't tempted my son—" Mardak began.

Kandler cut him off. "Don't finish that thought. Done is done. Give them both a stern warning and leave it at that. No use fighting old battles."

Rislinto shuffled uneasily.

Mardak lowered his head. "I apologize, old friend," he said. "That was beneath me."

"Then you think too highly of yourself," Rislinto said as he smiled and clapped Mardak on the back. The casual blow could have knocked the taller man over, but Mardak braced for it. Rislinto turned toward Kandler again. "I'll have a talk with my daughter."

"And I with my son," said Mardak.

"If they don't listen," said Rislinto, "I've a new set of chains in my shop to lock them in."

"Joke if you like," Kandler said, "but you've had worse ideas."

The room fell silent for a moment.

"What about yourself?" Rislinto asked. "What is your plan?"

Kandler hoisted up the bundle on the table once again and started for the door. "Someone," he said, "has to take care of our dead."

CHAPTER

3

Kandler bid the two men farewell and walked home. He avoided the main square, cutting between houses and through yards so people wouldn't see him and try to stop him. Luck was with him, and he was soon home. He set the bundle down on his front porch and washed at the pump before stepping inside.

Half in shadow, Esprë sat in a rough wooden chair at the shabby dining table in the dimly lit main room. The light poking in through the glassless windows was as pale as her porcelain skin, but her wavy, golden hair sparkled. Like torchlight on gold, Kandler thought. She was weeping, her face buried in her arms piled on the table's worn top.

As Kandler shut the door, Esprë looked up, her face puffy and red and her blue eyes shining with grief. She waited for him to step within arms' reach and then launched herself into his embrace. She wrapped herself around his chest, and he reached down to hold her and stroke her hair.

"Was it really Shawda?" she asked.

"Yes," Kandler whispered, and Esprë began sobbing once more. Kandler looked over at Burch, who sat silent and still in the darkest corner of the room, and nodded his thanks.

The shifter unfolded himself and padded forward to pat

Esprë on the back. "She's seen a lot of death. Too much."

"We all have," said Kandler. "It'll be all right," he whispered, although he didn't know how. He found tears welling in his own eyes, and he clamped down on them, willing them away. His stepdaughter needed him to be strong now, and he'd sworn long ago never to disappoint her in that way. He kissed her on the top of her head.

"No bad dreams last night?" Kandler asked Esprë. The girl shook her head against his chest. "Do you always remember them?"

Esprë nodded, then the tears overwhelmed her again, and she pressed her face against Kandler's shirt to weep.

Three sharp knocks rattled the front door.

Esprë jumped as if she'd been pinched.

"Open, Justicar!" boomed a deep voice. It was not a voice Kandler recognized. "Open I say! We must speak with you."

"Esprë," Kandler said. *"Leth! Leth!"*

The girl remembered her training, the hours of drills Kandler had forced her through over her protestations. Living so near the Mournland, one's life was always in peril, and surviving meant constant vigilance. Pushing away from Kandler, Esprë scrambled into the pantry, a shallow closet just off the main room, never uttering a word. She shut the thin door behind her on its oiled hinges, leaving it open only a crack, just enough for her to be able to see the front door.

Burch slinked back over into the dark corner near the fireplace. He unslung the crossbow from his back, cranked back its silent lever, and slipped a bolt into its temporary home. He signaled that he was ready, and Kandler opened the door.

Five people stood on Kandler's porch, each in finely polished chainmail. Long, crimson tabards covered them from shoulders to knees. A raging fire, stitched wholly in silver thread, shimmered on each chest, and a longsword in a gleaming, silver scabbard hung from each waist. They wore piety like robes of righteousness.

The man who knocked on the door stepped aside as Kandler

opened it, exposing the eldest of the visitors, who stood in the center of the porch. He stood an inch or two shorter than Kandler, but he was the tallest in the group. His years had not bowed his back, which was straight as a longsword's blade, but they had added depth to his clean-shaven face and grayed the receding hair that fell to his shoulders. He leaned on an arrow-straight staff of pale, polished birch, topped with a small magical flame that burned silver and cold.

"Hail and well met, my son," the silver-maned man said with a forced half-smile. "I am Sir Deothen and these are my traveling companions. We are servants of—"

"The Silver Flame," Kandler finished. As he did, he realized his hand was on the hilt of his sword. He left it there. "I've dealt with your people before."

The man's smile warmed at the recognition. "Then you already know of our holy calling to protect the good people of Eberron from the forces of evil."

Kandler said nothing but gazed out past the knights. At the edge of his ash-covered yard, five white horses stood tied to a hitching post. Each magnificent, snow-coated beast was fitted with a riding saddle and saddlebags that didn't seem as full as they must once have been. A crimson blanket edged with running embroidery of silver flames rested under each saddle.

"My friend," Deothen said, concern etched in his piercing blue eyes, "as one who lives in this desolate land, you must understand the desperate need for those such as we."

Kandler kept his other hand on the door as he spoke. "I understand what I need to. You're from Thrane."

Deothen frowned. "The deeds of the Last War are behind us, my son."

"Here we live with it every day."

Two of Deothen's fellow Knights glanced over their shoulders at the wall of mist that towered over the eastern horizon.

Kandler moved half a step back and considered slamming the door shut. He had more important things to do than coddle a bunch of knights.

"My son—" Deothen began.

"I'm not your son," Kandler said. "My father died in the war. Killed by Thranes."

The four other knights on the porch gasped that anyone would speak to their leader this way.

Deothen let his face soften. "You have my deepest sympathies, my . . . friend, if I might be so bold."

"That's bolder than I care for, but since you're knocking on my door, I already knew that about you."

"How do you prefer to be called?"

"I'm the law in Mardakine. The justicar."

"Justicar, then. We have come to petition for your assistance."

Kandler raised an eyebrow and moved half a step forward. "What do you want?" As he waited for the reply, he scanned the faces behind Deothen. They were all younger than their leader—some by many years. One youth was barely more than a boy, a thin lad with lanky blond hair and an upturned nose. His enthusiasm shone brightly against that of his more seasoned companions. He looked as if his sword would be too heavy for his arms.

The two other men seemed cut from the same mold, though slightly older. Although one was dark and the other blond, they wore their hair short and even, and they carried the seriousness of their position in their faces. Neither looked like they smiled much.

The last, the one hanging furthest in the back, was a beautiful young woman with sharp features. She had her long red hair tied back in a warrior's braid. Her wide mouth showed a determined set that matched the glint in her deep green eyes. Her gaze met Kandler's squarely before he turned back to listen to what Deothen was saying.

"Our Lady Tira Miron, the Voice of the Silver Flame, received a vision that a lost dragonmark has appeared in the Mournland. It is urgent that we find the person who bears this mark."

"Why?"

"If our foes—"

"Foes? Which foes?"

"The world is full of darkness, my s—er, Justicar. Should Karrnath gain control over this person, our fragile peace will be shattered. All of Khorvaire will could—"

"And if Thrane gets it instead, everything will be fine," Kandler said with a mirthless laugh. "You're standing in a crater left behind from the Last War. Left by Thrane."

"We did what had to be done!" the youngest knight shouted.

Deothen raised his hand with quiet authority, and the boy fell silent, his face burning red.

After a moment, Deothen spoke again. "Levritt is too young to remember much of the war. We cannot undo the past, but we can work to repair the damage done, whether purposefully or not. We ask you now to help us prevent a horror from transpiring. Is that not the greater good?"

"Good and evil are your domain. Mine's taking care of the people of this town."

"All we require is a guide into the Mournland. We were told you were the best in all of Mardakine."

Kandler shook his head. "I don't know who told you that, and I don't care. I knew Cyre once, but I'm not that familiar with her corpse. I can't help you."

"I can."

Kandler jumped at the sound of Burch's voice behind him. The shifter had slipped up behind him while Deothen had his attention.

"A shifter!" Levritt whispered.

Burch glanced at the boy as he shuffled around Kandler. Levritt averted his eyes and shuffled his feet.

"I know the Mournland," said Burch, stepping onto the porch. His yellow eyes blinked as he squinted in the light. "Better than anyone else around here. I could help."

Kandler reached out and put his hand on Burch's shoulder. "You know how dangerous the border's mists are," he said. "The land beyond them is even worse."

"That's why we need your aid," Deothen said, staring into

Burch's eyes as if into some deep, mystical mirror. He reached out to touch Burch's face, and the shifter stood impassive for the strangely tender gesture.

Kandler pulled Burch back like a child who'd stepped too close to the edge of a well. "Forget it," he said. "Neither of us is going anywhere." Turning to Burch, who had cocked his head at him, he muttered, "Quit looking at me like that." More loudly, he added, "We have enough on our hands here."

Deothen composed himself. "What could be more important than saving Khorvaire?" he asked. "Your people will not survive long if this lost mark falls into the hands of evil. What could be more important than that?"

"Than chasing off on a fool's quest into the deadliest lands because some prophet had a vision? How about a dozen people of Mardakine gone missing over the past two weeks—and one found dead this morning?"

Deothen frowned. "I am sorry for your loss," he said. "We knew not of your troubles here." He paused for a moment, arranging his thoughts. "Perhaps we can help each other. We would be glad to lend what aid we can."

Kandler shook his head. "We can manage fine on our own."

"We do not mean to insult you by trading for your services, justicar. We wish only to help. We expect nothing in return."

"Sounds good," Burch said.

Kandler glared at the shifter and then stared at the knights.

"Where can we start?" Deothen asked. "Our offer is given freely."

Kandler thought about it for a moment and then spoke. "You people have religion."

"Certainly," Deothen said, a relieved smile creeping across his lips.

"The dead woman's family worships the Sovereign Host." Deothen began to speak, but Kandler waved him down. "The Flame isn't the same, I know, but it'll be close enough."

"Do you not have a priest here who could comfort his flock?"

"He was the first to go missing."

Deothen offered a slight bow. "We would be honored to lend this woman's family what comfort we might. I understand you must burn bodies in the Mournland to ensure their spirits fly free. Before we meet with the family, we shall help construct a pyre."

"That would be a fine start."

"I assume the family has the remains."

Kandler shook his head. "Not yet. They won't want to see them before the burning."

Deothen raised his eyebrows. "Then where might these remains be?"

Kandler looked down at the bundle on the porch. "You're almost standing on them."

The younger knights gasped. Levritt stepped back off the porch to swallow some air and force down the bile rising in his throat.

Before the youth set foot on the ground, Deothen barked a series of orders. His knights set to work straight away, glad for something to keep their hands busy and their minds off of Shawda's death.

Deothen turned back to Kandler. "We will have a pyre constructed in the main square by afternoon. I suggest we conduct the cremation at least an hour before sundown."

"I'll spread the word."

The elder knight made a curt bow to Kandler, then left to join his fellows in their work.

❦

The knights labored hard throughout the day, ranging for miles about in a quest for enough wood, and by the time the sun was lowering in the west, they had completed the finest pyre Mardakine had ever seen. Kandler sent Burch to tell Mardak about the funeral plan, confident that Mardak's wife Priscinta would swiftly get the word to every person in town.

When the time for the ceremony came, Kandler and Burch walked Esprë to the main square. It seemed like the entire town was there. Shawda's family—including her husband Nortok and her daughter Norra—stood closest to the pyre. As soon as Esprë spied Norra, she ran over to her. Kandler started to stop her, but Burch stepped into his way, so he just watched.

Wet-faced and red-eyed, Norra held Esprë close, and they wept together.

Deothen gave them a moment before he lowered his head, extending his arms for those around him to do the same. Kandler looked straight ahead at the knight. The crowd fell silent.

"I am no priest," Deothen said as he raised his staff before him, its silver flame shining bright, even in the midday light, "although I feel the force of the divine in me, moving me, moving all of us. Today, I pray that this power—which my fellow knights and I know as the Silver Flame—shall move me to eloquence on behalf of our departed sister Shawda.

"I never had the privilege of meeting Shawda, but I know we had a connection. As people good and true, we shared a bond, just as she shared a bond with all of you. As a citizen of Mardakine, as a former daughter of Cyre, she was dedicated to standing up against the darkness, to lighting a candle, to saying 'No more.'

"Although I never knew her, I am lessened by her loss. We all are. For when one who stands against the darkness falls, the darkness grows. Only by standing together can the light from each of our candles join together. That light is enough to force back even the darkest night. Only by working together can we hope to prevail.

"And so I mourn the loss of Shawda with you. And I pray that the Silver Flame gathers Shawda's light into her own, now and forevermore."

Kandler nodded with respect for the knight. Deothen had not been idle while the others built the pyre. He'd obviously talked with some of the people in town. From the kind looks with which Norra and her father favored the paladin, it was clear he'd offered them some comfort.

Deothen's open plea to lend the knights aid was transparent, nicely couched as it was. Kandler felt a sense of duty to the world tugging at him, but protecting the people of Mardakine—especially Esprë—had to be his top priority.

When Deothen looked up from his prayer, he captured Kandler with his sky blue eyes. Kandler looked away, and his eyes met those of Burch, who gazed up at him like an expectant puppy. Kandler looked away from him too.

Mardak, standing a dozen feet to Kandler's right, cleared his throat. Suddenly remembering his duty here, Kandler stepped toward the pyre. He unfolded the cloak in which Shawda's body was bundled, exposing her remains to the sunlight so that the flames that consumed her could carry the smoke from her body straight into the sky.

Kandler winced as he completed the grisly job, knowing that the villagers would be able to see how viciously Shawda had been murdered. As he stepped back from the pyre, he heard a shout from the other side of the pyre.

"By the Flame!" Levritt said as he drew his sword and charged the pyre. Before anyone could stop him, the young knight swung his sword down and cleaved the remains of Shawda's head into clean halves.

Norra screamed. The assembled crowd, several score strong, roared in shock and rage. Kandler had his own sword out, its curved tip at the knight's throat before the youth could pull his blade free from the pyre. All around him, scores of rusty knives, daggers, and swords rattled free of their scabbards as the villagers leapt to join Kandler in the defense of Shawda's corpse. Levritt looked around him wide-eyed, seeing the knights outnumbered at least forty-to-one.

"I think," Kandler said to the young knight as he pressed his blade hard up under the youth's chin, "you have some explaining to do."

CHAPTER

4

A broadsword flashed out. Steel clanged against steel. The young knight yelped as Kandler's blade was pushed aside, its tip nicking the boy in the throat as it was forced from under his chin.

Kandler stepped back and swung his sword back around to his left at the attacker. The same blade parried his riposte. He found himself staring into the flashing green eyes of the lady knight.

"You shall not threaten a Knight of the Silver Flame," the woman said, holding her sword at the ready.

"Stand down," Kandler said, leaning his blade against hers, testing her strength. "Your friend just desecrated a good woman's corpse."

"Hold!" Deothen thrust his steel gauntlet into where the two blades met. "Hold friends! Words shall serve us better than swords."

"I don't know Thranite customs, but we don't butcher our dead here," Kandler said, never taking his eyes from the woman's. She met his stare without flinching and held her ground, but he could feel that she stood ready to counter any move he might make.

"It's her!" Levritt said, as he scrambled to his feet, his hand at his throat. When he brought his fingers away to point at Shawda's corpse, they were smeared with blood. He blanched at the sight. "Am I slain?" he asked weakly.

"Not yet," said Kandler. He glanced at the young knight's neck. The cut was shallow and small. He guessed that the boy had nicked himself worse the first time he'd tried shaving. The crowd pressed forward, and several men reached out to grab the young knight. They held him fast and snatched his sword from his hand. Levritt cried out in fear.

The lady knight used her sword to slap down Kandler's blade, then brandished it before her as she spun about. The townspeople who had been hoping to grab her fell back with a communal protest.

"Sallah," Deothen said in a firm tone, "these people are not our foes."

Sallah glared at Kandler and stepped back from the crowd, though she kept her sword at the ready. "Levritt did no wrong," she said.

Kandler opened his mouth to protest, but Mardak stepped between the justicar and the lady knight. Looking over the elder knight at Sallah, Mardak said, "We might see matters otherwise."

A cry went up from Levritt, and Kandler turned to see the crowd starting to haul him away.

"Hold!" Kandler said.

The people carrying Levritt away stopped in their tracks. When they saw that the justicar was speaking to them, they put the young knight down, although they still held him tight.

"These people aren't going anywhere," Kandler said. "I'd like to hear their explanation if they have one."

Some of the people in the crowd grumbled at this, but those holding Levritt let him go. One sandy-haired man to the side kept hold of the knight's blade.

Kandler looked to Sallah and sheathed his own blade. She lowered her sword but did not put it away. She hefted the hilt in her hand as if daring the people in the crowd to rush her.

Kandler looked to the shaking young knight. Levritt gulped and stood as tall as he could, glancing nervously at the angry people who surrounded him. "So," Kandler said to him, "what is your story?"

"Allow me," Deothen said. He stepped forward and stood next to Levritt, putting a warm hand on the boy's shoulder to calm him. "He is in my charge."

All eyes turned to the eldest knight. All voices fell silent but for the sound of Norra's muffled sobs.

Deothen cleared his throat. "This is not the first time we have encountered this woman whose body you are about to burn." Deothen glanced about at the crowd, gauging the reaction of those who heard his words. His eyes hesitated on Kandler for a moment, but the justicar offered no consolation.

Kandler was willing to give the Silver Knights a fair hearing. He'd seen too many people lynched during the war, too many innocent souls damned to satiate the rage of an angry mob. He'd do anything he could to keep that from happening here, but he was only willing to go so far. He had Esprë to think of now.

"We first met this woman—"

"Shawda!" said Mardak. "Her name was Shawda."

"Shawda." Deothen nodded his thanks. "We first met Shawda last night on the edge of your town, atop the crater's ridge. We reached your town after dusk and did not want to enter then for fear of alarming the watch."

"So you killed one of our citizens instead?" Mardak asked in barely controlled outrage.

Deothen ignored the interruption. "As we settled down for the night, we gathered around our campfire for a final prayer. Just as we finished, we heard someone crashing through the brush in the darkness, coming from the east, the direction of the Mournland. We drew our blades, not knowing what to expect. She appeared at the edge of the fire's light. Her clothing was rent and torn. Her skin was gray and streaked with dirt. I called out a greeting and welcomed her as a fellow traveler. I invited her to share our fire."

Deothen bowed his head for a moment to collect his thoughts. When the knight looked back up, Kandler could see tears welling in his eyes, and when he spoke his voice was raw.

"She snarled at us, an evil light dancing in her eyes. I called to her a second time. She lowered her head and charged straight at us, attacking with her bare hands. At first I feared she might be mad, and I ordered my fellows not to harm her. As she neared, though, I sensed the evil in her, and I called for them to attack. Sallah stabbed the woman through the heart. Such a blow should have been fatal, but your Shawda kept coming. With Sallah's blade jutting from her chest, she pulled herself further along its length until she could reach Sallah with her nails, which broke upon Sallah's armor. Levritt stepped forward and chopped at the intruder with his blade. His blow severed her arm, which then hung from where her fingers had caught along the edges of Sallah's breastplate. No blood flowed. The woman kept coming. She snatched her own arm from Sallah's breastplate and swung it like a flail. The palm of her detached arm smacked Levritt in the face and knocked him flat." Deothen glanced at the young knight before continuing on. "I have fought the undead before. I like to say I can smell them from a league away. I hadn't sensed that here."

"It's the Mournland," said Kandler. As he spoke, he gazed up at the wall of ash-colored mist. "Bodies don't rot there. There's nothing to smell."

"Perhaps. In any case, once I realized what it was we faced, I called for an all-out attack. We set upon the creature and made quick work of her."

"Is this what happened with Shawda?" Mardak asked, his voice held low. Kandler angled his body so that he could intervene between the knight and the mayor should Mardak lose control.

Deothen grimaced. "We had to be sure. As your justicar points out, we know little of the Mournland. We had no desire to have the creature return later in the night for vengeance, so we took steps to make sure that could not happen."

"You hacked her to bits," said Mardak.

Deothen gave a stiff nod. "And we spread those pieces far and wide."

"We couldn't find all of her," said Kandler. His voice was but a whisper, not out of respect for the dead, but so that Norra might not hear.

"That was the idea," Deothen said. Norra's sobs grew louder, and she punctuated them with a keening wail that put a halt to all other words.

Silence fell over the crowd. None of the people surrounding Kandler, Mardak, and the knights dared to breathe a word.

"So you say," Mardak said, restarting the conversation. Anger seethed between his gritted teeth as he spoke, each word uttered with deliberate force. "So you say, but you offer nothing to prove your words true."

Deothen stared at Mardak, indignation stitched across his brow. "We are Knights of the Silver Flame."

"Which means nothing here. This is not Thrane, and your goddess holds no sway in our town. Even so, how can we verify your claim? Perhaps you are brigands in knights' armor."

Sallah pointed a gauntleted hand at the mayor. "You are bordering on blasphemy. None can speak to Sir Deothen so. How dare you impugn his honor?" She kept her sword lowered, but she gripped it as if it might leap from her grasp and find itself in Mardak's heart.

Mardak spit at Deothen's feet. "What honor did you show Shawda?"

The crowd murmured in agreement. The three younger knights gasped. Sallah scoffed in disgust.

Kandler could see that this could soon become ugly. He looked around for Burch but couldn't spot the shifter anywhere.

Deothen remained impassive for a moment, then spoke plainly to Mardak. "What proof would you have me offer?" he asked. "We came to your town as soldiers of faith, on a mission handed down to us by our greatest prophet. We have no reason to kill your people. What of the others who are missing?"

"How do you know of these?" asked Mardak.

"I told him," Kandler said.

"We arrived only last night," Deothen said. "According to your justicar, whoever is responsible for Shawda's transformation has been taking victims from your village for weeks."

"Who's to say you haven't been lurking in the shadows until now?"

"Why would we reveal ourselves today? Why would young Levritt bring suspicion on us by attacking Shawda's corpse?"

Mardak shook his head. "It's not for me to fathom your reasons. The facts against you are damning enough."

Sallah brought up her blade toward Mardak. Kandler met its edge with his own. The two young knights still armed drew their blades and pointed them at Kandler.

"I have heard enough!" Sallah said to Kandler. Her eyes blazed with anger as she spoke. "We are leaving you ungrateful wretches and your horrid, little town."

"You really don't want to try that," Kandler said, staring into her emerald eyes above their crossed swords. Silently, he begged her to put down her blade, but he could see that this cause was lost.

"And why not?"

The sound of blades being unsheathed filled the air. Every able-bodied man and woman in the crowd stood with a weapon in hand, ready to fight. The children and elders scattered for cover without a word needed.

"These are not some farmhands you can scare with a bit of scabbard rattling," Kandler said. He kept his voice friendly and even, as if he was explaining the varieties of local crops. As he spoke, he gazed out at the people of Mardakine and hoped they would follow his example. His eyes landed on Burch in the distance, and he smiled. "Everyone here lived through the War. Most of us fought in it."

Sallah glanced around at the crowd, looking for an avenue of escape. Kandler grated the edge of his sword against hers and caught her eye. With a quick nod, he sent her eyes up toward the rooftop of the town hall overlooking the square. It was the largest building in town, big enough to hold all of Mardakine's citizens at once. A low-slung place, it was the oldest edifice in town, made of steel-gray bricks crafted from the ash that had once filled the bottom of the crater and still collected in thick drifts in the farthest edges of the place. On windy days, the breeze threw that ash swirling up into the sky, from where it later settled down upon the town like a patina of fresh-fallen, filthy snow. The roofs of the buildings in town huddled underneath layers of this ash, except directly after a rain. It had been a long time since the last rain, and the roof of the town hall was thick with the dusty stuff.

Burch stood there atop the roof, the steel-tipped bolt loaded in his crossbow pointed directly at Deothen's heart. The sun glinted off the bolt's metal tip as the shifter readjusted his aim.

"He can pick the balls off a rat at a hundred yards," Kandler said quietly. "If you attack, then he"—Kandler jerked his chin at Deothen—"is already dead."

Sallah gritted her teeth. The point of her blade wavered. Next to her, Levritt shook so hard his armor rattled softly.

"Please," Kandler said. He didn't want this fight. His job was to protect the people of Mardakine, and if a battle broke out here, people on both sides would be killed. The knights didn't deserve to die over this either. None of them did.

Deothen laid a hand on Sallah's arm. "Stand down," he said. She turned toward him, and he looked deep into her eyes. "These are good people. They are scared. We have no issue with them."

"But, sir—" Sallah started.

Deothen cut her off with a raised eyebrow, then he

reached down and unbuckled his sword belt. He wrapped the belt around his blade's scabbard and handed the bundle to Mardak. "These knights are my charges," he said as Mardak accepted the sword. "I am responsible for them and their deeds, whether good or ill. I shall bear the burden of your suspicions."

Mardak weighed the sword in his hands. "You are charged with the murder of one of our citizens. The penalty for this is death."

Levritt blanched. Sallah opened her mouth to object again, but Deothen silenced her with a wave of his hand. "Give them your swords," he said. He raised his voice to preempt any protests. "We are guests here. We will follow their laws."

The knights surrendered their weapons to Kandler. He handed them to Rislinto, one by one, marveling at them as he handled them. Each hilt was long and straight, of a piece with its blade, forged from a single length of the finest steel. Silver filigree wrapped around each crimson scabbard in the pattern of flames licking up the sheath's full length. The soldier in Kandler felt the urge to draw one of the swords, to test its balance and its edge, but he passed them along instead.

Rislinto blew out a sigh of professional amazement as he collected the blades. The blacksmith cradled them in his arms as if each was a fragile flower.

Deothen drew in a deep breath and addressed Mardak. "I place myself in your hands and trust your mercy."

"You are far wiser than your young charges," said Mardak, a hard smile growing on his face. "Now we must determine the truth of your words."

"How do you propose to do that?" Deothen asked, as serious as he had been while giving Shawda's eulogy. "Knights such as I have the power to separate truth from lies. Do you have one among your number blessed with such favors?"

Mardak shook his head. "Fradelko has been missing now for two full weeks. We will have to resort to more traditional methods."

"Wait," said Kandler. "I can poke around a bit at their campsite, try to confirm their story."

Mardak grimaced. "Do not waste your time, justicar. If these people could snatch so many from our midst without detection, then they could surely meddle with any such so-called evidence. We cannot trust our eyes or our hearts."

Kandler's stomach flipped over. He knew where this was going.

"Our course is clear," Mardak said. "Trial by fire."

CHAPTER

5

You're out of your mind," Kandler told Mardak. "Darguun may only lie over the other side of Point Mountain, but we aren't goblins."

The mayor of Mardakine narrowed his eyes at his old friend. "Perhaps you're forgetting who is in charge here, justicar," he said. "Our people follow my guidance, and they know I speak the truth."

Mardak turned and swept his arms wide, his ashen cloak swirling about him as he did. "My friends, Fradelko is with us no more. We have no means of extracting the truth from these intruders other than the tried and true methods our forebears used."

"We could take them to New Cyre," Kandler said, doing his best to be reasonable in the face of clear madness. The stress of having the citizens of Mardakine disappear one by one had taken its toll on the entire town, and it had affected no one more than Kandler. Still, he knew that the people were near their breaking point, and it seemed that Mardak was ready to snap them over his knee. "They have a priest there."

" 'New' Cyre," Mardak scoffed. "A town filled with those

Cyrans too fearful of what our home has become to live in its shadow as we do."

Kandler didn't like the way the conversation was headed. "Prince Oargev is the ruler in exile of Cyre."

"Exile?" Mardak said. His eyes widened in wrath. "Look to the east!" He pointed up at the gray tendrils sweeping high into the sky over the crater's rim. "We were not *exiled*. We lucky few happened to be outside our homeland the day it was murdered."

"Prince Oargev is the rightful heir to the throne of Cyre, and we should present these knights to him for judgment."

"What do you care about Cyre, Brelander?" Mardak said.

Kandler clamped down on his rising temper. Every time the two had a disagreement, Mardak would point out the fact that while Kandler had married an elf from Cyre, that land was not his home.

"I care about our home here," Kandler said, forcing the words out one at a time. "I will not let you turn these people into a pack of hobgoblins. We are civilized. We may not be a part of Cyre, but we follow Cyran laws, and they don't leave room for burning people we don't like."

"Cyre is dead."

Until that point, the crowd had murmured along with the argument, chattering support or disgust with each position. At that moment, everyone fell silent. This was the truth they all lived with but always refused to utter.

Kandler dragged the front of his hand across his mouth as if he hoped to pull out all of the evil things he wished to say before they escaped his lips. When he spoke, his voice was as calm and steady as an executioner's.

"If that's so, then we're in Breland. My homeland. We don't burn people to death here either."

"Times like these call for us to dispense with such niceties. We must use whatever means necessary to secure our safety."

"Like torture?"

Mardak's face turned stony. "Whatever means necessary."

Kandler locked eyes with Mardak and considered the meaning of the man's words. Eventually, Mardak looked away and scanned the eyes of the townspeople. Kandler didn't need to. He knew what he'd see—terror mixed with anger and just a dash of hope that perhaps killing these outsiders would end the disappearances.

"Fine," Kandler said.

Mardak's head snapped around and he goggled at the justicar. "I'm glad you've come to see it my way. You will take them into custody then." To Kandler's ears, this was more of a question than Mardak wanted it to be.

Kandler shook his head. "I'll take them. To my home. As my guests."

Mardak leaned forward and whispered to Kandler like a snake hissing through its teeth. "Do not defy my authority," he said. "If you break with me, our settlement—our cause—may fall apart. We are besieged on all sides and must speak with one voice. The people need a strong leader. Now more than ever."

"Then be one," Kandler said. He stepped back from the mayor and ordered the people holding Levritt to let him go. "These knights are my guests now. Mistreat them, and it becomes *my* problem."

Kandler looked to Rislinto. The blacksmith blushed.

"Give them back their swords," Kandler said.

Rislinto's eyes bounced back and forth between Kandler and Mardak. A bead of sweat rolled down his forehead and along his right cheek. His burly, hairy arms shifted nervously around the bundle of swords that he'd been cradling like an infant.

"You know where your loyalties lie, Rislinto," said Mardak. An oily sheen covered the mayor's upper lip. "With Cyre. And Cyre alone."

Kandler stepped up to Rislinto and relieved him of the swords. The blacksmith surrendered them without protest. "I'll take responsibility for these," Kandler said, "and their owners."

Rislinto nodded and stepped back into the crowd. He refused to meet Mardak's baleful glare.

Kandler turned to address the crowd. "You people have a funeral to finish. No matter what happened to Shawda or how she died, she was still one of us. She deserves better than this. Now see to it."

Rislinto ordered the men nearest him to fetch torches. Kandler turned away. The sooner he was out of here, the sooner Mardak could calm down.

Deothen approached Kandler and said, "We are in your debt, justicar. But you do not have to do this for us."

"I know," Kandler said as he beckoned the other knights to follow him.

Kandler glanced up at the roof of the town hall to see Burch still perched there, his crossbow now pointed at Mardak, who hadn't noticed. With a tug on his ear, Kandler waved the shifter off. He didn't bother to look up to see if Burch would comply.

One by one, the knights fell into line behind Kandler as he passed through the town square and headed for home. The townspeople parted before him as he went. None of them met his eyes, but they all looked after him and his charges as they passed.

Even Norra was silent now, her sobs faded to sniffles. As Kandler reached her, he put an arm around her and gave her a firm hug. Esprë, who stood next to Norra, her arm still around her, whispered something in her friend's ear. Norra nodded, wiping her tears and giving Esprë a quick embrace.

The young elf maiden reached up to take Kandler's hand, and they walked toward their home like that. As they left the townspeople behind, Kandler looked down at Esprë. They hadn't walked together like this in months.

Kandler didn't have any children of his own, and he treasured his stepdaughter's long childhood. He'd known her for six years already, and he'd raised her alone since her mother's death four years past. In that time, she had changed so little that she seemed to be the same person. He, on the other hand, had seen his thirty-fifth year, and he was starting to feel it.

Kandler squeezed Esprë's hand, and she looked up at him with her wide, almond-shaped eyes. "Thank you," he said softly. She smiled back at him, and he realized he'd been missing that smile for weeks.

CHAPTER

6

When Kandler and Esprë reached their home, the knights still in tow, Burch was sitting on the front porch waiting for them. "Took your time," the shifter said.

Kandler grinned. "Knights in armor don't move so quickly." He released Esprë's hand and guided her up the steps and into Burch's arms. She wrapped her arms around the shifter and hugged him so tight his yellow eyes began to bulge.

"Oof," Burch said. He pulled himself loose from the elf maid's embrace and favored her with a wan smile. "Be gentle with your friends." He tousled her long, blonde hair. Kandler smiled down at the scene for a moment, but a voice from behind interrupted him.

"Justicar," Deothen called from the edge of the yard, "you have our gratitude and that of the Silver Flame." He and the other knights unhitched their horses from Kandler's post as he spoke.

"Where do you think you're going?" Kandler asked as he turned to watch the knights work. "Just because I took responsibility for you doesn't mean you can just ride out of here. You owe me more than that."

Deothen shook his head. "Our horses need tending. It has

been a long journey for them, taken with all due speed."

Kandler tossed a thumb over his shoulder. "There's a full trough and some hay in the stable out back," he said. "You're welcome to what you need. Just watch out for Dargent and Cintila."

"You have other guests?" Deothen asked, his eyebrow arching high enough to match the path of his widow's peak.

"Other horses," Kandler said, "and they don't care much for strangers."

"Like most of the people around here, it seems," said Sallah as she led her horse around the side of the house, ahead of the others.

Kandler glanced to his left, but Burch was already gone around the other side of the house to keep an eye on the knights. The justicar looked back at Deothen. "When you're done," he said, "come inside. We need to talk."

❦

"Tell me again why you're here?" Kandler said. He and Deothen sat across the table from each other in the main room of Kandler's home. Esprë slouched next to Kandler in one of the room's other well-worn chairs. Even though a chair still sat open, Sallah and the other knights stood, each in a separate corner of the room, their swords once again buckled around their waists. Burch sat perched on the sill of one of the open windows, picking his teeth with a long, black fingerclaw as he glanced inside the house and out.

"Our Lady Tira Miron, the Voice of the Silver Flame, received a vision that a lost dragonmark has appeared in the Mournland," Deothen said. He stopped when Kandler held up a battle-scarred hand.

"You've said all that before. What more do you know?"

Deothen sat up straight and craned his neck at Kandler as if he could see straight through him to the opposite wall.

"You said you were in my debt," Kandler said. "It's time to start evening the score." He stared deep into the older man's piercing blue eyes, where he saw a natural distrust of outsiders warring with the duty to repay a kindness done. Duty won.

"We are looking for the Lost Mark," Deothen said.

"Which mark is that?" Kandler said.

"The Lost Mark," Deothen repeated, enunciating each word.

Kandler gasped despite himself. He shook his head in disbelief and said, "It has returned?"

"This is what Our Lady tells us. It is why we are here." Deothen was as somber as he'd been at Shawda's funeral.

Kandler felt a tug at his sleeve. "What's he talking about?" Esprë asked as he looked down at her. She seemed to have curled into a ball at the back of the chair's seat.

"It's nothing," Kandler said, but Sallah spoke up from a corner between two windows. The light streamed in around her on both sides, and the dust in the air swirled and danced in the beams as she spoke.

"The Thirteenth Mark," Sallah said in an eager voice. "Some say it was the first of the dragonmarks to appear, and the first and only to be lost."

"I've heard of dragonmarks," Esprë said in a voice that surprised Kandler with how grown-up it sounded. "They are magical tattoos that grant the powerful more power."

Deothen loosed a good-natured laugh. "Close, but not quite," he said. "They are birthmarks passed down through the strongest of bloodlines. A few rare and lucky members of the blessed peoples have them. These form the bases for the dragonmarked houses. They resemble tattoos, but they arise naturally in those born to them."

"Blessed peoples?" Esprë asked.

"Humans, dwarves, gnomes, halflings, elves, and some half-elves and even half-orcs."

"No shifters?" Esprë glanced at Burch. Kandler followed her eyes and saw his friend still sitting in the window, his clawed feet wrapped around the sill. He wore a smirk on his face.

Deothen sucked at his teeth. "No, child," he said. "No

shifters have ever been found with a dragonmark."

Esprë gazed at Burch for a moment. The shifter smiled back at her, baring all of his long, feral teeth. Her eyes flew wide as an idea struck her. "Maybe they're just hidden under all the hair," she said.

The room erupted into laughter. Burch nearly fell backward out of his window, but he managed to right himself in time. Esprë blushed with embarrassment at first, but when Kandler leaned over and gave her a one-armed hug, she joined in with the rest.

"What—?" Esprë said loudly. Kandler could tell she was eager to move on, so he motioned for the others to shush. "What is the Lost Mark the mark of?"

All laughter in the room evaporated like raindrops on hot coals.

"That's not important," Kandler said, trying to change the subject.

"I mean," Esprë continued, apparently not to be dissuaded, "there are the twelve regular marks, the Mark of Finding, the Mark of Making, the Mark of Storm, and so on. What's the thirteenth the mark of?" She leaned forward in her seat now, ready for the answer, no matter what it might be.

"The Mark of Death," Sallah said soberly. "The one who bears it has mastery over life and death."

Esprë's brows creased as she digested this. A hush feel over the house. The silence seemed to bother the dark-haired knight, who spoke. "Aren't there any birds here?" he said as he fidgeted against the wall.

"Nope," said Burch. All eyes turned to the shifter. "Too close to the Mournland. Not much grows around here, not enough for animals to feed on."

Deothen looked from Burch to Kandler. "Then how do you people survive?"

Kandler tapped his hand on the table a few times before answering. "We trade with New Cyre, mostly. Sometimes with Vathirond or Kennrun."

Sallah nodded. "We passed through Vathirond on our way here. The justicar there told us of this place."

"But what do you trade?" Deothen asked. "I can see your needs are many, but what would traders want from you?"

"Things from Cyre," Kandler said. He hesitated for a moment before he continued. He knew Mardak wouldn't like him talking to outsiders about such things, but at the moment he didn't much care what Mardak liked. "This town was founded as a base of operations for a group of people who want to learn what happened during the Day of Mourning. We've been here since the end of the war."

Deothen nodded. "Those must have been two long years. Have you discovered anything?"

"Only a lot of dead people," Kandler said. "We've never ventured farther than the Glass Plateau, a shelf high above the plains, filled with jagged formations of colored glass. The place is filled with never-ending spells that have come to life. And there are things more dangerous than that in the Mournland. Cyre is beyond dead. It's been . . . twisted." Kandler sighed deeply. "The ruins between here and the Plateau are filled with all sorts of things—stuff that used to belong to the dead whose bodies still lie there, never rotting. We gather up some of that and sell it to finance the town and our expeditions."

"You haven't gotten very far yet," Sallah said.

Kandler glared at the woman. She was beautiful but clueless. "Have you ever been to the Mournland?" he asked her.

Sallah shook her head. "No."

"Then you have no idea—" He stopped short at the sound of a quick two taps then three on the house's western wall. He glanced at the empty window where Burch had been.

"What is it?" Deothen asked.

Kandler patted Esprë on the back, and she scurried off to hide in her room, then he stood up and walked toward the door. "We've got company," he said.

CHAPTER

7

Kandler peered around the right corner of his front porch, back toward the town square. The knights lined up in the doorway behind Deothen, each of them peering over their leader's back as he kept a respectful distance from the justicar.

"Who is it?" Deothen asked.

"Stay here," Kandler said. *"Don't leave."*

The knights filed out onto the porch as Kandler leaped down and waited for Mardak and his followers to reach him. The mayor walked at the front of the pack of men, with Rislinto striding along next to him, arguing every step of the way. Behind them, they had a score of armed men.

The men chattered among themselves, their gait scattered and offbeat, nothing like the confident march of soldiers. Kandler had led each of them into battle before and knew them all like brothers. Pradak, the mayor's son, dogged his father's heels, his face a mixture of excitement and embarrassment. Temmah, the only dwarf in town, brought up the rear. Puffing along hard to keep up with the others, his long beard swayed before him, bouncing off the handle of the battleaxe he carried in both of his wide, meaty hands.

Kandler could hear the blacksmith growling at Mardak. "Stop this madness," Rislinto said. "The justicar is not our foe."

"We are at war here," Mardak said. His eyes darted from Rislinto to the men following them. He spoke as much to them as to the blacksmith. "An army requires a strong chain of command. He refused a direct order."

Rislinto put his hand on Mardak's shoulder. "This isn't an army. It's our home."

"All the more reason to protect it." Mardak shrugged off Rislinto's hand as they entered Kandler's yard. "We are being picked off one by one. Any of us could be next."

The hawk-faced man strode up to the justicar and said, "Kandler, you are under arrest."

A wry smile found its way to Kandler's lips. "What are the charges?" he asked. He looked into the faces of the others as he spoke. Only Rislinto dared to meet his gaze, puffing with indignity as he did. The rest bowed their heads sheepishly.

Mardak stabbed a finger at the justicar as he spoke and used it to punctuate his sentences. "You failed to protect us. You sided with these outsiders. You disobeyed me. This cannot be tolerated!"

With each word, Mardak's anger grew. By the end of his pronouncement, he was spitting out each word like bolts from a crossbow. It was then that a real bolt appeared between his feet.

Kandler cursed under his breath.

Mardak and his men looked up as one to see Burch perched on the edge of Kandler's roof, his crossbow in hand. He was already reloading.

"Archers!" Mardak said. A half-dozen townspeople broke off from the mob. In a handful of heartbeats, they each nocked an arrow, stretched their bowstrings, and took aim at the shifter. Burch ignored them and drew a bead on Mardak's heart.

"Stand down!" Rislinto said. "We've had enough mayhem today."

The archers hesitated for a moment. Two of them lowered their bows.

"There will be more if anyone disobeys another order," said Mardak. "Temmah! Take Kandler into custody!"

The crowd parted around the dwarf, who stood near the rear of the pack, thumbing the blade of his battleaxe. He noticed all eyes on him, and he cursed in the thick tongue of his people. "This is a hard vein of rock," he said, his face flushed red.

Temmah looked at Kandler. "Will you come peacefully, justicar?" His eyes pleaded with his friend to make this easy.

Before Kandler could answer, the knights stepped into the circle formed around Kandler, their swords drawn and ready. "He's not going anywhere," Deothen said.

Kandler shook his head in exasperation. He understood why Burch had loosed a bolt without waiting for a signal. Despite the shifter's laconic façade, he always stood ready for a good fight. Kandler had thought Deothen and the knights would have been better disciplined though. "Can't anyone around here do what I tell them?" he asked.

"By Dol Arrah's sacred sword," said Mardak, a dark vein pulsing in his forehead as he spoke to the knights, "this is an internal matter. It has nothing to do with you. I'll thank you to stay out of this."

"Don't do me any favors," Kandler said to Deothen. He tried to sound as confident about it as he wanted to be. "I can handle this."

"Really?" said Sallah. "You could take on a few score of battle-hardened veterans yourself? I'd like to see that."

"Step back, and you might get a chance," Mardak said, his voice dripping with desperate menace.

"Are you out of your mind?" called a strong feminine voice. Kandler turned back around to see Mardak's wife Priscinta smack him in the back of the head. He hadn't seen her march up with the others. She must have followed Mardak from the square and watched from a distance until she figured out what he and his people were up to.

Enraged, Mardak turned to slap his wife, but she snatched his arm before he could land the blow. "This is Kandler," she said, "not some wandering beggar worshiping some upstart god!"

Sallah started to object, but Priscinta kept talking. "Kandler founded Mardakine with you, and he's saved our little settlement more times than I care to count. Who slew that carcass crab when it came crawling out of the Mournland looking for a meal?"

Mardak opened his mouth to say something, but Priscinta kept rolling. "And Burch," she said as she pointed up to the shifter's rooftop perch, "he brought down three of that flight of harpies before these archers of yours even unslung their bows. I think they've earned their place with us."

Mardak took advantage of the fact his wife was looking away to slap her to the ground. Everyone gasped. Mardak looked down at his hand as if it had just come to life on its own. His face, red with anger only moments before, blanched pale as a skeleton left out in the desert sun.

Priscinta sat on the ash-coated crater floor, her hand covering the red mark Mardak's blow had placed on her ivory skin. She stood with painstaking care and brushed the ash from her skirts. Then she turned to her husband and spat blood from her mouth on the ground before him. Where it landed, it turned the ash black.

Without a word, Priscinta launched herself at Mardak. Before she could reach him, Rislinto stepped between them and held her at bay. "Don't!" he said. "He's not worth it!"

"He's not worth my blood, but he's already had some of that!" Priscinta said. "I was a warrior-maiden!" she said as tears streamed down her flushed cheeks. "I gave that up to bear your children, you spiteful bastard!"

"That's right," Rislinto said. "Your children. Like Pradak, who's standing right there!"

Priscinta turned to see her eldest son gaping at his parents. The fight fled from her. With that, Rislinto wrapped his thick arms around Priscinta, and she collapsed against his barrel chest. She pressed hard against him, muffling her sobs.

Mardak stared at his wife for a moment. Kandler could see the tears welling up in the man, but he knew that Mardak would never allow them to flow, never admit that he was wrong in front of so many other people. Mardak's eyes went to his son, and his face burned with shame.

"None of that matters right now," Mardak said, more to himself than anyone else, then louder he said, "We are under siege by forces unknown. If we are to survive, everyone must follow orders. No one is exempt." He turned to Kandler. The justicar could see that all of his old friend's shame and fear was now hammered into a red-hot blade of righteous rage, its new-forged tip pointed straight at him. "Not even our finest."

Kandler let loose a hard laugh. "So," he said, "what are you saying exactly?"

"You're not that dumb, justicar."

"Pretend I am."

Mardak sighed. "You and Burch shall surrender yourselves into my custody now."

"And if we don't?"

"Not even you two can stand against so many of us. You may manage to kill many who have called you friend, but we will bring you down."

Kandler scanned the faces arrayed against him. Many of them, like Temmah, refused to meet his eyes. They stood tall, though, with their hands on the hilts of their weapons. He had fought alongside many of them, and since the founding of the town he had trained with them all. He had worked to instill in them a sense of duty to their town, to each other. He had never guessed that this would be used against him.

How many of them could he bear to kill? If he tried to run, the archers would bring him down before he reached the crater's wall. If he stood and fought, he would be forced to murder his friends or die at their hands. Once such a fight began, there would be no turning back.

"Priscinta is right," Kandler said. "You are a bastard." He glared at the mayor, measuring the distance between the two. He knew he could draw his blade and slice through Mardak's throat before the man could even raise his sword. He considered it. The thought felt good.

"Sticks and stones, Brelander," said Mardak. "What will it be?"

CHAPTER

8

Y ou did a good thing," Sallah said through the barred window in the door of the jail. Her words echoed off the walls of the room dug deep into the stone beneath the town hall, and they sounded hollow in Kandler's ears.

The justicar sat up from where he'd been lying on the smooth, gray stone floor. The same material made up the walls, which were featureless but for two things—the anchors to which Temmah and Rislinto had attached the prisoners' manacles and the pair of cold fire torches that burned without smoke or heat, their flickering light lending a bit of illusory warmth that did nothing to push back the room's gravelike chill. Kandler's chains clinked as he stood up and stretched as far as the links would let him.

Across the room, Burch remained seated in his iron chains, the pupils of his yellow eyes gleaming in the torchlight. Still as a statue, he glared at the window in the door, the only window in the room, just as he had since he first heard the footsteps coming down the stairs. Kandler could feel the frustration radiating from his friend, as silent and cold as the unnatural torches.

"Temmah," Kandler said. "Is it our custom to let strangers visit with prisoners?"

"No," the dwarf called up at the window from the other side of the door, too short to speak directly through the aperture. "Well, actually, I don't really know. You two are the first prisoners we've ever had."

"Do you think I'd approve?" Kandler arched an eyebrow at the door. He thought he saw Sallah smiling at him through the bars. She turned away, though, before he could be sure.

Kandler could almost hear the dwarf pull at his beard as he puzzled over the question. "Normally, no," he said, "but these circumstances aren't particularly normal."

Kandler nodded, even though he knew Temmah couldn't see him. "You're one smart dwarf, Temmah," he said. "When your world changes, you change with it."

"I wish we could say as much of our town's leader."

Kandler and Burch both laughed at that. The echoes reminded them of where they were, and the sound trailed off fast. Kandler sat thinking for a moment. He wasn't sure just how he'd gotten himself into this mess, but he knew he needed to get out.

"How long we here for, Temmah?" Burch asked.

The dwarf hemmed and hawed for a moment. "Well, that all depends. We've never imprisoned any of our own before—or anyone else for that matter. You're our inaugural guests."

"Some honor," said Burch. Kandler knew the shifter would have preferred to fight, but once the justicar gave himself up, Burch followed his lead. They hadn't talked much since Mardak had thrown them in chains.

Kandler got up and started to pace the floor as far as his chains would let him. He could only go about three steps before he had to turn around. "This is a fine jail you built, Temmah," he said.

The dwarf laughed, a low merry rumble. "With all respect, you don't know what you're talking about. Compared to even the humble bolt hole in the Mror Holds where I was whelped, this is little more than an outhouse."

Kandler nodded. "It's better than any of the rest of us could have managed." He stopped pacing to turn to the door and ask, "What are the plans for us?"

Kandler saw Sallah look down at Temmah. When she looked back up, she passed along the dwarf's shrug.

"Any ideas at all?" Kandler said.

Sallah spoke, her voice calm and even. "Your leader doesn't seem to think there's any need for a trial."

Kandler smiled and wiped a hand across his brow. "Priscinta and Rislinto finally got him to calm down? That's a relief."

"Ah, no," Temmah called up through the window. "I'm afraid it's worse than that."

"Worse?" Burch asked. He leaped to his feet, his chains jangling around him. "What's worse than cooking to death?"

Temmah cleared his throat but no words came out.

"Temmah?" said Kandler. The dwarf's silence unnerved him, but he wanted an answer to Burch's question.

Sallah spoke up. "Mardak says your actions were treasonous. Everyone in town saw you, so there's no need for a trial."

"No cookfire for us, at least," Burch said.

Without taking his eyes from Sallah's, Kandler put up his hand to silence his friend. "What's the penalty for treason?" he asked.

The lady knight looked down at the ground, away from Temmah. "You're to be executed," she said.

Burch jumped back, rattling his chains. "That's a joke, right?"

"Sorry, lad," said Temmah. "They're dead—uh, I mean, they're entirely serious. At least Mardak is."

"Won't this Mardak see reason once he calms down?" asked Sallah.

A chill ran through Kandler's guts. "Maybe," he said. "Maybe not. He's had a bad few weeks, and today was the worst. We embarrassed him in front of the town."

"He hit Priscinta," Burch said.

"He'll pay for that for a while," Kandler said with a rueful smile. "Priscinta will get her pound of flesh from him a painful ounce at a time. But he knows that, and it won't improve his mood."

"He was wrong about us," Sallah said.

Kandler could hear in her voice that she knew how little comfort that would be to him. "Has he admitted that yet?"

"He's having dinner with Sir Deothen right now." Sallah gazed through the bars at Kandler. He noticed how green her eyes were in the light from the cold fire torch in the sconce outside the door.

"You weren't invited?"

Sallah smirked. "I was. I declined."

Kandler smiled and peered out at the knight's earnest face framed in the barred window. "So what are you doing here?"

"She wanted to say thanks," Temmah called up through the window.

Kandler thought he could see Sallah blush. She cleared her throat before she spoke. "As Knights of the Silver Flame, we're usually the ones who come to the rescue."

"Happy to oblige." Kandler tried to keep the irony from his voice.

"You saved the lives of many of your friends."

"I—" Kandler stopped. "Yeah, I suppose we did."

"We will not permit you to be executed for our sake, of course."

The shifter perked his ears at this idea. "How will you stop it?" Burch asked.

"As we speak, Sir Deothen is arguing for your lives."

The dwarf standing next to Sallah snorted. She glared down at him as if he was a beetle she wanted to stomp beneath her boot.

Kandler shook his head. "Temmah?"

"Yes?"

"What do you think of that?"

"Permission to speak freely?"

"Go ahead."

"That jackass needs someone to pay for his mistakes. You and Burch, you're at the top of his list."

"You don't think Deothen is going to hold any sway with him?" Kandler knew the answer, but he wanted Sallah to hear it.

The dwarf scoffed. "I'm surprised he didn't throw the whole lot of those armored pansies down here to rot with you. Begging your pardon, miss," Temmah said to Sallah, "but if Priscinta hadn't had Mardak scared enough to nearly wet himself, that's just what would have happened."

"That's appalling," Sallah said. "What about the Code of Justice?"

"You're a long way from civilization out here," Kandler said. He'd lived by the code of justice for most of his life, and he'd spent the last two years here enforcing it here. It pained him to see people he'd once trusted throw it aside so casually. "They don't hold trials by fire in Sharn."

"Nor in Flamekeep," said Sallah. "You are the justicar here. Do you not hold any sway over this place?"

"You're asking me that question through a set of bars."

"Rislinto," Burch said. "He'll stop Mardak. For sure." He started to pace the floor, just as Kandler had done before. The sound of his chains dragging back and forth on the stone floor seemed to soothe him.

For Kandler, the noise sounded horribly close to that of an executioner whetting his blade.

CHAPTER

9

"Temmah?" Kandler said, trying to keep any hint of cunning from his voice.

"Yes?"

"How late is it?"

"The sun was setting as we came in."

"You'd better start your patrol."

The dwarf gulped. "By myself?"

"I don't think Burch and I can join you tonight."

"All—all right."

Kandler heard the dwarf turn to go, leaving Sallah still standing at the door. The justicar waited for a moment, then said, "Temmah?"

"Yes?" The dwarf dashed back down the few steps he'd taken up toward the town hall proper.

Temmah was a good dwarf, but he wasn't the brightest star in the sky. Kandler feared that he'd really try to manage the patrol alone. "You're the justicar now. You can deputize some help."

"That's right!" The dwarf's voice brightened for a moment, then darkened again. "But who would be willing?"

"What about those men who brought Kandler and Burch

in?" Sallah asked. "They seemed handy enough with their weapons."

Kandler snorted. "Most of them haven't been in a fight since the end of the war. Two years is long enough for a blade to rust."

"They're better than nothing," Temmah said. "They were enough to haul you in."

"We surrendered," Burch spat. "If somethin' wanders out of the Mournland, it won't be so kind."

"Right," Temmah said, as if he'd somehow forgotten.

"What about your friends, lady knight?" Kandler asked. "They look sharp and ready."

"That we are," said Sallah, "but would Mardak allow them to serve?"

"He's not the justicar."

Temmah rumbled with laughter.

"Take them aside and ask them quietly," Kandler called to the dwarf. "Mardak doesn't need to know. If he finds out . . . well, it's easier to beg forgiveness than ask permission."

"Excellent!" Temmah said with a little laugh. "I'm off."

Before the dwarf got more than a few steps away, Kandler called after him once more. "Temmah?"

"Yes?" The dwarf dragged himself back to the door again.

"If you're going to leave this lady to watch over us, shouldn't she be able to open the door?" Kandler held his breath after the words left his mouth. He hoped his friend would either be dumb enough to fall for this or smart enough to play along.

Kandler heard the dwarf rummage around in his pockets. Through the window, he saw Sallah reach down to accept something from the dwarf, but then Temmah stopped. "Is this wise? She's a knight of Thrane."

"Aren't you about to deputize her friends?"

The dwarf didn't answer for a long moment.

"I can't see you, Temmah," said Kandler. "You have to speak."

"Uh, yes. I nodded yes. Sorry."

"Then . . ." Kandler said, drawing it out and hoping that Temmah would beat him to the punch. It didn't happen. "Make her your first deputy."

"A stupendous idea!" Temmah said. "Sallah?"

"Yes?" The young knight answered sweetly.

"Would you do us the honor of being a deputy justicar for the fair town of Mardakine?"

Sallah stifled a laugh, then said solemnly, "The honor is mine."

No one said a word for a moment. "Give her the key," Burch growled.

"Oh!" Temmah said. "Here you are, miss."

Sallah thanked him, then held the key up to the window for Kandler and Burch to see.

Temmah cleared his throat and spoke. "That's all there is to it?"

"Less even. You'd better find some deputies and get to work. It's sure to be dark by now, and the town lies undefended."

"Your Mardak didn't think this through well, did he?" said Sallah. Her eyes sparkled as she spoke.

Kandler smiled. "Go, Temmah," he called.

"Yes, yes!" The dwarf stumped up the stairs and was gone.

Sallah shook her head as she watched him go. Kandler could see her red curls swinging in the torchlight. She turned back to the cell and pressed her face between the cold, iron bars. "Why do you protect these people?"

Kandler raised his eyebrows. "That's a strange question coming from a Knight of the Silver Flame."

"You're not a knight."

Burch snorted at that.

"Keep walking," Kandler said, flicking his own chains at the shifter's heels.

"Well?" said Sallah.

Kandler drew in a long breath and blew it out. Sallah waited for him.

"They lost their whole country. When Cyre was destroyed on the Day of Mourning."

"You're a Brelander."

"I . . . I hadn't lived in Breland for a while."

Burch snorted. He opened his mouth to speak, but Kandler shut it with a blazing glare.

"Was your wife from Cyre?"

Kandler couldn't think of a thing to say. He noticed that Burch didn't snort this time. In fact, the shifter had frozen in his tracks. Kandler looked up at his old friend, his mouth a grim, bloodless line across his face.

"My apologies," Sallah said in a soft voice. "I didn't mean to pry."

"She was," Kandler said abruptly. "She died on the Day of Mourning."

Sallah nodded. No one spoke for a moment. Kandler wished that Burch would start pacing again, but the shifter stood rock still.

"She was an elf," Sallah said. It was not a question.

"How did . . . ? Ah." Kandler allowed himself a quick grin. "Esprë."

"You are no father to that girl."

Burch broke in there, striding toward the door as far as his chains would let him. "He's a fine father!"

"I'm sorry," Sallah said. "I meant by blood. I'm sure the justicar is a wonderful parent."

Kandler waved off the comment. "I wouldn't go that far," he said, "but we get by. Tell me more about this dragonmark you're looking for."

Sallah brightened at what seemed a welcome attempt to change the subject. "The Mark of Death, yes. It is imperative that we find the bearer—and soon."

"Are you looking for an infant then?" Kandler asked.

Sallah shot the justicar a confused look. "Of course not. Most dragonmarks appear in the bearer's youth, as they make the transition from child to adult."

Kandler nodded at that, trying to keep his face a mask. He feared what it might mean.

"Have you never seen a dragonmark?" Sallah asked.

Kandler cocked his head. "I've seen people who bear them—or so they claimed. Most people around here run about fully clothed. What do they look like?"

"They are rare." Sallah ran a finger across her lips as she thought about it. "I've only seen a few myself. They look like a tattoo made from black ink—sometimes bounded in red, as if it erupted from the skin."

"Like a mole?" Kandler asked.

"I suppose," said Sallah. "But no mole ever granted such power. Like a mole, however, these start out small and can sometimes grow larger. The bigger they get, the more powerful they become."

Kandler gazed off into the distance and nodded. "I was afraid of that."

Sallah narrowed her eyes at the justicar. "You don't strike me as a man who is afraid of much."

"So why do you do it?" Kandler asked, changing the subject. "Why are you a knight?" He wanted to talk about something else, anything else.

Sallah drew back from the bars a bit. Her face fell into shadow.

"I am a Knight of the Silver Flame, a paladin pledged to uphold the good and holy teachings of the Voice of the Flame and to bring justice and enlightenment to the world."

"I didn't ask who you are," Kandler said. "I asked your reasons for it."

Sallah stammered for a moment. "I was born to—Shush!"

"What?"

"Quiet!" Sallah held the palm of her hand up to the bars in the door's window as she moved a step toward the stairs that led to the main floor. Her armored boot scuffed on the stone floor. "I hear something."

Kandler stood up and moved as close to the door as his

chains would let him. He listened for a moment but couldn't hear a thing.

Burch held back and cocked his head to one side. Horror spread across his face. He rushed toward the door and held up his chains. "Let us loose!" he said.

"The dwarf charged me with keeping you here," said Sallah.

"Those are screams!" Burch said. "People are dying!"

Sallah looked to Kandler. He pleaded with her with his eyes, but she turned and started to leave.

"Stop!" Kandler shouted. "That's our town up there!"

CHAPTER

10

Kandler hoisted his chains and set his foot against the wall. "Help me!" he said to Burch. "Maybe we can break them together." He knew it was a long shot. Rislinto had forged each link with skill and care. Still, it seemed their only hope.

Burch rushed over to lend a hand. As the shifter began to pull, Kandler heard the sound of a key scraping in a lock behind them. The two looked back to see Sallah shove the heavy door in on its black, oiled hinges. They dropped Kandler's chains and turned to hold up their shackles up for her.

"No tricks!" the lady knight said as he stepped into the room.

"Hurry," Kandler said. He didn't want to panic her, so he kept his voice as steady as he could. He felt a small tremor in it, but he hoped she wouldn't hear it.

Sallah brought the key up to insert into the lock on Kandler's manacles, but at the last second she stopped and gave Kandler an appraising eye. "Maybe I should go up and check it out first," she said.

"No time!" said Burch. He snarled. Kandler realized that Sallah had gotten too close and the shifter was ready to strangle her with his chains. He put up a hand to stop his friend.

"Look," Kandler said, as he grabbed the knight's wrist, "if you go up there and get killed, we could be stuck down here for what little will be left of our lives."

Sallah looked at her wrist and then into Kandler's eyes. She pulled her arm free angrily. "I'll just have to chance that."

Sallah turned to leave. Kandler grabbed her by the gleaming metal collar of her armor and pulled her back toward him. "I can't let you do that."

Sallah swung around and backhanded Kandler to the floor. Incensed, she stomped over to where he was, pointed down at him, and said, "You can't stop me."

As the words left Sallah's mouth, the chain binding Burch's wrists sailed over her head. Before she could react, the shifter put his knee into her back and pulled the chain tight. It snaked up along her armor and came to rest under the chin where Burch pulled it taut in an instant.

Sallah dropped the key as her hands darted up to pull the chain from her throat. Before she could get a good grip, Kandler lashed out and kicked her feet from under her. The lady knight went down hard with Burch still on her back, pulling the chain even tighter.

"Hold her!" Kandler said as he scrambled across the floor to pluck up the key. "Try not to hurt her."

"I'm trying!" Burch grunted. Sallah struggled under him, swinging him to and fro on her back as her fingers sought purchase under the chain. "She fights like a troll!"

Kandler shoved the key into the lock on his manacles and turned. The shackles fell free.

Sallah, who had managed to get to her knees, growled with rage. "Whoa!" Burch shouted, as if he were trying to calm a bucking horse. To Kandler, this only seemed to make the knight even angrier.

Sallah was taller than Burch if no heavier. She stood and rammed her back toward the wall, crunching Burch between her armor and the unforgiving stone. The air rushed out of the shifter's lungs. When Sallah hauled on his chain this time, it slipped from his fingers, and she was loose.

"Let's talk this over!" Kandler said. He held both hands up in front of Sallah in what he hoped was a calming manner.

Sallah shrugged her way free of Burch's chain, and the heavy links fell on the shifter's head. She drew her blade and brandished it at Kandler as she spoke. "I will have that key," she said.

Kandler slipped back toward the wall to which he had been anchored, gathering his chain as he did. He began to swing the loose links before him, spinning his manacles about so the chain whirled like a spoke on a wheel. "You'll have to kill me to get it."

Sallah feinted at Kandler with her blade, and he knocked it away with his chain. As the lady knight searched for a hole in the justicar's defenses, she sidled away from Burch, who was still gasping for breath. "As you wish," she said to Kandler.

Kandler sent his chain whirring about faster. Sallah poked at his moving shield again. The chain knocked the blade away, but the contact disrupted the shield for a split second. She prodded at it twice more with the same result each time.

"We don't have time for this!" Kandler said. With the cell door open, he could finally hear the commotion in the town above. He hoped Esprë had found her hiding hole, just as he trained her to do, but he wasn't willing to bet her life on it.

Sallah drew back her blade and stabbed it at Kandler's chest, passing through his chain-shield near his hand. The chain wrapped around it like a constrictor.

Kandler wrenched at the chain, hoping to pull Sallah's weapon from her grasp. Instead of resisting the pull, though, the lady knight pursued it. As she closed, she reversed her grip and smashed Kandler in the face with the pommel of her sword.

The blow knocked Kandler from his feet, and he went down in a cascade of chain links. Sallah slid her sword free, and Kandler found himself staring down its point.

"I'll run you through," Sallah said. She held out her open hand for the key.

Kandler ran the back of his hand across his face. It came back blooded from a cut in his lip. As he held open his hand, the blood shone red against the silvered key in his palm.

The sounds of shouts and screams echoed faintly down the stairwell and into the open cell. Kandler moved to get up, but Sallah pinned him down with her blade again.

"You can't tell me—" Kandler started.

"Silence!" Sallah said. "I need to think."

The lady knight pursed her lips but never looked away from Kandler. A drop of sweat ran from her hair down her cheek. Her emerald eyes burned as she narrowed them in thought. Kandler realized he was holding his breath.

Sallah's mouth formed a frown. For a moment, Kandler's heart dropped into his stomach. "You are sworn to protect the people of this town?" she said.

"It's my job," Kandler said. He stared hard into her eyes. "Let me do it."

"Do you give me your word you will face justice when this is done?" Sallah glared around the cell. "Such as it is?"

"You'd trust a word given under duress?"

Sallah shook her head in frustration. "Bah!" she said. Then she swung her blade up over her shoulder and offered her left hand to help Kandler up. He took it and leaped to his feet.

"Looks like you'll have to trust me," Kandler said with a grim grin.

Sallah pointed at Burch. "Hurry and free your friend," she said. "And don't make me regret this."

Kandler tossed Burch the key. The shifter had his shackles undone in seconds. He rubbed his hairy wrists where the manacles had bit into his skin as he tried to strangle Sallah. "No hard feelings, lady," he said.

"No time for that," Sallah said as another scream sounded out above, much closer this time. She nodded at the others, then sprinted out of the cell and up the stairs beyond.

Kandler and Burch stopped only a moment to gather their weapons where they'd been stored on the landing at the bottom of the stairs. "Hurry!" Sallah said, waiting halfway up the steps.

Kandler buckled on his sword and stuffed his knife into the sheath on the back of his belt. Burch slipped his own sword belt over his shoulders and snatched up his crossbow. They nodded at each other and sprinted up the stairs, Sallah struggling to stay ahead of them.

As the trio emerged into the town hall, Kandler looked up and saw that someone—Temmah probably—had raised the tarp that usually covered the chandelier of everbright lanterns hanging from the large room's tall, peaked roof. The light spilling down from the ceiling lit the three long tables in the center of the room, but it cast the plain wooden walls in shadow.

The justicar glanced around and saw Temmah pushing against the heavy, wooden front doors of the place with all his might, although they stood closed and barred. Something outside banged on the doors hard enough to rattle the thick, ironbound bar that lay across them. The stout windows in the large, solid building were barred as well, as they usually were when the hall wasn't being used.

"What's going on?" Kandler asked.

Startled, Temmah screamed. Coming from the dwarf's normally deep-voiced throat, it was like cold steel sliding along Kandler's spine.

Temmah flipped around and pressed his back to the doors. "Thank Aureon!" he said as another blow shook the doors and rattled his teeth. "We're under attack!"

"Who is it?" Kandler motioned for Burch to grab the other end of a large table. They carried it over and shoved it against the door to lend it support. The banging continued.

"We don't know," said Temmah, his eyes wide with fear, his face and clothes spattered with blood. "I had just deputized a few men in the town square when they came in out of the darkness. Whatever they are, they tore Patelko's head clean off."

Kandler's mind zoomed through a list of possible attackers. The region had been quiet since the disappearances had started two weeks back. Perhaps whoever was behind the missing people had gotten tired of picking off the citizens of Mardakine one at a time. Privately, Kandler hoped so. All his investigations so far had borne little fruit, and he was ready to put an end to this.

"Is it a living spell from the Mournland?" Burch asked, his hushed voice just audible over the banging.

"Anything's possible," said Kandler. He glanced at Sallah. She was staring at the door—or, as it seemed to Kandler, through it.

"I can feel their evil," the lady knight said.

"They're trying to break down the door and kill us," said Kandler. "I'd say their evil is pretty well established."

"Hold on," Sallah said, still concentrating. "There are three of them right outside the door. One is far more powerful than the others. The darkness in him is deep."

The banging came faster and more furious. The bar bent. The doors began to give.

"Step away from the door," Kandler whispered to Temmah

Temmah's wide eyes goggled at the justicar. "I'm the only thing holding those creatures out!"

Kandler pulled his sword. "Move!" he whispered again.

"You're not the justicar anymore," Temmah said, as if he'd failed to convince even himself of that fact.

Kandler pointed his blade at the dwarf. "I'm reinstating myself. Consider this a direct order."

Temmah crossed his eyes at the pointed end of the sword before him, then grimaced. "All right," he said. Kandler had rarely heard such resignation in the dour dwarf's voice. "I just hope you know what you're doing."

Temmah leaped away from the doors. The attackers outside felt the loss of the dwarf's weight, and the pounding became worse than ever.

Kandler drew back his sword as if he was aiming a punch,

and he pointed his blade at the slim gap between the doors. Each time the attackers slammed into the doors, the gap between them grew a hint larger. Soon, the bar would break, and the doors would fling open under this terrible assault.

"Come on in and get it!" Kandler said.

A face appeared in the gap. It seemed human, but its skin was a pale white, more the color of bleached bones than flesh. Its lips were stained with crimson fluid that dribbled down its chin. Its eyes were wide and filled with the dark color of fresh, thick blood. It cackled as it thrust its face into the light, exposing a mouthful of sharp, pointed fangs.

"Yessss!" the face hissed.

CHAPTER

11

Kandler shoved his blade right into the thing's mouth. He felt it grate along the creature's spine and pop out through the back of its neck. Its eyes burned like glowing coals for a moment as it tried to scream. Kandler had never seen such unbridled hatred in a face that looked so human. His mind wanted to deny it could be. Then the creature disappeared in puff of smoke.

"That was a vampire," Sallah said as she scowled at Kandler in frustration, "and you just invited the damned thing in!"

The banging on the door stopped. "Seems to be working so far," Burch said as he cocked his ears, trying to hear where the creatures might now be.

Kandler cursed inwardly. He couldn't believe he'd been so stupid. Undead creatures like that were strong enough to break down the door anytime they liked. They hadn't been banging on the door. They'd been knocking on it.

The justicar sheathed his sword, then picked up a chair and smashed it over a table. Long, jagged parts of the legs remained in his hands. He tossed one of the legs to Burch. If they were going to survive this, they'd have to do it right. They couldn't afford any more mistakes.

"Where are they?" Kandler asked Sallah. His mind fled

to his house, to Esprë. Although he didn't believe much in the gods, he felt a strong urge to pray. He wanted to run out into the night, to race to his home, and to hold his daughter tight. He had to be patient though. If the creatures killed him, he'd be no help to anyone, and he certainly didn't want to lead them to his porch.

The lady knight stepped up to the battered front doors. There was still a gap between them, but although the bar had bent it had held. She touched it with her left hand while she drew back her sword for a blow with her right. She concentrated for a moment, then gasped. "They're gone."

"They're looking for easier prey!" Temmah said with a nervous smile. He flipped a quick salute at Kandler. "That was a dandy of a blow."

Kandler wanted to smile, but he knew better. "I didn't hurt that thing. Steel can't do the job. It'll be back." He glanced around the large, high-ceilinged room. The windows were all shuttered. The back door was barred too. "Any idea how they'll come?" he asked Burch.

The shifter shook his head. "Place is tight."

Kandler grimaced. "Not airtight. Now that I invited them in, they can just turn to mist again and flow right through the gaps."

Sallah put up her hand, and the others fell silent. "They're on the move. Oh!"

"What?" Kandler said as he moved closer to her. He hated relying on someone else like this, especially someone he didn't really know. And, he had to admit to himself, the fact that she was a paladin, a god's chosen knight, rubbed him the wrong way too.

The destruction of the Mournland had convinced Kandler that one of two things were true. Either the gods didn't care what happened to the people of Khorvaire, or the gods were out to get them. Either way, he wanted nothing to do with them.

Sallah pulled back her lips and revealed her gritted teeth. "There are more of them. Many more."

The banging started on the front door again. Temmah yelped, then slapped a thick hand over his red face and muttered an apology.

"I don't get it," said Temmah. "If they can come in, why the knocking?"

Kandler knew the knocking was just a distraction meant to focus their attention on the door while the vampires circled around and came in another way. He started to respond to Temmah, but Sallah cut him off with a sharp wave of her hand. She concentrated for a moment then performed a slow pirouette, her empty hand stretched out as if to feel for something. Her eyes flung wide, and she spun about and stabbed her finger at the back door. "There!"

Kandler turned to see a strange clump of mist swirling around the inside of the back door. A moment later, it coalesced into the vampire Kandler had stabbed.

"You are a rotten host," the vampire said with a grin, swirling his black cloak around him as he spoke. A crimson emblem of a gaping maw filled with fangs was embroidered on the cloak's left breast. "Do you stab all your guests?"

"What are you doing here?" Kandler said as he hefted the splintered chair leg in his hand.

"Oh!" said the vampire. "She hasn't told you yet?" The creature licked the blood from his lips. "How . . . *delicious!*"

"He's a Karrn," Sallah said.

"That's all I need to know," Kandler said as he advanced, holding the stake before him. The justicar didn't care much for people from Karrnath—especially if they were undead bloodsuckers bent on killing him.

Sallah matched Kandler stride for stride. Burch angled off to the right, and Temmah kept pressing his back against the front door as the creatures outside continued to pound on it

"He may have weaseled his way in here," Sallah said, "but he can't invite others. It's not his place."

"Correct, witch-knight," the vampire said, its eyes glittering red against its eggshell skin, its mouth a savage slash filled with teeth. "But wrong all the same." With a flick of his wrist, the vampire flung the bar from the town hall's back door.

Burch's crossbow twanged, and a wooden bolt pierced the vampire's heart and jutted from his chest. The undead thing collapsed without a sound, falling on the bolt and driving it further into its chest.

"Secure that door!" Sallah said.

Kandler sprinted over to the door picked up the heavy bar. Before he could drop it into place someone outside of the hall knocked the door inward and clean off its hinges. The justicar had to jump back to keep the slab of wood from falling on him.

Two creatures stomped through the naked portal. They walked like men and bore the arms and armor of great warriors, but their flesh was torn and rotten, hanging from their frames in ragged strips. Their eyes were dark, empty sockets. Their breastplates bore the same crimson symbol that appeared on the vampire's cloak. They snarled from their desert-dry throats, and they beat their blades on the ground as they stampeded in, daring any to stand before them.

"Zombies!" Burch said as he reloaded his crossbow.

"Karrn shocktroopers," Kandler said, recognizing the creatures' rotting uniforms. He raised his sword before him and leveled a swing at the first creature's head.

The zombie parried the blow easily, but it failed to counter Kandler's follow-up attack. The justicar's blade clanged off the creature's sword, just as he had intended, then slipped under the creature's blade and breastplate and sliced clean through its backbone. It hesitated for a moment and loosed a dry screech before it fell into two pieces. Its top overbalanced first and hit the ground before its knees, sending up a cloud of dust. Kandler almost choked on the stench.

The other zombie stepped forward, its jagged blade raised high as it aimed a blow at Kandler's neck. Busy with the first creature, he gritted his teeth and waited for the blade to slash at him. He hoped he'd be able to catch it on his armored shoulder rather than his face.

Sallah stepped between the two, shielding the justicar with her body. A silvery flame flickered along the length of her sword as she shoved it into the zombie's face. Its light illuminated the empty corners of the zombie's eye sockets.

"Get back!" Sallah screamed. "Your kind holds no sway here."

The zombie raised its arm to defend itself, as if the silvery light blinded its long-lost eyes. It let loose a dry, wordless scream as it turned and stomped out of the town hall the way it had come.

Kandler made to follow the creature, but Temmah screamed at the justicar to stop. "You don't know what's out there!" he said.

Kandler looked back at the dwarf. Temmah shook so hard that Kandler could hear his armor rattling from it.

"Esprë's out there," Kandler said. His voice felt raw with fear, but he hoped the others could not hear it. "That's all I need to know."

CHAPTER

12

A series of three short screams pierced the night. Each began full-throated with mortal fear, and each was cut horribly short. Deothen made the sign of the flame on his chest at the end of each one by drawing his fingertips down the length of his sternum in a wavering line. With the last, he stood and whispered a silent prayer that the Silver Flame would embrace the screamers with its cleansing tongues.

"By the Host!" Mardak said, leaping up from the head of his dining table, at which he had been hosting a meal with all the knights but Sallah.

The repast had been hastily prepared but tasty. Deothen suspected that Priscinta's pride wouldn't allow her to serve her guests a bad meal despite the way her husband had treated her earlier today. She had gone about the task of feeding the knights, her husband, and her son, never meeting their eyes, her cheeks burning with anger and shame. When Deothen had offered his thanks for the meal, she had coughed out a weak response and dashed from the room. He hadn't seen her since.

"What's happening out there?" Mardak said, panic stabbing through his voice as he stared out into the darkness through the dining room's large front window.

"Tira's tongue," Deothen cursed as he reached for his sword and his staff. "I thought we had more time." He turned to the three knights sitting around the table and began to bark out orders. They each complied without question or hesitation, their faces masks that concealed the terror Deothen knew stirred in their hearts. "Gweir, secure the back door!"

The blond-haired knight drew his blade and charged out of the room.

"Brendis, take the front!"

The dark-haired knight dashed for the porch.

"Levritt, you're in charge of Pradak."

The young knight nodded as he drew his sword and stood next to Mardak's son, his hand on the younger man's shoulder. The dark-haired Pradak trembled so that it seemed as if Levritt's hand actually held the boy from falling over.

"What should I do?" Mardak asked. The mayor's blue eyes darted nervously about the room, looking for danger from every quarter.

Deothen glared at the man. "Find your wife."

Mardak swallowed as he met the eldest knight's eyes. He reached up and pulled down his sword from where he'd hung it over the entrance to the room. As he'd done that, he'd explained to Deothen that it was a tradition of those who hosted meals in Cyre, designed to show both that the host was skilled in arms but also that he'd put all weapons aside for the meal. Mardak drew the blade from its scabbard slowly, almost ceremonially. Then another scream echoed through the town, and he nearly leaped from his clothes. Without looking back at Deothen, the mayor tossed the sheath and belt to one side and strode from the room.

Deothen closed his eyes and said a quick prayer as he touched the iridescent symbol embroidered across the front of his tabard. "May the power of the Silver Flame protect me against evil in all its forms." As he spoke, he felt the blessings of his god flow through his hands and throughout his body.

Deothen opened his eyes and listened. More screams

sounded in the distance. He hefted his staff, the silver light blazing from its tip and reflecting brilliantly in his icy eyes. Then he drew his sword, which burst into silvery flames as it left its scabbard. "And may we do what we can to protect these innocents," he said.

The senior knight strode out onto Mardak's porch. The edges of the crater that cradled the town lay enveloped in darkness. No moonlight broke through the layer of clouds that seemed to always swirl out from the encroaching edges of Mournland.

"The evil that lurks out there is in its element," Deothen said to Brendis, who stood beside him, peering into the night.

"The light of the Silver Flame will illuminate our path," the young knight said. Deothen saw the light from his staff glittering in the knight's eyes.

"Good lad," Deothen said. He clapped Brendis on his armored shoulder. "You have studied hard and well. Now it is time to put your lessons to the test. Can you feel them out there?"

Brendis concentrated and reached out with his soul. "No," he shook his head finally.

Deothen nodded. "Sometimes, lad, it's not a matter of how hard you look." A scream sounded from the direction of the kitchen behind them, and a shout followed from the back yard. "But where! With me!"

Deothen felt his joints creak as he sprinted into the house. Sometimes it seemed as if they were louder than the jangling of his armor. Brendis followed him into the house, where they bumped into Levritt and Pradak poking their noses out of the dining room. Both young men had their swords at the ready, although neither looked particularly ready to use them.

"Go to the kitchen to support Mardak and Priscinta," Deothen said to Levritt and his charge. "Brendis and I will lend Gweir our blades out back."

Deothen and Brendis charged out the rear of the manor.

There they saw Gweir facing off against five of the shambling soldiers from Karrnath. He charged into them, his blade blazing, and the dead things let loose a crackling laugh.

The two knights rushed to join the third, all three swords burning bright in the night, casting strange, silver-edged shadows as their steel lengths danced with those held by long-dead hands. Within moments, the creatures lay in several smoldering piles at the knights' feet.

Before Deothen could congratulate the younger knights on a battle well fought, another scream pierced the night.

"That came from inside," said Gweir.

"Priscinta," Deothen said as he ran back into the house. The high, throaty wail could belong to no one else. The elder knight wound his way through the home into the kitchen, with Gweir and Brendis clanging after him. They found Levritt and Pradak pounding on the kitchen door.

"It's locked," Levritt said as Deothen shouldered him aside. Fearful of what he might find inside, Deothen nodded to Gweir and Brendis, and all three lowered their armored shoulders and smashed into the door at once.

The knights stumbled over the threshold, past the splintered latch, and into the dimly lit room. In the red glow of the fire blazing in the fireplace against the far wall, they saw Priscinta brandishing a meat cleaver and a wooden spoon at a tall, pale man dressed in a flowing black cloak. Mardak's body lay at her feet, gouts of blood spurting from a gash in his neck.

The pale intruder whirled about as the knights burst in, turning his blazing red eyes on them and baring his face full of savage teeth. "Enter, Knights of the Silver Flame," he said. "I will extinguish your flaming brands with your own blood!"

Priscinta swung her cleaver down and chopped the head off of her wooden spoon, leaving only the pointed remnant of the handle in her hand. She stabbed at the vampire with it as the knights fanned out in the room, but her blow landed wide of its mark, puncturing the creature's shoulder instead of its heart.

"You'll pay for that, witch!" the vampire said through its bared fangs as it spun around and backhanded Priscinta away. She crumpled in a heap near the fireplace.

Pradak let loose with a feral howl and dashed past Deothen to hurl himself at the vampire. The creature smirked at the young man's effort and flung wide its arms to enfold Pradak in his unforgiving embrace.

The vampire cackled as he pulled back Pradak's head to expose the young man's unblemished neck. The walls of the kitchen echoed with Priscinta's horrified scream, a sound so terrible it chilled Deothen's bones. Before the creature could strike, though, the knight stepped forward and held his burning sword high before him. Its flames licked the ceiling.

"Abomination!" Deothen said to the vampire in a voice that rolled through the room like thunder. "You are an affront to the purity of the Silver Flame, and for that you shall be consumed!"

As Deothen spoke, the vampire froze in place, and his eyes wide in fear. Like a moth to the flame, he seemed unable to wrest his eyes away from the light of the flaming sword before him. He dropped Pradak and unleashed a final, horrifying cry, like metal scraping dry bone. A moment later, it turned into a column of dust that cascaded to the kitchen's cold stone floor.

Deothen grabbed Pradak by the shoulder and guided him into Levritt's grasp. "Escort him back to the dining room," the eldest knight said, "and this time keep him there!"

The young knight jumped to obey.

Deothen glanced around and listened for the sound of further threats. The only sounds were the breathing of the knights and Priscinta whimpering softly near the fire. "We seem to have repulsed the first assault," he said to Brendis and Gweir. "Resume your posts for the moment and prepare for battle. We will take this fight to them soon."

As the others left, Deothen knelt down to examine Mardak's body. The vampire dust coated the mayor's head and shoulders, the blood and ashen remains mixing into a thick, black paste where they commingled. The knight brushed the mixture aside with his mailed hand.

"I'm impressed that you were able to defend yourself so well," Deothen remarked to Priscinta as he examined the wound that had laid Mardak low.

"I was once a knight of the Sovereign Host," said Priscinta through her tears. Her voice was raw with sorrow and, from what Deothen could tell, rage. "I am no stranger to such creatures."

"It is too bad you couldn't say the same of your husband." The knight ran his finger along the length of the wound. The blow had nearly taken off Mardark's head. The cut was clean. The vampire had carried no weapon. Such creatures usually preferred to kill their prey with their bare hands.

"No," said Priscinta as she struggled to her knees, the cleaver still clutched in her hand. "He was a creature I knew far too well."

Deothen nodded and then ducked to the side at the last moment. He knew that Priscinta had seen him examining the wound, that he knew of her guilt. He'd hoped she'd simply confess to him, but she apparently wasn't going to make it that easy.

The cleaver in Priscinta's hand glanced off the steel spaulder protecting Deothen's right shoulder. Still kneeling next to Mardak's body, he whipped about and planted the point of his sword against the woman's chest. She froze.

As the knight stood, his blade's point still on Priscinta, he gazed at the woman. She had barely come out of the kitchen since the knights had arrived to break bread with Mardak. Her right eye was puffy and bruised from when Mardak had struck her earlier in the day. Her lip was broken and bleeding, but that wound was fresh. Fear warred with righteous anger in her eyes.

"It . . . it was the vampire," Priscinta said, stumbling over her words.

Deothen didn't need the favors of his god to know the words

were lies. This had been a good woman, he could tell, and such deceptions did not come naturally to her. He winced to hear her continue on.

"It bent Mardak's mind to its will," Priscinta said. "He attacked me." She fought back a dry sob. Madness danced in her eyes. "I had to defend myself."

Deothen pulled back his blade but held it at the ready. Priscinta dropped the cleaver and sagged. She looked a great deal older than she had that afternoon.

"Did you fear these dusty remains might have done the same to me?" Deothen whispered.

Priscinta shrugged and looked away. A single tear ran down her bruised and beaten face. "We live in a strange and unknowable world. Who can say what is possible?" Her gaze fell on her husband's corpse. Deothen could see that Mardak's eyes were frozen wide in surprise, although they were buried blind under a patina of the vampire's dust.

"Please don't tell my son," Priscinta said as she fell back on her knees, tears streaming down her face. She pleaded madly with the knight. "Isn't it bad enough he's lost his father?"

Deothen felt ill.

CHAPTER

13

A single light burned in the front window of Kandler's home as he approached it. No sounds came from within.

The justicar had left Burch and Sallah in the center of town to rally the townsfolk who had fled there. Burch had insisted on accompanying Kandler, but he had refused. "Esprë needs me," he'd said to his old friend, "but Mardakine does too. Stand here for us both while I find her."

The shifter had slapped Kandler on the back and wished him good speed as he dashed off toward his home.

The shutters on the front window of Kandler's home swung loose and wide. The hook that normally kept them shut after dark had been torn from its mooring. Kandler stopped and listened. Still no sound, not even the sobbing of a girl.

Kandler crept up his front stairs and over to the window, which gaped as wide as a dragon's maw. His sword before him, he poked his nose over the weathered, wooden sill. The lantern burning on the table in the center of the main room shed a flickering light on the scene. For a moment, the justicar saw nothing wrong. He blew out a long, silent sigh.

The sigh caught in his throat as the blood splashed across the room's rear wall caught his eye. It looked like it had been flung there by a careless artist working with red paint.

Kandler grimaced and ducked back below the sill. He considered sneaking around the back, but there was no telling who was hurt or how much time she might have left. He drew in a deep breath, stood, and wound his way around to stand before the door. He launched himself and threw his shoulder right at the point he knew would shatter the latch, but the door did not resist. It smashed open and bounced off the wall behind it.

The justicar's eyes darted about the room as he entered it. The stove was cold, as it always was at this time of night. Some of the furniture had been overturned. The table blocked his view of the bottom of the bloodstained wall. He barged past it, and he found a small body there, crumpled across a broken, toppled chair.

Kandler reached down with his free hand to pull back the girl's dark, matted hair, although he already knew what he would find. Norra's eyes were frozen wide with fear in a face still puffy from weeping most of the day. Blood trickled from her mouth and nose. It was too late for her.

A mixture of relief, terror, grief, and shame washed over Kandler. He was thrilled that the body hadn't been Esprë's, but that meant that his daughter was still out there somewhere. He mourned Norra, but the guilt over his relief colored that emotion.

The justicar lay Norra down on her back and tugged her eyes closed with the palm of his hand. He could do this much for her now at least. She might have given her life defending Esprë. He only hoped her sacrifice would not be in vain.

Kandler held his breath and listened again. A floorboard creaked low and soft in the back of the house. He recognized the noise. He heard it every time he stood next to the footlocker at the end of his bed.

His sword in hand, Kandler crept along the main room's back wall until he reached the door to his chamber. The door itself was a thin slab of wooden planks held together by a pair of crossbeams. It cleared the top and bottom of the frame by a few irregular inches. A dim light shone under the door, but as Kandler watched it went out.

Kandler raised his sword and kicked in the door. He blinked as his eyes adjusted to the darkness. The shutters on the room's sole window flapped open in the stiffening wind.

"Esprë?" Kandler whispered. As the words left his lips, he regretted them. If the girl popped out at him without warning, though, he feared he might kill her by reflex.

"It's all right, sir," a voice growled out of the darkness at him. A thin and wiry silhouette stepped partly from the shadows. "She's safe."

"Burch?" Kandler lowered his blade an inch. Something about this wasn't right. *Sir?* Burch never called anyone sir, even knights. "Where is she?"

"I sent her to Norra's house, sir."

Kandler let loose a false sigh of relief. "Thank the Silver Flame," Kandler said, his mind racing. Who was this creature that looked something like Burch, at least in the dimly lit room? Where was Esprë?

"Come on," Kandler said. He lowered his blade as he spoke. He needed this creature alive. "Let's go get her."

The justicar turned and stepped out of the room. As he walked into the light in the main room of his house, he heard the shifter step up behind him, just as he'd hoped.

Kandler reached back and grabbed the shifter by the arm. He spied a long, silvery knife in the creature's hand, and he knew that it had been meant for his heart, probably to be stabbed in from behind and up under his ribs.

Rolling forward, Kandler hurled the lighter creature over his shoulder and into the room, slamming him onto his back. The air whooshed from the creature's lungs, and Kandler pounced on him before he could recover.

The justicar kicked the creature in the ribs, once, twice. He felt the bones there snap under his assault, and he smiled. This creature was behind Esprë's disappearance, he was sure, and he wanted him to hurt for it. The third time Kandler kicked, though, the shifter grabbed his foot and twisted hard.

Kandler crashed to the ground. He landed on his sword arm but avoided slicing himself on his own blade, which went skittering from his hand. Frustrated at himself for letting his foe get the better of him, he lashed out with his free foot and booted the shifter in the nose.

The shifter let go of Kandler's foot and scrambled for the door. The justicar knew that if the creature reached the darkness outside of the house he might never find him, and then Esprë might be lost to him forever. He wasn't going to let that happen.

Kandler leaped to his feet and grabbed the nearest thing at hand—a frying pan hanging from a nail on the wall. He hurled it, and it caught the creature flat in the back.

The shifter tumbled down the front stairs of Kandler's home and into the night. Kandler had hoped the creature would trip on the porch or, better yet, fall back into the house. He cursed his luck and rushed forward, his heart pounding in his ears. The justicar dashed out the door and leaped down atop the creature, trying to crush it beneath his bulk.

Kandler fell on the shifter with all his weight. He felt the satisfaction of a rib or three cracking under him as he landed squarely on the creature. The shifter let out a high-pitched yelp.

Kandler threw his arms under the shifter's then reached up and laced his fingers behind the shifter's head. The creature thrashed about, trying to slip free, but Kandler just squeezed his arms together harder. This creature was his only link to Esprë, and he was never going to let go.

The shifter thrashed about like a wild animal, struggling to get free from Kandler's hold. The justicar pressed his elbows together, trying to force the fight from the creature. "Where is she?" he growled. Even to his own ears, he sounded desperate bordering on mad.

The creature in Kandler's arms became both taller and

broader. Its teeth morphed into tusks, and its skin grew rough and leathery. From the smell alone, Kandler didn't need to turn his foe around to know he was now holding something that looked almost exactly like an orc. The thing let loose a stomach-wrenching snarl.

Kandler pulled his elbows back nearly a foot, bending the orc's arms back nearly to the breaking point. Then he bore down and forward, slamming the thing's face into the ground. He felt the orc's snout smash into the crater's hardened floor. One of the creature's tusks broke off and stabbed it in the face. The creature yelped in pain. Kandler felt the blood pooling around his arms.

"I've dealt with your kind before, changeling," Kandler said. "I won't let go."

The justicar felt something tickling about at the base of his brain. His fingers started to go numb. It reminded Kandler of his youth in Sharn, the wondrous City of Towers. Once, at a friend's birthday party, a performer had asked him to come onstage to help out with a trick. The little gnome had reached into Kandler's brain and stunned him silly for a moment. He hadn't realized what had happened until he'd come to a moment later and saw everyone laughing at the way he was drooling down his shirt.

Afterward, Kandler had asked his father what had happened. "That was a psion, son," the old man had said, his huge paw of a hand on the young Kandler's shoulder. "They use their brains to mess with ours. You can't trust them for a second."

Still a bit confused, Kandler had asked his father what he should do if something like that happened again. The old man just flashed his son a rueful smile. "Me?" he said with an ironic laugh, "I'd kill him. But that's not for you, son. I'm just a soldier. You'll be better than that."

The efforts of the creature in his arms brought all the shame and confusion back into Kandler's head, and he used those emotions to force the tendrils from his mind. He found the outrage blazing in his heart and centered on that, shoving the invader back. He bore down harder and ground the orc's face into the dirt. What was left of its tusks scraped against the rocky floor.

"Get—out—of—my—head!" Kandler growled. He pounded the orc's face against the ground to punctuate each word. The sensation in the justicar's head vanished.

Kandler snorted down at the creature in his arms. "If I feel an inkling of you in my brain, I'll snap your neck." To emphasize his seriousness, he squeezed the creature's neck between the heels of his hands, and the fight slid out of it.

The creature in Kandler's arms slimmed down and grew shorter. Its hair lengthened, and its skin became smooth and pale. Its shape changed too, and Kandler realized he was now holding a woman.

"You're quite the warrior, justicar," the changeling said through lips now unbroken by an orc's shattered tusk. "It'll be a sad day when I have to kill you."

"Where's my daughter?" Kandler said. The creature's bravado hadn't unnerved him, but he struggled to keep his desperation about Esprë's safety from his voice.

The changeling snickered as best she could. "If I tell you, you'll kill me."

Kandler slammed the changeling's face into the ground again. "If you don't talk, I'll kill you for sure."

"You're bluffing," the changeling said. She morphed into something softer, sweeter—a slim lady elf with long, blonde hair.

It was the scent of her hair that informed Kandler instantly that he was holding the form of his wife again—the dear, deceased Esprina. For a moment, his grief over her death threatened to flood him, but he shoved it back. He hadn't been with his wife when she'd died on the Day of Mourning, and he'd spent many long, empty nights since wishing he'd had one last chance. This wasn't her though, and that thought made him angrier than ever.

Kandler ground the changeling's fine features into the

crater floor and flexed his muscles, pulling her arms back to breaking. He knew what had happened. The creature had pulled the image of his long-dead wife from his mind and transformed into her, hoping that the presence of his beloved would break his will. In that, she'd made a horrible, perhaps final mistake.

"Don't you *dare* use her against me," Kandler snarled, his ferocity surprising even him. "Last chance, then you die. *Where is my daughter?*"

The changeling cried out in pain but didn't say a word.

"I'll break your back and leave you for the zombies," Kandler said. "Read my mind, psion. Tell me if I'm bluffing." He forced aside any doubts he might have had about this course of action, and he hoped it would be enough.

Kandler flexed again and felt the changeling's arms start to pop. She yelped as she morphed back into her natural form. "All right!" she said. "All right!"

Kandler eased up on his hold, but just barely, enough to let the creature talk. "Where is she?"

"The others have her," the changeling said through gritted teeth, her cheek still shoved against the ground. "The vampires. She's in the main square." The battered changeling started to laugh. With Kandler's weight on her, it came out weak and shallow and set off a fit of coughing.

Kandler leaned over on the changeling so he could look in her pale, empty eyes. "What's so funny?" he asked, although he knew he wouldn't like the answer.

The changeling smiled. "I'm in telepathic contact with the vampire who has your daughter. With just a thought from me, he'll rip out her throat. Get off. Now."

It was Kandler's turn to be afraid.

CHAPTER

14

Kandler got to his knees, the changeling still in his grasp. For a long moment, he considered killing the creature then and there. If he was quick enough about it, she might be dead before she could even think about Esprë. It was impossible from this angle though. He could choke the changeling to death, but it would take too long. He loosed his hold and shoved the creature to the ground.

The changeling dusted herself off as she made her way to her knees. She winced at her cracked ribs and turned to look up at Kandler. The creature's face looked like a moon in the dim light spilling out of the house, soft and distant, yet still strongly feminine. The scratches and cuts on her rounded cheeks and on her thin slash of a mouth disappeared as Kandler watched. Her blank, white eyes seemed to glow softly in the darkness. She spoke as she started to her feet

"Now let's see who's in charge he—"

Before the changeling could finish, Kandler lashed out with his boot and caught her across the jaw. The blow stunned her, he saw, but it did not put her out. She reeled backward. Desperate to save Esprë, Kandler pressed his advantage, never giving her a moment's respite. He brutalized her with foot and fist, beating her until she stopped resisting, until she stopped moving.

Kandler grabbed the psion by the front of her tunic and hauled her toward the beam of light stabbing from his home's front door. Pinkish blood dribbled from her battered face. Her breathing was shallow but steady. He tossed her aside, picked up his sword, and dashed back into town.

With any luck at all, Kandler figured he would reach Esprë before the changeling regained her senses. He considered killing her there and then, but he feared he might need her later. Also, he didn't know if he could bring himself to kill her in cold blood. Taking a life in the heat of battle was one thing. Executing a helpless foe was something else altogether.

As Kandler sprinted toward the town square, he heard clashing swords and screams of terror and triumph up ahead. Someone had tossed more kindling on Shawda's still-smoldering funeral pyre in the main square, and the flickering light reflected off the low-hanging tendrils from the Mournland that were always reaching out over the Mardakine crater.

The justicar turned a corner, and battle lay before him. Men and women of Mardakine fought toe to toe with more of the tall, dusty figures dressed in ill-fitting armor forged in the fires of Karrnath. Their bones rattled as loudly as their swords as they clashed with the desperate townspeople.

"For Cyre!" Rislinto thundered, silhouetted against the flames. One of the strongest men Kandler had ever known, the warrior-turned-blacksmith bore a dwarven warhammer instead of a blade, his long years at the forge having made his skill with such a tool a second nature to him.

As Kandler ran to Rislinto's aid, the blacksmith's warhammer fell again and again, crushing undead flesh and snapping bones. "We lost one home!" the bearlike man thundered. "We won't lose another!"

At these words, a cheer went up from the townsfolk in the square, and they redoubled their efforts. As Kandler sprinted toward the action, he saw a pale, black-cloaked figure coalesce from a cloud of reddish mist hanging over Rislinto's broad shoulders. The justicar shouted a warning, but he knew it was too late. The blacksmith was too far away to hear him, and Kandler knew he'd never reach his old friend in time.

Kandler and Burch had scouted out this crater with Rislinto and Mardak back when the two sons of Cyre had first come up with the idea of establishing a settlement on the edge of the Mournland. The four had founded the town together, and now it was all falling apart. All Kandler could do was watch his friend die.

The telltale *clack* of Burch's crossbow sounded out, and the vampire behind Rislinto fell over with a wooden bolt in its heart. Kandler looked about for the shifter on the nearby rooftops as he sprinted toward the square, but Burch had already moved on.

As Kandler neared the square, he angled to the right, his eyes hunting for other black-clad creatures and for Esprë's shimmering golden hair. On the other side of the bonfire, he saw the flaming swords of the Knights of the Silver Flame swinging in the darkness, the light reflecting off their polished armor.

Right before the justicar, Priscinta and Pradak—mother and son—fought back to back, the Karrn zombies closing in on all sides. For a moment, Kandler wondered where Mardak might be, but he pushed the thought aside. It didn't matter. The important thing was that Priscinta and Pradak were outnumbered two to one. They would be dead in moments without help.

The justicar cursed. He needed to find Esprë before the changeling woke up, but he could not bring himself to abandon others so clearly in need. He charged into the relentless creatures from the rear, slashing all about with his sword.

Kandler's blade clanged ineffectively off the Karrn armor, but it just as often bit into rotted flesh and dried bone. The justicar hacked back and forth, spinning wildly as he went. He had to kill these creatures quickly, or Esprë would be doomed.

As Kandler cursed the vampires, the zombies, and the knights who he guessed might have brought them there, he glanced over and saw Pradak stumble before one of the undead Karrn warriors.

Pradak had been but a boy during the last days of the war, just four years past. Although he bore the promise of his father's legendary skill with a longsword, he lacked the hard-won experience earned only on the field of battle. Having laid one zombie low, he had stepped forward to press his advantage and slipped on his victim's corpse.

Kandler had seen many a young warrior make this same mistake. Few of them had lived to repeat it. War had no mercy, no matter how young the warrior.

The zombie standing over Pradak rasped a horrible laugh and raised its jagged blade high in both hands, its tip pointed toward the young man's chest. As the creature jammed the blade down to impale Pradak on its steely length, Priscinta dove at the zombie, bowling it backward. The two rolled away in a ball of thrashing arms and slashing steel.

Kandler ran over to Pradak and hauled the young man to his feet with his free hand. "You're a lucky boy," he said.

Pradak hefted his sword once again and began to offer his thanks. Before he could speak, the zombie battling Priscinta ran her through. The woman's gurgling cry ended with a snap as the Karrn bashed her with its free hand, and she fell to the ground.

Kandler reached out to try to stop Pradak from throwing himself into a suicidal attack to avenge his mother, but it was already too late. Mad with grief, Pradak launched himself toward his mother's killer.

What Pradak lacked in skill he made up for in rage. The youth lunged at the zombie standing over Priscinta, still gloating over its victory. Kandler watched as Pradak leveled a two-handed slash at the creature's neck, and an instant later its head spiraled away. Before the young man could enjoy his victory, another of the undead warriors laid into him.

Kandler stepped up beside the youth and lent his sword to his efforts. "Deothen!" he shouted. "We need a healer here!"

The senior knight did not respond. Kandler glanced over, and he saw one of the black-robed creatures turn to dust before Deothen's righteous wrath. The wind caught the dust and blew it into the fire where it formed an ascending spiral of glowing embers reaching into the night sky.

Deothen spat a single word at Sallah, who was standing next to him as the vampire vanished. While the senior knight directed the efforts of the others against the Karrn, she turned and ran over to Kandler. "Are you hurt?" she called as she ran, panting with the work of battle.

Kandler parried a blow from one of the undead Karrns and wrenched open its breastplate with his sword. The zombie screeched in surprise, but the justicar cut that short with a slash across the creature's exposed lungs. Two more quick moves, and the creature lay in a heap of bones and old, rotten meat at Kandler's feet, just as Sallah reached his side.

"Not us." Kandler pointed to the body lying at Pradak's feet. The boy stood staring wide-eyed out into the darkness, waiting for something else to come careening out at them. For the moment, the Karrns were elsewhere, but Kandler could hear the telltale sound of the shuffling gait of the undead circling out in the darkness.

"Priscinta," Sallah said.

The justicar scanned the darkness with one eye. With the other, he watched as the red-haired knight knelt beside Priscinta and checked her for signs of life.

"May the Silver Flame shine brightly on your final journey," Sallah said softly as she closed Priscinta's eyes. Pradak bent his head over her and wept.

Kandler bowed his head for a moment to fight back the emotions that threatened to overwhelm him. There would be time for grieving later. Right now, he had to find Esprë.

CHAPTER

15

"Where are the vampires?" Kandler asked Sallah.

Sallah looked up at the justicar blankly and shook her head. "When your friend Burch and I arrived, we saw a handful of them massacring the townsfolk who dared to stand against them. We set to them and drove them off. Burch brought down two with his crossbow." The lady knight hesitated for a moment. "Your daughter . . . ?"

Kandler could tell by her tone that she feared the worst. He shook his head. "I thought she might be here."

Sir Deothen and the three other knights arrived as Kandler spoke. "When we arrived, the vampires withdrew," the senior knight said. "They were content to let their undead underlings soften us up first, but such creatures could not stand long against the power of the Silver Flame."

Kandler looked around. The battle was over. The zombies either lay still or had fled. The survivors of Mardakine crept from the shadows to unite around the light of the pyre. In the distance, a pair of voices—human voices—shouted in agony.

Pradak knelt on the ground, cradling his mother's body as he shook with tears. Kandler wanted to lend the boy some comfort, but he had his own tragedy to prevent yet.

"Have you seen Esprë?" Kandler asked the knights. "My daughter?"

Deothen shook his head gravely. "Find the wounded and tend to them," Deothen told the other knights. "I must discuss with the justicar what will happen next."

The knights nodded and padded off to execute their orders. Kandler saw Sallah stop near the weeping Pradak for a moment, but she continued on. There were others who needed her help more.

Kandler ignored Deothen for the moment. If the knight didn't know where Esprë was, Kandler didn't care to talk with him. He knew he didn't have much time. He shaded his eyes from the firelight and peered into the darkness. "Burch!" he shouted.

The shifter appeared from behind a window set in a roof across the square. "Here, boss!" He waved his crossbow at the justicar.

Kandler's heart leaped. If anyone could have seen Esprë here, it would have been the sharp-eyed shifter. "Did you see Esprë?"

Burch shook his head. "Not a wink. Thought you'd find her at home."

Kandler felt ill. Perhaps he'd made a horrible mistake leaving the changeling alive. Maybe she'd lied to him about the telepathic link. He didn't know what to think. "Rislinto?" he called. "Are you still out there?"

"Aye." The blacksmith staggered around from the other side of the fire. He pressed his massive hand against his left leg, which bled through his fingers.

"Allow me," Deothen said to Rislinto. The blacksmith nodded his permission and removed his hand. The gash oozed blood.

"Where's Esprë?" Kandler asked as Deothen ministered to Rislinto's leg. The knight lay his hands on the wound and muttered a quick but heartfelt prayer. The skin and flesh knit back together under the soft glow that emanated between Deothen's fingers.

"Dunno," Rislinto said. "Haven't seen her."

"Not the whole time?" Kandler asked. "A changeling I met told me a vampire was holding her hostage here."

Rislinto's deep, humorless laugh rumbled through the square. "You trusted something a changeling told you?"

Ice water ran through Kandler's gut. "Damn, damn, damn!" He turned and raced back to his house.

❦

"It's all right, dear," Te'oma said as she stepped into Kandler's bedroom. "You can come out now." The changeling was bruised from head to toe, but appearances meant nothing to one as her. She used her shapeshifting powers to cover them up. To those who saw her, she would look as good as new, except she would look nothing like herself.

"Are you all right?" Esprë said as emerged from Kandler's wardrobe. The girl's blonde hair shimmered in the light streaming from the main room into the bedchamber. Her face was red as if she'd been crying—or at least trying not to. "I heard fighting."

"More of those creatures," Te'oma said. "Your father took care of them, but we have to leave now."

"Kandler? He's not my real father, you know."

Te'oma nodded as she escorted the girl into the main room. In the light, Esprë saw the same beautiful, dark-haired elf who had shoved her into the wardrobe when they'd heard someone prowling around outside.

"I know. Your father was a fine elf. We all miss him."

Esprë frowned. "I don't remember him. He died before I was born."

"I'm sure he'd be as proud of you as I am." Te'oma gave the girl a hug, even though the effort sent blazing pain through her cracked ribs. She guided Esprë through the main room and out onto the front porch. As she went, she kept her body between the girl and the body lying against the main room's rear wall. Once outside, she relaxed, but it didn't last long.

"Aunt Arnaya?" Esprë asked. "Where's Norra?" Te'oma heard fear creeping into the girl's voice. She had to act quickly or the girl would begin to panic.

The changeling-elf sat the girl down on the porch next to her and wrapped her arm around her. A breeze carried a chill through the air, ruffling their hair like dark and light flags behind them. The girl shivered and snuggled closer to the changeling.

"We must leave soon," the changeling said.

"How soon?"

"Tonight. Horrible things are happening in town, and we have little time to waste." Te'oma wished that the vampires would hurry up and come back. She knew the justicar wouldn't be fooled by her little lie for long.

Esprë thought about that for a while. "Is Valenar a long way?"

"It's a safe ways away. You'll love it there. You'll be with family again." Te'oma looked down at the girl as she spoke. The elf child's naïve nature was charming, and for a moment the changeling wondered how her life might have been different if she'd decided to pursue motherhood instead of . . . this. The thought unsettled her, but it evaporated when she hugged the child closer.

"What about Kandler?" Esprë looked up at Te'oma. "Isn't he coming with us?"

The changeling frowned at the thought of the justicar. "His place is here. His job is here."

Esprë smiled for a moment, then frowned again. "But won't Kandler at least say good-bye?"

"Not tonight, dear," Te'oma said. Lies came easily to her. As a changeling, most of her life was a series of lies as she changed herself about to look like something she really wasn't. Any pangs of conscience she might have felt over this had been buried by the lies long ago. "He asked me to start out with you right away. He said he'd catch up for good-byes soon. He wants to make sure you're safe and happy in your new home. But he has work here tonight. We must leave him to it."

Esprë smiled and hugged the changeling, who winced at the pain but kept silent. "I'm so happy you finally came, Aunt Arnaya."

"I am too." Te'oma stroked Esprë's long blonde hair.

"You have her? Excellent."

At the sound of the voice, Esprë jumped into Te'oma's lap, and the changeling yelped in pain.

A man stood nearby, surrounded in mist. He was tall and thin with high, wide cheekbones set in a gaunt, sculpted face. His skin was the color of the crater floor, and something dark dribbled from his chin. He wore his long, shiny black hair pulled back in a tight ponytail. His eyes glowed like dying coals.

Esprë screamed. She clutched at the changeling like a drowning dwarf.

"Look at me," the figure said. "Look at me!"

Esprë buried her head in the changeling's arms and continued to scream. As she wailed, she kept her eyes closed tight and kicked out with her feet.

Te'oma winced in pain as the child held on to her with all her might. She tried to pull herself free from the girl, but it proved impossible. She shot the man an angry look but kept her tongue.

The man snatched Esprë's legs with one hand and grabbed her head with the other. He pulled her away from Te'oma and held her up before him like a prize fish just pulled from the sea. She struggled against his iron grip, but he forced her face around to point at him. "Look at me," he said quietly.

Esprë closed her eyes tight and screamed again. "Aunt Arnaya! Help me!"

The impulse to leap to the child's aid surprised Te'oma as it awakened in her heart. She shoved it aside, suspecting it was just a side effect of throwing herself so completely into her role as the girl's aunt. Even if she wanted to do something for the girl, it was out of her hands now.

The man spit in the girl's face, and she opened her eyes in rage. Her voice caught in her throat, and Te'oma followed her gaze. Two other pale-skinned figures stood behind the first. Each wore a long, black cloak embroidered with a red mouth filled with teeth as pointed as their own. They glared at the girl.

"Look at me," the man holding Esprë said. Once the girl's eyes locked with the monster's, Te'oma felt Esprë's will slough off like an old snakeskin. She no longer felt the urge to scream, to fight, to flee. She awaited his orders, nothing more.

"Sleep," the man said, and Esprë did.

Te'oma caught the girl before she slipped to the ground. "Tan Du!" she said. "I had things well in hand."

"Would the justicar agree with you?"

"He interrupted me."

"We do not have the time to toy with our prey, no matter how pretty," Tan Du said. He took Esprë from Te'oma's arms and caressed her soft cheek.

"Where are the others?" Te'oma asked. "What happened to the foot soldiers?"

Tan Du grinned. "They were expendable."

"You lost two score of the finest Karrn zombies? And of the seven of your kind we started out with we now have only you three? You call that a success?"

"We have what we came for," said Tan Du. "That is all that should concern you."

Te'oma steamed at the vampire for a moment, then turned away. She couldn't bear to look at him.

Tan Du gazed down at the young elf in his arms. "Is your horse nearby?" he asked.

Te'oma looked back over her shoulder and nodded.

"Excellent. The others will lead you through the darkness."

As Te'oma watched, one of the vampires transformed into a massive, slavering wolf with glowing red eyes. The other morphed into a monstrous bat and flapped high up into the air on its leathery wings. No matter how many times Te'oma saw this, it always disturbed her. The changes weren't natural like hers. It was as if the vampires forced their new forms upon the world—as painfully as possible.

"They will cover the ground and the air," Tan Du said. "All you need do is follow them from here."

"What about you?"

Tan Du smiled. "I have business." He nodded for Te'oma to lead the way, and he followed. He carried Esprë in his arms as if she were as stuffed with feathers. When they reached Te'oma's horse, Tan Du and the other creatures stopped several yards away. The horse whickered at them. This brought a private smile to Te'oma, who felt pleased to be truly alive at the moment.

Te'oma continued on ahead. When she got to the horse, a massive black-coated gelding, she stroked his sides and face and whispered kind words to him. Once the horse was calm, Te'oma rummaged around in his saddlebags and pulled out a wax-sealed vial. She uncorked it with her teeth, which she altered to make as wicked as Tan Du's, and swallowed the pungent liquid in a single gulp.

The potion burned down her throat like homemade liquor and formed a lump in her stomach. She waited for a moment until she felt the warmth spread through her veins. In an instant, she recovered from the beating she'd taken at Kandler's hands, and she was ready to travel.

"Better?" Tan Du said as Te'oma walked back to him and took Esprë from his arms.

"I feel as good as I look," the changeling-elf said.

Tan Du smiled. "Good enough to eat."

Te'oma turned her back on the vampire and strode back to her horse. She pushed Esprë up onto the beast's back and then hoisted herself up behind the girl. She steadied Esprë in front of her and then looked down at Tan Du grinning at her. Te'oma wanted to wipe that self-satisfied look from his face, but she reminded herself that now was not the time.

"How long will you be?" Te'oma asked.

"Not long. Maintain your mindlink with me. I'll use it to follow you."

"As you wish."

Tan Du stepped toward Te'oma, and the horse skittered away. "Be off," the vampire said. "I can hear our guests arriving."

Te'oma turned and spurred her horse to a trot. She and Esprë rode off after the bat flapping away in front of them. The wolf dogged their heels, goading the horse to a gallop.

❦

Tan Du chuckled. Remembering his business, he leaped into the air and transformed into a bat. This was his favorite form. He loved to feel the breeze beneath him as he cut through the air with his light, lithe body.

The vampire flapped into the air until he had enough altitude, then glided down silently until he reached the roof of Kandler's house. He perched there and watched as Kandler, Burch, and Sallah sprinted toward the place.

As the trio charged up the path to the house, Tan Du resumed his normal form. With all their attention on the house's door, the three didn't see him until he announced his presence. "She is gone," he said from the edge of the roof.

The three stopped dead in their tracks and looked up at him. "Ah-ah-ah," Tan Du said as Burch raised his crossbow to fire. He always enjoyed torturing the living, and this encounter would be particularly sweet. "I've seen you with that thing, dogface. Put it away."

Burch held his weapon steady, still pointed at the vampire's heart. Kandler pointed his sword up at the creature. "What do you want?" the justicar said.

Tan Du stood and smirked. He could smell the justicar's fear rolling off him like a skunk. "To talk. Like civilized people." He gestured around him with a flourish and said, "I realize that this is not a civilized place, but I think we can rise above that."

"Where's my daughter?" asked Kandler.

"Ah, right to the point." Tan Du smiled, baring his fangs. "Very direct. I like that. It's refreshing."

"Answer me!"

Tan Du frowned, disappointed that the justicar didn't seem interested in sparring with him. "The girl is safe. For now. One of my associates has her. I believe you had the pleasure of meeting her earlier. She was a bit worse for wear after the encounter."

"I want her back here right now!"

Tan Du nodded, soaking up the justicar's rage. He loved few things more than making good men lose their temper. Irrational people were easy to manipulate. "I'm sure you do. What father wouldn't? But I'm afraid we can't do that."

Kandler shook his blade at the vampire in incoherent rage.

Tan Du spread wide his hands. "If you want to blame anyone," he said, "look at your new friends. They led us here."

"You blame the fox for running ahead of the hounds," Sallah said. The light from the silver flames of her sword flickered across her implacable face.

"The hunt is over now," the vampire said. "We're leaving. If you follow us, the girl dies."

Burch's crossbow twanged as Tan Du finished his sentence. The bolt shot straight for the vampire's heart, but it ricocheted off the creature's chest.

Tan Du knocked against his sternum with his knuckles, eliciting the same tinny response as the bolt. The armor plating he wore had held, but he knew that the shifter wouldn't make the same mistake twice. "That was your last chance," he said to the people below. "Leave us alone, or I'll wear that sweet little girl's heart on a necklace."

Before Kandler could respond, the vampire faded to mist and floated away.

CHAPTER

16

The lights in Mardakine's town hall blazed over the people assembled there. To one side of the long wooden table in the center of the large, open room stood Kandler, Burch, Pradak, and Rislinto. Deothen and the other knights faced off against them from the other side. The senior knight's white staff lay between them, its magical silver flame lending an unreal air to the scene.

Outside, Kandler could hear others dashing through the town, lending aid to the wounded and preparing the dead for burning. At the moment, he was more concerned with the living. He glanced at Pradak and saw the grief chiseled on the young man's face.

Kandler hadn't wanted to come back to the town. He was all for scouring the crater for tracks and heading out after the vampires right away. Burch was the best tracker in town, though, and he'd pointed out that following a flying vampire through the dark would be impossible even for him.

The justicar needed help, and he knew it. Even if he could catch up with the vampires, he still had to get Esprë from them, and that would probably mean a fight. Since he didn't know how many they had on their side, he was ready to ask for all the help he could get.

"Your troubles are not ours," Deothen said as he leaned over the table, his gauntlets scratching the finish as he did. "I am sorry for both you and your daughter, but we cannot compromise our mission."

"*You're* responsible for this," Kandler said, struggling to master his temper. "Look at us! Half the town slain and most of the place in ruins."

Deothen grimaced. "Surely you can't lay the blame for that at our feet. You cannot hold us responsible for the actions of those who would impede our efforts."

"You're damned right I do. You brought this little war of yours to our doorstep. It followed in your wake. It's your duty to make it right." Kandler hoped that the knights would accede to his reasoning, but he knew it wouldn't be easy.

Deothen started to respond and then stopped. He sighed and grimaced. "I understand how you feel."

"No, you don't," Kandler said, his temper rising. "How many children did you lose today?"

"Today?" Deothen snarled. "We risked the lives of every one of my knights to lend your people a hand."

"To defend us against a threat *you* dropped on our doorstep."

The senior knight threw up a hand. "I'm not finished." Deothen waited for Kandler to acknowledge his right to speak before he continued. "In the Last War, I lost many a knight— including two of my own sons. I do sympathize with you."

The thought of Deothen as a father put Kandler a step back, but he wasn't ready to give in yet. "Those were grown men who rode off with you to battle. I'm talking about an innocent girl."

"My sons sold their lives for the sake of such innocents! I put my life on the line for such innocents every day! How dare you question—"

"Hold!" Rislinto slammed his fist into the center of the table. Everyone in the room—Kandler, Burch, the knights, and Pradak—jumped. "Arguing like this doesn't get us anywhere."

"Agreed," said Kandler, "and with every word those blood-sucking ticks get farther away with my daughter."

"There's no following them tonight," Sallah said. She kept her tone even and reasonable. "None of us can see in the dark like they can. They'd tear us apart."

"Your swords are torches," Burch said.

Sallah nodded at the shifter. "True enough, but they can be as much a curse as a blessing. If we were to ride out into the darkness with those, every creature within miles would be drawn to us like moths."

"Then we leave at first light," Kandler said. "There's not a better tracker than Burch within a hundred leagues."

"And what would you do?" Deothen asked. "Charge off to certain death? Fight how many vampires? They might even have a platoon of those Karrn zombies in reserve."

"Can you seriously tell me they held back last night?" said Kandler. He shook his finger at Deothen. That wasn't an argument he cared to have. "Don't answer that. I don't care. I don't care if there are a thousand vampires out there waiting for me. I'm going after my daughter."

"My son," Deothen said with the gravity of a man who'd seen too much death in his life, "think clearly. Your people need you here. Don't throw away your life."

Kandler screwed up his face. "This girl is the only family I have left in the world. I'll be damned if I let her be taken from me."

Deothen flushed with anger, but he mastered it. "Kandler, listen to me. I know you don't want to hear this, but you must. I'll tell you what your heart knows as true."

Kandler stepped back from the table's edge. "What's that?"

"Your daughter is surely dead."

Kandler had been about to rage back at the knight, but he stopped cold. "First, don't call me 'son.' " He stabbed a finger at Deothen to punctuate each word. "Second, you can rot in Khyber you ice-hearted bastard."

Burch reached over and clapped Kandler on the back. "I'm with you, boss," he said, "either way."

Kandler stopped flat and turned on Burch. "What are you saying? That's Esprë's dead?" He heard his voice rising as he spoke, but he couldn't seem to bring it under control.

Burch shook his head. "No. She's alive."

Kandler narrowed his eyes. "Why are you so sure?"

"If they'd wanted to kill her, she'd've been dead before they left. They went to a lot of trouble to get her out alive, then hang back to warn us not to follow. Why? I got no idea. But she's alive."

"What if they killed her after they left town?"

Burch shrugged. "Why take her at all then?

"But what if they did?"

"Either way, we hunt them down and kill them. Rescue or revenge."

Kandler smiled and clapped him on the shoulder. "Burch, my friend, I like the way you think."

"Still, we should wait for dawn," Burch said.

"Every second Esprë is out there, her life is in danger." Kandler could feel himself getting heated up again.

Burch raised his claw-tipped hands to placate the justicar. "We go out there in the dark, we die, and we're no good to Esprë dead. Vampires have to rest during the day." Burch made a stabbing motion with his finger. "Find them then and pop them in the heart."

Kandler sighed. He lowered his head and buried his face in his hands. He hadn't wept since Esprina had died, but he was sorely tempted now.

The justicar had been holding something back since the knights had arrived. From the very moment they mentioned the Mark of Death, he'd had his suspicions, and it had finally come time to voice them. They almost sounded insane, even to him, as they danced in his head, but he needed help now, so it was time.

Kandler raised his head and looked Deothen in the eyes, then he scanned the faces of the others—Sallah, Gweir, Brendis, and Levritt. Each of them met his gaze with grim determination, even young Levritt. The justicar knew they wouldn't follow him any other way. Only the truth—the full truth—would do.

"She has the mark," Kandler said. He meant to say the words clear and strong, but they came out barely a whisper.

Deothen leaned across the table and stared deep into Kandler's eyes. "What mark?" the knight said with terrible calmness. "Who?"

Kandler glanced over at Burch. The shifter's yellow eyes stared back at him wider than ever. The justicar hadn't shared his suspicions with anyone, not even his best friend. The thoughts had been too horrible to contemplate, but now it was time to drag them out into the light for all to see.

"The Mark of Death," Kandler said. As he spoke, he heard Rislinto gasp. Everyone else was dead silent, even Pradak, who had stopped weeping. "I think Esprë has it."

"It's a lie," Sallah said softly as she stared at Kandler. "It can't be."

Deothen shook his head. "I can see how a father might try such a desperate ploy, but we can pierce such attempts with the help of the Silver Flame."

Kandler smiled mirthlessly. "Be my guest," he said.

Deothen hefted his staff from the center of the table and passed his hand through the flame three times as he bowed his head and muttered a prayer to the Silver Flame. "May the tongue of the Silver Flame burn bright enough to put the lie to those whose tongues speak falsely," he said. As he did, the light from the staff ran down his hand and up his arm until it encompassed his head. When Deothen looked back up at Kandler, the Silver Flame burned in his eyes.

"So," Deothen said in the tone as serious as a dying man making his final request, "what makes you think your daughter bears the Mark of Death?"

"I've seen it," Kandler said. He ran a hand over his face before he continued. "I don't even think she knows she has it. It's very small. On her back. I saw it one morning when she came out of her room for breakfast."

Burch nodded, realization dawning on his face. As he spoke, his smile revealed his pointed teeth. "That was when you made her give up her favorite shirts for those fuller ones."

Pradak piped up at that. "We—I mean, me and the other boys . . . well . . ." He blushed as he spoke. "We figured it was because she was hitting . . . um, womanhood. We thought you were just being overprotective of her."

Rislinto smiled. "My wife was thrilled about that. You bought a whole week's worth of clothing from her that day."

Deothen looked at the other knights. "They speak the truth," he said in a hushed tone, then he turned back to Kandler. "How do you know this is the Mark of Death?"

"I don't. Not for sure. I hoped it wasn't, but after what you said . . ." Kandler ran a hand through his hair. "I don't know much about Esprë's heritage. Her mother didn't talk about it, and I never met her father."

"She is a full-blooded elf?" Deothen asked.

Kandler shrugged. "As far as I know. She doesn't seem to have a drop of human blood in her. From what I know about dragonmarks, elves these days only ever manifest one kind."

"The Mark of Shadow," Deothen said. "The bloodline of the Mark of Death died out centuries ago."

Kandler's spine filled with ice. He turned away from the table and walked over to a black-cloaked pile of ash near the door, a mound of dust that had once been a vampire. "What was the name of the house that once held the mark?"

Deothen hesitated for a moment before he spoke. "The House of Vol," he said. "They were said to experiment with the abomination of breeding elves and dragons together for the purposes of furthering their power. The other elves and the dragons banded together to destroy them all long ago."

Kandler reached down and picked up the black cloak at his feet. Holding it at arm's length, he shook the dust from it. When it was done, he turned the cloak about to expose the crimson insignia embroidered on its left breast.

"This is the symbol of the Blood of Vol," Kandler said, "a religion devoted to blood and death." He looked straight into Deothen's silver-flamed eyes now. "But you knew that already, didn't you?"

The senior knight nodded gravely. "The bearer of the Mark of Death can only be a direct descendant of the House of Vol. There were always rumors of at least one survivor, and the followers of the Blood of Vol always pursue them vigorously. But no one in Flamekeep believed them . . . until the prophecy that brought us here."

Kandler shook his head. "I can't swear that Esprë doesn't have the Mark of Shadow. I'm a fighter, not a scholar. I couldn't tell one mark from the other, I'm sure. It seems the bloodsuckers who followed you here are confident she bears the Mark of Death, though. Can you bet on them being wrong?"

The light flickering in Deothen's eyes faded and went out. "No," he said. "The light of the Silver Flame brought us here, but I was too blind to see it."

CHAPTER

17

The overcast sky above the house was barely a shade lighter than the pitch black of night, but Kandler had charitably decided to call it dawn. The others—Burch and the five knights—hadn't disagreed, so they all found themselves standing in Kandler's yard, their horses each packed and ready for a long, tortuous trip. The knights were dressed in their full, gleaming suits of armor and their crimson tabards, their swords and shields buckled in various places, ready to be put to use at an instant's notice. Kandler and Burch wore less armor than the knights, but they moved more surely for it—a compromise between protection and speed Kandler was always willing to make.

"What do you say, Burch?" Kandler stood over the shifter as Burch examined the ground.

Kandler could barely see even his own footprints on the ground, but the shifter sauntered around the place as if the noontime sun had burned through the clouds and exposed the secrets on every inch of ground.

"They came this way," the shifter said. He knelt down and ran his hand over the thin, gray, weedy grass that made up Kandler's lawn. "Two people—both in boots—and a big dog."

"Vampires often take the form of wolves," Deothen as he climbed astride his white stallion. Each of the knights followed his example.

"Fits," Burch said.

"The one we saw turned to mist," Kandler said. "I hear they can fly as bats too."

"All true," Deothen said.

"Then there's no way to tell how many of them there are," Levritt said.

"It doesn't matter," said Kandler. "We'll kill them all."

The shifter followed the tracks for a while on foot, his russet-coated mount—a shorter, shaggy-coated horse known as a *lupallo*—close on his heels. The others trailed after him in single file—first Kandler, then Deothen, Sallah, Levritt, Brendis, and Gweir, each of the knights on their snow-colored horses.

After a short while, Burch raised his hand to call a halt. The others spread out behind him as he studied the ground before him. "A horse waited here. The two pairs of boots lead right to it. The wolf and the horse went off that way." He pointed eastward.

"Were the two people Esprë and the changeling?" Kandler asked.

Burch rubbed his chin. "Maybe the changeling, but the other one wasn't Esprë. Both sets of footprints are too big for her. The changeling was hurt bad too, but better now."

"How could you know that?" Gweir asked.

Burch reach down and picked up a small, metal vial. He raised it to his nose and sniffed. He wrinkled his nose and then tossed the vial to Deothen, who plucked it out of the air. "Healing potion," Burch said. "Powerful stuff."

"It might have been the vampire," Levritt said.

"Healing magics harm the undead, my son," said Deothen. "That would have been like poison to one of their ilk."

"The horse's trail is clear as a road," Burch said. "Let's ride."

The shifter mounted his *lupallo* and spurred it to a trot, heading to the northeast. The others fell into line behind the squat, powerful steed.

The hunters rode without speaking, the rhythm of the horses' hooves the only sound they made. Soon, the edge of the crater reared up before them. Burch picked out an aggressive switchback path that worked its way up the curve of the crater wall, winding its way through the scrub. As the riders rose along the ever-steeper wall, they grew closer and closer to the swirling gray mists that obscured the crater's edge. The air grew close and oppressive.

"Is it always like this?" Brendis asked.

"Ever since the Day of Mourning," Kandler said, relieved to have something to think about other than Esprë. "This wall of fog rolled out to the edges of what was once Cyre, and no one's seen a ray of sunshine in the Mournland since, even four years on."

"I thought we were already in the Mournland," said Sallah.

Deothen chuckled at that but allowed Kandler to explain.

"Mardakine is on the edge of the Mournland. We're low enough that the mists rarely reach the crater floor, and we're close enough to the border that we sometimes see the sun. If the wind blows in the right direction, we can get full days during which you'd think we were in Breland's green and fertile fields."

"They say little can live in the Mournland," said Sallah. "You have a solid people here, but I wondered how even they could manage in such a place."

"That's life on the edge," Kandler said. "If it wasn't for the crater being right where it is, I don't think we could make it this close to this place."

"Then why are you here?" asked Deothen. "This seems an inhospitable place for a town."

"Everyone in Mardakine except for Burch and me hailed from Cyre—even Temmah. After the Day of Mourning, the people had nowhere else to go."

"Other refugees fled the place," Deothen said. "Your people could have joined the others in New Cyre or Sharn."

"That's deep in Breland, not Cyre."

"But your King Boranel granted them the land for New Cyre, and the town is run by none other than Prince Oargev. How much more Cyran could it be?"

Kandler laughed. "Look around you. You see this place, how gray and horrible it is? The people of Mardakine love sunlight as much as the next person. No one enjoys living in the shadow of the largest mass grave in recorded history."

"Then why?"

"Back when there was a Cyre, this crater was part of it. The people of New Cyre hope to one day return to their homeland. The residents of Mardakine live that dream every day."

"Seems like a nightmare to me," Levritt said as the hunters trotted further into the mists.

"Boy," Kandler said, motioning to the mists, "this is nothing. You're looking at the shroud over the body."

The mists grew thicker until it was nearly impossible for Kandler to see farther than the horse before him. Burch called a halt. While the others calmed their mounts, which were all a bit unnerved by their strange environs, the shifter pulled out a long length of rope and used it to tie their horses together.

"What's this about?" Gweir said. "We are experienced riders, and these are the finest horses."

"You can still get lost," Burch said. "That would slow us down."

"Birds lose their way in this stuff and fly into the ground," Kandler said. "Even I get turned around sometimes, and I've been through here dozens of times. The mist is miles thick, and most who wander into it never wander back out again. Burch is the only one I trust here."

"If you get separated, don't move," the shifter told the knights as he double-checked the knots in the line. "Don't run. You could fall off a cliff or into a gully. Stay where you are and stay quiet."

"Shouldn't we yell for help?" asked Brendis.

"Only if you're already under attack," Kandler said.

Burch frowned. "Stay quiet. I'll find you."

"What if you don't?" asked Sallah.

Burch walked back to the front of the line and mounted his horse. Just two horses separated him from Sallah, but the mists were already too thick for her to see him.

"Yell all you want then," Kandler said. "Better to die fighting."

The hunters fell quiet then. Only the sound of their horses' hooves broke the silence. The mists muffled the noise as if they were made of cotton. It was like riding through dark, angry clouds, waiting for the storm to break all around. With no sun to guide them, it was impossible to judge the time. Kandler counted for a while but gave up when he neared a thousand.

After what seemed like half a day, Brendis spoke. "How long does it go on like this?" His tone mixed reverence with fear, as if he found himself in the house of an angry god.

"Miles," said Kandler, "sometimes more than others. Or at least it seems that way. It impossible to tell while you're in here."

"Haven't we already gone for miles?" asked Levritt.

"It's slow going," Kandler said. "Burch is barely able to see the trail as it is. You can thank your god we have a trail to follow. It beats falling into a sinkhole or wandering into a trap."

"Yes," said Deothen. "I was just thinking how easy it would be to set up an ambush in a place like this. Assuming you could see through the mists."

"Or turn into it," said Sallah.

"They won't chance it," Kandler said. As the words left his lips, he wondered if he should be as confident as he sounded.

"Why not?" asked Sallah. "They could destroy us before we could draw our blades." She rested her hand on the pommel of her sword and peered into the mists.

"For one, vampires like to sleep during the day. Two and three, they're powerful and immortal, so they're arrogant and think they have all the time they need. Four, they're cowards. If there's even an off chance one of us could do something to part the clouds for a minute, they don't want to mess with us. Five"—Kandler smiled—"because I say so."

"Who's being arrogant now?" Sallah asked.

The hunters fell mute again and rode on. After what seemed another few hours, the mists began to thin.

"We must be near the end of it," said Brendis.

Gweir smiled. "Finally! I can't wait to feel the sun on my face. I shall almost be glad to hear Levritt whining about how hot it is under his armor again."

The young knight began to protest, but Deothen cut him off. "You are Knights of the Silver Flame, not children. Behave—"

Deothen's voice stopped dead as the mists swirled back and revealed the blasted landscape of the Mournland to him for the first time. The hunters found themselves atop the crest of a hill overlooking a wide valley that stretched on for miles to the north and south. The grass their horses trod upon was dead and gray, as were the few trees scattered on the opposite hill in the distance. A tar-black river ran through the center of the valley.

No animals moved here. No birds sang. The only sound was that of the wind rustling through the grass and the scrub and the rumble of distant thunder. The whole of the land lay under the shadow of a thick, unbroken layer of gray cloud. Miles to the north, lightning flashed, but it came down in all colors of the rainbow rather than electric white. Some of the discharges were a bright black.

A trail ran down the hill before the hunters and crossed the river at a shallow ford. The rocks shoved up through the water there like broken bones through skin. Things lay all about the ford, scattered in various formations that were hard on the eyes, as if the mind did not dare to examine them too closely.

"What are those?" Deothen asked as he came to a halt next to Kandler and Burch.

"There was a great battle at that ford on the Day of Mourning," said Kandler. Thousands died."

"But that was years ago," Deothen said as he made the sign of the flame in front of himself. "Did the victors leave behind the losers' armor?"

"There were no victors," said Kandler. "They all died. Those are their bodies."

CHAPTER

18

Deothen frowned. Sallah's eyes widened. Gweir and Brendis offered up quick prayers to the Silver Flame. Levritt retched over the side of his horse.

Kandler stared out at the hard land below. He knew Burch was looking back at him, but he ignored it. He didn't think he could bear seeing the pain in his friend's eyes. The shifter never liked it here in the Mournland, and Kandler felt guilty for having to drag his old friend back here once more.

"I heard the tales," said Deothen, "but they were impossible to believe."

Kandler nodded for Burch to lead the hunters down the trail. "You're sure to see stranger things."

The hunters rode down the hill after Burch in single file. Gweir and Brendis continued praying, and Levritt joined them. Soon they began a solemn hymn.

Deothen turned in his saddle to scold them. "Quiet, please. If the Blooded are out there, I'd rather not alert them." He called to Kandler before him. "I believe the servants of Vol have been spying on us since we left Thrane."

"All the way through Breland to here? That's bold."

"Not during the day, of course, but every night when we

staked camp I could feel them out there watching us."

"Did you ever see them?"

"Once," Deothen said. "One of them got close enough for Gweir to hit with a burning arrow. They stayed farther away after that."

Burch looked over his shoulder at Kandler and Deothen and shushed them. "You're worse than the singers," he said.

"Where are we going?" Kandler asked.

Burch pointed toward the ford. "Tracks enter the river there. Hard to tell after that."

Kandler cursed. "It would have to go through there, wouldn't it?"

"Shouldn't we ride faster?" Sallah asked. "Now that we're free of the mist, what keeps us from moving at speed?"

"Respect for the dead," said Kandler, gesturing at the bodies mounded ahead of them. "Once we're past the battlefield, it's a race to see who can find these Blooded of yours first."

As the hunters neared the battlefield, Levritt retched again. Kandler wrinkled his nose at the scent, but he refused to comment. It was never easy to see this much death. He'd been here more than once, and it still turned his stomach. Everywhere lay bodies, right where they'd fallen four years past. Many of the faces still turned toward the sky, their open eyes and mouths full of water from a recent storm.

Not a spot of rot touched the skin of the fallen forms. Some of the suits of armor bore spots of rust, their luster long since tarnished away, as did many of the weapons, several of which were still coated in the dried, black blood of their owners' foes.

"This would be a thieves' paradise," Deothen said as he marveled at the scene.

"Most thieves value their lives more than the number of rusty suits of armor they could stack on a wagon," said Kandler. "Only the desperate enter the Mournland."

"What's that over there?" Deothen asked. He pointed at

fractured stone spire stabbing toward the sky at the edge of the ford. The top part of it lay in pieces near its feet.

Kandler cocked his head at it. "That's the monument the Mardakines put up here after the end of the War. Old Entiss carved the symbol of the Sovereign Host into an obelisk he cut out of the floor of the crater. About forty of us carted it out here one day and set it up. That's when we cleared the path through the corpses. We figured moving them was more respectful than running them over."

"How long has it been since you've seen it?"

"Burch and I haven't pierced the veil for the better part of a year. The last time we came this way, the monument was untouched."

"The trail passes right by it, boss," said Burch.

"We'll check it out."

As the hunters rode through the battlefield, Sallah sneezed. "What is that smell?" she asked. "It's not rot. It's . . . something else."

"Old flesh," Burch said. "Rust. Stale water."

"All three," Sallah said before she sneezed again.

Kandler gazed out over the hundreds of yards of bodies. Near the path, they were stacked three and four deep, but they thinned out farther away. Some were in pieces, hacked apart during the battle before the event that killed the rest.

Others were whole, their skin intact, their armor unpierced. Their faces, though, bore looks of terror far worse than the pained grimaces of those who had met an earlier death.

"What in the light of the Silver Flame happened here?" Deothen asked.

"The Day of Mourning," Burch said, just as if those four words said everything there was to be said.

"We know that," said Sallah, "but just what does that mean?"

"No one knows for sure," said Kandler. He struggled for the right words. "In 994, the War heated up again. Cyre was situated in the middle of Old Galifar, the old empire, which forced it to fight battles on many fronts. Thrane, Breland, Darguun, Valenar, Karrnath—they all charged into Cyre at one point or another."

"Who fought here on that day?"

"Whose bodies are we riding through?" Kandler gazed out at the time-frozen carnage, rain-washed clean of all but the most encrusted of the blood spilled there long ago. "This was a three-way affair. Breland ran Argonth up along the Howling Peaks and the Seawall Mountains until it reached the tower at Kennrun, right where the mountains came to an end. Its army got off there and marched the rest of the way into Cyre, hoping to take the Cyrans by surprise."

"Argonth?" said Brendis. "The Floating Fortress? I hear it's as large as a city, big enough to blot out the sun. Have you seen it?"

Kandler nodded. "I served on it. Burch and I watched the Breland army march into Cyre, off to its doom. Soon after, our scouts brought word of a goblin force marching north from Darguun. It launched out of Gorgonhorn, a fort just on the other side of Point Mountain, the last of the Seawall Mountains. The Llesh Haruuc, the hobgoblin leader, wanted to extend the goblins' reach, and like most scavengers he figured that he'd clean up after the real fight was over. The goblins got there too early, though, and their warchiefs couldn't hold them back. The sight of the Cyran and Brelander armies clashing in this valley got their blood up, and they charged right in."

Kandler stopped talking for a moment.

"What happened then?" Sallah asked.

"No one knows for sure. The battle raged on for three days, and at the dawn of the third day, everyone died. Whatever happened, it probably didn't start here. We're almost on the edge of the Mournland. Most people think something horrible happened in the Cyran capital. Some figure the princess made a bad, desperate deal with the Dark Six, maybe just the Devourer, and it finally came time to feed the beast. Others guess that one of the other countries involved in the war caused it, but they all deny it. If they did, they probably didn't get what they wanted out of it. The creation of the Mournland ripped the heart out of Old Galifar. Most of the smarter people I've met—wizards, mostly—think it wasn't any of that. They have this theory about different 'planes of existence' that orbit our world, waxing and waning with respect to us like the moons. They think the planes aligned in a once-in-forever kind of event that broke down the space between us and those places."

"What do you believe?" Sallah asked.

Kandler grimaced as the hunters trotted the last few yards toward the broken monument. "I look out there," he said, "and I sometimes think that if any part of the world looks more like Dolurrh I've never seen it."

The justicar dismounted and walked up to the monument. The others did the same and joined him. The river gurgled a stone's throw away. Kandler knelt next to the toppled part of the obelisk and closed his eyes. Deothen put a hand on his shoulder.

"You surprise me," the elder knight said. "I didn't think you were a believer."

Kandler brushed the man's hand away and stood up. "I'm not," he said. His eyes burned red with suppressed grief, but his face remained grim. "Before we put up the monument, some of us searched the battlefield for our friends."

Kandler strode over to the wider end of the stone and knelt down to examine the break. "I buried my wife here," he said.

Sallah gasped. "Here, among all this death? Why did you not take her from this place and give her a proper burial?"

Kandler shook his head. "This is the way she would have wanted it. Out there . . . that's not her homeland. For better or for worse, right where we're standing, this is Cyre." Kandler bit the side of his thumb until the urge to weep went away. "This was her home. She belongs here. Someday, maybe it will belong to her again."

CHAPTER

19

Everyone lapsed into a respectful silence, and Kandler turned back to examining the damaged monument.

"It wasn't lightning," Burch said. He had come up behind Kandler to peer at the broken end of the obelisk too. "No scorch marks."

Kandler nodded, ignoring the confused looks from the others. "See the marks here near the break?" he said. The place where he pointed was covered with the marks of dozens of tiny chips smashed off the obelisk. "Looks like a warhammer or mace."

"Maybe both."

"Maybe lots of them."

"Whoever it was, they wanted this thing down bad."

"Who?" asked Deothen. "More importantly, why?"

"Does it really matter?" Sallah asked.

Kandler stood up. Before he could speak, Burch cut him off.

"Hostiles! All around!"

Kandler glanced at Burch, but before he could ask what his friend meant, bodies on either side of the path around them erupted. The horses screamed and bolted.

The hunters drew their weapons. A score of armored creatures stood up from underneath the corpses arranged near the river and staggered toward them. "Zombies!" Levritt shouted, his voice shredded by panic.

"We can handle this," Brendis said, clapping the youngest knight on the shoulder as he spoke. He looked back at Deothen and said, "Stay back and witness the power of our faith." He, Gweir, and Levritt stepped forward, leaving Deothen and Sallah behind with Kandler and Burch.

As the creatures stomped closer, their armor clanking all about them, the knights raised high their silvery swords, which burst into sparkling flame. "We are the defenders of the weak and foes of the darkness!" Brendis shouted. "Your kind cannot stand before our righteous light!"

The creatures halted for a moment just outside of the swords' reach. They gazed up at the blazing blades in what the young knights could only believe was awe.

And then the creatures laughed.

It was a hollow, tinny laugh, as if the suits of armor were empty and the sound echoed inside their breastplates before making its way out.

The three young knights glanced at each other, confused and filled with a doubt they'd rarely known. While their blades were still held high, the creatures leaped forward and stabbed at the knights' exposed middles.

One of the creatures ran Gweir clean through. The knight fell over the sword and coughed up blood onto his attacker's arm. He tried to scream, but he just spurted more crimson from his mouth instead.

Brendis managed to bring his sword back down in time to offer some defense, but two of the creatures bowled into him and knocked him over. They kept on him, pinning him to the ground, and began poking at his defenseless form with their blades. He screamed as he was stabbed again and again.

Levritt stumbled backward and fell. As he went down, Burch's crossbow twanged, and the creature about to drive his blade down through the young knight's heart fell over dead.

Kandler and Sallah dashed forward. Deothen held his blade before him and called on the Silver Flame to protect the knights from these creatures.

"It's not working!" Kandler said to the senior knight. "We're on our own here!" He cut down one of the creatures with a single blow then parried attacks from two others. They were fast but unimaginative in their savagery. Kandler could almost predict exactly where their blows would be aimed each moment, and this gave him the kind of advantage he needed over their superior numbers.

"Does the Silver Flame's light not reach into this damned land?" Sallah asked as she stepped into the fray, swinging her sword left and right.

"Blasphemy, daughter!" Deothen said, staring at the flames dancing on his sword. "I can feel the Flame's power coursing through me and my blade."

Kandler kicked one of the creatures off of Brendis, then decapitated the other with a single, well-placed blow.

The severed cranium sailed through the air and bounced off Levritt's head, knocking him back to the ground and conveniently out of the way of a slashing sword. As he scrambled to his feet again, he looked down at the thing's face. It was made of cast metal bolted to a skull, and all over it was carved intricate runes, the color of which faded from red to black as he watched. The thing's jaw flapped loosely from a pair of rivets as its leathery tongue lolled out of its mouth. Its blank, obsidian eyes stared back at the young knight like those of a statue, with as little life left in them.

"By the Silver Flame!" Levritt squealed. "What is that?" The knight stumbled backward away from the skull, waving his sword recklessly before him.

Kandler stepped in front of the downed Brendis. As he did, another of the creatures stepped up to face him. Its body looked more like that of a living statue than a man. Plates of metal and disks of stone overlaid muscular fibers flexing beneath. The creature stood as tall as a man, had the same shape, but it fought with the tireless fury of the undead.

Kandler recognized what the creature was. He'd fought against some of them in the Last War, both in Breland and abroad. "Warforged!" Kandler shouted. He continued to hack away at the creatures, peeling their armored skin from them with his blade, then taking them apart a piece at a time. "They fight like animals but die like men! Keep at them!"

The warforged were the monstrous creations of wizards who served kings that were running out of warm bodies to place into a soldier's garb in the final decades of the Last War. They were constructs somehow gifted with humanoid sentience, creatures like the unliving golems that served in many a wizard's tower, but imbued with the power to reason, as well as what could only be called a soul.

Deothen stepped into the fray, standing back to back with Sallah as the creatures surrounded them. As each of the warforged stepped forward to brave an attack, the knights made them pay. Soon, the ground around them lay covered in pieces of these strange constructs.

Using his clawed hands and feet, Burch scaled the obelisk and stood atop its broken shaft. From the safety of this vantage, he rained bolt after bolt down on the creatures. Many fell with the shifter's steel-tipped missiles jutting from the spaces between their metallic plates.

Brendis struggled to his feet and stood with his back to Kandler. His left arm was hurt, and he held it close to his side as he blocked blow after blow from the warforged. The justicar rolled around to the knight's left side to protect the young man from attacks from that direction

With Kandler's flank protected, he lay into the warforged who came at him, weaving a steely net of death with his blade. They fell before him, one by one, and it was not long before only three of the creatures were left.

Sallah knocked the warforged in front of her flat with her pommel, then stabbed it through the chest with her blade. The creature screamed as it expired, and in spite of herself Sallah whispered, "May the Silver Light guide your final journey."

Levritt found himself facing one of the last warforged. It circled around him, putting his body between itself and Burch. The young knight lunged at the creature with his sword, but it parried the blow. Its riposte tore open a gash in Levritt's cheek.

The young knight fell over in pain and shock, clutching his face. As he tipped over, he left the warforged standing over him exposed. A bolt from Burch's crossbow punched through the creature's obsidian eye and buried itself in its fibrous brain.

"Cursed breathers!" a warforged fighting Kandler said. "The Lord of Blades rules this realm. Leave or be killed!"

Kandler removed the warforged's sword hand at the wrist. He'd heard rumors of the Lord of Blades from the infrequent visitors to Mardakine, people passing through on their way out of the Mournland or in. The most revered of the warforged, this creature hoped to establish a homeland for its kind in this most desolate land.

Few but the orphaned offspring of Cyre would envy the Lord of Blades' choice. The unforgiving Mournland suited the warforged, who could go without food, water, or even sleep. Most people were happy to leave the creatures to their own devices in this blasted land. Others, though, feared what the Lord of Blades might do with an army of dispossessed ex-soldiers who were literally created to kill.

At that moment, none of that mattered to Kandler. These creatures were just another obstacle standing between himself and his adopted daughter. Standing here on the site of his wife's grave, Kandler's recalled what Esprina had said to him the last time he'd seen her. She said the same thing every time they parted.

"Take care of Esprë," Esprina whispered as she caressed the curve of his face. "She had nothing else in the world but me."

"And me," Kandler said, just like always.

Esprina smiled, and the sight caused Kandler's breath to

catch in his chest. "You are more of a father to her than any other has been," she said.

"And I always will be," Kandler said, taking her hands in his. "I promise."

"I know, my love." Her smile turned wistful here, as if she somehow knew the fate that would befall her soon after. "I know."

Brendis collapsed against Kandler, nearly knocking the justicar from his feet. He had to leap forward to avoid falling. As he did, the warforged before him lashed out with its remaining hand and caught Kandler around the throat. It pounded him in the face with the severed stump at the end of its other arm.

Kandler tried to pull the warforged's grasp from his throat, but the creature's thick three fingers held him like a vise. He brought up his knee into the warforged's groin but only bruised his knee on thing's metal codpiece.

"Your time on this world is over, breather!" the warforged said as it squeezed Kandler's throat. The justicar felt his world begin to go black.

CHAPTER

20

Seeing Kandler's plight, Deothen forced his aging muscles into action. He had not seen this much action since the final days of the Last War, and his body had grown soft in the intervening years. He ignored its pleas to sit, to rest, to slow down. There was no time for such things now.

The knight leaped forward and slashed across the back of the warforged's knees with his flaming sword, slicing through the fibers there. Unable to support its own weight, the creature fell to its knees, dragging Kandler down with him it.

Deothen shoved his sword through the warforged's back. Dark fluid flowed from the wound, and the shock of seeing it almost made Deothen lose his grip on his hilt. He pushed the blade in harder, and it jammed against the inside of the creature's chestplate.

Deothen twisted the sword furiously, trying to slash through something vital inside. He didn't know if the warforged had organs like a man, but if it did he was determined to find them. The sweat running down his brow stung his icy eyes and he fought with the creature for its life. After a moment, the creature let go of Kandler's throat and fell forward onto its face, wrenching Deothen's blade from his hands as it went.

Kandler rubbed his throat and croaked out a word of thanks to Deothen. The knight nodded a response at the justicar as he scanned the battlefield for more of the warforged. All of the ambushers lay dead or downed around them. No one besides the hunters stirred.

Burch clambered down from atop the broken monument and dashed to one of the warforged with a bolt in its neck. He turned the creature over, and it snarled. "Thought so," the shifter said. He smacked the warforged with an open hand. "This one's still alive, boss!"

Kandler strode over to Burch and leaned over the fallen warforged. Deothen followed close behind. The warforged that lay before them growled and snapped its head about like a mad dog as it tried to bite them, but it couldn't seem to move anything below its neck.

"Stinking breathers!" the warforged said. "One day, the Lord of Blades will turn you all into meat."

"I thought your kind didn't eat," said Kandler.

"We'll feed you to animals. Your time is over!"

Burch kicked the creature in the ear. It snapped back at him, but its teeth found only air. "Did someone else come this way?" the shifter asked. Burch was still sweating from the exertion of the battle, and to Deothen's nose he smelled like a wet dog. The knight did his best to ignore it.

"Do you plan to kill them?" the warforged asked. The hopeful tone made Deothen uncomfortable.

Kandler looked at Deothen, and the knight nodded. As a matter of honor, he didn't care to lie to the creature, but he was ready to let Kandler say whatever he liked.

"They have my daughter," Kandler said through gritted teeth. Deothen admired the depth of the justicar's emotion for a child not even of his own blood.

The warforged pulled the edges of its mouth apart in what Deothen could only guess was a smile. "Two breathers on a horse came through earlier today."

"Did you hurt them?" Kandler asked.

"They galloped straight through."

"Which way?"

"If I tell you, will you kill me?"

Before Kandler could respond, Deothen spoke up. "I sense no evil in this one's soul," he said, pointing down at the warforged, "although he is clearly misguided."

"Does he have a soul?" Kandler chucked the warforged under its jaw with his boot. "Do you have a soul?"

"More precious than yours."

Kandler shrugged. "Soul or not, makes no difference to me. Which way did the others go?"

The warforged narrowed its obsidian eyes at Kandler. It surprised Deothen to see such a human expression on the creature's face as it sized up Kandler's intent. "North," it finally said.

Burch reached down and picked up a nearby helmet. "Thanks, and good night," the shifter said. He jammed the helmet down backward on the warforged's head and strapped it on tight. The creature cursed as loudly as it could, but the helmet muffled the words enough to make them unintelligible.

"Do you have to do that?" Deothen asked the shifter.

Burch shrugged. "You'd rather have him screaming for help? Take the helmet off yourself then—once we're gone."

Kandler, Burch, and Deothen walked over to where Sallah and Levritt were looking after Brendis. "How are you?" the senior knight asked the injured young man.

"It hurts, sir," Brendis said, "but I'll live." Deothen could see that the knight was putting on a game face for his leader, and he appreciated the effort.

"And young Gweir?" Deothen turned to look at the other knight's form where it had collapsed nearby.

Sallah and Levritt looked up at Deothen. Their eyes were puffy, and the streaks of tears mixed with the rivulets from the sweat of battle on their faces. Levritt's skin burned with shame as well.

"Ah," said Deothen as his heart fell into his polished,

armored boots. He looked at Kandler and Burch. "Please pardon me."

The elder knight walked over to Gweir's body. With reverent care, he closed the dead knight's eyes, then laid him flat on his back and folded his hands over his heart.

When the five knights had left Flamekeep, Deothen had promised the parents of each of his younger fellows that he would treat them each as his own children. He'd seen plenty of death in the Last War, but those days now seemed long behind him. He'd grown close to each of his young charges throughout the journey, and Gweir's death shook him harder than he cared to admit.

Deothen muttered the last rites of the Silver Flame over Gweir's body. As he spoke, he pushed back the tears that threatened to overwhelm him. He kept his voice low for fear that it might crack at any moment—and he along with it. The others needed him to be strong now, to lead them, and he refused to let them down as he had Gweir's family.

While Deothen tended to Gweir and composed himself, he listened to Sallah lend comfort to Brendis.

"Levritt and I have done all we can," she said. "Once Sir Deothen completes his duties, he'll take care of you."

"I don't mind the pain," Brendis said. "I deserve it."

"How do you figure that?" Kandler asked.

Deothen glanced over. Brendis started to point toward Gweir, but the pain was too much. He jerked his head in that direction instead. "Gweir and I entered training together. We've always watched each other's back." The young knight bowed his head. "When he needed me most, I failed him."

Sallah patted Brendis on his back. "None of us saw it coming," she said. "Not even our vaunted tracker."

Anger filled Kandler's voice. "What's that supposed to mean?" Kandler said.

Deothen turned from his duties to watch the justicar glare down at Sallah.

Sallah glared right back. "You two are our guides here. You're supposed to know the land."

"You're supposed to have your own special god on your side. Why didn't it say anything to you?"

Sallah stood up, her emerald eyes blazing. "How dare you blaspheme to me?"

Deothen could see where this was headed. He stood and walked back to the others, ready to intervene.

A full head taller than Sallah, Kandler leaned over the lady knight. Neither backed down an inch. "I didn't put that blade in that boy's guts," he said.

"Your hand wasn't on the grip," said Sallah, "but you failed him."

"We all did," Deothen said before Kandler could respond. He placed a hand on Sallah's shoulder to comfort her and hold her back. "I understand your anger here, daughter, but it is misplaced. We are Knights of the Silver Flame, and we cannot expect any to protect us but ourselves. If there is anyone here to blame, it is us."

"Or him," Burch said, pointing a thumb at the paralyzed warforged still shouting wordlessly into the helmet bound across his face.

"He is no threat to us now," Deothen said. Although he did not approve of having to muffle the creature's shouts, he understood Burch's reasons. "I applaud your mercy."

Burch flashed a cold smile that bared his sharp, wolfish teeth. "That thing could live there forever like that, blind and trapped. I don't call that mercy."

"Killing the helpless is an evil act," Deothen said. "You avoided that path."

"Barely," Burch said, fingering his crossbow.

"We need to get going," said Kandler. "Do what you can to get Brendis fixed up."

Deothen shook his head. "We need to bury our dead."

"That will take too long. This fight slowed us down enough."

Deothen remained clam and steadfast. This was not an issue on which he was prepared to negotiate. "Our traditions demand that we dig our fellow knight a proper grave. Under better circumstances, I would insist that we bring his body back to Thrane to find its home in his family crypt. We need to press forward, true, but not before we administer the final rites in full."

"If we don't get moving now, my daughter may soon need the same ceremony." Kandler stared at the knights in disbelief. "The man is dead. There is nothing else to do for him, and a girl's life hangs in the balance."

"We have our duty," Deothen said. He understood the justicar's anxiety, but the traditions surrounding dead fellows were long established. The knight feared to fail to respect them in such a horrid land.

"Aren't you so-called knights sworn to uphold the greater good?" Kandler asked, his rage evident in his voice. "Or does your 'good' only cover what's good for you?"

Sallah took two steps forward and slapped Kandler in the face. "You will not speak to Sir Deothen like that!"

Kandler rubbed his jaw. Deothen put his hand on the hilt of his sword, afraid that he might have to step in to defend Sallah from the justicar's fury. He was happily surprised to see Kandler speak reasonably instead. "You just lost a friend," the justicar said, "so I'll let that temporary lapse into insanity slide."

Sallah tried to slap Kandler again, but he caught her wrist. "You only get one," the justicar said.

This only angered Sallah more. Deothen put his hand on her shoulder. At his touch, she seemed to remember her station and her duties—and neither involved fighting the justicar. She flushed with embarrassment, then pulled her hand from Kandler's grasp and walked back to look after Brendis.

"Trail's getting cold, boss," said Burch. The shifter moved to his shaggy horse.

"We must adhere to our traditions," Deothen said in a tone he hoped brooked no argument. "Gweir deserves a proper burial, don't you think? Didn't you bury your wife?"

Kandler screwed up his face and spit on Deothen's polished steel boots. The senior knight refused to acknowledge the act, waiting for the justicar to speak.

"My wife lay here for nearly three years before I could come back for her," Kandler said, growling out each word like a sword on a grindstone. "The whole of the Mournland is an open grave."

"Not for Gweir."

"I didn't realize the Silver Flame was a cult that cared more about the dead than the living."

"Without our traditions—our religion—our lives are worthless."

Deothen said a silent prayer that the justicar might somehow understand. When Kandler turned and strode away, Deothen knew the effort had been in vain.

Kandler mounted his horse. He sneered down at the knights before he left. "You're already worthless to me. Bury the dead, if you like. But you're on your own."

The justicar and the shifter spurred their horses toward the black waters of the ford and put the knights behind them.

CHAPTER 21

Kandler and Burch rode hard through the black waters of the ford. The tar-colored liquid seemed to pull at their horses' legs, but they spurred the beasts on and won their way through. Once across the river, they turned north and headed up the valley.

The two friends galloped along in silence, giving the horses their head. As their mounts began to tire, they slowed to a trot.

"Still got the trail, Burch?" Kandler asked.

The shifter nodded. "Like following a herd of hammertails."

Kandler looked sidelong at his friend. "What do you know about the big lizards?"

Burch paid no attention to Kandler's surprise. The justicar knew the shifter enjoyed these rare moments but would never admit it to him. "Scouted the Talenta Plains five years back. Rode with the little people."

"The halflings? On those clawfeet?"

"Clawfoots. Good mounts. Not fast as these, but bigger teeth."

The two trotted on for a moment. "You always manage to amaze me," Kandler said.

Burch said nothing for a while, and they put a good two miles behind them. Finally, Burch spoke. "I'm thinking, right?"

Kandler glanced at him, then back at the trail. "What's on your mind?" he said as evenly as he could. He recognized Burch's tone. He took it when he wanted to bring up something Kandler wouldn't like.

Burch wrinkled his broad, tanned forehead. "Those knights. We could use their swords."

Kandler nodded. He knew what the shifter wanted to say, but he didn't agree. "We could use the swords, but they could be hours digging a grave and praying. Hours. And every minute Esprë is farther away. We'll do all right without them. Did you see how those warforged mangled them? They'd just get in our way."

"That old knight saved your skin."

"You'd have done the same for me."

Burch looked up at Kandler on his taller horse and nodded. "True enough. Then we'd be even up."

"I thought I had two on you these days."

"Forget about that siren?"

Kandler laughed. "She *wasn't* going to kill me."

"She'd have had you first, then killed you." Burch smiled. "Like a spider."

"There are worse ways to go." Kandler said. They both laughed at that, and for a moment the Mournland didn't seem like such an awful place.

The sensation didn't last. As the two rode, the sky grew a darker shade of gray. The lightning in the distance grew closer.

"That a real storm?" Kandler asked.

Burch shaded his eyes and squinted at it. "Looks like it's on the ground."

"Think it's a living spell?"

"Chain lightning like that isn't natural. Got to be a spell. Might be hunting."

"What does a spell eat?" Kandler tossed it out as a rhetorical question. He should have known that Burch would tackle it. The shifter seemed to have an answer for everything. He didn't talk much, but that's because he was always thinking. When he did speak, you knew he meant it, that he'd given the matter due consideration. Kandler liked that.

"It doesn't eat. It . . . zaps."

"What?"

"Everything has a reason to live. A living spell like that lives to be cast, over and over. A living lightning spell zaps."

Kandler thought about that for a moment. A notion sprang into his head that he could not get rid of. "Think it might zap Esprë?" he said.

Burch cracked his neck. "It'll zap the changeling first."

Kandler frowned. "Let's hope so." He spurred his steed on faster, and Burch pushed his mount to match his stride for stride.

Darkness closed in on the two hunters. Soon after, Burch reined his horse to a halt. "Can't see the trail," he said as Kandler's horse stopped beside his. "Don't want to lose it."

"We can break out an everbright lantern," Kandler said. He steered his horse around Burch's pony and kept riding.

Burch urged his horse to trot after him. "Not good enough," he said. "I can't see the trail from my saddle."

Kandler wasn't ready to stop. "Then we can walk."

Burch kept at the justicar. "The torch'll show the way. But the light'll make a good target. Those vampires can see us, and we can't see them. I don't like it."

Kandler spat on the ground. "Esprë's still out there," he said. "We can't leave her with them for another night."

Burch rode alongside Kandler for minutes in silence. The land grew darker by the moment. Soon, all the two could see was a sky that was just a shade less black than the valley floor. The living lightning wandered off behind a bend in the distance and robbed them of even that occasional flash to break the monotony.

"All right," Kandler said. He felt sick that they hadn't caught up to Esprë yet, but he knew they wouldn't do her any good dead. "You're right. Let's make camp."

The two dismounted. Kandler pulled out a capped everbright lantern from his saddlebag and removed the top. The heatless flames trapped inside leaped to life once again. "Let's be quick about it," he said. "Anyone within a mile can probably see this thing."

Burch found them a flat patch of ground within a minute, and the two unpacked their sleeping rolls with the ease from long hours working together. Once they were settled, Kandler capped the torch again and set it down beside his bedroll.

"Your turn to get dinner?" Kandler said.

"Can you see past your nose?" Burch asked with a laugh.

"No."

"Then it must be my turn."

Kandler heard Burch rummaging around in his saddlebags for a moment, then the shifter handed the justicar some cheese and cured meat. The two munched on their cold meal in silence and sipped from their waterskins.

"Think the knights know not to drink the water here?" Kandler asked. He was starting to regret leaving the others behind. It had been a rash act, a gamble that they might be able to catch up with Esprë before dark, and it had not paid off.

"Think I care?" Burch laughed. A moment later, the shifter added, "They're not that dumb."

"I hope so," Kandler said. As the words left him, he found he really did.

The two finished their meal. Burch cleaned up and packed away the scraps.

"Do you have to do that?" Kandler asked.

"Don't want to attract animals." Burch kept scuffling around in the dark.

"Are there any out here? I haven't seen any."

"Never know," said Burch. "Better safe than sorry. Besides, it could be worse."

"Worse than what?"

"Animals."

Kandler thought about that for a moment. "Good point. Good night."

"Night."

Burch took the first watch as he always did. The shifter liked to claim he was nocturnal, and that usually suited Kandler fine. Burch's eyes worked much better in the dark, and at the end of the day Kandler was often too tired to argue.

Kandler tried to sleep but couldn't. The air was so still and the sky so black that he could almost convince himself he was sleeping back in his house in Mardakine. The ground was only a bit harder than his bed.

He wanted to get out of his bed and check on Esprë. He hadn't done that much since the end of the War. For the first two years after Esprina died, Kandler had checked on Esprë almost every night. He tiptoed into her room and stood there watching her until he was sure he could hear her breathing. One night Esprë had woken and screamed. Kandler stopped coming in so often after that, and he hadn't done it once in the past year.

As he lay on the hard ground of the Mournland, he held his breath and listened for that noise, but the only sound he heard was that of Burch breathing. He closed his eyes and let that steady rhythm lull him to sleep.

In his dream, Kandler walked through the Mournland. It was day, and bodies covered the ground from one side of the misty borders of the place to the other. They were all face down, and Kandler stopped to turn them over one by one, looking for Esprina. He couldn't find her anywhere, no matter how many bodies he disturbed. Row upon row he went, turning dozens, then thousands.

When he turned over the last body, Esprë's face looked back up at him with empty eyes. It was then that he realized that every body he'd looked at had borne Esprë's face. He stood and looked around the valley to see that the bodies all faced the sky now. Each of them looked like Esprë.

The Esprës stood up and began walking toward him. They were zombies like the Karrnathi ones Kandler had killed the night before, but they had his daughter's features and her long, blond hair. His held his sword before him, but he could not bear to strike the creatures, any of them. Instead, he ran.

The Esprë-zombies stampeded after Kandler, their feet tearing at the earth and raising a cloud of dust in their wake. He ran until his sides ached and his breath came in like a jagged knife. Every time he looked back, they were just behind him, no matter how hard he ran.

The wall of mist that defined the border of the Mournland rose up before him. He knew if he could reach it he would be safe. The creatures would not follow him in there. As he sprinted for the mist, though, it never seemed to get any nearer. The footsteps pounding behind him drew closer and closer with every second. He reached for the mist, but as he did a thousand undead hands grabbed him by the back.

Kandler woke with a start.

The pounding footsteps still sounded in his head. He sat up and called out for Burch.

"Right here," the shifter said. He stood next to his own bedroll, the uncapped torch stabbing out of his right hand and parting the night.

"What are you doing?" the justicar asked. He shook his head, hoping to make the pounding go away, but it just got louder. "You want to bring every creature in the valley down on our heads?"

"Too late." Burch pointed into the distance. "We got company."

CHAPTER

22

Kandler stood and peered into the darkness. Off in the direction in which Burch had pointed, the justicar saw four torches bouncing closer to them with every second. "Horses' hooves," he said. "I heard those in my dream. And those aren't torches, are they?"

"Swords."

Kandler shook his head. The knights either didn't realize that anyone could see them coming from miles around, or they didn't care. "It looks like they are that dumb after all," he said. He patted Burch on the back. "Good thing you uncapped that torch. They might have run around all night waving those damned things around."

"Moths to a flame," said Burch.

"Who are the moths? Us or them?"

"The vampires maybe."

Kandler scowled at that. His friend had a way of voicing his worst fears at the worst moments.

Burch held the torch high and waved it at the riders. They waved back in response and turned toward the light.

"Know what happens to those moths?" Burch said.

Kandler smiled despite himself. The shifter might have a

dark view of the world, but that never dampened his bravado. "They get burned," Kandler said.

"Hail and well met!" Deothen shouted as the four knights rode into the meager camp.

Kandler signaled Burch to cap the everbright lantern. As the shifter complied, Kandler stepped forward and addressed the knights. "I thought we'd seen the last of you."

"We would not abandon good people in their hour of need," Deothen said.

"Not as long as they're still useful to you." Kandler said. He found it hard to bite back his bitter feelings about the knights' pursuit of Esprë.

"That our goals match is a happy coincidence." Deothen smiled, either unaware of Kandler's pique or willing to ignore it. Kandler saw that this was a pattern with the knights. He often couldn't read their intent, but he supposed it didn't matter much. Actions spoke louder than words.

Kandler watched the knights dismount. Deothen looked hale and hearty, as if the fight and the ride through the night air had lightened his spirit. Sallah frowned at Kandler and kept a careful eye on both he and Burch. Levritt's eyes were even wider than normal, and they kept peering into the darkness.

"How are you?" Kandler asked Brendis.

The young knight moved his arm without defect. "In body, I am fine, but my heart is heavy."

"I am sorry about Gweir. He was a good soldier."

Kandler looked at the others and had to shield his eyes from the lights of their blades. "Could you put those things out?" he said. "All sorts of creatures come out around here at night. I'd rather we didn't invite them into camp."

Levritt and Brendis sheathed their swords, extinguishing the flames as they did. Sallah continued to carry hers about like a torch. Deothen stuck his point first in the ground in the center of the camp and let it burn.

"Let them come," the senior knight said. "The power of the Silver Flame will keep us safe."

From somewhere nearby, unseen in the darkness Burch snorted. "It didn't save Gweir."

Kandler shot the shifter a look that he doubted his friend could see. Exposed out here in the Mournland at night, this was no time to start a fight.

Deothen nodded. "The warforged caught us unawares. It won't happen again."

"Excellent!" a low, raspy voice said from behind the knights. "I'd hate to think this was a surprise."

Sallah screamed and nearly dropped her sword. Kandler stepped toward her and drew his own blade. The time for hiding in the dark was over.

Before Brendis and Levritt could draw their swords, two dark-cloaked figures stepped from the darkness, their hands and faces luminous like moons in the light of the two still-blazing swords. They grabbed Brendis and Levritt and held them fast. The knights struggled but the vampires' arms had the strength of steel bands, and they froze when they felt fangs against their necks.

"Hold still, little knightlings," the same voice said, "or my friends will tear out your throats."

Kandler recognized the voice. It belonged to the creature he'd last seen perched atop his roof like a monstrous bird of prey. As he watched, the figure melted into the light, as if it was the worst part of the night become solid, Kandler's worst fears become real.

Deothen went for his sword, which still stabbed into the ground in the center of the camp near Kandler and Sallah. He didn't get three feet before the leader called for him to halt.

"That's far enough, great paladin," the creature said. "I saw what you did to my fellows in that crater-town. If you touch that sword, we will kill your young charges before you can draw it from the earth."

Deothen froze, his arm already reaching for his sword's hilt. He drew his hand back and held it in the air. "As you say," the senior knight said through bloodless lips.

Kandler stepped forward and stood near the sword.

"That goes for you, too, Justicar," the leader said. "We can keep this civilized, can't we?" The creature permitted himself a bloodless smile, baring his long, ivory-colored fangs. "Forgive my rudeness," he said. "My name is Tan Du."

"I'll carve that on the marker over your grave," Kandler said as he reached out and rested his hand on the pommel of Deothen's sword. Brendis and Levritt cried out in fear as the beasts holding them tested their teeth on the skin of the knights' necks.

Kandler barked a short, mirthless laugh. "Go ahead," he said, praying that the vampire would not call his bluff. It was a risky gambit, but he wanted everyone's attention on him right now. "Kill them," he said coldly. "They're nothing to me."

The two other vampires drew back their fangs and looked at Tan Du for guidance. The beast bared all his teeth at Kandler in a vicious smile. "Of course," he said, "but we have you by a different set of hairs."

Tan Du raised his right hand high in the air. A voice rang out of the pitch-black night.

"Kandler!" It was Esprë. The voice was faint, distant, but there was no mistaking it. "I'm all right!"

The justicar left Deothen's sword and stepped toward the vampire, his heart in his throat. "Bring her to me," he said, struggling to keep the desperation from his voice. "Now."

It was Tan Du's turn to laugh. It was the worst sound Kandler had ever heard. No death rattle seemed as dark and final. "I thought I told you to leave us alone," the vampire said.

"I haven't done a thing to you," Kandler said, trying to keep the shaking from his voice. "Yet."

"Let me explain in terms even you could understand," Tan Du said. "Go back to your little crater-town. Now. And never come out."

"Or what?" Kandler hated to ask the question—he knew what the answer would be—but he needed more time.

"Or we'll kill your little girl."

Kandler reached back and pulled Deothen's sword from the ground. The knights all held their breath to see what the vampires would do. The two holding Brendis and Levritt squeezed their charges harder, and the youngest knight let out an involuntarily whimper.

"I'm going to kill you either way," Kandler said, steeling his heart to the fate of the knights. They might very well die here, but he was willing to risk that to get Esprë back. He knew that if she truly did bear the Mark of Death, then Deothen would be willing to do the same thing. Despite that, he never looked to the senior knight for approval. Instead, he held up the knight's sword before him.

"Do you have any idea what's at stake here?" Tan Du hissed as he fell back before the silvery flames.

Kandler strode toward the vampire, keeping the sword between them. "The only thing about to be on a stake is your heart."

Snarling, Tan Du locked his gaze into Kandler's eyes. The justicar felt the vampire trying to bash his way into his mind. When the psion had tried this stunt, it had felt like a worm trying to burrow into Kandler's skull. This was more like a battering ram trying to smash a gate.

The justicar felt nauseous for a moment, as if he were reeling, but he continued toward the vampire. As he walked, he drew upon all the fury he felt over Esprë's kidnapping to shove the rough probing aside. "That might work on little girls," he growled at the vampire, "but you're playing with grown-ups now."

Tan Du backed down before Kandler's advance, his attention focused entirely on the justicar. He didn't notice Deothen charge up behind him.

"Master!" the vampire holding Levritt cried out.

Kandler cursed. He'd been taking a calculated risk, but Deothen hadn't been part of the plan. Until now, he thought he'd had the situation under control, but in an instant it spun out of his grasp.

Tan Du turned, but he was too late. Deothen rammed into him, wrapped his arms around the creature's middle, and slammed him to the ground.

The vampire holding Brendis sank his fangs into the young man's neck. Brendis screamed, his knees gave out, and he would have fallen if the vampire had not held him in a tight embrace.

Kandler started toward Brendis, but before he could reach the knight, a bolt appeared out of the darkness and pierced the feeding vampire's heart through its back. The creature fell over on top of Brendis, dead before it hit the ground. The young knight screamed in terror and scrambled to pull himself out from under the vampire's body.

The vampire holding Levritt tossed the knight before him to one side. Kandler dashed forward and caught the boy in his arms, dropping the swords in his hands as the creature dashed over to help his fallen compatriot. Before Kandler could even see if Levritt was all right, Sallah sprinted past them, aiming a terrible blow at the neck of the vampire about to tear Brendis apart.

Deothen bore all his weight into Tan Du. "You are all dead!" the vampire hissed as the pair hit the ground. "I'll feast on your hearts!"

Kandler was sure the vampire was right. Even if they succeeded, what might happen to Esprë? Inwardly, he cursed the Silver Flame and all who followed it. Convinced Levritt was fine, he let the young knight slip to his knees, and he scrambled for his saddlebags.

His hands were shaking, and he had trouble untying the knot. As it finally gave, he heard Deothen chant a prayer to the Silver Flame. Kandler turned to look. The elder knight slapped his hands over the vampire's eyes. Light stabbed forth from between the knight's fingers, and Tan Du howled in pain.

The vampire shrugged Deothen off with his superhuman strength. "What have you done?" Tan Du said, his face glowing like the sun. "I can't see!"

As Kandler dug around in his saddlebag, he watched Sallah thrust her sword into the side of the vampire attacking Brendis. The monster screeched in pain as the burning blade pierced its flesh. It stood, wrenching the blade it was impaled upon from the lady knight's grasp.

"You'll pay for that, you bitch!" the vampire snarled. He started toward the unarmed Sallah, her sword still protruding from the side of his chest. Before he got two steps, another bolt emerged from the darkness and impaled the vampire's heart.

Kandler's hands closed on a set of wooden stakes in his saddlebags. He knew his blade was useless against vampires, so he had packed these as well. "Catch!" Kandler shouted as he tossed one of the stakes to Deothen. The old knight snatched the length of wood out of the air and stalked after Tan Du.

Deothen drew the stake over his head with both hands and stabbed down at the vampire leader's heart. The wooden point blunted on the thick armor plate and twisted wide of its mark, plunging into the vampire's side instead.

Tan Du bellowed in rage and pain. He lashed out in blind anger and smashed the old knight in the chest, sending him sprawling across the half-dead grass.

Kandler hefted the other stake in his right hand and sprinted off, circling to Tan Du's right. As he did, the vampire turned, always keeping Kandler to his front.

"I can hear you stomping around like a bull, coward," Tan Du said. He pulled his hands from his face. The light poured from his eyes as if he was lit from within.

"I haven't lived for over a hundred years by being foolish," the vampire cackled. "Besides, I don't want to kill you until you find your daughter's body torn into bite-sized pieces."

The very thought spurred Kandler to desperate action. He knew he only had once chance here, and he had to take it no matter what might happen to him. He dove at Tan Du in a last-ditch effort, the stake held before him.

The vampire seemed to fade, the darkness bleeding into him, and he melted into mist. Kandler hit the ground hard, wrenching his shoulder. The justicar howled, the stake still in his hands. "Come back!" he said to the air. He got up and spun around, swinging the stake back and forth wildly. "Come back and fight! Give my daughter back!"

The mist hung in the air over Kandler for a moment, then faded into the blackness. The justicar went back on his knees and screamed. He pounded his fists against the ground until Deothen came over and patted him on the back.

Kandler stood and glared at the knight, but he bit back the venom he wanted to spit at him. Instead, he turned and strode over to where the other knights had set the bodies of the downed vampires next to one another.

Esprë was somewhere out there in the darkness, Kandler knew, but she might as well have been a thousand miles away. He'd never find her, not until the dawn. But right here in front of him there was something he could do.

Kandler picked up his own sword from where it lay and decapitated the corpses with two clean, savage cuts. Then he hacked the rest of them to pieces.

While Kandler chopped away at the bodies, Burch stole up beside him. The shifter put a hand on Kandler's sword arm, and the justicar stopped, his chest heaving from his efforts.

"Couldn't find her, boss," Burch said. "Too dark, and even I can't track mist."

Kandler nodded at his old friend as he put an arm around him and drew him into a sidelong embrace. He hoped Burch wouldn't realize he was shaking not with rage but fear.

CHAPTER

23

A chill had settled over the Mournland as the sky grew darker, and the changeling feared the girl might catch a cold. Te'oma had not packed a bag for Esprë before leaving Kandler's house. There hadn't been time, and the girl had only what she wore on her back.

Esprë had slept throughout most of the journey into the Mournland. Tan Du's control over the girl's mind had kept her in half a stupor during the few times she'd awakened. It kept her from screaming and drawing Kandler and the knights to them—or any of the other monsters that stalked this forsaken place.

The girl was awake now though. Tan Du needed her to speak to punctuate the statement he planned to deliver to the justicar and his friends. "Keep her quiet until then," the vampire had ordered.

Te'oma had watched the vampires fade into mist then picked up her everbright lantern and raised its front shield just enough to show her the way to where the girl lay on the ground. The changeling knelt down and roused Esprë by stroking her long, blonde hair. The girl woke as if from a pleasant dream she didn't want to leave behind.

"Mommy!" Esprë said as her mind wandered back to her. The word sent strange flutters through the changeling's heart.

Te'oma, in the guise of the girl's elf aunt again, clapped a hand over Esprë's mouth and shushed her. "You must be quiet, sweetheart, or we are all doomed."

Esprë's eyes widened. In the light escaping from the lantern, the whites showed all the way around. "Aunt Arnaya?" she said, but the hand over her mouth muffled the rest of her words.

"Yes," Te'oma whispered. "I'm here. You're safe." She glanced into the darkness. "And we'll stay that way as long as we keep quiet."

The girl nodded and reached up to pull Te'oma's hand away. The changeling clamped down harder. "I can let you speak," she said to the girl, "but only if you swear to keep it to a whisper."

Esprë nodded seriously, and Te'oma removed her hand. "What's happening?" she asked in whisper so soft that Te'oma had to strain to hear her.

"We're in the Mournland," Te'oma said. Esprë drew in a deep breath for a scream, but the changeling clamped down on her mouth again before she could let loose.

"Esprë!" Te'oma said. "This is a matter of life and death. You *must* be quiet."

The girl's eyes widened even more. After a while, she nodded, and Te'oma removed her hand again.

"Why are we here?" the girl asked in a small voice.

Te'oma reached out and felt Esprë's soft, round cheek as she searched for the words that would comfort the girl. "These are desperate times."

"How did we get here?" Esprë asked as she took Te'oma's hand. "The last thing I remember is . . ." The girl shuddered and fell silent.

"Yes." Te'oma nodded. "We are prisoners of those creatures now."

Esprë sat up and glanced around. "Where are they now?"

Te'oma grimaced and wished the girl would just sit quiet and stop asking so many questions. Why couldn't she just enjoy the illusion of an aunt and niece sitting together in the dark?

"They've gone off to speak with your stepfather."

"Kandler!" Esprë's voice started to rise, but she clamped down on it before she finished the word. "Where is he?"

Te'oma stood up and pulled the girl to her feet. Just on the edge of adulthood, Esprë was barely a head shorter than the changeling. Her piercing blue eyes scanned the darkness for any break in the black.

"There," Te'oma said, pointing behind the girl.

Esprë turned and saw three rods of silvery light in a valley below, dancing together in the darkness. Shadowy shapes moved through and around them.

"There," Te'oma said again. "Do you see the figure closest to us? That's Tan Du, the leader of the vampires."

"Is he terribly dangerous?"

"He likes to think he is."

"Will he kill us?"

Te'oma frowned. "Let's hope not." She put an arm around Esprë's shoulders and drew her close. It felt good to comfort the girl, even if she knew she was leading her like a lamb to the slaughter. The two watched the scene in the valley below.

"What's going on?" Esprë asked.

"Tan Du is trying to make a deal for your life."

"What about you?"

Te'oma said nothing. The girl actually cared for her, and for a moment words left her.

"What about you, Aunt Arnaya?" Esprë looked up at the changeling.

Te'oma let a wistful smile spread across her lips. "Your stepfather doesn't know me, dear," she said.

Esprë looked back out at the scene below and leaned into the changeling. "Don't worry Aunt Arnaya," she said. "Kandler won't let you down."

"Ah," Te'oma said. "Here comes your cue. Tan Du needs to

prove you're still alive. He's raised his hand to signal us. When he brings it down, call out to your stepfather."

Esprë squinted at the figures near the flickering silver lights. When she saw the figure's arm fall, she looked to Te'oma, who nodded at her. "Kandler!" the girl said at the top of her lungs. "I'm all right!"

The shout echoed off the walls of the valley, and the words bounced back and forth until they died.

Te'oma pulled the girl closer. "Well done," she said to Esprë. "Now keep quiet again."

The girl pressed her lips tight, but it wasn't long before she opened them again. "Shouldn't we try to escape?" she asked.

"Where would we go?" Te'oma asked. Inwardly, she smiled at the girl's spirit. She was a fighter, this one. "In this horrible place, we're safer with the vampires than we would be without them. They, at least, have some reason for wanting us alive."

"What's that?" Esprë asked.

Te'oma did not answer. As the two watched, a fight erupted in the valley. They could not make out most of the details, but they heard the screams of pain and anguish as they rang throughout the valley.

"We could go now, Aunt Arnaya," Esprë said. "We could ride straight down there and help."

Te'oma shook her head. "It's too dangerous," she said. "We could get killed. We'll wait here until we know who's won."

Esprë started to protest, but Te'oma cut her off. "I didn't come all the way here just to lose you again."

Te'oma held the girl close as they watched the fight below. It was over in a matter of minutes.

"What happened?" Esprë asked. "I can't tell."

"Patience," Te'oma said. "We'll find out in good time."

As the words left her mouth, Kandler's voice rang out. "Come back! Come back and fight! Give my daughter back!"

Esprë sprang out of Te'oma's arms and started down the hill toward the voice. Before she got three steps, Te'oma tackled her to the ground. The changeling fell on top of the girl and wrapped her hand over her mouth to stop a scream.

"Quiet!" Te'oma whispered in the girl's ear. "Be quiet, or you're dead."

The changeling cursed her luck, the mighty Vol, and most of all Tan Du. The vampire was the purported leader of this mission, but his arrogance had consistently cost them lives. Now, she knew, it had robbed her of the girl's trust.

Once Esprë got her breath back, Te'oma removed her hand.

"You're not my aunt, are you?" Esprë whispered.

"What makes you say that?"

"She would want me to live."

Te'oma growled in frustration as she resumed her natural form. She grabbed Esprë and turned the girl around to face her. "You're a clever girl," she said, "but that doesn't change a thing. I'm still the only friend you have here."

Esprë stared at Te'oma, taking her all in. "How do you figure that?"

Te'oma stood up and dragged Esprë to her feet. "I want you alive, which is more than I can say for Tan Du. If he had his way, we'd just tote your body along with us."

"I may still have that chance," Tan Du said as he materialized from the darkness, his face still glowing with light.

Esprë screamed in shock and fear.

The vampire strode forward blind and smacked the girl across the face. She fell to the ground, bleeding from her cheek. He licked his fangs as he stood over her, his eyes shut tight against the light still flowing from his face.

"Get her up and on your horse, changeling," Tan Du said. "If she utters another word, I'll tear out her throat—and yours, too." He turned to mist again and hovered near the horse to wait.

Te'oma scooped Esprë from the ground, placed her on the front of her saddle, then slipped in behind the girl and spurred the gelding forward. "Don't worry," she whispered into the girl's ear as they took off at a gallop. "I'll keep you safe." She surprised herself with how much she meant it.

CHAPTER

24

The scream pierced the night like a banshee's cry, freezing Kandler's heart. For a moment, he wasn't sure the noise hadn't come from one of those fearsome spirits, then he recognized the voice.

"Esprë!" he said. "Burch, we have to try!"

The shifter nodded. "I'm on it," he said. As he spoke, his voice turned from its regular low rasp to a bestial growl.

Burch flexed his wiry frame about as he howled at the moonless sky. His wide, yellow eyes seemed to glow in the silvery light of the knights' swords. Levritt drew back as the shifter snarled at them and bared his pointed teeth. Burch's head snapped around from left to right, and he trotted off in the direction in which the vampire had vanished.

"This way," he said.

Kandler stopped long enough to gather their waterskins and food, but he left their other gear behind. The justicar grabbed the reins of Burch's *lupallo*, mounted his own horse, and opened his mouth to shout at the knights to hurry. But he kept quiet when he heard Deothen saying a solemn prayer over Brendis and placing his hands on the young man's neck. As the elder knight pulled his hands away, Kandler saw that the fang marks there had disappeared, although the spilled blood stayed behind.

"My thanks, sir," said Brendis, and offered a small bow.

"My honor, young knight," replied Deothen. "Now hurry and mount up. Every moment is precious."

Sallah and Levritt helped their fellow knight into his saddle, where he swayed a moment before pushing his mount forward. Kandler led the way out of the camp after Burch. The other knights followed.

Burch sprinted along for half a minute and then ground to a halt. When the others trotted up with their flaming swords, he turned to Deothen.

"Can you do that again?" the shifter asked. "Make a light for me?" He held his sword up to the knight.

Deothen nodded and said a quick prayer to the Silver Flame, then reached out and laid his hands along Burch's blade. It began to glow as if fresh from the forge, brighter than any torch.

Burch nodded his thanks to the knight then leaped into his horse's saddle and gave it a quick kick. He held his sword aloft before him as the animal broke into a slow gallop. Kandler snapped his reins, and his mount gave chase.

"Can he follow the trail like this?" Deothen asked as he spurred his horse to match the gait of Kandler's stallion.

"We have to try," Kandler said. He heard his frustration creep into his voice, and he tried to stamp it out. "This may be our only chance."

Burch ran his horse straight up the rise on the side of the valley. He veered neither left nor right as he forced the *lupallo* to pull itself upward on its short, powerful legs. Soon, the hunters found themselves at the valley's crest.

As Burch's horse topped the ridge, he whipped his head left and right, then steered his horse into a tight circle. A lump rose in Kandler's throat as he worried that the shifter might have lost the trail. As Burch completed the round, though, he snarled, turned his horse to the north, and started off again.

The others followed.

Forty yards farther on, Burch reined his horse to a halt and held his glowing sword out high. "Here," he said. "Four or five people. One horse. Most of the tracks stop here."

The shifter jumped down, his nose almost to the ground. "One track in or out. The horse." He scanned the matted grass for a moment more. "It was lighter coming in, heavier going out."

"Better than the other way around," Kandler said. He allowed hope to swell in his chest. "Which way did they go?"

Burch hauled himself back into his saddle and pointed his glowing sword to the north.

The shifter led the others off along the edge of the ridge. He held his sword-light before him as he scanned the ground, looking for signs of the horse's trail. Every so often, he signaled for a halt and rode out in a wide circle around the others. Each time he did, he led them again to the north.

The hunters rode hard for hours, slowing only to spare their horses. The sky became less dark in the east.

"The vampire cannot stand the light of day," Sallah said. "He must stop and find shelter soon."

Kandler shook his head. As much as he'd like to believe that, he couldn't. "Not in the Mournland," he said. "Pure sunlight here is rarer than diamonds."

"So they could continue on forever?" Sallah asked.

"The vampire may not tire," Deothen said, "but the mount we follow will tire soon."

Sallah reached down to pat her own horse's neck. "How much longer can it hold out? Our own mounts are close to breaking."

"Keep riding or get left behind," Burch called back.

Sallah's eyes burned holes in the shifter's back, but Kandler appreciated the shifter's sentiment. This was no time to talk about slowing down.

Sallah eased her horse back a bit to check on the wounded knight.

"How's Brendis?" Deothen asked.

Kandler looked back. Even in this light Brendis's skin was sallow, and dark circles had formed under his eyes.

"I'm all right," Brendis said gamely. "We're not going to lose two of us in one day."

"It's nearly the next day," Sallah said.

"Good. I think I can make it that far."

The young man summoned up a grin both wan and determined. He looked up ahead of them as if he could see the end of a long journey stampeding toward them, then he narrowed his eyes in concentration.

"My wounds must be catching up with me," Brendis said as he gripped the rim of his saddle with both hands.

"What do you mean?" Sallah asked. She reached out a hand toward him, ready to catch him should he start to topple from his mount.

Brendis pulled one of his hands free from its grip on his saddle and stabbed a finger toward the sky. "Look," he said. "Can the sky here be clear?"

As one, the other hunters lifted their heads. All of them had been either following the trail or watching Burch's progress. None of them had seen the circle of blue sky forming in the heavens before them as they rode up a gentle rise in the land.

Kandler's jaw dropped. He felt like a dragonfly could knock him out of his saddle. "That can't be!" he said. "This is the Mournland. The sun never shines here." He stopped himself. "Not until now."

"The world changes," said Deothen. "Better to see the changes than ignore them."

As the senior knight spoke, the hunters crested the hill, and a wide vista came into view. Another valley opened below them. The wall of mist that bordered the cursed land still hung like a curtain across the river and miles off to the west. To the north and east, the half-dead grassland sprawled wide and open.

The circle in the sky grew wider as the hunters watched, still galloping along. The sun was still too low to shine through it, but a steely blue sky peeked through the mists over them.

Kandler's eyes left the hole in the otherwise solid blanket of clouds and looked straight beneath it. There on the ground stood a mound of mist that seemed as if it might have fallen from the empty spot in the sky and crashed on the land beneath.

"What in the name of the Silver Flame is that?" Levritt asked.

"The light of knowledge shines on those who venture into the darkness of ignorance," said Brendis.

"What's that supposed to mean?" said Kandler.

"How should I know?" the young knight smiled. "I'm dizzy from the loss of blood."

"Look!" Burch stood up in his saddle at the front of the riders, pointing at something on the valley floor. Kandler craned his neck around to see what it was.

A horse bearing three riders—two adults with a child before them—sprinted across the valley, straight for the mound of clouds. Kandler's heart bounced with hope. He'd recognize Esprë's flowing, blonde hair anywhere.

"It's them!" Kandler said.

The hunters spurred their horses, and the faithful steeds called upon their last reserves of energy to heed their masters. They pounded down into the valley at breakneck speed. The horse they chased, though, was too far ahead. As the hunters watched, their prey rode headlong into the dark, swirling, earthbound cloud and disappeared.

Kandler howled in frustration as he urged his stallion ahead even faster.

CHAPTER

25

The swirling mists enveloped Te'oma's horse like the waves of an ocean. The dark, musty wisps encircled the three riders in all directions, blocking out the sky. Te'oma could barely see her horse's ears. The creature rode blind.

The changeling hauled hard on the horse's reins. The beast ground to a halt and let out a grateful whinny.

"What are you doing?" Tan Du said as he slapped Te'oma in the back of the head. "Keep going!"

"I can't see a thing," the changeling said as she twisted in her saddle to sneer at the vampire behind her. The glow had faded from his face, and it was no longer painful to look at him. She fought an urge to smack him back. "We could ride straight into a canyon or worse."

Tan Du snarled at Te'oma. "Stay here then, you spineless chameleon."

The changeling began to spit a retort at the vampire, but he was gone. As he faded into mist, the fog seemed to absorb him into its oppressive mass. "I hope it never lets you go," Te'oma said.

She turned back to the girl in front of her, who hadn't said a word since they'd gotten on the horse last night. "Esprë? He's gone."

The girl drew in a deep breath and screamed at the top of her lungs. The changeling nearly jumped out of her saddle.

As Esprë drew in another breath, Te'oma's hands darted out to cover the girl's mouth and stifle another scream. "Quiet!" the changeling said. "Would you like him to come back here and silence you forever?"

Esprë pulled back a little then lunged forward and bit into the fleshy part of the palm clamped over her mouth. The changeling shouted out in shock and pain and let the girl go.

Esprë leaped, hit the ground running, and disappeared into the mists. Te'oma heard her scrambling away.

"Have you lost your mind?" Te'oma said as she leaped down from her horse. She followed the noises Esprë made, leading her horse behind her by its reins.

For a moment, Te'oma considered letting the girl get away. It was a pity that such a sweet child found herself bound up in the machinations of greater forces, but there was little that Te'oma could do about that. She often felt unable to escape her own fate. How could she hope to set someone else free from such entanglements?

Te'oma knew one thing. If she didn't get the girl to Karrnath, all her dreams would be dashed. The Lich Queen herself had sent Te'oma and the others out on this mission, and to fail Vol was death. Whispered promises of immortality swirled through Te'oma's head like the mists through which she walked. No matter how much she might like the girl, the sacrifice of one small elf seemed a small price to pay for such a gift.

Te'oma knew that Vol wanted the girl alive, and that sparked a bit of hope in the changeling's cold, dark heart. She still wasn't entirely convinced Esprë even had this Mark of Death, and it mattered little to her one way or the other. But Vol and her lackey Tan Du certainly believed it, and Te'oma knew the Mark of Death was useless if the bearer was dead. Tan Du had scoffed at this restriction, pointing out that the Lich Queen had spells available that could resurrect the dead, but Te'oma knew such things were risky. It was better to deliver the girl safe and sound, with as little trauma as possible. Besides, the Lich Queen's orders had been specific. *Bring the girl alive.* Tan Du might put on a brave front, but even he was not foolish enough to cross her.

Te'oma could still hear Esprë running, but she seemed to be farther away.

"Stop!" Te'oma shouted, fearful that the girl might hurt herself while sprinting blindly about. The changeling kept a tight hold on the horse's reins and charged into the mist, stabbing out with her free arm.

It was too late. Te'oma heard the girl stumble and fall, but the child did not scream. For that reason alone, the changeling held out hope. "Esprë!" she called. "Are you all right?"

As the last word left the changeling's lips, she stumbled into the girl, who was sitting where she had tripped, right on the edge of a massive abyss. Esprë went sliding forward, but she flailed out to find something to grab on to. Her hand landed on Te'oma's boot and held. The sudden weight on the changeling's foot pulled her into the chasm after the girl.

Te'oma screamed as she fell. She was sure she was dead, but the reins wrapped around her left wrist pulled taut and arrested her fall. Esprë's weight on her leg wrenched at her hip and shoulder, and she cried out in pain.

Te'oma felt the girl clutching her boot with all her strength, and she heard her whimpering through gritted teeth. The two hung there for a moment, and all the world seemed to stop, then the horse bent forward its neck to relieve the weight upon it, and they slid downward again.

Both Esprë and Te'oma screamed. The noise scared the horse, and he tried to pull his head back up against the awkward weight hanging from his reins. The exhausted beast whined at the effort.

Te'oma reached her right hand down toward the girl. "Esprë," she said, "climb up me. Quick!"

"No!" the girl said. "I'll fall! You'll kick me off!"

"I would have already!" Te'oma said. "You're wasting time. Climb!"

Te'oma heard the paralyzing fear in the girl's voice as she whimpered, "Pull me up!"

"I can't reach you! Climb!"

"I can't!"

The horse dipped his head, and Te'oma and Esprë slipped back down again. The girl swung back and forth at the end of the changeling's foot.

"My boot is slipping off!" Te'oma said. "You have to do it now!"

Tears running down her cheeks, Esprë clawed her way up the changeling's front. As she reached Te'oma's shoulders, she flung her arms around the changeling as if she might never let go.

"There, there," Te'oma said. "Good job. You did great. But we're not done yet."

Esprë pulled her face away from Te'oma's tear-stained shoulder. "What do you mean? Pull us up!"

Te'oma shook her head. "I can barely move my arm. You have to climb up first."

Esprë looked into the changeling's all white eyes for a moment, then nodded. She wiped her face on Te'oma's shirt and said, "All right."

The girl pulled her way up along Te'oma's over-stretched arm until she reached the horse's reins, then swung her feet out toward the chasm wall and scrabbled up until she was out of sight.

"Thank Vol," the changeling said softly. Once the girl was clear, she tested her arm. Agony lanced through her shoulder. She tried to swing her good arm up to grab the reins, but her fingers fell inches short.

"Esprë?" Te'oma said. "Where did you go?"

There was no response. The horse twisted its neck back and forth, wiggling the reins. Black spots danced before Te'oma's eyes for a moment, but she fought them back. When she looked up, she saw the girl standing next to the horse at the edge of the chasm.

Esprë held the horse's taut reins in one hand. A sharp knife glittered in the other. "I found this in your saddlebag," she said.

"No," Te'oma said, tears welling into her eyes. Inwardly, she kicked herself for this. Every time she'd ever done someone a kindness, it had come back to haunt her. It seemed this time was no different. "Please, Esprë. Don't."

"You're not my friend!" Esprë said. Her rage marred her tender young face. "You're not my aunt! You kidnapped me! You were going to kill me!"

Te'oma shook her head as she strained to peer through the mist and into the girl's eyes. "No, Esprë. No." Her voice grew hoarse with emotion and desperation. "I never would have killed you."

"You're a liar!"

"No." The knife came closer to the reins, glinting dully in the half-light. "I mean, yes! It's true—I am a liar. I lie all the time." Te'oma swallowed hard. "But I'm not lying now."

Esprë brought the knife to the reins. "Swear it," she said. "Swear you won't hurt me."

Te'oma nodded. "Yes! Of course, I won't!"

"Say it."

"I swear it!"

"How sweet," said Tan Du, as he appeared from the mists next to Esprë. "You two have formed such a lovely bond."

Te'oma screamed.

Esprë turned and stabbed at the vampire with the knife, but he caught her wrist and sneered down at her. "Admirable, but predictable," he said.

Tan Du grabbed Esprë's chin and forced her to look into his eyes. "Have you forgotten who's in charge here?" he asked.

The fight left Esprë's arms and her eyes. She stood before the vampire, her mind a blank, awaiting his next instructions.

Tan Du let go of the girl's chin and grinned. "Don't let me interrupt you," he said. "Go ahead and do what you were going to do."

"No!" Te'oma said. She had known she couldn't trust the vampire, but she was shocked that he would cut her loose so carelessly. "You bloodless bastard!"

Tan Du smiled down at the changeling, baring his white fangs. "It seems to me that our partnership has reached a cross-roads. Since you've taken such good care of our little friend here, I think it's only fair that she determine your fate."

The vampire turned Esprë around and put placed her so the knife in her hand rested against the horse's taut reins once again. "Go ahead," he said to the girl. "Make your choice."

CHAPTER

26

Te'oma closed her eyes for a moment, then opened them again. "Please!" she whispered at the girl.

Esprë hesitated, the hand with the knife trembling over the reins. Her grip tightened, the blade touched the edge of the reins, and Te'oma held her breath. In one fluid movement, Esprë twisted the knife, turned, and plunged it into the vampire's belly. He winced, then looked down at the blade.

"You are an interesting child," Tan Du said as he wrenched the girl's hand off the knife and removed the blade, "as determined as the justicar. I see his influence upon you." The vampire stooped over to look into Esprë's eyes. "It's almost a shame what will happen to you. Now step aside."

The girl obeyed, and Tan Du reached out and grabbed the horse's reins. He snarled at the poor, tired beast, and the horse kicked backward, its terror overcoming its exhaustion. As the horse scrambled back, it pulled Te'oma up and over the chasm's edge.

When she was safe, Te'oma flipped her injured arm free of the reins and collapsed. She hugged the ground like an old lover she'd never hoped to see again.

"Get up," Tan Du said. "I have something to show you." He

turned to Esprë and spoke. "As for you, behave yourself and stay with the changeling. You seem to be able to count on her to keep you safe."

"What is it?" Te'oma asked as she struggled to her feet. Her arm hung loosely at her side. What little feeling she had in it was only pain.

"Something unbelievable." Tan Du looked at Te'oma's useless arm. "It's a pity you used your last healing potion."

The changeling used her good arm to pull her injured limb and stuff its hand across her body and into her belt. "Don't worry about me."

The vampire grinned. "Do you think it's in my nature?"

He turned and walked off to the left of the chasm.

Te'oma grabbed her horse's reins with her good hand and led the animal after Tan Du, following the edge of the chasm. Esprë scrambled up onto the horse's saddle where she rode in silence.

"What is it?" Te'oma asked again when they caught up with the vampire, who stood waiting for them.

"As always, changeling," Tan Du gestured toward the nearby chasm, "you manage to find the obstacles that lay in our path, while I"—the vampire stepped aside and bowed, revealing the end of a lowered drawbridge behind him—"I find the solutions."

"After you," Te'oma said.

Tan Du strode out onto the ironbound oak planks of the bridge. Te'oma led the horse after him, the girl still silent in the saddle.

The changeling stayed in the center of the drawbridge. She looked back to see Esprë leaning out from the saddle and peering into the abyss below. The changeling's eyes followed the girl's, but the mist obscured everything. The chasm could have been a dozen feet deep or a hundred. It was impossible to tell.

The wall of the tower seemed to grow out of the mist as the travelers approached. It stabbed high into the swirling grayness, or so it seemed. Te'oma could not even see the top of the arch that stood at the drawbridge's base.

The trio passed beneath the arch and found themselves in an open courtyard. Tan Du led them forward until they came to large, wooden door, in which was set an ornate, iron knocker cast in the shape of a gargoyle's head with a large, thick ring in its mouth. He presented the door to Te'oma and said, "Here you are. I believe this sort of thing is your specialty."

"Why don't you just turn to mist?" Esprë asked from atop the horse. Her voice sounded distant.

The vampire looked up at the girl with a bloodless smile. "I have to be invited," he said. He looked at Te'oma. "But I think we can arrange that."

Te'oma handed Tan Du the reins to her horse and stepped forward. The vampire tied the animal to a hitching post near the door and pulled Esprë down from the saddle. They stood back and watched as the changeling examined the door.

Te'oma ran her eyes across the door's surface first, scanning for any traps—in the Mournland one couldn't be too careful—then ran her good hand in the same pattern. Nothing happened. She reached out for the knocker with one eye open. Her hand touched it. The metal felt cool, if a bit moist from the mists.

The changeling pulled on the knocker, then pushed, and nothing happened. The door did not give an inch. Te'oma tried twisting the knocker, but it wouldn't budge. In frustration, she pulled the ring up and then slammed it down.

The door swung open, creaking on its rusty hinges.

Te'oma looked back at Tan Du, who motioned for the changeling to enter. She pushed the door open and peered inside.

The swirling mists stopped outside the door. Te'oma could see all the way across the large, brick-walled room.

Shelves of books and scrolls stacked floor to ceiling lined the walls. Papers spilled out of some of them and on to the floor. The clutter almost obscured the sumptuous red rug that covered all but the few feet on the edges of the polished wood floor. Ink spots were splattered all about the place, many of which trailed from a pot sitting on the corner of the massive desk in the center of the room.

Te'oma slipped into the room and padded to the desk. She could not read the writing on the pages there, but she recognized the strange notations of a wizard's instructions for spells. She reached out and ran her finger along the edge of the desk. It came back covered with dust. She noticed, though, that the pages atop the desk's dark, mahogany surface were clean.

Windows lined the walls. They were wide and unglazed but the mist outside stopped just before their edges anyhow, almost as if each wisp feared to be sucked into the building. No light shone through them.

A long set of wooden stairs snaked back and forth along the rear wall and disappeared through a hole in the ceiling. There was no telling how far up it might continue or how many other floors lay above.

An iron chandelier hung from a long chain in the center of the ceiling. The tips of the bars glowed with a magical light that hurt to look at. Te'oma shaded her eyes with her hand and squinted at the structure long enough to see that it was wrought as a symbol of a god.

Te'oma turned back to see Tan Du and Esprë peering through the doorway at her. "We may not be welcome here," she said.

"There is no one here," the vampire said. "The place is empty."

"You can't be sure of that."

The vampire bared a wicked smile. "If it's not empty now, it soon will be. Invite me in."

For a moment, Te'oma considered defying the vampire. If she did, she would be safe, at least until she had to leave. The girl, though, would still be in his grasp. "Come in," she said.

Tan Du strode across the threshold, pulling Esprë along behind him. Once inside, he let her go.

Esprë wandered about the place without a word, her wide blue eyes taking in everything. She looked up at the chandelier and said pointed. "That's the symbol of Aureon, the god of magic." She bowed her head. "My mother wore a medallion of it around her neck."

"Then your mother must have been a good and powerful wizard," a voice said from the top of the stairs.

Tan Du, Te'oma, and Esprë looked up to see an emaciated elf coming down the steps. She was dressed in fine robes of green- and blue-patterned silk that draped over her pointed shoulders and gave the illusion that there might be some volume to her under them. Her sunken eyes, cut-like mouth, and knife-sharp cheekbones under paper-thin skin belied that impression. She moved with purpose and economy, as if every gesture caused her a pain she refused to express.

"She was a sorcerer," Esprë said.

The elf favored the girl with a half smile. "I do not receive many visitors," she said. "The mists keep them away."

"We came seeking shelter," Te'oma started.

"From the sun," the elf said. "I know. Who do you think opened the skies?"

"You forced us here?" Tan Du glared at the elf.

The gaunt wizard nodded. "I predicted your arrival. I know who you are, I know what you are, and I know what you are about."

Tan Du frowned. "Then you should know better than to interfere."

The elf coughed up a dry laugh as she descended the final stairs and stood before the trio of intruders. "I do not fear your lich-goddess. True power comes from the light, not the dark. She is but a shadow of what she could have been."

Tan Du's frown deepened to a scowl. "You blaspheme. Apologize, or I will tear your heart from your chest."

Te'oma reached out and took Esprë's hand. The girl did not pull away. Without taking her eyes from the wizard, Te'oma

began to creep backward, a step at a time, bringing the girl
with her.

The elf squinted at Tan Du. "You are a pawn and a fool. Do
you not realize what you are in the presence of?"

"A dead elf," the vampire sneered. He lashed out, and his
hand closed around the wizard's bare, thin throat.

The elf's eyes narrowed in delight. Her smile showed all
her teeth like a corpse's rictus.

The flesh on Tan Du's hand burned. Te'oma heard the
sharp hiss of burning skin and saw smoke rising about the elf's
face.

The vampire's eyes flung wide in terror. "What—?" he
said.

He drew his hand back and stared at it, stunned. It was red
and blistered as if he'd pressed it on a hot stove.

Te'oma hustled Esprë behind the wizard's desk. She didn't
know what might happen next, but she hoped the wizard would
be reluctant to attack someone hiding behind her spellbook.
She held the girl to her chest, keeping Esprë from watching the
pair near the stairs, but she found herself unable to avert her
own eyes from the scene.

The elf chanted a few quick words and presented a pearl
between her fingers. It burst forth with the heat and light of
the sun.

Tan Du cowered before the light and screamed. "No!" he
said. "I cannot fail! You cannot—!"

The vampire stopped protesting and turned to run. The
elf followed him with the light still blazing from her hand. He
stumbled into the side of the wizard's desk opposite Te'oma and
bounced off it toward the door. Esprë let out a little scream and
clung to the changeling tighter. Te'oma ran a hand through her
hair and shushed her gently as she craned her neck around the
desk to watch the vampire flee.

As Tan Du moved, smoke curled from his bare flesh and
from under his clothes. The vampire reached for the door,
but it slammed shut as he did. Bellowing in frustration, he

hauled at it with all his supernatural might, but it refused to give.

The vampire turned to face the elf, his body burning now, flames licking up all around him. His hair caught like a torch, and his skin blackened and began to peel away. He let loose a final agonized scream before he collapsed. Moments later, all that was left of him was a smoldering pile of ashes spilling out of his scorched clothes.

The light in the elf's hand went out, and she turned to smile again at Te'oma and Esprë. "Now," she said, "shall we get to know each other a bit better?"

CHAPTER

27

"We have to go in," Kandler said, staring up at the mound of mist that sat in the center of the valley. From this close, it looked more like the wall of a tomb. "I'm through wasting time."

"You can't see a thing in there," Deothen said. "It's suicide."

Kandler turned on the old knight. "You have a better plan?"

The knight nodded. "We set up positions around the place and wait for them to come out."

Kandler goggled at Deothen. "My daughter is in there!"

"It is a sound plan."

Frustrated, Kandler pointed at the rest of the hunters. "Do you see how many of us there are left?" The others stared at him. "There's you, me, Burch, and three knights so green they have grass growing out of their armor."

Sallah opened her mouth to protest, but Kandler kept talking. He stared at Deothen. "What makes you think the six of us can surround this place? And if they come out of there, how are we going to catch them? How long are we going to wait? When night falls, we won't be able to see a thing." Kandler pointed up at the hole in the cloud cover. "And what about that? As soon as that goes away, which could happen any second, they can just ride away again."

Deothen raised his hands to calm the justicar. The gesture just made Kandler even more angry. "I understand why you are upset," Deothen said. "but you must think about this clearly."

"I'm not going to think about it like a coward." Kandler turned to speak to the others. "I'm going in. Now." He looked each of the knights in the eye. "Who's with me?"

Burch raised his hand, and Kandler cracked a quick smile. "Thanks, Burch," he said. Then he glared at the others. "Who else?"

Deothen sat on his mount in stony silence. Levritt looked to the senior knight for guidance and avoided Kandler's stare. Brendis started to speak but then shut his mouth. He frowned at the justicar and sagged in his saddle.

"I'll go," Sallah said.

Surprised, Kandler nodded his thanks. "All right."

"No, daughter," Deothen said. "I cannot permit it." Kandler started to respond, but Deothen cut him off. "I am your commander. I am responsible for your life and that of every other knight that rides with me."

"Nice going so far," Burch said. "One dead and one nearly killed."

"You will speak to Sir Deothen with a civil tongue!" said Sallah.

Deothen ignored Burch and spoke to Kandler. "I will not permit one of my charges to risk her life needlessly."

"But, Sir Deothen," Sallah said, "the girl—"

"Is trapped in there with her kidnappers. They are going nowhere. We should wait for them to come to us."

"Are we not charged with the protection of innocents?" Kandler could hear a trace of desperation creeping into Sallah's voice.

"You are, as am I, but there are larger issues at stake here. They want the girl alive."

"How can you be so sure of that?"

"If her life was so cheap to them, they would have killed her already. You know that, justicar."

Kandler shook his head in frustration. "You can sit out here and argue about it all you like. I'm going in." He nodded at the shifter and brought his horse around. "Come on, Burch."

"Sir Deothen," Sallah said, "should we not lend them aid? They will defy your wisdom no matter what, but can we not take advantage of that? Let me accompany them. They may need my prayers if not my sword."

Kandler and Burch hesitated for a moment to hear what the senior knight would say. The old man's face fell. "Very well," he said, looking deep into Sallah's green eyes. "Do as you will, daughter. And may the Silver Flame guide your way."

Sallah brought her horse around to face toward the wall of mist. She snapped a quick salute to Deothen and the other knights then gave Kandler a sharp nod. Without another word, they plunged into the unknown.

The gray mist curled around Kandler like a blanket. He could barely see his horse's ears much less Burch or Sallah, but unlike the mists that bordered the Mournland, which were chill and stifling, this was simply . . . mist. Cool and damp, yes, but just mist.

His steed tried to pull up short, but he goaded the stallion on.

"Should we tie our horses together again?" Sallah said. Her voice came from somewhere over Kandler's shoulder.

"Burch and I did that already," Kandler said. "Did we miss you?"

"You know you did," Sallah said, irritation tinged with fear creeping into her voice. "Throw me a—ow!"

"Sorry," Burch said, in a voice untainted with regret. "Got the rope?"

"I do now," Sallah snarled.

The trio started forward again. Burch led the way with Kandler and Sallah riding behind, their horses each tied to the shifter's stocky, sure-footed *lupallo*.

Sallah held up her sword and set it ablaze with a short prayer to the Silver Flame. In here, the blade seemed brighter than it had since entering the Mournland. Still not quite a pure flame, it nonetheless burned with an eager light. The mists seemed to part before the fire, and soon Kandler could see both her and Burch.

Burch looked back and nodded his approval. "Keep that burning," he said.

"Can you follow their trail?" Kandler asked.

The shifter got off his horse and scanned the ground. "The ground here is nothing but rock. No trail to follow."

"Can you sniff them out?"

"Maybe." Burch huffed and flexed for a moment as he drew upon the powers of his werebeast ancestors. He crouched low to the ground like an animal and rumbled out a low snarl. He put his nose in the air and sniffed, then scampered about for a moment until he found the direction. He pulled his horse along behind him, leading the others by the rope that bound them together.

"Got it," the shifter said as he padded ahead. "Sweaty horse, and . . . that muddy scent is the changeling. And I can smell . . . rose petals."

"Rose petals?" Sallah asked.

Kandler's throat tightened, but he managed to speak. "We traded for them two months ago. Esprë sleeps with them in her pillow."

"There's something else," Burch continued. "Something . . . foul. Like a dank tomb."

"The vampire?" asked Sallah.

"Yeah. Probably."

The trio walked in silence for a moment. The only sounds were that of their horses' hooves and Burch sniffing the air.

"Whoa!" the shifter shouted as he skidded to a stop. The *lupallo* halted behind him. Kandler and Sallah reined in their horses.

"What is it?" Kandler asked.

"Come here," Burch said. "But get off the horses."

Kandler and Sallah dismounted and walked toward Burch. As they moved closer, Sallah's sword melted away more of the mist, and Kandler saw that the shifter stood on the edge of a vast chasm. Both the bottom and the other side were invisible in the mist.

"Did they . . . ?" Sallah said. She gulped as she went to one knee and peered over the edge. "Did they fall?"

"Smells like . . ." Burch stopped and sniffed the gray air. "Stinks like fear." He looked at Sallah and smiled. "And not just from you. Stay here."

Kandler looked at Sallah. "Are you blushing?" He hadn't thought such a strong-willed woman could ever be embarrassed.

"It's natural to be afraid here," the lady knight said. "This is a fearsome place."

"No doubt about that," Kandler said as he peered through the thin swirls of fog at Burch.

The shifter stepped back from the edge of the chasm and walked back and forth along it, sniffing as he went. As he went to the left, he sniffed harder and faster. "Here," he finally said. "This way."

Kandler and Sallah followed Burch, each of them leading their own horses on foot. "Could some of them have fallen?" Kandler asked.

Burch shook his head and sniffed again. "They went this way. And the horse. Esprë was with them." Soon the trio came upon the drawbridge. "They crossed here."

Kandler nodded at the shifter, and the three led their mounts across the bridge. The hooves and footsteps rang out on the oak planks.

"That's the horse," Kandler said as they entered the mist-shrouded courtyard. The animal stood tied to the hitching post outside the cream-colored tower's closed door. He and Burch drew their swords as all three of them eased their way up to the door.

Burch pressed the side of his head to the door and listened.

"Two voices," he whispered. "Can't make out the words."

Kandler beckoned the shifter back and then gestured with his sword. Each of the three held their weapons at the ready. The justicar lowered his shoulder and charged.

The door swung wide on creaking hinges. Kandler burst into the room with Burch and Sallah close on his heels. All three blinked at the bright light from the chandelier hanging from the ceiling.

As the trio entered, the two people standing at the desk in the center of the room looked up. "Kandler!" one of them shouted with glee.

Esprë dashed around the table and flung herself at her stepfather. Relief washed over Kandler like a wave. He gathered her up in her arms and hugged her tighter than he had since her mother's death.

"It's all right," he said softly in her ear, tears rolling freely down his face. "I'm here now."

"Boss?" Burch said as he tapped Kandler on the shoulder. "Want to say hello to our host?"

The shifter's tone told Kandler that something was wrong. Kandler swung Esprë around in his left arm and held his sword at the ready in the other. He looked up and saw a gaunt elf standing behind a desk nearly covered with a book and papers coated with arcane writing.

"Two sets of visitors in one day," the old elf woman said, her voice like rustling leaves. "This is a special day."

Before Kandler could respond, he heard hoofbeats in the courtyard—a sudden clatter followed by the sound of the horses leaving. Kandler turned and raced back out the door, Esprë still in his arms and clinging to his neck. Burch and Sallah were hot on his heels.

As he reached courtyard, he saw all four horses stampeding away across the drawbridge. The changeling stood in the stirrups of the beast in the rear, urging them all forward into the mists.

CHAPTER

28

Is the changeling leaving without a farewell?" the elf said as she emerged from her tower. The others parted before her as she stepped into the courtyard. "I can't tolerate such rudeness."

With a gesture from the wizard, the drawbridge began to rise. Still crossing it, the horses whinnied in fear as they felt the planks move beneath them, but Te'oma shouted and kicked her heels into her mount's sides, urging them on.

The far end of the bridge continued to rise. The horses raced toward its limit at top speed, and when they reached it they leaped out into the mists.

Kandler's horse cleared the gap with Burch and Sallah's close behind. Te'oma's mount seemed to almost lose its nerve, but the changeling spurred it hard, and the beast jumped over the abyss.

The horse's rear hooves scrambled as it landed on the far side of the chasm and it slid backward toward certain doom. Esprë squealed in fear and reached out to the changeling, although there was nothing she could do. Kandler pulled the girl back toward him, never taking his eyes away from the scene before him.

With a desperate effort, the gelding's rear hooves managed to find a crack in the rock, its hoof caught, and it pushed itself up and forward to safety. It galloped off into the mists, carrying Te'oma away with it.

Kandler raced a few steps forward and shouted after the fleeing changeling. "No!" Then he realized he still had Esprë in his arms, so he turned back and handed her to Sallah, who held the girl away from her at arm's length, as if she'd been tossed a wild animal.

Kandler raced up to the bridge and started to hunt for a winch, lever, or any sort of mechanism that would let him bring the bridge down. Behind him, he heard Esprë say to Sallah, "You can put me down. I won't bite."

Kandler glanced back to see Esprë back on the ground for just a moment before the girl hurled herself at Burch and wrapped him up in her best impression of a bear hug.

The justicar gave up and stormed back toward the others. "Lower the bridge!" he said to the elf. "We have to go after her."

As the justicar waited for a response, he took a good look at the elf for the first time, and his jaw dropped. Her yellowed, wizened skin stretched thin over her skeleton like old parchment, but out here in the dimness she seemed to be glowing from within, like a light blazing behind a leathery shade.

"It can't be," Kandler said, stunned by what he saw. "I mean, you . . . you can't be."

The elf smiled, revealing her teeth, which seemed to be barely attached to her faded gums. She shook her head. "I'm not," she said. "Close but not quite."

"Not what?" Sallah said.

"One of the ascendant councilors," Kandler said, nearly every other thought fleeing from his head. "The ancient dead of the elves."

"I am dead," the elf said, "but still I walk this world." She looked out at the mist. "At least as far as I care."

Sallah stepped back and put her still-blazing sword between

herself and the elf. "No undead creatures can stand before the light of the Silver Flame," she said.

"So I am told," the elf said. She reached out and patted Sallah's hands on the hilt of her sword. "But I am not one of those abominations that stroll about at the whim of some lowly necromancer. No." She shook her head. "I am one of the deathless."

"I beg your pardon, my lady," Kandler said in the elf tongue, his wits returning to him. "Could you see fit to lowering your drawbridge so we can pursue the thief who has entered both your house and mine?"

The deathless elf smiled and answered him in her native language. "You are mannered. You may call me Majeeda."

"My Lady Majeeda," Kandler said with a worried smile, "could you find it in your heart to lower the bridge for us? We thank you for your hospitality, but urgent matters call upon us, and we sadly must part company with you."

"What are they saying?" Sallah whispered to Burch.

The shifter shrugged. "Do I look like an elf?"

"He's asking her to let us go," Esprë whispered.

Majeeda threw her hands wide. "Why should you wish to do leave so soon?" she asked. "Do you not have what you came for?"

She looked over at Esprë and smiled. The elf girl clutched Burch tight and sidled around far enough behind him that Majeeda could only see her face.

"Of course," Kandler said. He smiled at Esprë, and the girl relaxed a little. Burch reached back and tousled her hair. "But there is the matter of the one who recently abandoned your graces. She must be punished for her actions, or I fear that she may repeat them."

Majeeda nodded. "I understand your concern, but I wish for you to stay with me a while longer. The changeling you seek has already left my home. She no longer offends me or concerns me."

Kandler held back a frown. "I appreciate your thoughts

and your offer of continued hospitality. It saddens me that this changeling who caused you such concern should roam unpunished, but that is a matter I can hope to take up with her at a later date."

The justicar licked his dry lips before he broached the next subject. Dealing with ancient elves was always tricky—he remembered how difficult it had been to ask Esprina's parents for her hand in marriage—but this was worse. Esprina would have married him either way. He sensed that Majeeda's wrath was not something he wished to incur.

"I know your feelings on the matter of undead," the Kandler said. "I share your revulsion at the horrible monstrosities. When we pursued the changeling in here, she was in the company of one of the most terrible breeds of these creatures."

Majeeda raised her painted-on eyebrows. Kandler could hear her skin crinkle with the movement. "The vampire, you mean?"

Kandler nodded and waited.

A thin smile crept across Majeeda's dry-leaf lips. "He is no longer a concern to anyone, least of all himself."

"What happened?" Kandler asked, forgetting the mannered patterns of the elf language for the moment and slipping into the common tongue.

"He tried to leave without my permission." Something close to anger clouded the deathless elf's eyes. "I granted his wish for an early departure, although not perhaps in the means he would have preferred."

Kandler switched back to the elf language again. "I hesitate to trouble you with matters so mundane my Lady Majeeda," he said, "but could you elaborate upon the vampire's ultimate fate?"

"In what fashion?"

Kandler could tell the elf was being deliberately obtuse. She seemed to enjoy forcing him to drag every detail from her papery lips. "Forgive my vulgarity, my lady," he said with a grimace, "but is he dead?"

Majeeda opened her mouth and laughed out loud. The sound rustled like a child dashing down a leaf-strewn lane in late fall. "My dear," she said, "I haven't laughed like that in over a century. That creature of which you speak died a long time ago." She patted her chest to calm herself down. "But I . . . eradicated his corpse, yes."

Kandler bowed then turned to speak to Esprë, Burch, and Sallah. "Lady Majeeda here," he said in the common tongue, "has asked us to stay a while and enjoy her hospitality. It would be in our best interests to take her up on her kind offer."

"What about the vampire?" Sallah asked.

"Already taken care of," Kandler said.

Burch looked around at the mists. "Is this safer than the Mournland?" he whispered.

Kandler glanced at Majeeda. "I think so. At least for tonight."

"For any day or night," said Majeeda. "I want you to be comfortable here in my home for as long as you stay."

"But I can't," Sallah started, but Kandler cut her short with an angry glare. She tried again. "My thanks for your kind offer, my lady. We would rather not impose on your good nature for any longer than we have to."

"It's no imposition at all," Majeeda said. "I assure you."

"How long might you expect us to enjoy our time with you?" Sallah asked.

Kandler's stomach flipped at the question. He wanted to know the answer himself, but he'd hoped to not learn it until there was no other option.

The deathless elf smiled. "Not long at all, my dear," she said. "A blink of an eye. Only until it's safe for you to go."

"When's that?" Burch asked.

Majeeda's pleasure dimmed only a bit at the sound of the shifter's voice. "Why, until Cyre is restored and the Mournland is no more," she said.

CHAPTER

29

A shout went up from Levritt's position to the north of the mound of mist. In another land, Deothen might not have been able to hear it over the sounds of chirping birds or crickets, but in the stillness of the Mournland Levritt's call carried far.

The senior knight stood and scanned the distance. Levritt was right where he'd been ordered to be, at one vertex of a triangle that surrounded the mist, allowing the three knights to each see a half of the misty mound and both of their compatriots at the same time.

Leaping in the air, Levritt waved at Deothen with one arm and pointed to his right with the other, toward the spot at which Brendis had been sitting near his horse. Deothen turned to look for Brendis and saw the other knight waving as well and climbing upon his mount. Once in his saddle, Brendis pointed off toward Levritt and then spurred his steed in that direction.

Deothen climbed atop his white horse, his bones creaking with the effort. The rest after the long ride here had been good for both himself and his mount, but his muscles had stiffened up in the short time he and the other knights had kept their watch. With a grunt, he kicked his heels into his steed's sides and galloped off after the others.

Deothen rode down the side of the valley toward the mysterious mound of mist, along the shortest route to where Levritt and Brendis were headed. As he neared the mists, he veered to the right and gave the place a wide berth. He didn't know what might be concealed within them, but thoughts of a dragon's wings or a hydra's head snaking out to pluck him from his saddle danced in his head.

When Deothen made it around to the other side of the mist he saw Levritt and Brendis speeding ahead of him, off to the northeast. He lowered his head, nudged a bit more effort from his mount, and they thundered after the two knights at full gallop.

The blasted landscape fell away before Deothen and the knights and then rose into a hilly stretch of ground that rolled off into the distance. Deothen poked up his head to see what his young charges might be after. It took him a moment, jangled as he was by his horse's pounding hooves, but he spotted it—a lone figure on a massive black horse galloping straight for the hills.

At this distance, Deothen couldn't be sure, but he would have bet his last copper that the rider was the changeling. The patch of sunlight over the mound of mist had long since faded, the hole in the thick, dark cloud cover now just a strange but happy memory. It could have been the vampire astride the horse, but Deothen's gut said different.

The knight looked back over his shoulder, wondering if he'd see the vampire come flapping out of the smoky area on a bat's wings now that the knights were on the chase. Perhaps it was all some devious trick meant to draw the knights away while the vampire escaped with Kandler's stepdaughter.

If so, it was too late for the knights to change course. Brendis and Levritt had raced ahead rather than wait for their commander, so Deothen had little choice but to try to catch up with them. He prayed it wasn't the wrong path.

It bothered Deothen that this course of action forced him

to leave Sallah behind, but he saw no alternative. He prayed the Silver Flame would keep her safe.

Levritt and Brendis seemed to be enjoying the pursuit. They hunched high in their saddles and urged their horses beyond breakneck speeds. Deothen heard the two laugh out loud as they glanced at each other.

The land started to rise. Deothen looked ahead and realized that they had no chance of catching the changeling before she topped the first hill. Levritt and Brendis were gaining on her by the moment, but she had too much of a head start. She must have come barreling out of the mists as if all the demons of Dolurrh were on her tail.

The young knights didn't seem to care. They spurred their mounts on faster and faster, never breaking stride as the ground rose. They used the momentum from their headlong sprint downhill to propel them upward fast as they could.

As Deothen watched, the changeling and her mount disappeared over the crest of the hill. The young knights reached the same spot only half a minute later. They hauled up short for a moment and glanced all around.

Levritt turned back to Deothen and pointed off to the right. The senior knight signaled for the young men to slow down for a moment longer so he could catch up with them. Too eager to run their prey to ground, they never saw the gesture.

Deothen shouted at the young knights, but they plunged over the crest of the hill and out of sight, the thunder of their hooves drowning out the old man's protestations. Although his mount was laboring at the effort now, he pushed the horse hard up the hill.

Once Deothen topped the rise, he hauled his steed to a halt and scanned the land around. The hills stretched away before him, dipping and rising in an easy, patternless way.

The knight knew that Levritt and Brendis had sped off to the right. A low valley presented itself there, and the obvious path quickly turned around a bend. Deothen could see the path of divots in the grayish grass and rock that the young knights' steeds had torn up as they raced in that direction.

The elder knight was not so eager to give up the high ground. Instead, he plunged down into the small valley and then up the other side to the next hill's top. Then he turned his horse to the right and drove it along that hill's crest.

As Deothen rode, he squinted into the distance, scanning the land for a sign of some kind of trap. He thought perhaps he'd see the changeling crawling along a hilltop with a wand of some sort, ready to rain magical death down on the hapless young knights. Or maybe the vampire would appear, spring upon Levritt and Brendis, and tear them from their saddles.

Deothen shivered as he recalled how the other vampire had sunk its fangs into Brendis's neck. If it hadn't been for the shifter's bolt, the young man would surely be dead. Despite all the training Deothen had striven to instill in the young knight, he'd been helpless before the evil creature's overwhelming power.

Those thoughts brought Deothen's mind to the fate of Gweir. He didn't know what he could have done to save the knight from that kind of an ambush. How could he have predicted so many warforged would be hiding under those long-dead bodies? The concept was almost unthinkable for the old warrior.

Deothen had already prayed long and hard for the Silver Flame to forgive these inadequacies in himself. He hoped that Gweir's parents could find it in their heart to do the same. Deothen did not relish bringing them the news of their son's demise, no matter how heroic it might have been or how noble the cause. He prayed he wouldn't have to make the same visit to any other parents once this mission was done.

How was he going to be able to find Sallah again after this? Of all his young charges, he trusted her abilities the most. He hoped he would see her again before too long.

It was then that Deothen spotted the two knights as they trotted along the floor of the twisting hollow before him, which was coming to a dead end. The changeling was nowhere to be seen, and Deothen imagined the young men were discussing just how they should proceed. He called out to them.

Brendis and Levritt turned in their saddles to wave back at their commander. As they did, Deothen spotted something on the ridge to the left above them. He thought it might be the changeling, but another silhouetted form joined the first, and then another.

Deothen shouted out a warning to the young knights, but they were unable to hear him. They cupped their hands to their ears as more and more of the forms rose from the ridge. Deothen stabbed his finger into the air behind the two knights, over and over, but they didn't seem to understand.

Deothen snapped his reins and spurred his mount to a gallop as fast as he could. "Get out of there!" he screamed. "It's a trap! Move! Now!"

Brendis figured it out first. He glanced over his shoulder to see the creatures standing over them, and he slapped Levritt's horse on the rump to make it move.

As the youngest knight's mount leaped forward, a few of the creatures atop the ridge let loose a volley of arrows. Most flew wide of their mark, but one pierced a spot right below Brendis's left shoulder. The knight was able to kick his steed into action before he slumped down over his reins.

It was suicide, Deothen knew. There was no way that the knights could stand against so many attackers. Their only hope was to outrun them, and here he was racing straight for them.

CHAPTER

30

Do you get many guests here, my Lady Majeeda?"

The deathless elf looked across the dining table at Kandler, an amused smile swimming across her face. "You are not the first to have supped at my table since the Day of Mourning," she said. "Is the repast not to your liking?"

Kandler surveyed the wide oak table before him. He sat at the foot of the table with Majeeda across from him at the head. Sallah fidgeted to his right, while to his left Burch perched on the edge of an ornate chair covered with elven carvings. Esprë sat between Burch and the wizard. Kandler had tried to jockey for Esprë to sit near him, but Majeeda seemed to have taken a liking to the girl that was just as strong as her revulsion for the shifter.

The food was wonderful. The tasty roast had just a bit of pink in the middle. The potatoes were creamy and light. The vegetables were fresh and savory. Even the apples were crisp and tart.

"My compliments," Kandler said.

The wizard laughed again, the sound rattling in Kandler's ears. "Oh, you are a prize," she said. "No hands touched this food. I conjured it myself from thin air."

Burch choked on a piece of meat he'd been chewing. He reached out for a goblet of mead with which to wash it down but stopped and tried to hack it up on his own. When it was clear that wouldn't work, the shifter snatched up the goblet and threw back the golden liquid so fast that Kandler couldn't tell if Burch had swallowed it or just opened up his throat and poured it in.

Majeeda wrinkled her nose at the shifter as if someone had brought a half-trained animal to her table. He smiled at her and belched loud and long.

"Good grub," he said.

The wizard buried her face in a long, spindly hand and shook her head in disgust.

"When did you last entertain?" Sallah asked. "You seem well versed at it."

Majeeda turned toward the knight and smiled at the compliment. "I have had few guests here since the Day of Mourning, but I do what I can to keep them happy for as long as they are with me."

She pushed away the plate in front of her. Although it was heaped with food, she had pointedly left it untouched.

"To answer your question," Majeeda said, her eyes focusing into the distance. "The last party I held here was for a small group of fortune hunters—adventurers, they called themselves—who were wandering through the Mournland in search of treasure. Can you imagine such a thing?"

Kandler and Sallah shook their heads. Burch ignored the question as he turned back to gorging himself on his meal. Esprë flashed a wide smile at the wizard.

Majeeda reached out and patted the girl's hand before continuing with her tale. "There were five of them, a priest of Dol Dorn and a sorcerer among them. The others were their bodyguards, ready to defend them in case of physical peril. At least that's what they said. The little one always looked at everything I owned as if it might turn to gold on the spot."

"How did they get here?" Kandler asked. "I'll bet more

than one set of potential visitors has fallen into your moat."

Majeeda cackled at that. "Oh, there's no water in there. Hasn't been for years. It's just a sheer drop, fifty feet down."

Kandler felt an urge to offer the elf a drink for her parched throat, but he was sure that no fluids had passed her lips since before he was born.

"Has anyone ever survived it?" Esprë asked with wide eyes.

"It's possible, I suppose," Majeeda said, "but they could never climb out before the oozes that live down there swept the place clean. The poor dears get so little to eat these days. It used to be you could count on a rabbit or even a deer to fall into the place every now and then, but in these dark days that happens so rarely."

Sallah's fork clattered to her plate. To Kandler, she looked a little green.

"Please don't be upset about it," Majeeda said to the knight, as she wrinkled her thin brow at her. "It's not a matter of good or evil. It's just the circle of life."

Burch looked up for a moment from the bone he was gnawing on to belch a greasy agreement.

"But that's not how my last visitors got here," Majeeda said, turning away from the side of the table at which Burch sat. Kandler saw the shifter grin.

"How did they arrive?" asked Sallah.

"They flew here in airship," the wizard said.

Esprë's eyes flew wide. "Really?"

The wizard nodded at her. "It's magical, of course, something along the lines of the lightning rails."

"The first one I saw was flying over Flamekeep while I was attending the Knights' Academy," Sallah said to Esprë. "They're huge—almost like a galleon, but much sleeker."

"How do they move?" Esprë asked. Kandler smiled at her eagerness to learn more.

"House Cannith builds them in Fairhaven, up in Aundair. Their dragonmarked shipwrights bind an elemental creature of fire to the vessel. When the ship moves, the elemental appears as a ring of fire that runs around its middle." Sallah drew a vertical circle in the air in front of her to illustrate.

Majeeda shook her head condescendingly. Kandler could tell she was irritated that someone else might have Esprë's attention. "The ship these people came in on was much smaller than that. There were only the five of them on it. They spotted the mists surrounding my tower here and came to investigate. They set down inside the moat and announced themselves." The wizard laughed again. "They hardly needed to say anything. With my magic, I saw them coming from miles off. Even without my crystal ball, I could hardly have missed the ring of fire surrounding their vessel. It nearly burned the mists away. It took me hours to get it all right again."

"Where are they now?" Sallah asked.

Kandler winced as Majeeda turned her full attention on the lady knight. The wizard's papery lips trembled as she spoke.

"They did not appreciate my hospitality. They turned on me. They . . ." Majeeda covered her face with her skeletal hands. "They tried to kill me."

Sallah reached her hand across the table toward the wizard but pulled back when Kandler shook his head at her. "That's terrible," she said. "Wh-what did you do?"

Majeeda removed her hands from her face and wiped away her nonexistent tears. Kandler almost thought he could see trails of dust on her face instead.

"I did what I had to do. What they forced me to do." Her face turned grim and determined. "I, well . . ." She looked sidelong at Esprë, who was hanging on her every word, then she put a hand to the side of her mouth to block the girl from seeing her lips and whispered, "I eradicated them."

CHAPTER

31

Burch watched Esprë's eyes grow wide. He tried to kick her under the table to tell her to be quiet, but the wizard spotted him and her scowl sent him back to perching on the seat instead. Majeeda turned to the girl and stretched out her hands.

"I'm sorry, my dear," the deathless elf said. "I didn't mean to disturb your young mind with such terrible tales about such horrible people. Please forgive me."

Esprë glanced at Kandler, who nodded at her. The girl looked back at the wizard and gulped. "I'm fine," she said. "I was just thinking about that vampire and how you got rid of him." The girl let a smile poke through her fear. "That was a good thing you did."

A grin grew across the wizard's face, so wide that it seemed her jaw might fall off into her lap. "I'm so glad you think so," she said. Her pale, sunken eyes sparkled with joy, and the light within her glowed a bit brighter.

Majeeda beamed at each of the people around the table with her, even Burch, although less so when she saw the shifter wiping his face with her table linen.

"It's so good to be surrounded by such fine people again, people who understand me." She sighed. "It's been so long."

"We're glad to be here," Kandler said. "This is far better than spending another night in the Mournland. We spent most of the night chasing that vampire and changeling."

With that reminder, Esprë covered her mouth as she tried to stifle a long yawn.

"Where are my manners?" Majeeda said. "I forget that the living tire so easily, and you must have had such a harrowing ordeal. Can I show you to your chambers?"

The guests nodded as one and followed as the deathless elf rose and strode from the chamber. She walked over to the stairs in the north wall and ascended another flight to the next floor up.

"The guest chambers are up here," Majeeda said.

They emerged into a sitting room about a third of the size of the dining hall or the library on the first floor.

Overstuffed chairs sat scattered about the room in pairs, accompanied by low tables for resting feet or drinks upon. A roaring fire blazed in an open hearth near the rear wall, showering the room in warm, flickering light. Two closed doors stood at opposite ends of a wooden wall, otherwise covered with gold and red tapestries that ran across the tower from side to side.

"Ladies reside on the left," Majeeda said. "Gentlemen on the right."

Burch leaned in to whisper something to Kandler. The justicar turned to their hostess and spoke to her in her native tongue again. "My compatriot here"—he pointed to Burch—"prefers to sleep outdoors. We'd be in your debt if you could find appropriate arrangements for him."

Majeeda frowned for a short moment. "You think he'd fare better in the courtyard?" she responded in the common tongue.

Burch's face lit up.

"I think so," said Kandler as he rubbed his eyes. "Otherwise, he's liable to start howling and keep us all awake."

Majeeda inclined her head at Kandler. "Allow me to take care of this matter for you."

Kandler glanced at the shifter, concern etched on his face. Burch recognized the "Are you sure about this?" look. In response, he gave Kandler a single, serious nod. To Burch, this seemed like their best chance for escape, and he wasn't going to back down now.

"Our thanks for your kind consideration, my Lady Majeeda," Kandler said.

Esprë ran over and gave Kandler a big hug before following Sallah through the left door. Kandler watched her go and waited for the door to close before he took the door on the right. Burch gave him a quick wink just before the justicar shut the door.

"Follow me," Majeeda said to Burch. She turned and walked off without looking back to see if he would pursue her. He did.

When they reached the stairs, Majeeda climbed upward instead of going down. Burch hesitated for a moment but then started up after the deathless elf.

There was a landing at the top of the stairs, and Majeeda waited for Burch there. When he caught up with her, she pointed at an ironbound trapdoor hanging in the ceiling above them. "That leads to the roof," the wizard said. "Please show yourself up and close the door behind you. I trust you will be comfortable up there."

Burch hesitated for a moment. He wanted to be put in the courtyard, but he supposed that getting outside at all was a good first step. He nodded at her without a word.

"Excellent." Majeeda gestured for the shifter to proceed.

Burch clambered up the short ladder to the trapdoor and slid aside the thin metal bar that kept it locked from below. He pushed the heavy door up until it fell back on its hinges, and he pulled himself through the opening and onto the roof.

Chill winds whipped around the top of the tower. The mists here were still so thick that the shifter could not see through them to the sky or even much farther than his feet. He sighed as he breathed in the open air again. Even clogged as it was with the swirling gray mist, it still tasted better than the mausoleum atmosphere below.

"Don't forget to close the door," Majeeda called up from the landing. "It does rain out there sometimes. I'd rather it didn't flood me out."

Without a word, Burch leaned over and pulled the trapdoor shut, letting its weight slam it closed. He stood there for a moment listening, and he heard Majeeda tap the door with her bony fingers.

When Burch was sure the wizard was gone, he pulled on the trapdoor's iron ring. The door didn't budge a hair.

Sleep called to Burch, but the shifter decided to tour his surroundings. If he was trapped up here, he'd need a good idea of what "here" was like. The assurances of the wizard aside, this was still the Mournland.

He had hoped the wizard would put him in the courtyard where he might be able to escape and find Deothen and the other knights so he could lead them back here to fight the wizard. The plan still sounded like suicide in his head, but Majeeda had foiled even that idea.

Burch padded to what he thought should be the north. Within just a few steps, he found the edge of the roof. A waist-high shield wall topped by a battlement lined it.

The shifter leaned out through one of the gaps in the battlement. The wall dropped away from it at a negative incline, slanting in toward the rest of the tower. The stones from which the exterior of the tower was made were all cut neat and fitted well and smooth. He had considered scaling his way down to the courtyard, but that seemed impossible now.

Burch picked up a small stone from the roof and dropped it over the edge of the battlement. He listened but never heard it hit bottom. Whether that meant there was no bottom to the moat or that it was filled with those oozes the deathless elf had talked about, the shifter couldn't tell.

He walked a slow circuit around the perimeter of the wall, keeping his hand on the top of the battlement, bouncing his hand from one high section to the next. He walked for a long while, hoping to find a corner as a point of reference. It was then he realized that the top of the tower was not square but round.

A moment of sharp panic raced through the shifter's mind. He didn't know how he'd ever manage to get back to the trapdoor in this mist. He could crisscross the top of the tower time and time again without finding it, he was sure.

Then Burch realized it didn't matter. The trapdoor was locked, maybe by magic. Even if he found it, he wouldn't be able to open it. He was stuck out here until Majeeda came to let him back into the tower again.

His mind more at ease, the shifter decided to take a stroll across the roof, just to see if he might stumble across the trapdoor anyhow. That small victory would make him feel better, no matter how hopeless the situation now seemed.

Burch padded across the rooftop, scanning the floor ahead of him and to both sides as he went. He did so twice and never found the trapdoor. He decided to keep at it for a while, to work off some of his nervous energy. He never liked feeling like he was in a cage, even one without a roof.

Burch had lost track of the number of times he'd crossed the top of the tower and was considering giving up when he tripped over something. He danced across it, regaining his balance, then spun about to see what it was.

Burch got on his knees. Instead of the iron ring in the trapdoor he'd hoped for, he found a large, iron mooring cleat that had been mounted in the tower's roof with huge spikes. He poked at it for a moment, unsure what to make of it.

Then Burch noticed the rope still attached to the cleat. It was slack, so he picked it up in one hand and followed it. Perhaps there was enough of it for him to lower himself over the side of the roof and to the ground below. He might even be able to swing out wide enough to cross the chasm.

As Burch crept along, the rope cradled in his hand as if it was spun from gold, he realized that the line left the roof and wandered into the sky. Mystified, he followed it until it pulled out of his reach, then he backed up and gave it a tug. It was hanging from something.

Burch scratched his head. "It can't be," he said with a grin.

"One way to find out," the shifter answered himself. He grabbed the rope in both hands and began to climb.

CHAPTER

32

Kandler looked around the bedchamber. Four different beds lined the walls, each made of polished mahogany with a tall, white canopy. A thick oak panel separated this bedchamber from the ladies', just like the one that partitioned off the sitting room from the rest of this level of the tower. Wide, unglazed windows stood in the tower's outer wall. As with the windows on the other floors, the mists dared not cross over their thresholds.

The justicar ran a finger along the edge of one of the ornate nightstands that stood next to each bed. It came back covered with dust.

Kandler heard the trapdoor in the tower's roof slam shut. He returned to the door and pressed his ear against it. He could hear someone walk down the upper stairs and stop in the sitting room.

Majeeda's voice muttered something in the arcane tongue of wizards. After a moment of silence, footsteps receded down the stairs from the sitting room to the lower levels. When Kandler was sure his host had left, he tried the door. It didn't budge, no matter how hard he shook it.

The justicar strode over to the windows and peered into the

mist. He couldn't see anything other than the swirling clouds. He poked his head outside, and the cloying mist clung to him. Even at this altitude, it was so thick he couldn't see anything below or above.

Kandler peered off to his left where he guessed there would be a window looking out from the ladies' bedchamber. If there was, it remained hidden to him.

"Esprë," the justicar called through the mist. He feared that Majeeda might hear him, but he was ready to risk it. "Sallah, are you there?"

"Kandler!" Esprë sounded excited. "We're here. I can't see you."

"Stand aside, child," said Sallah. "The light of the Silver Flame will help here."

Kandler saw a light come shimmering out of the darkness to his left. It burned away at the mist, and soon he could see Sallah's sword flickering with its silvery fire.

"Have you tried your door?" Kandler asked.

"It's locked," Esprë said.

"Magically," said Sallah. "And don't think about trying to scale these walls."

Kandler ran his hand along the stones near him. "Too smooth. I left my ropes in the saddlebags too."

"What about the bed sheets?" asked Esprë.

Kandler snapped his finger. "Good thinking. I've got lots of them, plenty to reach the ground."

"Are you sure?" Sallah said. "We don't know what's straight down from here. It could be that chasm or something even worse."

"Worse than the chasm?" Esprë asked in disbelief.

"I don't see where we have much of a choice," said Kandler. "Majeeda's several arrows shy of a full quiver. The longer we stay here, the better the chance that she'll do something to us."

"Sir Deothen will not abandon us in here," Sallah said. "We need only wait for him and the others to come to our aid."

"Even if they could somehow get across the chasm, Majeeda would spank them like babies. If they're lucky, they'd end up here with us, which leaves us in the same spot."

"So what do you propose?"

Kandler rubbed his chin for a moment. There were no good options, but one was clearly less worse than the others. "We have to give it a try. I'll make a rope from the sheets over here. Get started over there too."

"We're going to use separate ropes?" Sallah asked.

"I'm coming over there first. If I get to the bottom and it's safe, I'll tug on the sheets. Then you can follow me down."

"This is insane."

"Welcome to the Mournland."

Kandler went over to the beds, tore their dusty sheets from them, and began knotting them together. The sheets were old, and they had a musty scent that made him sneeze, but they were rough enough that he thought the knots would hold. He wondered how long it had been since someone had slept in them.

The justicar soon had a makeshift rope he was confident would be long enough reach to the ladies' bedchamber. He needed something to weigh down one end of it, though, so he could throw it. He glanced around and on one of the nightstands he spotted a small statue, a bust of an elf carved from jade. As he picked it up, he wondered if it was a likeness of Majeeda in life. If so, she'd been beautiful. He tied the end of the sheet-rope around it and stepped over to the window.

"Ready," Kandler said. Sallah's sword reappeared at her window.

"We're still working in here," Esprë called out.

"I'll give you a hand when I get over there. I only made enough to get from my room to yours."

"We're ready," said Sallah.

Kandler leaned out the window and swung around the bust-weighted end of the sheets in a wide circle. "All right," he said, "catch!"

The justicar flung the bust toward the sword. "Ow!" Sallah

said. There was a clatter, and Kandler could see the knight's sword almost fall away into the mist. When the bust hit the end of the sheet-rope's length, it tugged hard. Kandler felt himself being pulled through the window, but he hauled himself back in at the last moment.

"You could say something when you tie a chamber pot into the end of something you're throwing at me," Sallah said.

"It was a jade bust," said Kandler. "And now you know." He hauled up the sheet and started swinging the bust around again to give it another try.

"Incoming!" the justicar said as he flung the bust over once more. This time, he heard a satisfying grunt on the other end.

"She got it!" said Esprë.

"Perfect. Now tie your end to something solid. I'm coming over."

Kandler anchored his end of the sheet-rope to the nearest bed's leg and tested it with his full weight. It held.

"Ready!" said Esprë.

"Here I come."

Kandler pulled his legs over the edge of the window and looked down into the nothingness of the mists. For a moment, he wondered if this was what the realm of the dead looked like, then he rubbed his hands together, took a deep breath, grabbed the sheet-rope, and swung himself out.

The sheet-rope gave a bit under Kandler's weight. He swung for a moment, trying to regain his equilibrium. When he was ready, he moved hand over hand along the rope.

The distance between the windows hadn't seemed so far when Kandler made the rope. Throwing a jade bust the thirty feet or so was easy. Crossing the gap himself was a bit more treacherous.

Kandler was about halfway to his goal when he heard a sheet behind him start to give. The tearing noise pierced the mist-shrouded air like a shout. He recognized it and flung himself along the rope as fast as he could go.

The justicar only managed to get another swing in before the rope separated. It tore right where it had been rubbing against the corner of the windowsill, and Kandler fell.

Esprë screamed.

Kandler yelled as he swung out into the mists. He clung to the rope with all his might. When he reached the bottom of his swing, his hands slipped along the rough, musty sheets. The skin burned from the palms of his hands, but he held on tighter, trying to slow his descent.

Kandler's grasp came to a knot in the sheet, and he stopped hard. His momentum kept going, though, and he swung far out away from the tower's wall.

When Kandler reached the end of the swing, he breathed a sigh of relief, despite the pain in his hands and his arms. It turned into a gasp of fear as he swung back.

Kandler's back slammed into the tower's wall, knocking the air from his lungs and wrenching his arms. Still, he managed to hold on, and he hung there until he could breathe again, grateful that the swinging had stopped. The mists swirled hungrily below him, and for a moment Kandler considered letting them have him. Maybe Esprina would be waiting for him on the other side.

"Kandler!" Esprë said. The voice shocked Kandler out of his daze.

Sallah joined her. "Kandler!"

"All right," the justicar said. He still had work to do here. He couldn't leave Esprë and the others to the mad elf's whims. He choked on his words until he cleared his throat. "I'm all right," he said. "Be right up."

Kandler stretched his shoulders a bit, testing to see if they would still work. He took a deep breath and started pulling himself hand over hand up the sheets. He had only made it a few feet when he heard the sheet start to tear again. This time, the sound came from above him.

CHAPTER

33

I's tearing!"

Esprë's scream rang in Kandler's head. He looked up and saw her reach out and grab the sheet just past the point where the rip had started.

"Kandler!" she screamed as she wrapped her little fingers around the rough fabric and pulled.

"Get off the rope!" Kandler said as he pulled himself higher. It was bad enough he was going to die here. He wasn't going to drag his daughter down with him. "Esprë, you're not big enough!"

Sallah shouldered the girl aside and snatched the tearing end of the sheet-rope from her. "I have you!" she said.

"Who's got you?" he said. "Let go!"

Sallah ignored the justicar. She pulled on the rope with all her might, but it didn't come up an inch. He was a full-sized, fully armed man, and he was just too heavy.

Esprë started to wail with fear. Kandler's stomach turned. The girl had lost both her parents already, and now she was going to watch him fall to his doom. He kept climbing.

"Be quiet!" yelled Sallah.

Esprë's wail ended as if Sallah had sliced through it with a sword.

"Quick!" Sallah ordered. "Hand me the other rope!"

A moment later Esprë appeared at the window with rope that she and Sallah had been working on. She tossed it down to Kandler. "Here!" she said. "Grab hold!"

Kandler reached out and grabbed the other rope just as the first gave way. He had barely enough time to wrap it around his wrist before he fell. The other rope still had a lot of slack in it, and it snaked out the window after Kandler as he dropped away into the mist.

The rope finally played out and snapped tight, and Kandler felt as if his arm was pulled from its socket. He growled in pain and then felt himself swinging back toward the tower again. This time he was able to brace himself for the impact. He hit the hard stone, and his shoulder burned as if a red-hot brand had been shoved up his sleeve.

Kandler hung there at the end of the rope from his bad arm, trying to recover his strength. He couldn't tell how far from the window he'd fallen or how close the ground might be. He thought he heard something wet and sticky far below—perhaps a beast smacking its lips over an anticipated meal or the bubbling of a pit full of tar.

"Pull!" Sallah shouted.

Kandler heard something above him crack. The image of a spitting bedpost flashed through his head, and he closed his eyes and thought of his wife.

The sheet jerked as whatever it was anchored to started to give, and pain lanced through Kandler's arm. The agony jabbed him into action. He reached up with his good arm and started pulling himself up. Each time he used his left arm, his shoulder protested, but he kept climbing through the pain. He used his teeth to hold on to the sheets when his arm hurt too much. The musty smell reminded him of a funeral shroud, and he gagged at the taste.

The air behind Kandler grew warm, and he heard a noise like a crackling bonfire all around him. For a moment, he feared he was already dead, that the heat came from the Keeper welcoming him into the fiery afterlife. He wrapped the rope around his good arm and turned to meet his fate.

A large circle of fire cut through the mist straight for Kandler. Orange tongues of flame crackled as they pushed the ring closer. As Kandler watched, the ring grew larger and larger until it seemed it must be the maw of a dragon come to pluck him from the side of the tower wall.

Kandler grunted and started climbing again. He pulled himself up as best he could with his injured arm, fighting for every inch. He could feel Sallah and Esprë tugging on the sheet from above, but they weren't able to move it. He heard Esprë screech in frustration, and his heart sank.

When the justicar glanced back again, he saw that it was hopeless. He'd gained a few feet, but the fiery ring looked large enough to swallow his house whole. There was no way to escape it. He clung to the rope with his teeth and hands, hoping to at least make the creature work for its meal.

Something large and heavy struck the tower below Kandler. The structure shook to its foundation. Esprë's scream punctuated the smash.

The bedpost anchoring the sheet snapped, and Kandler fell, pulling the sheet after him.

"No!" Sallah shouted. Esprë let loose with a long, heartbroken wail.

Kandler kicked off from the wall as he fell, in a vain hope he might find some kind of water below to cushion his landing. After only a dozen feet, the justicar crashed onto something solid and flat. He cried out in agony and surprise.

Kandler reached out around him and felt the wooden planks of a deck swaying beneath him. "What?" he said, then he looked around and was struck dumb.

Half of the ring of fire towered over Kandler like a blazing rainbow, crackling as it burned where it hovered in the air. The flames forced back the mists, and he could see along the length of the ship's deck on which he stood. The vessel looked like a large cutter but stretched out as if a giant had picked her up and pulled her hard at both ends so he could better hurl it through the air. Instead of sails, the ship had a carved wooden harness that arched high out of the bridge and hooked around the ring of fire at its apex.

Burch waved at Kandler from behind the ship's wheel. "Ahoy, castaway!" the shifter called.

"Ahoy, the ship!" Kandler said as he struggled to his feet. The deck pitched beneath him. "Permission to come aboard?"

Burch barked out a laugh. "Granted!"

Kandler raced along the ship's deck and up to the bridge. "How?" he asked. "Where?" He just stopped and stared at the shifter. "There's a legend in this, I'm sure, but we have to get Esprë and Sallah out of the tower now."

"Think that bang woke up Majeeda?" Burch asked with toothy grin. "I can't steer this thing worth a damn."

"Let me give it a shot," Kandler said. He took the wheel from Burch and felt the polished wood in his hands. As he did, something poked around the corners of his mind.

"It's the elemental," Burch said. "The ring. It's a creature made of pure fire."

Although Kandler had never ridden an airship before, he understood the basic principles behind them. He reached out with his mind and urged the burning thing to move the ship higher. At first, it resisted, content to burn away in its mystical, circular cage, but eventually it gave in.

Kandler looked up at the window of the ladies' bedchamber. He saw Esprë and Sallah gaping down at them, and he waved. Esprë squealed with joy.

Kandler noticed that the wheel didn't move with the ship. It didn't turn at all. It was just a conduit by which the ship's pilot could reach the elemental that kept the thing aloft. He willed the ship to come to a stop at the window, but he misjudged the distance in the mist. The ship came to a crushing stop as the starboard railing caught under the window's stone sill.

Kandler left the wheel and dashed over to the window.

Burch was already there, taking Esprë from Sallah's arms. Kandler reached out to help the lady knight over the railing too.

At that moment, the door to the bedchamber burst open. Majeeda came shuffling through as fast as her withered legs would carry her.

"No!" the deathless elf screeched. She reached out toward Kandler with a bony hand, raw energy arcing between her fingers.

CHAPTER

34

Kandler grabbed Sallah by the arm and kicked at the stone windowsill with all his might. Already damaged by the ship, the sill gave way. Sallah fell into Kandler's arms as the ship lurched toward the mist-shrouded sky. The two fell to the deck in a tangle of arms and legs.

"Stop!" Majeeda said. "I command you to stop! You must stop!"

The deathless elf screeched something unintelligible at the people on the ship, and each of them froze in place, unable to move a muscle. Kandler found himself lying underneath Sallah's armored form, incapable of doing more than breathe at her. He couldn't even blink.

The airship kept rising.

"No!" Majeeda shouted at the ship from below. "Don't leave me here alone! You can't!"

No one on the ship replied. Kandler had a lot of things he wanted to say to the insane wizard, but his tongue refused to move.

"Damn you all to Khyber then!" Majeeda said. "If you won't stay, then you can all die!"

Kandler heard the wizard chanting again, and then

something came crackling at them from below.

A scorching explosion shook the entire ship, tossing it up and to port as if a whale had hit it from below. Kandler and Sallah tumbled across the deck toward the railing. They smashed into it hard, unable to brace themselves for the impact.

The ship pushed higher into the mist, faster than ever. As she righted herself, Kandler realized he was lying on top of Sallah at an awkward angle that threatened to break his wrist under her armored form.

The dark, cloying mist became thinner and lighter as the ship rose higher. Far below now, Majeeda screeched out in anguish. "Don't leave me!" she said. "Please!"

The ship broke through the darkness of the mist and into the dimness of the Mournland's overcast sky. After so long in Majeeda's domain, even this weak light hurt Kandler's eyes. He winced, and in so doing realized he could move his eyes.

Kandler rolled off of Sallah, who scrambled away. He cast about for Esprë and spotted her several feet down the railing, rubbing her head. He dashed over to her and snatched her up in his arms.

Esprë wailed in fear as Kandler held her. "It's all right," he said to her, most of his body aching as he patted her on the back. Her sobs slowed as he spoke. "We're safe now."

"Don't be so sure about that," Sallah said. "I smell smoke."

Kandler pointed up at the circle of fire that encircled the airship like a ring on a finger. "There's fire all around here," he said.

"Fire below, boss!" Burch called from the bridge. Kandler saw the shifter was leaning over the port side of the ship and looking at the hull.

Kandler dashed to the rail and stared downward. Flames billowed from the bottom of the ship.

The justicar sprinted up to the bridge, Esprë still in his arms. Burch already had his hands on the wheel.

"We have to bring her down," Kandler said.

"We're still going up," Burch pointed out. "We have to stop that first."

The shifter handed the wheel to Kandler. He put Esprë down and grasped the wheel in both hands. He reached out with his mind and felt the elemental out there, just like before. This time, though, the creature wanted nothing to do with him. It liked flying straight into the sky, away from Majeeda and her tower, and it wasn't going to stop no matter how much Kandler might want it to.

Kandler tried again and again, but it was no good. "We're in trouble," he said to Burch. "How high are we?"

The shifter leaned over the back railing and looked down. "Fatally," he said.

Kandler let go of the wheel and scanned the bridge, hunting for something, anything that would help. "Maybe we can toss a mooring line overboard," he said.

"There's nothing for it to catch on," Sallah said as she joined them on the bridge.

"We can't just go up forever," Kandler said, striving to keep the panic from his voice. "It has to stop sometime."

"Says who?" Sallah asked.

As the knight spoke, the ship stopped rising so fast that Kandler was almost lifted from the deck. Startled, he spun around to see Esprë holding the wheel. "How?" The justicar knelt down next to his stepdaughter and placed a hand on her shoulder. "How did you do that?" he asked.

Esprë beamed down at him sweetly, reminding Kandler of her mother. "You just have to ask nicely," she said.

Kandler tried to keep from laughing, but failed. Sallah joined in, and Esprë too. It was Burch who brought them back to earth.

"We're still burning!" the shifter shouted.

"Good point," Kandler said. He stood up behind Esprë and put his hands over hers on the ship's wheel. "We need to land this thing fast."

"Where?" asked Sallah

Kandler scanned the land all around. There were no ponds, rivers, or even a stream in Majeeda's valley. To the north, a series of low hills rolled away.

"Head over there," Kandler said to Esprë. "We need to smother the flames. If we can skim the top of one of those hills we might be able to snuff the fire in the grass."

"Or crash," Burch said. He ran off to the bow of the ship to play scout. Sallah moved down to the main deck after him.

"Just give it a try," Kandler said to Esprë. He knew they didn't have much time, but scaring the girl would just cause her to freeze up. He needed her to be calm now, so he kept his voice modulated and cool.

"Too fast!" Burch called back.

Kandler looked out at the ground and saw it speeding toward the ship. "Take us back a little," he said to Esprë. The ship's nose yanked upward.

"Whoa!" Esprë said. Her voice was steadier than Kandler would have guessed. After a moment, he realized she was enjoying this.

"Easy," Burch called back.

Kandler leaned over and pointed out a place that he thought they might be able to land, right along the crest of the first hill.

"This is fun!" Esprë said as she aimed for it.

Kandler smiled at her. The wind blowing in her long blonde hair reminded him of her mother again—her mother, the sorcerer. It seemed Esprë had inherited some of Esprina's talents. He leaned over and gave her a small kiss on her on the cheek.

"You're doing great," he said. "Take it easy. I'm right here with you."

Sober again, Esprë looked up at Kandler and nodded.

Kandler looked down and saw the ends of a leather belt hanging from around the wheel. He grabbed them and fastened them around both he and his daughter, then attached them to the wheel's post. He called for Burch and Sallah to join them.

The shifter came bounding up with a big grin for Esprë. "Nice work, pup," he said. He and Sallah found a set of leather straps mounted in the bridge railing and wound their wrists into them.

The hillcrest came rushing up at the ship. Kandler looked down at Esprë and saw her concentrating with all her might as she jutted out her chin and chewed on her lower lip. "Slow down just a bit," he said quietly. "Just take it in right there." He arced his hand as if it were the ship angling along the hill's crest.

"We have all the time in the world," Kandler said. It was a bad lie, and he knew that Esprë wasn't fooled, but he hoped it calmed her nerves all the same.

The ship hit the hilltop hard. Had Kandler and Esprë not been wearing the wheel's belt, they would have been thrown from the bridge. As it was, Kandler struggled to hold them both in place, his injuries screaming in protest.

"Hard to port!" Kandler said. "Left!"

Esprë almost jumped from between his arms, but the ship swung hard to port and ran the burning part of her hull against the hillside. She scraped along, the boards of her shell groaning in protest.

"Bring it up now," Kandler said. The ship came off the hill and righted itself.

"Report!" the justicar said to the shifter.

Burch let go of the straps and peered over the side of the ship. "That did it!" he said. "The fire's out!"

Kandler sighed with relief and he felt Esprë sink back into his arms. He hugged her tight, then said, "Bring her up just a bit." The ship nosed higher into the sky.

Kandler undid the belt around himself and Esprë, then reattached it around the girl. Sallah removed her hands from the straps she'd used and came over to Esprë with a wide, proud smile.

"Where to now?" said Burch, who was scanning the countryside below. "I don't see the changeling anywhere."

"Sir Deothen!" said Sallah, as if ashamed the thought had just struck her. "We have to go back for them and the others."

Esprë nodded and brought the ship around to point south again. Under Kandler's direction, she headed for the south end of Majeeda's valley but gave the mists surrounding her tower a healthy berth, keeping them always to the starboard.

Kandler marveled at the airship's speed as she flew toward the other side of the valley, the heat blasting from the back end of the fiery ring pushing them along. Unhampered by the drag of the ocean's waves, it moved faster than any seagoing ship. It seemed like the finest horse would be hard pressed to keep up with her, even on a flat stretch of land. The way she sailed straight and smooth above the valley floor was unmatchable.

As the ship came up on the spot where Kandler and the others had left the knights behind, he frowned. "I don't see them," he said.

Sallah climbed down from the bridge and ran out to the tip of the ship's stem. She leaned over the bow and peered out at the long southern slope and into the valley. She stood up and pointed down.

"That's where we were," she said. "They're gone!"

CHAPTER

35

Kandler looked to Burch. "What's your best guess?"

The shifter leaned over the nearest railing and gazed down at the terrain below. Although it was rock and hard-packed dirt near the chasm and mist-shrouded tower, beyond the sickly-looking grass sprouted again, and the soil was a bit softer.

"Trail's clear," the shifter said. "From here, I can see where horses trampled grass. They were moving fast."

Kandler whispered something to Esprë, and the girl brought the ship back around until it was headed back toward the mound of mist.

"What happened?" Kandler asked.

Burch stared down over the railing and tried to decipher the signs scattered on the ground below.

"The changeling bolted that way," the shifter said, pointing to the northeast. "Then the knights followed." He stared off to the left and right. "They were posted all around tower, but they chased her together." He jabbed his finger to the northeast again. "Into the hills."

"That's the way the changeling was headed before," Kandler said.

"You're going after them, aren't you?" Sallah demanded

as she rushed back from the bow. "We can't just leave them out there."

Kandler smiled. "What kind of rogues do you take us for?"

Sallah narrowed her eyes at the justicar. "The kind that might turn around as soon as they got what they came for." She glanced at Esprë, still standing at the wheel. The girl blushed.

"That's a good point," Kandler said as he looked down at Esprë. "I hadn't thought of it that way." He reached out and put an arm around his daughter.

"You can't be serious," the lady knight said. "Without them you never would have gotten this far. You never would have rescued her."

"Maybe," Burch said. The others turned to look at him. "But I'm interested in something else."

Sallah sneered at the shifter. "Getting home safe to the town that threw you in prison?"

Burch smiled at the knight, showing all his sharp teeth. "No," he said. "I want that changeling's head on my wall."

"No!" Esprë blurted, taking her hands from the wheel. The ship bobbled in the air for a moment as if it had hit a rock. Esprë grabbed the wheel again, and the ship straightened out. "You don't have to do that," she said to Burch once she was back in control. "Not for me."

Kandler wrinkled his brow at his Esprë. "This lady kidnapped you. She used you as a hostage. She could have killed you."

"But she didn't," said Esprë. "She wouldn't have. She saved me from those vampires."

Kandler put a hand on the girl's shoulder. "She saved you for herself, I think."

"I know," said Esprë softly, "but you don't have to kill her, do you? Not for me."

Kandler sighed then kissed the girl atop her golden locks.

"But you have to go after her!" Sallah said. "You can't let her get away."

"I thought you wanted to save your friends," Burch said.

Sallah snarled in frustration at the shifter. "They were going after her. You find her, and you find them."

Kandler smiled. He hadn't thought the knight could be that bloodthirsty, and he was happy his instincts had proved right. "Good. Then we're headed in the right direction. Right, Burch?"

The shifter nodded. "Straight over that ridge, then follow the hollow."

"Don't worry, ladies," Kandler said. "We'll find your knights," he said to Sallah, then he turned to Esprë, "and we'll leave your friend alone, assuming the knights don't get to her first."

Esprë let go of the ship's wheel with one hand and hugged Kandler tight.

The ship scudded through the sky. Sallah watched the mists swirling overhead for a while then gazed out at the landscape below, marveling at the grace with which they moved. Under Burch's guidance, Esprë kept the ship low, only a few score feet above the crests of the hills. Each time the shifter signaled her, she reined the ship back from its top speed to give him time to spot the changes in the trail.

Sallah walked back to the bridge and put a hand on Kandler's arm. He winced. "How are you?" she asked.

"I've been better."

The lady knight looked at him. "Is it your shoulder? You wrenched it when you fell, didn't you?"

Kandler started to say something then shut his mouth and just nodded.

"I can help," Sallah said tentatively.

"You or the Silver Flame? Healing magic doesn't work well in the Mournland," Kandler said, rubbing his shoulder. "It won't even heal on its own until we get out of here."

"What I'm offering isn't magic," Sallah said. "The chosen knights of the Silver Flame have their own kind of power. As you saw with Brendis, it seems to work here."

"This must be my lucky day."

Sallah stepped back. She wasn't used to having anyone talk to her like this. Her fellow knights always treated her with respect, especially since Jaela Daran, the Keeper of the Flame, a girl not much older than Esprë, had called out her name in the course of the prophecy concerning the Mark of Death. Since then, they had been almost deferential. She liked the fact that someone would treat her more like an equal, but she bristled at Kandler's obvious distrust of all things holy.

"Would you like my help or not?" Sallah asked, letting the exasperation show in her voice.

Kandler flexed his shoulder and winced again. He pushed it toward her and nodded.

With Kandler's permission, Sallah slipped her hands up the sleeve of his shirt until she reached his shoulder. She offered up a short prayer to the Silver Flame that ended with, "May the light of your kindness shine on this heathen. Amen."

Kandler drew in a breath to protest, but he stopped when Sallah's hands warmed up and a soft glow arose under his shirt. The warmth moved from Sallah's hands into his shoulder. As it washed away, she knew it took the hurt with it.

"How's that?" asked Sallah.

Kandler flexed his shoulder again. "My thanks," he said.

As the ship rounded a bend in the hollow, Burch held up his hand and called out, "Hold it!"

Esprë hauled the ship back until it stood hovering in the air. "What is it?" she asked.

Sallah followed Kandler as he ran forward to peer around Burch at the ground. Below, she could see the signs of a fight. A few pieces of armor lay scattered about the place, and the grass was all torn up.

"What happened here?" Sallah asked Burch, not at all sure she wanted to hear the answer.

"A big fight," the shifter answered.

"I think we can see that much," Kandler said. "What's all that armor doing down there?"

"That's not armor," the shifter said as he looked closer. "Those are pieces of warforged. They must have come from three soldiers, at least."

"Can you tell anything else?" Sallah asked.

Burch shook his head. "Hard to say from up here." He motioned for Esprë to bring the ship lower.

"Keep going," Burch said. At the last moment, he held up his hand to stop. "Good!"

The ship bumped against the ground. "Close enough?" Esprë asked, blushing.

"By the Silver Flame," Sallah said, "be careful!"

"It's just a bump," the justicar said. "It's not easy to control this beast."

Sallah turned and pointed to the ring of fire surrounding the ship. She understood that Kandler wished to protect his daughter, but this was too important to tiptoe around.

"You see that?" she said to Kandler.

"It's hard to miss."

"That's an elemental creature of fire," she said. "The dragon-marked shipwrights who created this craft bound it into this ring with powerful magic. Just look at the carvings along the retaining arch." Sallah paused to calm herself down and to let her words sink in. "Break that arch, and you let loose the elemental. It might not be too happy about being bound up all that time. It might decide to take it out on the child behind the wheel."

"Or the mouthy lady in the armor," Burch said. "Point taken." He signaled Esprë to bring the ship up a bit. The ship lurched upward into the sky and hovered a few feet over the ground.

Sallah scowled at the shifter, but before she could respond, Kandler tapped her on the shoulder and pointed down the length the ship's rail. "There's a rope ladder there," he said. "Let's take a look."

The two scrambled down the ladder and onto the hill. Kandler scanned the crest while Sallah strode down into the hollow.

"The warforged must have started out here," Kandler said loud enough for Sallah to hear over the crackling of the fiery ring. "I'd guess they ambushed the knights when they rode into that hollow."

Sallah bent over and ran her hand along some of the stunted, gray grass. Then she stood and held it up. Crimson stained her fingers.

"They're not here anymore," Kandler said. "Who do you think won?"

Burch looked down at Sallah from the ship and said, "Warforged. No doubt."

The knight shook her head. "If that's so, where are the bodies?"

"What's that over there?" Burch said, pointing down to a fold in the hollow. "Something shiny."

Sallah hissed and launched herself up the hillside, uttering a silent prayer to the Silver Flame as she went. Kandler dashed along the crest of the hill and beat the lady knight to the spot. He knelt down reverently before the things Burch had seen from the ship. As Sallah reached him, he turned to let her see what they were.

"Their swords," Sallah said, horrified as she looked down at the sacred blades of her fellow knights. "No knight would ever willingly give up his sword to a foe. They must be dead."

CHAPTER

36

Tここ aren't any bodies," Kandler said as he looked up at Sallah. She seemed so hurt, he needed to hold out some hope for her to cling to. "They could still be alive."

Sallah shook her head as tears welled up in her emerald eyes. "They are sworn to keep their holy swords by their sides at all times. They would have fought with them till their last breaths."

Kandler stood and put his arms around the lady knight. She lowered her head but managed to fight back the tears. She did not pull away.

"Trail goes that way," Burch called down from above. "Lots of people." The shifter scanned the grass along the top of the ridge. "Some dragged."

Sallah pushed away from Kandler and craned her neck to talk to Burch. "You think they were captured?"

"Warforged don't eat."

"By the Flame!" Sallah said, shocked at the shifter's words. "What made you suggest that?"

"You only carry bodies for food—unless the bodies aren't dead."

The knight nodded. "I suppose so." She looked along the

ridge in the direction Burch had pointed. "Then there's still time. We must go after them."

"Come on," Kandler said as he reached for the rope ladder and handed it to Sallah. "Even I can see the trail. Warforged leave large footprints."

Sallah hauled herself up the rope ladder and then reached back behind her for the swords of her fellow knights. Kandler handed them up to her one at a time, hilt toward her, then followed her up the ladder.

"Let's go," Sallah said to Esprë. The girl smiled as she brought the ship a bit higher into the air. Kandler joined his daughter on the bridge while Sallah found Burch peering over the bow, where they both hunted for signs of the trail.

Esprë nudged the airship forward at Burch's signal. As the ship moved along, Kandler looked up at the ring of fire.

"What do you think our chances are of sneaking up on anyone in this thing?" Esprë asked.

"It depends how fast you're going," Kandler said.

Esprë coaxed a bit more speed from the airship and let the wind blow through her hair. She looked up at Kandler and smiled. He smiled back.

The sky had grown a darker shade of gray. Esprë rubbed her eyes, and Kandler remembered that he hadn't slept since the night before—and not much then. The cool air whipping past him made him more alert, but he longed for his bed back in Mardakine.

Remembering his home, he remembered his last few days there, and the weeks before that. Anxiety had been gnawing at him for some time as his suspicions about his daughter grew. Kandler reached around and pulled the collar of Esprë's shirt away from her back.

There it was, just above her shoulder blades. A dragon-mark. When he'd first seen it, he'd thought it was black, but this close he could see it was mottled with many colors, mostly vivid blues and greens. Around the sharply defined edges, her skin was marbled with red, almost as if the mark had sprung painfully from the flesh beneath.

"I . . ." Esprë said quietly. Her smile vanished. "I didn't think you knew about that."

Kandler let the collar go. He'd seen enough. "I didn't think you did either."

"It itched when it first came in." One of Esprë's hands snaked back past her neck to scratch at the dragonmark, as if even thinking about it irritated the skin again. "Then it *burned*. Now, I don't notice it much."

Kandler stood there mute. He didn't want to have this conversation. He just wanted his daughter back, for them to have their old life back.

"Are you going to arrest me?" Esprë asked in a small voice.

Kandler was so surprised he coughed. "What? No! Why would I do that?"

"Because," Esprë said. A tear rolled down her cheek, but she kept her eyes glued to Burch and Sallah at the bow. "I . . . I killed all those people."

It took Kandler a moment to figure out what the girl meant. Then it hit him. The people of Mardakine who had disappeared. He shivered in the evening air then reached out and hugged his daughter, shaking his head.

"You didn't kill them," he said. "The vampires did."

It was Esprë's turn to shake her head. "I think they turned Shawda into that thing that attacked the knights," she said. "But she was already dead."

Kandler narrowed his eyes at the girl. "What makes you say that?" he said slowly.

Esprë bowed her head. "Every night before each person went missing, I saw them. In my dreams. I saw them running." She held her breath for a moment and closed her eyes. "I saw them die."

Kandler ran his hand through Esprë's hair. "Those were just dreams," he said. "You can't control those."

Esprë looked up at Kandler, her face soaked with tears now. "That," she said, "is what I'm afraid of."

Kandler hugged the girl tighter as he wiped her eyes dry.

"It's all right," he whispered. He tried as hard as he could to believe that.

❧

"Up there!" Burch called from the bow.

Kandler looked to where Burch was pointing. In the distance, smoke rose from a hollow in the hills.

"Does the trail head that way?" Kandler asked.

"Straight," said the shifter.

"What's the plan?" Sallah asked.

She and Burch turned back to look at Kandler. At Kandler's direction, Esprë brought the ship in low over the crest of a hill and nestled it into the deepest part of a hollow.

"Does this thing have an anchor?" Kandler asked Burch.

"Didn't see one," the shifter said. "Just mooring lines."

"Nothing around here to tie off to, though," Kandler said, thinking out loud. "It's just as well, I suppose. We're not all going."

Sallah snorted. "I should have known. Very well. I will go alone."

"I'm in," said Burch. "You'll need a tracker."

"I think I can follow the smoke," Sallah said.

"You need to get back, too."

The lady knight nodded at the shifter as a soft smirk played across her lips.

"Very well," she said, gathering up her fellow knights' swords. "Let's go."

"I'll come!"

All three of the adults turned in shock. Esprë looked up at them bravely, her eyes still red from weeping. "You need all the help you can get, right?"

Kandler leaned over and put his hand on Esprë's neck. "That's very brave, but no."

"But, Kandler—"

"Forget it. You're not coming. Besides"—the justicar smiled—"we need someone to stay back here and fly to our rescue."

"I knew you'd come, boss." Burch grinned.

"You're going to leave a child alone in the Mournland?" asked Sallah. She slung the other knights' swords across her back.

"It's safer than coming with us," Kandler pointed out. "Besides, she's the only one who can fly the ship."

"I haven't tried it yet."

"But you're going with us."

Sallah grimaced. "You should stay here with your child."

Kandler looked down at Esprë. He wanted to stay with her—he'd risked so much to make sure she was safe—but he couldn't leave the knights to die.

"Where's the honor in that?" Kandler said with as much bravado as he could muster. He turned to Esprë and put his hand on her shoulder. "You'll be fine. Haul the ladder up after us, and don't let it down until you hear me call your mother's name."

The girl nodded.

"Your place is here with the girl," Sallah said. She stepped between Kandler and the ladder.

Kandler looked down into Sallah's eyes. "If those war-forged took down three knights, then you need my blade."

Sallah glared at Kandler for a moment, then turned and lowered herself down the ladder. "We don't have time to waste," she said as she disappeared behind the railing.

Burch followed right after the knight, stopping to give Esprë a quick kiss on the top of her head before he left.

"I'll be fine," Esprë said as Kandler turned to her.

"I know you will."

"Just come back alive, all right?"

Kandler kissed the girl on the forehead. "We'll be right back," he said as he started down the ladder.

When the justicar reached the ground, he gave the ladder a sharp tug. Far above, Esprë pulled the ladder up.

"Not until I hear mom's name!" she called as the others padded off toward the smoke.

The trio kept to the hollows as much as possible, creeping along the crests of the hills only when necessary. Soon they made it to the final crest. Burch lay on his belly and peeked over the top then beckoned the others to follow.

A dozen or more tents stood scattered about the bottom of the hollow, all loosely gathered around a central campfire from which a large plume of smoke curled up to disappear into the darkening Mournland sky. Other than a few lanterns glowing in a tent here and there, it was the only source of light in the entire camp. Warforged lumbered about the place on their business, ducking in and out of tents as they went.

"They seem riled up," Kandler whispered.

"I don't see Sir Deothen or the others," said Sallah.

"There," said Burch, pointing to the largest of the tents. Its front flap faced the trio and opened onto the circle around the fire.

"How do you know?" asked the knight.

"Trail goes there," the shifter said. "Plus, it's the busiest."

Sallah stared at Burch in disbelief. "You can follow the trail through all that traffic by watching from here."

Burch grinned. "I saw a knight when the flap opened."

The knight slapped the shifter affectionately on the back. "I'll never underestimate you again," she said. She turned her attention back to the camp. "I don't suppose you know the best way to get in there?"

"We don't have to," said Kandler.

"And why not?" The lady knight glared at the justicar.

Kandler pointed down at the tent. "They're bringing them out."

The front of the flap opened wide, and a warforged emerged. The three knights followed him, each with his own warforged escort. The knights' hands were bound, and their legs were hobbled with rope. Their faces were cut and bruised. One of Brendis's eyes was swollen shut, and Levritt walked with a limp. Another warforged wearing a white tabard followed them out.

The warforged who had led the procession from the tent cupped his metal-plated hands around his lipless mouth and called out to everyone in the camp. "Gather round! The breathers refused to talk. They are no longer useful, so it's time to shut them down!"

"Shut them down?" said Sallah. "What does that mean?"

Kandler answered. "They're going to execute them."

CHAPTER

37

The warforged gathered in the center of the camp as the three guards brought their charges out and forced them to kneel in front of the fire. Deothen resisted, but two of the warforged stepped forth and kicked him in the back of his legs. The elder knight fell on his face but did not cry out. The two warforged who had kicked him hauled him back up on his knees and held him there.

The last warforged who had followed the knights out of the tent did not take part in the abuse. He wore a white tabard over his metal carapace. The cloth was stained and grimy with dark, three-fingered handprints. "Superior," he said to the one who had called all the others around, "is this truly necessary?"

The warforged leader laughed. The sounds echoed in his metal-lined chest and cheeks. "Breathers aren't welcome in the Mournland, Xalt. That's what Bastard says, and he gets it straight from the Lord of Blades."

"These men can harm us no longer," Xalt said. "We have pulled their fangs."

Superior slapped Xalt on the back. The blow landed with a metallic ring. "The Mournland belongs to us now," he said.

"These breathers invaded our territory. We must teach them a lesson."

"What lesson is good to the dead?"

Superior shook his head. "You always twist my words, greaser. The lesson is for the other breathers. We need to send them a message, one that says, 'Keep out!' in letters drawn in their stinking blood."

"Who would get that message here?" Xalt asked. "It would be better to shove them into the mists bordering our land. If they make it through, then they can tell the tale of their terror to their kind."

"That's just it," Superior said, slamming a fist into its hand. "Breathers don't listen. The only thing they understand is death. Why do you think they made us?"

"We weren't all made to be soldiers, Superior," said Xalt. He gestured at his own soiled tabard.

"Artificers made to fix soldiers are still soldiers, greaser. Now close your mouth and let me get on with this."

Xalt shrugged and stepped to one side. Deothen cursed. Pinning his hopes on the artificer had been a long shot, but it had seemed like his only choice. He looked to Levritt on his left and Brendis on his right. Their eyes were filled with mortal terror.

"Have faith, my sons," Deothen told the other knights. "The Silver Flame will keep us, in life or death."

"Death, I think." Superior chortled as he stood before the three knights.

"My fellow createds," the warforged leader said, turning and spreading his arms wide to encompass the entire camp, "while we work to establish a homeland for ourselves, we are constantly assailed on all fronts by these foul, stinking breathers. Their repellent hunger for land, for food, for air—for things to consume—places them always in opposition to us. We know their nature. They made us in their image. They built us to fight in their war. And now they must pay the price." Superior stopped for a moment to look down at the kneeling knights. As he did, he drew his sword. "Your deaths will send a message to your kind. The Mournland is no place for breathers."

Deothen could contain himself no longer. "You cannot do this!" he shouted at the warforged leader.

In a scornful voice, Superior said, "You cannot stop me."

Deothen bowed his head and uttered a final prayer to the Silver Flame to accept his soul into the purity of its presence. He closed his eyes when he heard the warforged step forward and raise his sword.

There was a sickening chopping sound. It took Deothen a moment to realize it hadn't happened to him. He opened his eyes to see Levritt fall over next to him. The young knight's head rolled in the opposite direction.

Deothen glared up at Superior, who stood laughing over the fast-cooling corpse. He prepared to curse the warforged as he'd never done before, but before the words could escape his lips, a shout went up from the other side of the camp.

Deothen looked past the warforged leader to see Sallah sprinting down the side of the valley, her blazing sword flashing before her. A smile spread across the knight's face, and Superior stopped laughing.

A bolt stabbed through from the center of the warforged leader's chest. Superior looked down at it in astonishment, then fell over atop Levritt's corpse.

Deothen heard someone laugh. He turned his head to see Brendis cackling next to him, half-mad with hope or relief. Deothen turned his attention back to Sallah. He spied Burch high up on the ridge, peppering the warforged with bolts as they turned to meet the lady knight's attack. Some of the missiles bounced off the creatures' armored skin, but others found homes in their most vital parts. Two others lay dead, and three wounded had fallen.

Sallah's fury surprised the warforged. Many of them hadn't drawn their weapons when she reached them, and they fell without a word before her wrath.

When Sallah finally reached foes ready for her, the ring of clashing blades sounded to Deothen like a clarion call to battle. He struggled to reach his feet, but a warforged guard behind shoved him back to the ground.

When Deothen looked back up, Kandler was storming his own way down the hill. The sight brought a smile to the knight's battered face. He watched the justicar battle his way through to Sallah in the thick of the brawl.

"I have your back!" Kandler roared over the din of combat.

Blood trickled from a cut on Sallah's forehead and ran down her cheek. She nodded her thanks to the justicar then turned away and continued fighting without a word.

Kandler and Sallah fought on, warforged bodies stacked at their feet. One warforged charged out from a nearby tent, a massive flail in his armored hands. Before he could reach the battling duo though, he tripped and collapsed in the dirt, a bolt protruding from its side. He dropped the flail and tugged at the shaft in an attempt to remove it. The next bolt pierced his eye. He fell with a crash and did not move again.

Beside Deothen, Brendis let out a little hoot. A warforged still guarding the prisoners backhanded the young knight from behind, knocking him face first into the dirt. Brendis kept right on cheering.

Sallah cried out and fell, clutching her leg. A warforged stood over her, ready to stab down into her with its long, heavy sword. Deothen prayed to the Silver Flame, promising his god anything in return for sparing the lady knight's life.

Before Sallah's attacker could finish its job, Kandler's blade slashed out and cut the creature across the eyes, drawing sparks and a cry of anguish. The warforged fell back, clutching its face.

Another warforged tackled Kandler from behind, and the two went sprawling forward over Sallah, pinning her to the ground. An ironclad foot stomped on Kandler's hand, and the justicar dropped his sword. A mass of three-fingered hands fell on him from all sides.

Deothen bowed his head again. He refused to weep for himself, although he could hear that Brendis's cheers had turned to sobs. He did not begrudge the young knight his lack of composure.

When Deothen looked up, he saw the warforged lift Sallah and Kandler to their feet and carry them over to deposit them next to him and Brendis. Both of the fighters were badly battered, bleeding from a half-dozen cuts each.

A warforged stood before the prisoners and kicked Superior's body aside. "I'm Superior now," he announced to the others.

None of the others objected. At their new leader's direction, the warforged holding Kandler moved Levritt's corpse aside and put him in the dead knight's spot on his knees. Sallah wound up on Kandler's other side, and other warforged grabbed Brendis and propped him back up on Deothen's right.

Deothen looked to the other knights. Sallah's face burned with anger and shame. Brendis's face was streaked with dirt still wet from his tears, but he had stopped weeping. His eyes stood vacant and distant.

Deothen lowered his head and began to pray. After a moment, the other knights joined in, recited the long-practiced words along with him.

Kandler leaned over and said, "Put in a good word for me."

Deothen raised his eyes to look at him. The justicar's eyes remained defiant. "I already have." The battered knight shook his head. "You should have left us to die."

"Coming down here wasn't my idea," the justicar said. He glared at Sallah.

Deothen's lips spread in a smile that spoke of the weariness of all his years. "She is sworn to defend the helpless and to come to the aid of her fellow knights. You have no such duties, yet here you are. It was brave."

Kandler shook his head. "Just stupid."

"You got that right, breather," Superior said. He threw a

heap of swords in front of the prisoners. There were four of the knights' swords, with Kandler's own blade mixed into the lot. "You just added your own head to the tally."

The warforged named Xalt stepped forward. "Superior," he said. "This must end. We were built for violence but are not compelled to perpetuate it. We have free will. We have a choice. We can choose to put an end to this."

Superior clapped Xalt on the back. "You speak well," he said, "but we have lost many of our own the hands of these breathers. For that, they must pay."

Xalt looked down at Levritt's head, which had rolled near the fire. "This is barbaric. We cannot build a new homeland on the bones of our neighbors. How will we ever live in peace?"

Superior laughed. "We were made for war, and in war we shall live forever. Don't deny your pattern, Xalt. We are all soldiers here, and soldiers are good for only one thing—killing." He looked down at Kandler and the knights. "Or dying."

Superior glared at the captives, each in turn. "You fought well, breathers, but your time has come to an end. Someday, your kind will know better than to invade this land. The first of our messages to them will be written in your blood."

The warforged leader stepped back and nodded at the warforged standing guard over Kandler and the knights.

"Kill them."

CHAPTER

38

The moment the justicar, the shifter, and that lady knight left the airship, Te'oma saw her chance. She'd spotted the airship scudding across the gray Mournland sky toward her soon after it entered the air over the hills north of the crazed wizard's tower, and she'd hidden under some low brush until the thing sailed by.

So far, this had turned out to be a lucky day for Te'oma. First, the old elf wizard had rid her of Tan Du. He'd been a useful ally in the Mournland, but entirely too unstable. One more mishap on their mission, and Te'oma knew she'd have been the vampire's next meal. Then the justicar and the lady knight arrived at the tower and provided her with cover for her escape. And when racing away from the other knights, she'd spotted the warforged patrol before they found her. Dismounting and sending Te'oma's horse on alone to gallop past the patrol had been a stroke of genius. It left the changeling without a mount, but it alerted the patrol to the presence of the knights in time for them to form a hasty ambush.

Once the knights had all been captured, Te'oma had been at a loss for what to do. Without Esprë, she had failed at her mission, so going home was out of the question. In any case, without a mount she faced a long, hard walk out of the Mournland. More than one traveler had stepped into the mists around the borders of the place never to be seen again.

Then she spotted the airship. She didn't know who was driving it, but she decided against hailing the captain and pleading for a ride. Using her mental powers, she projected her senses aboard the ship's deck for a look around. Once she saw Esprë and Kandler behind the wheel, she knew her instincts had been good.

The ship moved slow but with purpose. Te'oma guessed that the people aboard were hunting for the other knights. Once the ship had passed overhead, she followed, trying to stay as close as possible without being seen. This soon proved impossible, but no one ever looked back to see her sprinting after the ship, racing up and down the hillsides as she worked to keep them in sight.

When the ship came to a stop, Te'oma crept up the side of the hill and peered over the edge. She watched and listened as the adults threw the rope ladder down and disembarked from the airship. She waited for them to disappear over the crest of the next hill before she stood up.

The changeling padded down into the hollow in which the airship was nestled and then up the other side to where the end of the rope ladder had been. When she got there, she morphed her form until she looked something like one of the Knights of the Silver Flame that had chased her out here—the young one with the blond hair. Her clothes wouldn't change, but she'd just have to deal with that.

Te'oma peeked over the edge of the hill to make sure that Kandler and the others were long gone, then she whistled up to the ship's deck. "Hello?" she called. "Anyone there?"

The changeling had to call out three times before Esprë poked her nose over the ship's railing.

"What do you want?" she said.

"Thank the Flame you're there!" said Te'oma. "I just ran

into your father, and he sent me back here. They're off to rescue the others."

"Why aren't you?"

The changeling patted her leg. "They cut me pretty good. I
can't move well enough for a fight. I barely made it here."

"Why are you dressed like that? What happened to your
armor?"

"Warforged took it," said Te'oma. "They'd already killed
the changeling, so I took her clothes."

The girl chewed on her lip for a moment, thinking all this
over.

"What do you want?" Esprë asked. Te'oma could hear the
suspicion in the girl's voice.

The changeling gazed up at the girl as innocently as she
could. "Could you throw down a ladder? I think I could make
it up. Once I get on the ship, I should be all right."

Esprë narrowed her eyes at the knight standing below.
"What's the password?" she said.

Te'oma had heard Kandler's parting words to the girl. The
psion thought she remembered the name of Esprë's mother
from when she'd scanned the girl's mind before, but she did it
once more to be safe.

"Esprina," the changeling said.

Esprë frowned, thought a moment more, then finally
picked up the rope ladder and unfurled it over the railing. It
landed right before the changeling's feet.

Te'oma climbed up the ladder and bounded aboard the airship. She gazed all around and took it in. "What an amazing
craft!" she said. "I've never been on anything like it."

"What's your name?" Esprë asked.

"Mardak," the changeling said as she pulled up the ladder
behind her.

The girl's jaw dropped.

"Wait," Te'oma said. "That's not right, is it?" She looked at
Esprë. "It's, um, Levritt."

Esprë screamed.

Te'oma snatched up the girl in her arms and clamped a hand over her mouth. Esprë kicked and thrashed about like a beast in a net. Te'oma reached out with her mind and tapped the girl's brain hard. She fell limp in the changeling's hands.

Te'oma lay the girl down on the deck and said to her. "Don't make this harder than it has to be. I can keep doing that all day if you like."

Esprë blinked and sat up. She looked at the changeling, still in the form of a blond knight, and said, "It's you again, isn't it?"

The changeling smiled at the girl. "You just can't get rid of me, can you?"

Esprë stuck out her bottom lip. "Am I your hostage again?"

Te'oma shifted back to her normal form as she reached out and tousled Esprë's hair. "Let's just say we're going for a ride together."

"What about Kandler and Burch and the knights?"

"They're not invited. This trip is just you and me." The changeling glanced around at the airship, at the ring of fire that encircled it. "At least we'll be traveling in style."

Esprë drew in a breath to scream, and Te'oma put a single finger over the girl's mouth. "Ah-ah-ah," the changeling said. "None of that. Play nice now, or I'll tap your brain again. We have many miles ahead of us, and screaming for help every chance you get will grow tiresome very fast." The changeling stared into Esprë's sky-blue eyes. "If I take my hand from your mouth, do you promise not to scream?"

The girl hesitated for a moment before she nodded. Te'oma removed her hand.

"Now," the changeling said. "How do you operate this thing?"

Esprë shrugged. "They didn't tell me. Kandler barely lets me drive a wagon around Mardakine."

Te'oma curled her lip at the girl. "Yet they left you here all alone?"

"They knew there could be fighting where they went."

The changeling shook her head in disbelief. "I suppose," she said. "*I* wouldn't have left you here."

Esprë cocked her head at Te'oma. "What would you have done?"

"Left those other knights to rot. They're doomed as it is. No reason to put your heads on the block next to them."

"You'd leave your friends to die?"

"I don't have any friends." As the words left her lips, Te'oma realized they were true. She felt a pang of regret at this, but she shoved it aside.

"What about the vampires?" Esprë pressed.

"What about them?"

"Weren't they your friends?"

Te'oma laughed. The girl's ability to surprise her was delightful. "Vampires don't have friends. Not among the living."

"Are you alive?"

Te'oma goggled at the girl. "I'm a changeling not a zombie. I breathe. I bleed the same as you."

Esprë thought about that for a moment. "I've never met a changeling before."

"Maybe you have and didn't know it."

"I doubt it."

"What about Gurn?"

Esprë's eyes grew as large as a pair of moons. "The baker? That couldn't be!"

Te'oma smirked. "Think whatever you like. You'll never know now, will you?"

The girl considered this for a moment before she spoke. "He never kidnapped me," she said.

"We're not all so talented."

"Esprë!" a voice called out from below.

Te'oma dropped to one knee and swung the girl around in front of her, a hand clamped over her mouth. "Vol's black blood!" she said. "It's that shifter."

Te'oma knew she could take no chances, so she stunned

the girl with her mind again. When she let her go, Esprë stood there quietly, her mouth slack and her eyes blank.

"Esprë, toss down the ladder!" Burch said. "We got big trouble and no time!"

Te'oma whispered into the girl's ear as she reached into her mind and mentally wiped the last several minutes from her brain. "As far as you're concerned, I was never here," she said softly, "but I'll be seeing you soon."

With that, the changeling padded off to a hatchway and slipped down into the hold below the main deck. She didn't like letting the shifter back onboard, but she knew she couldn't fly the airship by herself. Better to stowaway and get a free ride out of the Mournland than to have to walk out alone.

CHAPTER

39

Kandler stood on his knees and waited to die. He figured it was only a matter of moments before the new Superior gave the order. He wondered if Burch was still alive, and if so, what was keeping him.

"Don't do it!" Xalt said to the warforged guards standing behind the kneeling prisoners. "I'm warning you."

Superior stared at Xalt for a moment then threw his head back and let loose a tinny laugh. "I'm impressed, greaser," he said. "I didn't think you had that much metal in you."

"I'd hoped you were better than the last Superior. It seems I was wrong. Your soul is twisted."

Superior shook his head. "You spent too much time among the breathers," he said. "They built us, put a sword in our hands, and pushed us out the door to kill. It's what we were made for. It's what we're good at. We have no souls. Soldiers don't need souls. They just get in the way of what we need to do. Maybe that explains it. You weren't created to kill. You were built to fix. You're a patch instead of a blade."

While Superior ranted on, Kandler looked around for a way out. As he turned his head, the guard behind him slapped him across the face. It felt like getting smacked with the flat of a sword.

Superior didn't miss a beat. "Maybe your makers gave you a soul," he said to Xalt. "They wanted you to care about the rest of us. Otherwise, you'd just cower behind a rock while we died, calling for you to help us. I hope that soul rests easy inside of you. The rest of us, we don't want them. We don't need them. We just need these trespassers dead."

"Say what you like, Superior," Xalt said as he tapped a thick metal finger against its chestplate. "There's something that moves us more than the magic that first sparked life in our shells. I've seen it in every one of us. I've even seen it in you. As your 'greaser,' I see us each at our lowest points, when we need someone, when we're in pain. I see how the others come by as I work on a fallen friend, wanting to know if there's a chance. I've watched you all grieve at funerals held over our lost compatriots' graves. I've seen souls—in all of us."

Kandler stared at the artificer. He had never known warforged to be so eloquent. Until now, he'd only met them on the field of battle. There they seemed like nothing more than remorseless killing machines. At the moment, Kandler believed Xalt would be shedding tears if he could.

"Call it what you will," Xalt continued. "Deny that you even have one. But my soul cries out against this injustice."

Superior slapped a massive, three-fingered hand over its face and shook its head. "Justice is a breather concept," he said. "It means nothing in the Mournland."

"It means nothing to you."

Superior nodded. "In the end, it's the same thing. If you have a problem with that, you can take it up with Bastard."

"I could go straight to the Lord of Blades."

"Let me know when you do. I'd like to add your head to my collection." Superior turned to the guards standing over the kneeling prisoners.

"Is there a means of appeal?" Deothen asked.

Superior waved the question off. "Don't let this greaser give you hope. This is your end."

"Go ahead and kill us," Kandler said. He wasn't sure where he was going with this, but he hoped it would buy him and the knights a bit more time. "You warforged are all cowards. We couldn't expect a fate better than this."

Superior folded its arms across its chest. "Cowards? Who attacked us out of nowhere? Who invaded our camp?"

"We came to save our friends."

"By killing us?"

"You killed Levritt. It seems death is the only thing you understand."

Superior stood as still as a statue then unfolded its arms. "What would you have me do? Release you so we can slay you in the heat of battle? Would that satisfy your breather sense of justice?"

As Kandler shook his head, an idea blossomed. It was crazy, but he didn't see how he had anything to lose other than the chance to be the first one executed. "I challenge you to a duel, one on one. If you win, you can do with us as you wish. If I win, you let us go."

Superior stood stock still again. Kandler was unable to read the creature, no matter how he tried. Then the warforged shook its head at the justicar.

"You must think they made me with half a mind." Superior looked up at the guards over the prisoners and said. "Kill them."

"No!" Xalt said.

The guards raised their swords high in the air.

Xalt held out its clenched fist. A wide band of gold shone on its thick, outside finger, a ring forged for a warforged. "Stop!" he said.

Superior scoffed, but the guards stayed frozen with their arms in the air. After a moment, the warforged leader lost his patience.

"What's going on?" Superior said. "Kill them!" He tried to point at the prisoners, but his hand couldn't move either.

Xalt walked up to Superior and flicked a finger into the center of the leader's face. It rang like a muffled bell.

"You!" Superior growled. "What have you done, greaser?"

Xalt turned to the prisoners and gestured for them to rise. Sallah and Brendis looked to Deothen for guidance. Kandler jumped to his feet and helped the old man to stand. The other knights rose, and Sallah freed Brendis from his bonds as Kandler untied Deothen.

"Xalt!" Superior said.

The artificer in the grubby tabard turned back to Superior. "You mean, 'greaser?' " he said. "You called me that to disparage me. You never thought much of me until something broke on you. Until you needed me."

"Undo this, Xalt," Superior said, desperation creeping into its voice. "It's not too late. I understand your frustration. Put an end to this, and all will be forgiven."

"I don't need your forgiveness," Xalt said. "I wanted respect, from you and the others." He put his hands to the sides of its head. "How I ever expected to get that, I don't know. That's how we got into this situation. It's why you insisted on killing these people. You don't respect any life but your own!"

"Xalt. I am . . . I am sorry."

"You're a bad liar." Xalt knelt down and picked up the prisoners' swords. Deothen's staff lay among them. The warforged handed them back to their owners one by one. "You'd better go now," he told them. "They won't be frozen for much longer."

"What did you do to them?" said Kandler.

Xalt chuckled. "A little invention of my own. I worked on everyone in this camp at one point or another. It wasn't hard to guess that I might want a fail-safe installed on each of them at some point."

Kandler clapped the warforged on the back. "Smart," he said.

"Not smart enough!" Superior said. He drew his sword.

Xalt stood stunned, frozen to the spot like most of the other warforged around. "H-how?" he said.

Kandler brought his blade up to parry Superior's blow, but

it wasn't aimed at him. Instead, it sliced into Xalt's hand. The thick finger bearing the golden ring tumbled into the dirt.

"You think I didn't see what you did?" Superior raged at the maimed warforged. "I found what you implanted into me. I removed it weeks ago."

"But—but . . ." Xalt stared at its unmoving finger lying on the ground.

"I faked being frozen when you betrayed us," Superior said. "I wanted to give you a chance to redeem yourself. I believed you were still one of us."

Kandler spun about, his blade at the ready. The other warforged were no longer frozen. They surrounded him and the knights.

"You made your choice, greaser," Superior said. "You chose to stand with the breathers. Now you're going to die with them."

CHAPTER

40

Kandler slashed at Superior with his blade, but the war-forged leader stepped back and waited for his fellows to join in. The justicar took advantage of the momentary space to reach down and scoop up Xalt's severed finger. It was cool to the touch, wet with whatever fluid passed for warforged blood, and not as heavy as Kandler had expected.

The knights formed a tight circle, covering each other's back. Sallah reached out and pulled Kandler in to join them. As he fell back, he grabbed Xalt by the collar of its grease-stained tabard and pulled him into the circle's center. He was busy binding his wound, trying to staunch the flow of his own blood.

While the other warforged surrounded Kandler and the knights, their swords rattling in anticipation of the coming fight, the justicar tossed Xalt his loose finger. The greaser caught it with his good hand, bobbled it for a moment, and then cradled it close to its chest.

"Surrender!" Superior said. "Don't make this any harder than it has to be."

"On you or us?" said Kandler. "Aren't you going to kill us either way?"

"You are good and valiant foes," Superior said. "If you put down your swords, I guarantee you passage from this land."

"We will die before we submit to you again,".Deothen said. "You tricked us into lowering our weapons once. We will not fall for such chicanery again."

"I promised you passage from this land," Superior said with a chuckle that raised Kandler's hackles. "I just didn't mention it would be into the afterlife—assuming you have those souls you believe in so much."

"Step a little closer," Kandler said, brandishing his blade. "I'll give you a chance to tour the next world yourself."

A shadow fell over the combatants. Even in the dimness of the Mournland, Kandler felt the change. He stabbed out at Superior, testing the warforged's skill, and glanced into the sky as the inevitable parry came.

A smile split Kandler's face as he looked back into Superior's eyes. "Surprise," he said.

The shadow grew larger around them. Superior stepped back out of Kandler's range and looked up to see what had made the justicar so happy. He gasped and staggered back.

The other warforged looked up to see what had their leader's attention. As one, they goggled at the airship as she sailed down at them from out of the sky.

"Scatter!" Kandler shouted. "The ring's coming right for us!"

The warforged turned and ran. Brendis and Sallah started to follow, but Kandler reached out and hauled them back. "That was just to scare them off. Stick close to me. We're hitching a ride as soon as that thing come down low enough."

Sallah pointed to the rope ladder dangling down from the side of the ship. "We can't all climb that at once. They'll cut us to pieces."

"That's not the only way to get on that ship." Kandler's stomach flipped as he spoke. While he was thrilled to not be executed, the thought of Esprë diving so bravely into danger made him nauseous. He hoped Burch was with her.

Deothen stared at the justicar. "Where, by the light of the Flame, did you find an airship?"

Kandler herded the crew over to one side of where he thought the ship would land. "It wasn't through a life of prayer," he said.

Brendis stared at Sallah. "It's the prophecy," he said. "Only a fate as large as yours could command such fortune."

"Quit yapping and get ready to jump on the lower arch when it hits the ground," Kandler said. He didn't know if the arch would come that close to the ground, but he hoped that Esprë and Burch would brave it.

"When it hits the ground?" Sallah said. "If that arch breaks, the entire ship might explode."

"It's that or the warforgeds' blades. Take your pick."

"I'll go with you if I may," said Xalt. Kandler could hear the pain in the warforged's voice. "I think I've worn out my welcome here."

Kandler glanced at the greaser and grinned. "It's the least we can do."

As the ship neared the ground, Kandler shoved the others ahead of him toward the fiery ring's lower arch. "Hit it hard, and hold on tight!"

Superior looked back from the edge of camp where he'd fled and realized what was happening. "No!" he shouted. He launched himself toward the ship. The other warforged held back, unwilling to risk their lives to take on a flying ship in hand-to-hand combat.

The ship smashed into the ground with a loud crunch. The ring of fire flared out and scorched the nearby earth. A couple of warforged who had crept too close were engulfed in the flames, burned to metal-clad crisps before they had a chance to scream.

The rest of the warforged scattered before the landing—except for Superior. He charged at the escaping prisoners and slashed at them with it blade.

Kandler turned to face the warforged leader. He needed to

buy the others some time or Superior would cut them all down as they fled. He parried the first blow, but Superior lowered his shoulder and plowed him back into the dirt. The justicar's head landed less than a foot from the ring of fire.

"Get off!" Kandler roared at the creature trying to crush him. As the pair struggled, the others clambered onto the fiery ring's lower restraining arch. Sallah boosted the battered knights and the wounded Xalt up ahead of her, then turned her attention to Kandler's plight.

The justicar struggled to escape, but Superior laid into him with all its weight, pinning him down. It was all he could do to draw a ragged breath.

Kandler had a hand on the warforged's sword arm, trying to keep the creature from impaling him on its blade. But he was no match for Superior's strength, and the warforged pressed the tip of its sword inexorably toward the justicar's throat.

Kandler knew he had to do something fast. He looked up and saw the ring of fire roaring only a few scant feet from his head. His hair smoldering from the heat, Kandler rolled away from the fiery ring as hard as he could. Determined to prevent his victim from getting away, Superior pressed back in the other direction with his full bulk

Instead of continuing to struggle against the warforged atop him, Kandler switched directions and allowed Superior's momentum to carry the warforged over him and into the fire. Immediately, Superior realized his mistake and clawed at Kandler to try to prevent himself from rolling over into the ring, but it was too late.

Superior screamed as the flames swallowed its head and shoulders. He tried to pull free from the fire, but Kandler held him there, the skin on his hands and arms blistering.

"See you in Dolurrh," Kandler said as he shoved Superior off him. He scrambled away from the fiery ring and toward the restraining arch.

Sallah saw the justicar coming. She pounced upon the arch herself and reached back to give Kandler a hand up.

"Go, go, go!" Kandler shouted as soon as his feet left the ground. The airship leaped into the air. As she went, the carved wood of the mystic arch creaked, complaining about the abuse of the landing and the load of its passengers, but it held.

As the ship gained altitude, the warforged in the camp peeked out of their hiding places. Some of them brought out bows.

"Archers!" Sallah shouted out above the noise of the raging fire.

Kandler smiled despite himself and shouted, "Hold on!"

CHAPTER

41

The airship lurched skyward and leaned to port. Arrows whizzed past. The few that found any mark either lodged themselves in the restraining arch or incinerated on contact with the ring of fire. As the ship raced away, Kandler waved the warforged camp a heartfelt goodbye.

Just when Kandler began to relax, the maimed warforged who had risked his life to save the intruders slipped out toward the edge of the restraining arch. He hung from a corner of the arch for a split second, his feet swinging free in the sky. Kandler's free hand darted out to him, catching him before he fell. Seeing the justicar's predicament, Sallah grabbed the back of his belt with her free hand.

"Let go!" Xalt said. "I will survive the fall."

"And then they'll kill you," said Kandler.

With Sallah holding onto his belt, the justicar reached out with both hands and pulled the warforged in. It wasn't until later that he realized how easily he'd trusted the knight with his life.

An arrow bounced off Xalt's carapace as he scrambled atop the arch. Xalt clung to the justicar with both arms as the ship veered back and forth in an effort to protect those on the arch from the arrows.

The airship soon sailed over the crest of the nearest hill and out of sight of the camp. She stopped bobbing and weaving, and Kandler extricated himself from the warforged's viselike embrace.

The justicar looked out at the blasted hills of the Mournland below as a stiff breeze ruffled the green-gray grass that lined them like a day-old beard. The sky grew darker by the moment, and it would soon be pitch black again.

As the airship's fiery ring propelled them forward, Kandler looked at the others in its hot, flickering light. Sallah tended to Brendis's wounds while a battered Deothen looked on, waiting for the younger knights to be healed before he would call attention to his own injuries. Xalt held his severed finger in his good hand, examining both it and the damaged hand as he looked for a way to match them together.

Kandler stood and balanced on the restraining arch as the airship lowered itself into a hollow several miles away from the warforged camp. He leaped to the ground and helped the others to the turf and then up the rope ladder to the ship's deck. He climbed up last. When he reached the top of the ladder, Esprë met him with a hug neither of them ever wanted to break.

"Glad to see you," he said. She looked up at him then backed away long enough for him to climb over the railing.

Kandler looked up at the bridge, and Burch waved down at him. The justicar strode up to his old friend, Esprë under his arm, and clapped him on the back. "Did you do all that fancy flying?" he asked.

The shifter smiled. "You have Esprë to blame. That was some sharp stunt, pup."

Kandler gave Esprë a proud hug. "You did great," he said. "You saved us all."

Esprë didn't say a word. She just beamed up at Kandler, soaking up his adoration. The justicar looked up at the ring of fire blazing overhead. From there, against the darkening clouds, it reminded him of the Rings of Siberys that soared across Eberron's night sky.

"So where now?" Kandler said. "Back to Mardakine?"

The shifter shook his head. "Others might think different." He jerked his head toward the knights on the main deck, where they huddled around Xalt.

Kandler left Esprë at the wheel. "I'll be right back."

As the justicar strode over to the knights, he saw Deothen shaking his head. "I'm afraid there's nothing more we can do," the senior knight told Xalt. "At least not until we get to Flamekeep."

The artificer held up his wounded arm, the finger back in place. For a moment, Kandler thought that the knights had been able to reattach the digit, but then Xalt pulled the finger from his hand and stuffed it into a pouch on the inside of his white tabard.

"You say the clerics there can repair such damage?" the warforged said in a hopeful tone.

"The favors of the Silver Flame are available to all those willing to open their hearts and minds to its sacred light," said Deothen.

"Careful," Kandler said as he approached. "Give them a chance, and these knights will induct you into their order."

"Would that be so bad?" Xalt asked, his wide obsidian eyes focused on the justicar like those of an innocent puppy. "I wouldn't think so."

"I don't speak ill of my traveling companions," Kandler said with a smile.

The warforged just looked at him, confused.

"Our undying thanks to you for all your help," Deothen said to Kandler. "Without your aid, not only would we have failed in our mission, we would all be dead, I'm sure."

"Don't thank me," the justicar said, pointing a thumb over his shoulder at the people on the bridge. "Without Burch and Esprë, I'd have died alongside you."

"I'll express our gratitude to them as well when I put in our traveling orders."

"What orders?" Kandler said. He peered into Deothen's

eyes and glanced at the other knights. Brendis refused to meet his gaze, and Sallah looked away.

"We need to return to Thrane at once," Deothen said. "We have rescued the girl, and now we must take her to Flamekeep."

Kandler eyed the senior knight. "Do you even know that she bears the dragonmark you're looking for?"

Deothen shook his head. "No one has seen this mark in centuries. With a ship like this at our disposal, we can be in Flamekeep in a matter of days, and the scholars there can confirm or deny my suspicions."

Kandler did not like the way this conversation was going. "I don't recall giving you ownership of this vessel," he said.

Deothen smiled. "Of course. You and your friend found her, and for that we are appreciative. However, we must commandeer her. Once we are in Flamekeep, you will be paid handsomely for your troubles."

"I'm not interested in going to Flamekeep," Kandler said. "I have a girl here that I need to get home. Don't tell me you propose to 'commandeer' her, too."

Deothen raised his eyebrows at that. "Of course not. However, if she proves to have the Mark of Death on her, then she will need our protection. She will not be safe in Mardakine. You must understand that. There is no place safer for her than Flamekeep."

"How convenient for the Church of Silver Flame." Kandler could not keep the sarcasm from his voice.

Deothen's face turned red. "What else would you propose?" he asked. "Returning to Mardakine? Do you think they will welcome you back with open arms? When we left, the town was in a shambles, which may have been the only thing that kept the people from forgetting that you were supposed to be imprisoned."

"Mardak would have let me out once he cooled down."

"He's no longer alive to rescind his orders—nor is his wife."

"Rislinto wouldn't keep me in chains."

"Is he in charge now?"

Kandler could see that Deothen sensed he was winning the argument here. The knight continued to press his point.

"What about that boy, Pradak? Does he inherit his father's position now? If so, do you think he'll be as forgiving?"

Kandler had heard enough. He put up a hand to cut the knight off. "You're missing the point. Esprë is my daughter, and you're not taking her anywhere. Also, Burch and I found this ship. She's ours to do with as we like."

"Stole her, you mean," said Brendis, who turned an accusing glare on the justicar.

Kandler stared at the young knight. He couldn't believe he was hearing this. "From a crazed wizard who was holding us prisoner," he said. "Who had taken her from people she killed."

Deothen reached out and put a hand on Kandler's shoulder. "For the good of the world, we must return to Flamekeep straight away. There is no higher priority. And if not for the world, it really is best for the girl."

Kandler looked over at Sallah, but she continued to avoid his gaze. He'd hoped that she would be on his side at least.

"If you like, we can drop you off in Mardakine on our way to Flamekeep," Deothen said softly.

The justicar shrugged Deothen's hand from his shoulder. "Esprë is coming with me," he said. "We're going south, to Sharn. I know people in the City of Towers who can help us. We'll drop you off anywhere along the route that you like."

With nothing more to say, Kandler turned his back on the knights to return to the bridge. He'd only made one step when he heard swords being drawn.

"You must be joking," the justicar said as he turned back around to face three blazing blades. He gaped at Deothen. "I thought you were supposed to be the good guys."

The gray-haired knight flushed with shame, but he refused to back down. He nodded at Brendis, and the young knight stepped forward to strip Kandler of his weapons.

"Sometimes," Deothen said, "you must commit a wrong to further the greater good."

"As long as *you* get to decide which good is greater, right?"

"What's up, boss?" Burch called down from the bridge, where he stood next to Esprë, who peeked out over the wheel. He had his crossbow out and pointed at the knights.

Kandler looked to Deothen. "Are you going to threaten my life to get him to surrender?"

Deothen tapped Kandler in the center of his chest with the tip of his blazing blade. The hot metal seared a black mark into the justicar's shirt. "I hoped we could be more civilized than that."

"We just need to go to Flamekeep," Sallah said, her eyes begging Kandler to be reasonable. "All of us. I swear to you, this is the right thing for your daughter. I understand how you might disagree, but please think about it. Is that worth dying over?"

Kandler shook his head at her sadly then turned to look back at his daughter and friend standing on the airship's bridge. "The question is whether it's worth killing over."

CHAPTER

42

Te'oma's heart skipped several beats when the hatch to the hold opened. She scurried back into the darkness, as far toward the bow as she could, and waited. She willed her skin, hair, teeth—even the whites of her eyes—to turn black. Her clothes remained the same nebulous color, but there was little she could do about that. She pulled a dull, black knife from her belt and held it before her, ready to strike from the inky shadows.

The justicar entered the hold first, slipping down the steep wooden steps, the shifter close behind. In the flickering light from the ring of fire that cascaded through the open hatch, the changeling could see that neither of them were armed. When the two friends reached the hold's floor, they looked up at someone through the hatchway.

"How long are you going to keep us down here?" Kandler asked.

"At this speed, we should reach Flamekeep in a matter of days," said Deothen's voice, tinged with regret.

A waterskin fell through the open hatch, a pack right behind it. "Most of our supplies ran off with our horses," Deothen said. "Make this last."

The hatch closed, plunging the hold into total darkness. Kandler fumbled around near the stern. "I thought I saw—ah!"

He uncovered the lens of an everbright lantern set in the ceiling, and that end of the hold flooded with light. Te'oma didn't move a muscle, striving to blend in with the shadows that still surrounded her.

The hold was sparse but not bare. Hammocks made of netted ropes lined a short walkway that ran the length of most of the hold. Kandler picked up the waterskin and pack and then walked over and rolled into one of the hammocks. The ropes cradled him, and he swung gently with the movement of the airship.

"Should have let me shoot, boss," Burch said as he paced through the airship's tight hold. The floor curved up sharply to where the changeling hid, and the shifter never came close to her, turning aside and going back the other way instead. "That old knight'd be dead."

"I know," Kandler said in a resigned voice. He shaded his eyes against the lamp and peered up at the ceiling as if he could see through the planks in the ship's deck. "I just hope Esprë's not too scared."

Burch snorted in disgust. "Bolts through all three hearts before they got near her."

Kandler put his hands over his face for a moment then dragged them down past his chin. "We're here, all right?"

"We're going to Flamekeep, not home."

"He was right about Mardakine. It's not an option." Kandler opened the pack and found some cheese and dried beef wrapped tightly in dry cloths. He helped himself to a meager portion and tossed the pack to Burch, who stopped pacing. "I would have preferred Sharn, but Thrane's not all bad."

"Been there?" The shifter fished out some food for himself and set to it.

"Once. On assignment from King Boranel."

"Kill any knights?"

Kandler took a pull from the waterskin before he answered. "Not too many."

Burch stopped chewing. "That a problem, boss?"

Kandler sighed. "I don't think I'm wanted in Thrane. If I was, Deothen would have slapped me in chains days ago."

Burch nodded and went back to his pacing. When he reached the bow again, the floorboards groaned. Te'oma's stomach dropped through the floor, and she held her breath tight.

Kandler sat up in the hammock. "Step back from there, Burch," he said. "Quick."

"Just a creaky floor," the shifter said.

Te'oma measured the distance between herself and the shifter. His back was turned to her now. With luck, she could kill him with one strike, but that would leave her trapped in the hold with Kandler—a prospect she did not relish. Still, the justicar was unarmed, and she had her knife and the power of her mind.

"That's where Majeeda's spell hit the ship," Kandler said. "It might not have holed the hull, but I wouldn't walk on it."

Burch sidled away from the damaged spot, and Te'oma let out a silent sigh of relief. When the shifter reached the ship's stern, he sat down on the hull's rising arc.

"It's late," Kandler said. He took a last pull on the waterskin and tossed it to Burch. "Can you cover that lamp?"

"You can sleep now?"

"Burch, it's been a damned long day. Last night, we fought a pack of vampires and chased that changeling into Majeeda's tower. The night before, we broke out of prison so we could rescue Mardakine. It's going to be a while before we make it to Flamekeep, and I could sleep through a war right now."

The shifter reached up and pulled the lamp's cover shut, plunging the hold into darkness.

"Thanks," Kandler said before he drifted off.

Te'oma heard the sounds of Burch munching on a bit more of the food and then climbing into a hammock across the aisle from Kandler. The shifter grumbled to himself a bit and started snoring soon after.

Te'oma waited until she was sure both Kandler and Burch were sound asleep. She considered knifing both of them, but she feared that wouldn't help her get out of the hold. If the knights came down here and found their prisoners dead, they would scour the hold until they found her, and she wasn't ready to take them all on.

Te'oma was still sitting awake in the dark when the hatchway opened. The sky outside was only a few shades lighter than the ceiling of the hold, but the light from the ring of fire played off the edge of the folded-back hatch and the top of the ladder beneath it.

"Kandler?" a voice called down. It was Deothen. "Burch? Are you ready to come up and speak like civilized people?"

"We're not the ones who tossed their friends into the hold, sir knight," said Kandler.

Te'oma started at the sound of the justicar's voice. She'd been sure he was asleep.

"I am comfortable with my decision," the senior knight responded, although an edge in his voice belied his words. "The Silver Flame lights my path, and it is clear."

"Then we're happy down here in the dark," Kandler said. "And we're sleeping. I'm not getting out of this hammock to make you feel better about betraying us. Good night, good knight."

Deothen sighed and the hatch closed once more.

Te'oma waited, stretching her limbs where she sat in the dark. She heard footfalls overhead, but they soon tapered off. When the ship had been silent for many minutes, the changeling slipped from her perch and tiptoed over to the ladder below the hatch. Reaching out with her mind, the changeling visualized the restraining bolt holding on the other side of the hatch. Once she had it, she tapped it with her mind. Above her, the bolt slid aside, unlocking the hatchway. Te'oma nudged the hatch upward an inch and then another. When there was just enough room, she peered out through the narrow gap she'd made and surveyed the airship's deck.

The bridge stood above and behind the changeling. She knew that anyone up there could not see the hatchway. The console on which the ship's wheel hung blocked the view straight down.

She opened the hatch just enough to see down the length of the rest of the deck, all the way to the bow. Three forms lay huddled near that end of the ship, perhaps trying to escape the heat of the fiery ring for comfort as they slept. One of them was dressed in white. At first she thought it was Esprë, but upon closer inspection she realized it was too large and bulky. A newcomer then. The others had to be knights, although the changeling could not tell which.

Beyond the bowsprit stood the Mournland's mist-shrouded border. Clouds of the same color and texture filled the sky above. Te'oma smiled, baring her blackened teeth.

"Burch?" a voice behind her whispered. "Is that you?"

Te'oma froze.

CHAPTER

43

Kandler rolled out of his hammock and padded toward the ladder. "How did you get the hatch open?" the justicar whispered.

The hatch flew open, and in the sudden light that poured through from the ring of fire surrounding the ship, Kandler could see that whoever was on the ladder, it was not the shifter. The figure was far too lithe and held herself with a distinctly feminine grace.

"Hey!" Kandler shouted and charged.

The intruder hauled herself up the ladder and onto the deck. Just as the figure was about to clear the hold, Kandler's hand stabbed out and caught an ankle.

"Come back here!" he said.

The justicar yanked the intruder halfway back through the hatchway. As she landed with her belly on the edge of the hatch, she lashed out with her free foot and caught Kandler across the chin. Determined not to let go, the justicar held on through the first blow, but the stranger knew where to find him now. A second kick in the face smashed his nose flat. With a third kick, the intruder wriggled free and pulled herself out through the hatch.

Blinking away tears, Kandler wiggled his nose and decided it wasn't broken. He lunged for the ladder, but just as he reached it the figure slammed the hatch shut.

"Huh?" It was Burch, stirring from sleep. "What's going on?"

"The changeling!" Kandler said as he climbed the ladder. He shoved his head and shoulder up against the hatchway and pushed with all his might. He managed to leverage the lid up and back, and the intruder jumped away.

As Kandler stuck his head through the hatch, he saw the changeling standing above him, her form silhouetted against the raging ring of fire, the light of which reflected warmly on the gray clouds of the Mournland sky above. The thought that the creature had been on the airship with them—down in the hold with him!—made him roar with rage.

As Kandler scrambled through the open hatch, he heard Esprë's scream from the bridge above him. Kandler stood and scanned the deck. Deothen, Sallah, and Xalt sat near the ship's bow where the justicar guessed they'd been dozing. Kandler glanced up at the circular blaze. They were so close to the layer of clouds overhanging the Mournland that all he could see was the gray above and the black emptiness along the ship's sides, as if they were floating through some nether realm far beyond the world he knew.

"Kandler!" Esprë screeched when she spotted the justicar from her spot on the bridge.

He turned and flashed a quick grin at Esprë then snapped his head about to look for the changeling. His daughter seemed safe, but no one on the airship would be out of danger until the changeling was dead. It was hard to pick the creature out in the dim light and flickering shadows, but the sound of Brendis drawing his blade brought Kandler's gaze back to the bridge. There! He saw the changeling facing off against the knight.

She feinted a charge at the knight, and Brendis stepped backward, maintaining his guard.

"We finally meet," the young knight said to the changeling.

Even to Kandler's ears, his bravado seemed strained.

The changeling smiled at Brendis. As she did, she let her gray cloak unfurl around her. The edges of it splayed out farther, wider, and as the fabric thinned it became leathery and more formed.

Brendis watched in horror, holding his burning blade before him like a shield as the cloak fashioned itself into a massive set of batlike wings.

The changeling allowed herself a short laugh as she leaped onto the rear railing of the ship. The young knight recoiled, bumping into Kandler as the justicar came storming up on to the bridge.

"It's a flying cloak!" Kandler snapped. "Now fight or get out of the way!"

The justicar snatched the sacred blade from Brendis's hand. The young knight, still stunned by the changeling's transformation, did not protest.

Kandler swung the burning sword at the changeling, but she sprang backward and fell into the inky night. "No!" he shouted. "Come back and fight!"

The changeling laughed again as she let her magical wings catch the air and bring her soaring back up toward the ship. "How stupid do you think I am?"

With that, she glided back into the darkness again.

Frustrated, Kandler snarled at the young knight. Brendis stepped back clear of the reach of his sword, still in the justicar's hand.

"Burch!" Kandler said.

"Right here, boss!" the shifter called as he emerged from the hold. "Where's my crossbow?"

"Get back down that hatch!" Deothen said to Burch as he stormed along the deck, brandishing his sword at the shifter. "We have the matter under control."

"Saying it don't make it so," Burch scoffed. He spat at the senior knight and headed for the bridge.

Before Burch reached the narrow stairs, Sallah called out

to him and then slid his crossbow across the polished deck at him. He stopped it with his foot, then kicked it up and snatched it from the air. "Thanks," he said as he cocked it. Sallah slid over the quiver of bolts next.

"Sallah!" Deothen roared. "Stop arming our prisoners!"

Burch turned and pointed his crossbow at the senior knight. Deothen ducked to his knees, and the shifter's shot sailed over his head. A cry pierced the black night beyond the ship's bow, and Kandler caught a glimpse of a winged shadow turning back into the mists.

Burch snarled and stepped past the knight, swinging his weapon around to cover as much of the sky as he could. "She gets near the ring again," he said, "I'll drop her."

Kandler lowered the flickering blade in his hand and scanned the darkness. On the ground in the Mournland, the air usually seemed still as a grave, but up here, with the airship soaring along, the wind whipped through him like a cold knife. Only the heat from the fiery ring dulled its edge.

As Kandler's gaze hunted through the sky, Brendis stepped forward to take the weapon back from him. The justicar elbowed the young knight back. "Stay out of my way," he said.

Sallah drew her own sword and set it ablaze with silvery fire as she raced across the deck, her long, red curls flapping behind her like a battle standard. She clambered onto the bridge where she found Esprë huddled next to the wheel.

"Don't let her get me again," the girl said. "Please!"

Esprë was gripping the wheel of the airship in white knuckles, and her entire body was shaking. She squeezed her eyes shut, and Kandler saw the red glow of the fire reflected off tears. The airship lurched slightly upward. Perhaps it was only the ship catching a pocket of air, but it was then that Kandler noticed a distinct trembling in the deck. Esprë was terrified, and it was affecting her control over the ship.

Sallah knelt down next to Esprë and stroked the girl's golden hair with her free hand. "She won't get past me," the knight said solemnly. "I promise."

Kandler reached down and patted Sallah on the back. When the lady knight looked up at him, he nodded his thanks.

Deothen stood in the center of the deck, directly under the crackling ring of fire that propelled the ship through the night. "Where is she?" he asked. "Has she fled?"

"There!" Kandler stabbed his silver-flame-coated blade past the ship's rear railing. "She's out on the rudder!"

As Kandler watched, the changeling slashed at the rudder's leathery fabric with a black knife, trying to shred it to ribbons. The material resisted her blade's edge, but she kept at it.

Kandler spied a mooring line lashed around a cleat on the rear railing. He picked up the loose end of it and threaded it through the rear of his belt. With a series of deft moves, he tied a tight knot and then leaped up to the rear railing. From there, he stepped out on to the rudder's top spar and crept forward, balancing on the narrow beam of wood as the winds whipped around him.

"Kandler!" Esprë screamed.

A crossbow bolt sailed past Kandler and buried itself in the rudder's frame. The changeling saw it, hissed, and took a step back. Kandler glanced over his shoulder. Burch was coming at them, reloading as he ran. He turned back just in time to see the changeling drop away into the darkness below. Kandler heard the *clack* of Burch's crossbow followed by the whisper of a bolt shooting past.

Kandler looked back over his shoulder as he stood crouched on the spar, Brendis's burning sword still in his hand. "Did you get her?" he asked Burch.

Before the shifter could answer, the changeling came around behind Kandler and blind-sided him from his perch. As the justicar toppled into the blackness, he swung about, let go of the sword, and grabbed the changeling, hauling her down with him. Brendis's glittering blade arced out and away from them and tumbled through the dark toward the unseen ground far below.

CHAPTER

44

Kandler wrapped his arms around the changeling's waist, and she battered at him with her fists as they plummeted through the inky blackness, the wind whipping around them as they fell. The arc of their dive reached the end of the mooring line on the justicar's belt with a tug that bent him in half and knocked the breath from both of them, but his hold on the changeling never weakened.

The pair's momentum swung them back and up toward the bottom of the ship's hull, only feet away from the lower part of the fiery ring. In the blazing light, Kandler could see the changeling's face clearly for the first time. She was beautiful in her own formless way, her black hair fluttering behind her.

"Release me," the changeling demanded, "or I cut this line!"

She pushed the edge of her knife against the rope that kept Kandler from following the sword down to his doom. Kandler rammed his head into the changeling's nose. Red blood spurted onto her ebony skin. He reached up, grabbed her wrist, and pulled the knife away from his lifeline.

"The chase is over," the justicar said.

Kandler forced the knife around lower, readying it for a stab into the changeling's exposed side. As he did, he felt something foreign jab into his mind, probing for a weak spot, a switch that would turn him into a drooling madman or a gibbering fool. He fought with everything he could muster, but he knew it was only a matter of time before the psion battered down his defenses and destroyed his mind. Kandler stopped trying to force the knife lower and swung it back up toward the rope instead. It bit into the line above him, splitting some of its vital fibers. The pressure in his head spiked, and he growled like a cornered beast.

"Stop it! These wings won't hold our weight!" The changeling hissed the words into his ear. "You'll kill us both!"

"Fine. With. Me." Kandler spat through gritted teeth. He had let this creature kidnap his daughter once, and he wasn't going to let her get away with it again. Try as he might, though, he couldn't force her from his mind.

As the pair struggled, they swung back out behind the airship again. A bolt sailed through the air as they hit the apex of their swing. It grazed the changeling's shoulder, and she howled in pain.

The pressure in Kandler's head disappeared. He grinned down at the bloodied changeling in his arms as they swung back under the airship again. "It's over," he said as he reached up to pull the black knife from the rope so he could finish her off.

The changeling lunged forward in Kandler's arms and sank her teeth into his neck, biting and tearing like a mad dog. He shrieked and shoved the changeling away from him as hard as he could. The changeling kicked off from the justicar and, free at last, arced backward into an elegant dive. She spread her arms, and her wings unfolded around her. They caught the rushing air and buoyed her up again into the sky. The light of the airship's ring of fire reflected off the wings for a moment, making her seem like some sort of demon, then the mists swallowed her again. Kandler snarled in frustration.

One of his the rope's strands popped under his weight. His head snapped up, and he saw the changeling's knife still stabbed through the rope. With every motion, he pulled the rope against the blade, shredding a few more fibers.

Kandler reached up and grabbed the rope above the knife. Grunting with the effort, he began hauling himself hand over hand up the long line. After a moment, he realized the rope was moving upward, too—and fast.

As the justicar reached for the ship's railing, a mailed hand met his. Brendis pulled Kandler up and helped him onto the bridge.

"That was the most amazing thing I've ever seen," the young knight said.

Burch and Deothen dropped the end of the rope they'd been hauling on. The shifter reached over and grabbed Kandler into a bear hug. The justicar pounded his friend on the back and grinned.

"Sorry about your sword," Kandler said to Brendis as Burch let him go. He stuck out a hand to the young knight.

"It was a sacred blade awarded to me by the Council of Cardinals," Brendis said. "It can never be replaced. But it was lost in a good cause."

"Yes," Deothen said as he picked up his own sword from where he'd dropped it on the deck. "You can use the justicar's for now. He won't have any use for it."

Kandler stared at the senior knight. "You can put that away," he said. "I won't fight you, but I'm not going back into that hold."

"The situation has not changed," Deothen said. "We are still going to Flamekeep."

Kandler glanced behind the gray-haired knight and saw Esprë huddled in one corner of the bridge with Sallah's arms around her. The sight warmed his heart, and he smiled. That disappeared as a thought struck him.

"Who's flying this thing?" he asked, staring at the abandoned wheel.

Esprë pulled herself from Sallah's arms. "The elemental!" she said through her tears. "It can't see where it's going, but if you set your direction and altitude, it can fly all by itself. I figured it—"

One moment Kandler was reaching out to give Esprë's shoulder a proud squeeze, then the changeling, gliding in on silent wings, swooped down and snatched her away from his outstretched hand. There was only an instant of hesitation as the wings adjusted to the added weight, then both changeling and Esprë disappeared into the night. The girl's scream echoed in the justicar's ears long after she was gone.

"Esprë!" Kandler shouted as he dashed toward the airship's rail. He stared out into the darkness, looking for any sign of the girl or the changeling. All he saw was the mists of the Mournland, now pulsing a sickly red from the light of the airship's ring of fire. He heard Esprë scream again, but the sound ended horribly short.

"Burch!" Kandler said.

The shifter was already scanning all around, his crossbow hungry for a target.

"Don't!" the justicar cried. "They'll both fall to their deaths."

Burch growled in frustration at the sky. "Doesn't matter anyhow," he said. "There's nothing. She's gone."

Kandler cast about desperately. "The changeling can't get far on those wings," he said, thinking out loud. "They weren't strong enough to carry the two of us."

"You're a bit larger than your daughter," Sallah said.

Kandler looked over at the woman. Her face was flushed with shame for letting Esprë get away from her, even though the girl had been walking between the two of them at the time. The lady knight would barely meet the justicar's glance, but he could see tears of frustration welling in her eyes.

Kandler nodded at Sallah in agreement as he lay a hand on her shoulder in forgiveness. Sallah hadn't snatched his daughter away.

"You are wounded," Xalt said to Kandler.

Kandler put his hand to where the changeling had bitten him. It came away wet and red. "Doesn't matter now," he said. "We have to go after Esprë." He looked up at the mists swirling past above as they sailed along and held up his hand to the sky. "Can anyone stop this ship?"

"By the Flame," Sallah said, "you're right! We're being carried farther away with every minute."

Deothen launched himself at the wheel.

"No one's been able to fly this thing but Esprë," Kandler said.

Deothen flashed a grim smile as he gripped the wheel. "I think you'll find I'm as strong willed as anyone."

The ship braked to a halt so fast that Kandler found himself nearly thrown from the bridge. He righted himself and stared at the gray-haired knight.

Deothen raised an eyebrow at him and said, "They don't put just anyone in charge of a mission like this." He nodded at Sallah. "Get the justicar fixed up. I'll bring the ship around."

"But Esprë—!" Kandler started.

"Is out of our hands until dawn," said the senior knight. "You need to be ready to fight if you're to help her when we find her again. Get that wound cleaned before it festers. You're no good to your daughter dead."

Kandler started to argue with the old man, but the wisdom of his words sunk in. He suddenly realized how tired he was and how much his neck hurt. He climbed down onto the deck, and Sallah knelt down beside him. She reached up and tilted his head away from her, angling his neck so she could see the wound in the light from the ring of fire above. She grazed the opened skin with her fingers, and the justicar winced.

"You're lucky to be alive," Sallah said. "If she'd bit a little deeper, you'd have bled to death before we could've hauled you aboard."

"If I hadn't been locked in the hold, this might never have happened," Kandler said bitterly. He held onto that feeling for a moment before he looked down at Sallah's face.

Sallah ignored him and concentrated on the wound instead. "He's a good man in a bad position," she said.

"That's how you tell who's good," Kandler said. "It's easy to behave when everything's going well. Ow!"

"Hold still," Sallah said. "I want to make sure I get all of this." She tugged at the collar of Kandler's shirt to expose every bit of the wound.

"Ouch! Are you sure she wasn't a vampire too?" Kandler said.

Sallah peered at the wound. "Teeth marks are too even. No sign of fangs." She lay her hands atop the savaged skin and spoke a solemn prayer to the Silver Flame. Her hands glowed with an argent warmth that spilled into Kandler's flesh. When she lifted her hands, his skin was whole again.

"Thanks," Kandler said, looking into her eyes as he rubbed his healed neck with a rough hand.

Sallah returned his gaze. "I'd do the same for anyone."

"Any of your prisoners?"

Sallah smiled. She stood and wiped her bloodied hands on her white tabard. "Almost anyone."

"I'm honored," Kandler said. He glanced back at the bridge and noticed Deothen watching them. When the old man saw that he had caught the justicar's eye, he beckoned the pair to join the others back on the bridge.

"At my best guess, I've brought the ship back around to where we were when Esprë was taken from us," Deothen said, gazing out into the seamless night. "Unfortunately, I don't think there's much we can do until the dawn."

Kandler nodded reluctantly.

"Where to then?" Sallah asked. "By morning, the changeling will have had hours to get ahead of us or to hide. She could be anywhere."

Kandler frowned. "Those wings of hers aren't all that strong. She'll be stuck on foot, dragging Esprë along behind her. She'll need food and water, too, neither of which is easy to find around here. I bet she'd kill for a horse."

"My best guess?" Burch said. "She'll head northeast again. The way she was going before we ran into Lady Majeeda's tower."

"What's off in that direction?" Sallah asked.

Kandler shook his head. "I don't know. Burch and I never made it this far into the Mournland before."

"I wasn't asking you," the lady knight said. "Xalt is the native here."

The warforged rasped a soft laugh. "Nothing, I fear. This is the Mournland."

"There has to be something," Brendis said. "Maybe she went for one of the old lightning rail lines."

Deothen grunted. "Those haven't run since the Day of Mourning. They'd be useless to her."

"There is something that may be off to the northeast," Xalt said. "But the changeling couldn't possibly know about it."

"She's a psion," Kandler said. "A mindreader. If you know about it, there's a chance she might know about it too. Who knows how long she was in that hold scanning our thoughts?"

Xalt nodded then said one word. "Construct."

Kandler cocked his head at the warforged. "What's that?"

"Construct is a town the Lord of Blades founded after the end of the Last War as a warforged settlement. It's meant to be our capital someday."

Deothen curled his lip at this. "I've heard rumors of this place," he said. "Different reports have placed it in every part of the Mournland, but no one's ever been able to confirm them. The place is like a ghost."

"Almost like it moves," said Xalt.

Sallah's eyes grew wide. "It's a moving city? Like Argonth?"

The warforged nodded.

Burch whistled. "That explains a lot," he said.

"But how can anyone find such a place?" Brendis asked. "It would be almost impossible."

"Not if you knew when it was coming," Kandler said. He looked at Xalt.

"It was scheduled to meet with Superior," the warforged said, "later today."

CHAPTER 45

There it is, boss," Burch said. He handed Kandler the spyglass he'd found in a compartment on the bridge.

Standing in the airship's bow, the wind whipping all about him as they sailed forward at top speed, the justicar lifted the spyglass to his eye and gazed off in the direction Burch had pointed. Even at this distance, he wasn't sure how he could have missed it. The city had to be half a mile long and perhaps a hundred yards wide. It was built on a series of interlocking platforms that crawled along the ground. Smoke billowed from great furnaces in the factories that rose from the center of the town. Guard posts lined the edges of the place, each outfitted with a massive set of ballistae and a squad of well-armed soldiers.

"If there was ever a good reason for people to stop making warforged, that's it," said Burch.

"We are not all bad," Xalt said from over the justicar's shoulder.

"Staggering," said Sallah, who stood next to the warforged and peered over Kandler's other shoulder. "I've never seen anything like it." She turned to Kandler. "How does it compare to your Argonth?"

Kandler handed the spyglass to the lady knight, who looked through it and gasped. "It doesn't," said the justicar. "Argonth is a floating fortress built from the start for war. It's the most powerful weapon in Breland. An entire army can travel on it at once.

"This looks like it just grew. There's almost no plan to it, other than the guards on the perimeter. I bet you could take any of those platforms off and run it around by itself too. In an emergency, they could split the place into as many parts as they like and run them in different directions. Imagine being surrounded by a city like that."

"Argonth is taller," said Burch.

"With Construct," said Xalt, "each platform can tilt independent of the others. If you built up too high, the tops of the buildings would crash into each other."

"Why did they build it like that?" Brendis asked.

"It has to do with the terrain around here, doesn't it?" said Sallah.

Xalt nodded. "A flat-bottomed structure like Argonth would never work here. How would such a thing traverse a hill? Or climb the Glass Plateau?"

"Good point," said Kandler. "Argonth works in Breland because it sticks to the flatter parts of the country. There's a reason the fortress has never been used in an invasion. It would have a devil of a time getting past Breland's own natural boundaries."

"But how does this thing move?" asked Brendis. "If it doesn't hover by magic, what pushes it along on those wheels?"

"May the Flame protect us," Sallah said in awe as she lowered the spyglass. "Those aren't wheels under those platforms. They're legs. Are those warforged?"

"That's impossible," said Deothen, as he strode up behind the others. "That would mean there are thousands of them there." He took the spyglass from Sallah. "Maybe tens of thousands," he said.

"Were that many warforged made?" said Brendis. "How can that be?"

Xalt laughed. "Those are not warforged," he said. "My people are free here. They would never submit to such mindless drudgery again."

Kandler turned to look back at the artificer. "Then what are they?" he asked.

"Walkers," the warforged answered. "Metal golems that consist of little more than a platform on legs."

Kandler's breath caught in his chest. He heard Sallah gasp.

"You're jesting," said Burch.

The artificer shook his head. "Many wizards use them, and you can find them in the warehouses and factories of the wealthiest houses in Khorvaire, where they are used to help transport goods."

"If you know how to make them," Kandler said, "then making lots of them is just a matter of time."

"Precisely." Xalt nodded.

"Thank the Flame they haven't figured out how to create their own kind," Deothen breathed.

"If the changeling is in there, we'll never find her," said Sallah. "The place is too big."

"Get me in there," said Burch. "I can pick up her scent."

"She might not even be there," Deothen pointed out.

Kandler nodded at this. He'd had the same thought but been reluctant to voice it. "Well," he said, "I don't think we have any other choice. We have to go in to find out."

"How do you propose we do that?" said Deothen. "Shall we simply fly this airship in and set down in their central square?"

"I've heard of worse ideas," said Kandler. "It might give us the element of surprise."

"It also might give those ballistae a chance to knock us out of the sky," said Deothen. "I doubt we could take too many hits from those. An expert pilot might be able to avoid them, but not I."

Burch pointed up at the ring of fire that surrounded the airship. "They see us already, boss."

Kandler looked around at the ring. "I suppose you're right."

"They don't seem to have raised any kind of alarm," said Brendis. "If I saw an airship on its way toward me, I'd have something to say about it."

"Dragons don't worry about mosquitoes," Kandler said.

"Can't a mosquito bite a dragon?" asked Sallah.

"Sure," said Kandler, "if the mosquito doesn't mind being crushed afterward."

"We're more than a mosquito," said Brendis. "If we crashed the airship into the center of their town, that would loose the fire elemental. That would get their attention."

"And how do you suppose we'd walk away from that?" Kandler asked.

"It is a good thought, Sir Brendis," said Deothen, "but we're not here to get their attention. We want to get in and find out if the girl is there. If she is, we rescue her and leave. If not, we leave and look elsewhere. The changeling was traveling northeast with undead Karrn warriors. It's safe to assume she's headed to Karrnath."

"So how do we get in there?" asked Sallah. "We're not all warforged. They'll spot us at once."

"True," said Xalt. "But there are many breathers in Construct."

Sallah's face lit up. "Excellent! Are they merchants, diplomats? I'm sure we can pose as them and sneak in. It's just a matter of doing it right."

Xalt shook his head. "They do get such people from time to time, but they are rare enough that they always draw a crowd."

"You said there are many 'breathers' in town," Kandler said. "Why are they there?"

Xalt paused a moment before speaking. "Slaves."

Everyone stared at Xalt.

"You saw Superior's attitude toward your kind," said Xalt.

"He is not alone in such beliefs. Among my people, I am somewhat of a . . . rarity."

Kandler tapped his forehead. He didn't like the idea that sprang into his head, but there was nothing else there. "All right. We can pose as slaves and you"—he pointed at Xalt—"you can be our master."

"You would trust him that far?" Brendis asked.

"You saved my life when you had no reason to do so," Xalt replied. "I am in your debt. I will pose as your master, if that is what you wish."

Deothen fell a half step back. "Never," he said. "The Knights of the Silver Flame are no slaves. There is no honor in such a deception."

"The honorable route would be suicidal," said Kandler, frustrated. He had known that Deothen would find some way to object. "You can't just announce yourself and walk in. They'll tear you apart."

"Actually," said Xalt, "they would probably take you before the town's ruler for judgment. Then they would either enslave you or tear you apart."

"Who's the town ruler?" Deothen asked, a tad too imperiously for Kandler's taste. "Perhaps he is a creature who can be reasoned with. We have no issue with him. We only want the changeling and the girl, neither of whom are his concern."

"He's a lieutenant of the Lord of Blades," Xalt said. "Each of them is named after a particular kind of sword or knife. They are his tools, after all, his weapons in his war on breathers."

"What's this one call himself?" asked Kandler. The artificer's hesitancy had piqued his curiosity.

"He calls himself after the hand-and-a-half sword, the kind that you can fight with in one hand or switch to a two-handed grip for a more powerful blow. He uses the colloquial term for it—Bastard."

Deothen's face fell, and Kandler couldn't help but smirk to himself.

"The Knights of the Silver Flame are not slaves," Deothen said firmly.

"We'd just be *posing* as slaves," said Sallah. To Kandler, she sounded like the voice of reason, but it seemed that Deothen didn't share the justicar's opinion.

The senior knight spun about as if he'd been stabbed. "I can't believe I'm hearing such words from your mouth, my daughter!"

"Please hear me out," the lady knight said. "While it is beneath a Knight of the Silver Flame to engage in such deception, there is something else to consider here—the life of the child and the fate of our mission. We can adhere to a strict code of honor here and all end up dead and the girl in enemy hands. Or we can . . . bend the code. These are extraordinary circumstances, after all."

"Listen to Sallah," Kandler urged. "Would you rather ride in with your head held high and have it handed to you or swallow your pride and get the job done?"

Deothen stood before the justicar and steamed, unable to bring himself to speak. Kandler looked the man dead in the eyes and shook his head.

"Never mind," the justicar said. "Burch and I are going in anyhow. With or without you. If you want to charge in after us, just don't give us away."

"Wait!" said Sallah. She turned to her commander. "Sir Deothen, I beg your leave to accompany the others into the warforged city. They may have need of a knight's talents."

Deothen grimaced as he considered the request. As Kandler saw it, this was a way for the knight to be able to do the right thing while still keeping his own precious pride. He just hoped the knight would agree.

"Very well," Deothen said finally. "Brendis and I will stay here in the airship, ready to come to your aid at your signal."

Kandler nodded. "What kind of signal would work for you?"

Deothen gave Kandler a hard look and said, "If I see the

light of the Silver Flame dancing along Sallah's sword, we will immediately fly to your aid."

Kandler saw what the knight was doing. If the only signal Deothen would pay attention to was Sallah's sword, then the justicar would be compelled to help keep Sallah alive.

"Fine," he said. He turned to Sallah. Her face was flushed, but whether from the impending action or just standing in the whipping wind, he couldn't discern. "You in?"

The lady knight offered a small bow. "To the end. My sword is yours."

The justicar turned to Burch and Xalt. "Let's go."

CHAPTER

46

The trail to Construct was not an easy one, but Kandler ignored its challenges. He was too eager to get to the moving city to worry about such things. He'd had Deothen set them down in a hollow out of sight of the warforged capital, and from there they had hiked along in the city's wide wake.

"Did I have to leave my armor behind?" Sallah said as she hurried after the others, dressed in a large, formless shawl that covered her from chin to waist. Burch walked right in front of her, with Kandler next to him. Xalt led the way toward the mobile city, which grew closer to them with every step.

"We're posing as Xalt's slaves," Kandler said. "Didn't you hear Deothen explain how a knight would never be a slave?"

Sallah sighed and rested her hand on the pommel of her sacred sword, which she had disguised by wrapping it in a dull cloth she had found in the airship's hold. "As a Knight of the Silver Flame, I am trained for battle, not subterfuge. This makes me"—she searched for the right word—"uncomfortable."

Kandler looked up at the rolling sections of Construct as they neared it. The low, gray buildings on the dozens of platforms sprawled away from them like a string of massive barges scudding across the gray-green land. He was thankful that the walkers under the city moved so slowly, but it irritated him that the place was moving away from them at any speed. It made the journey seem much longer than it should.

"If you're afraid of going into that place . . ." he said.

"I didn't say I was afraid."

"You should be. I am."

"Me, too," said Burch.

"How about you, Xalt?" said Kandler.

"Had I skin, it would be white as a sheet." The warforged gazed along the length of Construct's platforms. "Even without a gang of breathers tagging behind, I never liked this place."

"Why?" said Kandler. "It looks like a warforged paradise."

Xalt shook its head. "This is a place dedicated to conquest and war. As the lady just said, such things make me uncomfortable."

Burch stared at the moving city as they it grew closer. "Must be heavy," he said. "Moves slow."

"When Bastard wishes, the city can move much faster."

"What happens if we run into one of the warforged from Superior's camp?" Sallah asked.

"We won't," said Xalt. "Bastard does not smile upon failures. None of the patrol's survivors will be willing to come here to report what happened and risk his wrath. Warforged have been dismantled for far less."

As the quartet neared the rear of Construct, Xalt waved at a squad of warforged soldiers standing on one of the ballista-bearing platforms that lined the edges of many of the platforms. A soldier draped with a wide red collar returned the gesture.

At the squad leader's signal—a series of stomps on the platform below it—two of the walkers at the end of the rear platform slowed their strides. As they did, the end of the ramp they were standing under pulled out atop them while the city moved on ahead until the other end of the ramp caught on its hinges. Then the two walkers crunched themselves down as low as they could while matching the pace of the city. When they were done, they only stood about a foot tall but still moved as fast as the others in front of them.

"That's amazing," said Sallah. "I'm surprised they can make themselves so thin."

"This is nothing," Xalt said. "When they stop moving entirely, they can fold themselves down to a height of only a few inches. Sometimes a roving animal gets stuck under a platform when this happens. It's always a mess." Xalt lowered his voice as they made up the distance between themselves and the end of the ramp. "Remember, you are slaves. Do not speak unless spoken to. Do not meet the eyes of any warforged but me. And you must obey my every word. There is far more to a slave's proper etiquette, but that should suffice for our purposes."

Kandler put his hand on the hilt of his sword. "You're sure we're okay with these swords?"

Xalt nodded. "You are my bodyguards. It's dangerous for anyone to walk through the Mournland alone, even a warforged."

As Xalt said this, Kandler saw the artificer look down at the stump where its finger had once been.

When they reached the ramp, Xalt jumped up on and walked up to the squad leader. The others followed the artificer and stopped behind him, keeping their eyes low. As Sallah cleared the far end of the ramp, the walkers carrying it along stood up, raising the ramp, and walked it toward the city platform, shoving the ramp back into its home.

"Business?" the squad leader said to Xalt.

"I am an artificer. I have come to offer my aid."

The squad leader surveyed the people behind Xalt. "Business must be good for you," he said.

"There never seems to be a shortage of injuries among our kind."

The squad leader nodded. "You won't find one here. Report to the central workshop. They should have plenty of work for you."

"My thanks," Xalt said. He strode into the city, the others following right behind.

"That went better than I hoped," said Kandler. Sallah slapped him on the back of the head. He turned and glared at her. "What was that for?"

"Were you spoken to?"

"Quiet!" Xalt said. "When we find our quarters, I will have to whip you all for your impudence!"

Kandler and Sallah glanced around to see the other warforged on the platform looking at them. As one, they bowed their heads and said, "Yes, master."

The quartet moved further into the city, Xalt leading the way. Each platform seemed to have a purpose of one kind or another. Some were forges, others homes, still others open spaces where warforged either sat and meditated or trained with various sorts of weapons. The spaces between the platforms were covered with wooden gangways that moved and shifted with the vagaries of the walkers underneath them and the terrain they were covering. When moving between platforms, most people walked along the gangways unless they were just hopping over to the next platform. Once the quartet passed the first few platforms, they saw few others.

"Where is everyone?" Kandler whispered.

"Patrol, most likely," Xalt said. "Construct is a base of operations, not a home. We're rarely all here at the same time."

Kandler stared around him at the eerily empty platforms. "What do the people here do then?"

"Study, train, undergo repairs. They gather to watch our finest warriors battle each other in the main arena for sport, then it's up to artificers like myself to piece the losers back together."

"That's barbaric," said Sallah.

"It's the curse of being a young people," Xalt said. "We are still struggling to find our way. Most of us aren't much older than five years old, although very few are less."

"The Treaty of Thronehold barred the creation of more

warforged," Sallah said. "All known creation forges were ordered destroyed."

"Good thing, too," Burch said softly.

"It was a crime," Xalt said. Kandler could tell by the artificer's tone that this was no joke to him.

"Why is that?" asked Sallah.

"It was an atrocity. To deny a people the means to reproduce . . . it is one of the reasons the Lord of Blades finds so many of the warforged willing to flock to his banner."

"But the treaty granted you all the rights of sentient beings," the lady knight said.

"We were already sentient beings," Xalt said. "That part of the treaty only recognized what was already a fact."

Sallah frowned. "But we couldn't let every country continue to produce warforged without restriction," she said. "They would have outnumbered the other peoples in a matter of years."

"Centuries, perhaps. It's not so easy to create a warforged as you might think."

"Still, I think you can understand the fear."

Xalt nodded. "But I find it hard to accept the actions taken. Look around you, and you can see the direct results of these restrictions. The Lord of Blades is in the process of creating a nation of disaffected soldiers. Someday, the warforged of the Mournland will grow restless in their harsh homeland and start to look outside their borders. What do you think will happen then?"

Sallah shook her head.

Xalt turned to look past Kandler and Burch at the lady knight. "A conflict that will make the hundred years of the Last War seem like a pit fight."

Kandler raised his eyebrows at Burch. "What do you say?" the justicar asked.

"Think more about Esprë and less about politics," the shifter answered.

"I knew there was a reason I liked you."

Burch smiled and lowered his head. He snorted and snuffed for a moment, flexing his arms and twisting his head. When he looked back up, his eyes were wider and more yellow than ever, and his nose a bit wider too. He sniffed at the air and then ran his tongue across his sharp, pointy teeth.

"What's the word?" Kandler asked.

Burch turned his wolf's eyes on his friend. "Esprë's scent," he said. "Roses. I got it."

CHAPTER

47

"You will like it in Karrnath," Te'oma said to Esprë across the single table in the tiny room, "for as long as we're there. Of course, after the Mournland, I think anything would be an improvement."

The girl glared up at the changeling but didn't say a word. She'd been utterly silent since the two had slipped into Construct just before what passed for dawn in the Mournland, and it was starting to grate on Te'oma's nerves.

"It's a long trip not to say a word the entire way," Te'oma said. There was still no response.

The changeling sighed and stood up. She knew she'd been fortunate to find this abandoned warforged shelter—it was too bare for her to think of it as a home—before any of the guards had spotted them, but she was already tired of being in the dim room. She'd spent time in jail cells that were roomier and more welcoming.

Warforged needed no rest, water, or food—three things Te'oma wanted badly, and she suspected Esprë did as well. The girl had dozed with her head on the table for a bit, but Te'oma was too wary of every sound she heard outside their borrowed quarters to let sleep take her. The constant tromping of the walkers' feet beneath the city's floor didn't help any, although it lent the entire place a gentle sway that Te'oma thought might have been able to rock her to sleep under more pleasant circumstances.

The changeling started to pace the room. The place was so small that she had to turn around after every few steps.

"I'm thirsty," Esprë said.

The sound startled the changeling, although she tried not to show it. She covered by leaning across the table at the girl and saying, "Ah! She speaks!"

Esprë ignored Te'oma's sarcasm. "I'm hungry, too."

The changeling sat down in the rough wooden chair across the unpolished table from Esprë. She looked at the walls and ceiling around her, fashioned from thin panels of wood painted with something the color of ash. A flimsy wardrobe stood in the corner, empty but for a pair of threadbare tabards. The only light in the room streamed in through a high window above the place's sole door, which was made of the same material as the walls.

The utilitarianism of the warforged of Construct astonished Te'oma. As a changeling, appearances were vital to her. She spent much of her spare time studying the way others looked and behaved, how they spoke, and what they wore. It seemed to her that imitating a warforged would be a simple thing, as most of them seemed almost identical, various styles of interchangeable cogs in a long-defunct war machine—if only she could make her skin seem like metal.

Te'oma leaned across the table, looked into Esprë almond-shaped, blue eyes, and said, "Why don't you do something about it?"

The girl sat up straight in her chair with an offended look on her face. "Isn't that your job? You're not much of a kidnapper."

Te'oma stared at the girl for a moment with wide eyes, then threw back her head and laughed. "Believe it or not, I don't kidnap many children," she said. "I wasn't aware of the protocol."

"What do you usually do then?"

Te'oma stopped laughing. "What do you mean?"

She suspected the girl was just trying to get her off guard so she could attempt an escape, but Esprë had been silent for so long that Te'oma was willing to indulge her for a moment.

"What do you spend your time doing when you're not kidnapping innocent children?"

Te'oma flashed the girl a savage smile. "Don't play innocent with me," she said, leaning closer across the table. "I know *all* about you."

Esprë screwed her face up at that. "What's that supposed to mean?"

Te'oma stood and walked around the table like a hunting cat on the prowl. As she crept behind Esprë, she pulled the girl's collar back and looked down her shirt at the dragonmark that lie hidden there.

"Hello, killer," Te'oma said.

Esprë jumped as if the changeling had stabbed her. "Get away!"

Te'oma danced away, feigning fear. "Don't kill me," she said in a falsetto tone. "Just like all those people you killed in your dreams."

All the color drained from Esprë's face.

"That's right," Te'oma said as she moved to put the table between her and the girl again. "I know all about that. Your mind is an open book to me. It's been an interesting read. A little short though."

"Shut up," Esprë said sullenly.

Te'oma leaned across the table again and leered into the girl's eyes. "You might as well face up to it," she said softly. "You are a killer. Just like me."

"I am nothing like you," Esprë said, her voice just a bit louder.

"Of course you are," Te'oma pressed. "You come from a long line of killers. Your mother fought in the war. Do you think she had no blood on her hands?"

Esprë swallowed hard. The color returned to her face, but her eyes sank with barely suppressed rage.

"Your father was probably a killer, too," Te'oma continued. "And Kandler. That man leaves a wake of blood behind him wherever he goes."

"Shut up," Esprë said through clenched teeth.

Te'oma softened her tone. She'd been using vinegar. Time for a little honey. "There's no crime in killing. Birth, life, death . . . it is the way of the world."

"I'm *not* like you."

"Not yet, no," Te'oma smiled. "The difference is you have no control. You kill without meaning to. Innocent and guilty alike, you've killed them."

"I—" Tears welled in the girl's eyes.

"It's all right, Esprë," Te'oma knelt beside the girl. "I know you didn't mean to. It wasn't your fault. But"—she put a bit more steel into her voice—"it won't stop just because you don't like it. You have to sleep sometime. If you don't learn control . . ."

Te'oma didn't complete the thought. Let the girl finish it herself.

"You just need time to grow. There's a reason you bear that dragonmark, Esprë, when no one else has had it for over twenty-five hundred years." Te'oma bent far enough over the table that she could have reached down to kiss Esprë on the nose, then she whispered at her. "You're destined to be the greatest killer of all time."

"That's not true!" Esprë raged. The girl stood up and threw herself at the changeling.

Te'oma retreated back across the table, and Esprë's hands missed her by scant inches. The changeling knocked over the chair behind her as she retreated to the far corner of the room. The girl followed her straight over the table, screaming in frustration as she went.

"Take it back!" Esprë roared. "It's not true! Take it back!"

The girl lunged at Te'oma, and the changeling caught the

girl's arms by the wrists. "See!" the changeling said. "Do you see? Look at your hands!"

In the heat of her anger, Esprë glanced at her hands, which she had formed into talons to scratch out the changeling's eyes, and she saw that they were glowing a malevolent red that oozed and flowed around her palms and fingers like living blood.

"That's it!" Te'oma said triumphantly. She let go of Esprë's wrists, and the girl reeled back from her and into the table. *That's* the power of the Mark of Death, to kill with but a touch, and you have it."

Te'oma hadn't been positive about Esprë's dragonmark. She'd seen a drawing of the last known dragonmark of that kind, but the legends that swirled around the Mark of Death made anything about it hard to believe. Now she was sure. Te'oma breathed an inward sigh of relief. She'd taken a chance in provoking the girl, but she had needed to know if the girl was the one. If not, Te'oma didn't see the point in hauling her all the way to Karrnath. Now that she knew she was right, all the challenges that lay before them would be worth it. And the rewards . . .

"I should kill you!" Esprë said, tears of rage rolling down her tender cheeks.

Te'oma grinned. "You know better than that. Like it or not, you need me."

"I do not!"

"Look around you," Te'oma said, swinging her arms wide. "You're in the middle of the Mournland on a rolling city filled with hundreds of hostile warforged. Are you going to hike home on your own?"

The cold facts of her situation slashed through Esprë's anger. The tears stopped flowing, and her color slowly returned to normal. The changeling had her just where she wanted her.

"Even if you somehow managed to get off Construct by yourself and make it to the border, do you think you could get through those mists alone? On foot?" Te'oma shook her head. "And what if you do make it back to that ramshackle slum you called a home? Will you go back to that life, killing townsfolk in your sleep? Killing is a fine art, and you may one day be its finest practitioner, but you *must learn*."

"I don't want to learn!" Esprë said. "I'll never be like you. I hate you."

"Fine. Hate me. But you know I speak the truth. You are a killer whether you like it or not. That dragonmark is part of you. Learn to control it, and you may choose to never kill again. Let it control you, and . . ."

"And what?" Esprë sniffed and wiped her tears away on her sleeve.

"You know what, girl," Te'oma replied. "You're not stupid. Just scared. And I don't blame you. But you must learn to control your dragonmark, Esprë. Until you do, you are a danger to everyone you know and love. I can take you to people who will teach you to control your gift."

"Why? What kind of people would know such a thing?

Te'oma smiled. "There is a queen in the north, far in the north. She is a distant relative of yours, an elf of such great age and power that the old crone we met in the tower would cower before her. You weren't raised among the elves, Esprë. You don't know their ancient ways. You are of this queen's family, and the queen protects her own."

CHAPTER

48

"This is it," said Burch.

The quartet stood before a door that looked like most of the others they'd passed as they meandered through Construct, following Esprë's scent. It was tall and gray, with a simple mechanical latch in its handle.

"Are you sure?" Kandler asked.

The shifter nodded. "Scents don't lie."

Burch put his ear to the door and listened for a moment. Kandler saw Xalt glancing nervously up and down the gangway that ran in front of the door.

"Someone's moving inside," Burch whispered. He glanced left and right. "No one's watching."

"Hit it," said Kandler.

Kandler and Burch took two steps back. On three they lowered their shoulders and charged into the door. It gave way, and they plowed in.

"Quick!" Xalt said, pushing Sallah through the door. "I hear someone coming." Once inside, he slammed the door shut again. It fit poorly on its frame now, but it still closed.

Kandler surveyed the room. It was furnished with simple but sturdy furniture. The walls were unadorned. There were no doors other than the one through which they'd come. A wardrobe stood in one corner, opposite a table and two bare chairs.

"Where is she?" Kandler whispered.

Burch sniffed at the air one last time. When he looked at Kandler, his eyes were back to normal. "Smells strong," he said. "She has to be close."

"B-Burch?" a little voice said.

"Esprë!" Kandler said. "Is that you?"

"Kandler!" Esprë said as she burst out of the wardrobe. She dashed into his arms and hugged him tight, silent tears rolling from her eyes.

The justicar pulled the girl away from him for a second and used his hand to brush her hair back from her face. "Are you all right?" he asked. "Did she hurt you?"

Esprë shook her head as she gasped through her sobs of relief. "She left me here, and when I heard you outside I didn't know who it was. I hid in the wardrobe."

Kandler swept the girl up into his arms and held her tight. "It's all right now. Don't worry."

Esprë sunk her face into Kandler's shoulder and wept. He held her and rocked her back and forth as he thought about the things he'd like to do to the changeling who had put his daughter through so much.

Sallah put a hand on Kandler's back. "I don't want to break up this happy reunion," she said, "but we need to get out of here. The changeling could come back at any moment."

"You don't say." The door opened. A gray-cloaked figure stood there silhouetted in the dim, gray daylight of the Mournland sky. "What an interesting scene to come home to," the creature said.

Esprë looked up at the figure in the doorway, her blue eyes wide and red and magnified by her brimming and spilling tears. "Te-Te'oma?" she whispered.

Kandler gathered Esprë up in his arms as he stood. He told himself that he had what he came for. There was no reason to start a fight here in the middle of a warforged capital if he could help it. His first priority had to be getting his daughter out alive. He looked the changeling dead in the eyes and said, "Because she's not hurt, I'm going to give you one chance to run."

Te'oma chuckled, and the sound set Kandler's teeth on edge. "Give me the girl," she said.

For a moment, Kandler couldn't believe his ears. He was stunned that the changeling could be so brazen. "You're out of your mind. We're four to your one."

"Don't fool yourself. The game is over. You're going to give me the girl and walk away, or I'm going to call the entire city down on your heads."

Burch reached back and slapped his crossbow into his hands. Before he could loose a bolt, the changeling dove out of the doorway. As she went, she let out a scream worthy of a banshee.

"Help!" Te'oma cried. "Breathers!"

"Stop her!" Kandler shouted. He considered launching himself after the changeling, but he couldn't find it in his heart to put Esprë back down. At the moment, he felt like he never would.

Burch leaped across the room, Sallah close behind him. The shifter slid through the open doorway and to the left, giving the knight enough room to barrel past him as he took aim at the changeling. He let fly, but Te'oma ducked around the next corner, and the bolt sailed wide.

The shifter and the knight raced after the changeling, elbowing past the few warforged who poked their heads out of their doors to see what all the noise was about. Within a matter of seconds, they were gone.

Clutching Esprë close to his chest, Kandler ducked through the doorway after the others. "Hold it!" he said as he burst into the narrow alley between the platforms.

Xalt misjudged Kandler's abrupt stop and slammed into the justicar's back as he emerged from the tiny room. Kandler,

Esprë, and the warforged went down on the gangway in a tangle of metallic and fleshy limbs.

Kandler struggled to his feet, Esprë still hanging around his neck. "Burch!" he shouted. "Sallah! Come back!"

The shifter and the lady knight were already out of sight and apparently earshot. Kandler reached back and helped Xalt to his feet. "Damned shifter temper!" the justicar said.

He held Esprë to him and started off after his friend.

Kandler glanced back at Xalt. "Where are they headed?" he asked the artificer.

"In the wrong direction," Xalt said as he trotted along behind the justicar.

"Why's that?" asked Esprë. Hanging on Kandler's neck, she could see right over his shoulder to the warforged.

"That way lies the arena, the main barracks, and Bastard's headquarters," Xalt said. "This is suicide! We should let them go and save ourselves."

As Kandler leaped over a warforged who Burch and Sallah must have knocked down a moment before, he squeezed Esprë tight, and she hugged him back. He wondered if Xalt was right. He'd risked so much to rescue his daughter. Was he throwing it away now?

"What do you think?" he asked Esprë.

"No!" Esprë said. "You don't leave friends behind."

"That's my girl." Kandler grinned as he stiff-armed a warforged that leaped out from a nearby intersection. "I sure miss your mother."

Esprë kissed Kandler on the cheek. "Me, too," she said softly.

As he ran, Kandler kept catching and then losing sight of Sallah and Burch as they chased Te'oma deeper into the city. The canny changeling kept ducking down side passages, turning back and forth as often as she could, never giving the shifter the time to bring her down with a well-aimed bolt.

From up ahead, Kandler heard a dull noise, like the murmur of a thousand tinny voices. As he got closer, an excited roar went up.

"Are we ready to give up?" Xalt said from behind.

Kandler heard a tremor in warforged's voice.

"Never!" Esprë shouted back at the artificer. The justicar just held her tighter and smiled.

They turned a final corner, and there—across an open set of platforms that formed a barren sort of park, complete with low benches but missing plants or trees—a huge wall appeared before him, at least forty feet high. The noise came from behind it. The wall stretched almost entirely across the city, leaving perhaps a single column of platforms untouched on either side of it. Open portals pierced it at regular intervals, each standing empty. Kandler saw the backs of his friends disappear through the portal straight in front of him, which formed a long, dark tunnel. A moment later a roar went up from the other side of the wall.

"By the forge that made me," Xalt said, reaching out his good hand to slow Kandler down. "Tell me they didn't go in there."

The warforged dragged the justicar to a stop and stared up at the wall with his jaw wide open. The structure stood four stories tall and stretched from one edge of the city to the other, at least a hundred yards across at this point. With the exception of the tunnels that ran through its base at regular intervals, it was a solid wall of graying tarpaulins stretched taut over an intricate wooden frame, the outlines of which were visible beneath the thick, oiled canvas.

Kandler spun back at the stunned artificer. "What is it?" he said.

The warforged didn't seem to hear him.

"Xalt!" the justicar said. "What's through there?"

"This is bad," Xalt said. "Not just bad. Awful."

Kandler stepped into the artificer's face. "Can you be more specific?"

Xalt brought his obsidian eyes back down to look at Kandler. He focused on the justicar as if he were seeing him for the first time. "It's the arena," the artificer said. "And from the sound of it, there's a match going on."

Kandler closed his eyes.

"What is it?" Esprë said as she turned around in his arms to stare at Xalt. "What's going to happen to Burch and Sallah?"

The justicar kissed the girl's cheek, never taking his eyes from the artificer. "How many warforged in there?" he asked.

Xalt shook his head. "That must be why the streets are so empty."

"How many, Xalt?"

The greaser spoke slowly, as if waking from a deep sleep. "A few score at least. Hundreds? Maybe more."

Kandler grimaced as another roar sounded from inside the arena.

Esprë pulled back from Kandler's neck and sat on his hip. She furrowed her brow at him. "What's going to happen to them?" she asked.

Kandler looked back at her, and her eyes were as blue and wide as he had ever seen them. He reached up with his free arm and brushed the blonde hair back from the elf-girl's face. Even in the Mournland's half-light, it seemed to glitter.

"I just found you," he whispered.

Kandler kissed Esprë on her forehead and handed her to Xalt.

"Get her out of here," he said. "Take her someplace safe till things quiet down, then get her back to Deothen."

Xalt nodded as the girl slid from Kandler's arms and grabbed his thick, three-fingered hand. She bit her lip and said, "Wait! I can help."

Kandler shook his head. "The world needs you safe," he said, "but our friends need me." He drew his sword and stared down the black tunnel toward the circle of dim light at the other end. "I have to go."

"Wait!" Xalt said. "What is the plan? What are you going to do?"

Kandler glanced back over his shoulder as he left and said, "I'll be damned if I know."

CHAPTER

49

As Kandler reached the end of the tarpaulin-lined tunnel, he saw Burch and Sallah racing into the middle of a sawdust-floored open area that seemed to stretch on forever. The shifter loosed his crossbow at something above, and Kandler poked his head out of the tunnel to see Te'oma flapping away on her cloak, which had transformed once again into batlike wings.

The justicar craned his head around to see the entire arena. Rough-hewn bleachers lined both of the longer sides of the place, each of which stood behind a system of split-rail fencing that kept the crowd separated from the arena floor. Hundreds of warforged stood in them and stared at the shifter and the knight who had just barreled into the place.

For a moment, it seemed that the observers thought the intruders were part of the show, but when Burch's errant bolt sailed into the stands on the opposite side of the arena, the crowd leaped to its feet and roared in outrage. In the center of the arena, two of the largest warforged Kandler had ever seen turned from where they had put a halt to their fight and stomped toward the intruders.

"What in the name of the Silver Flame are those?" Kandler heard Sallah shout to Burch as she pointed at the massive creatures. They looked something like a warforged, but they stood over twenty feet tall, even hunched over. The plates of armor that formed their skin were each at least an inch thick, and foot-long spikes rose from their backplates and the backs of their limbs. In place of hands, their arms terminated in massive weapons. The right was a massive hammer made of battered granite. The left was an axe-head nearly as tall as a man.

As the creatures lumbered toward Burch and Sallah, they rasped their weapon-hands together. The edges of their steel axes drew huge lines of sparks from their hammers' stony surfaces.

"Titans!" Burch exclaimed.

The arena floor shook with the massive creatures' every tread.

Kandler glanced behind him and saw a squad of five warforged warriors stomping up the tunnel behind him. "So much for the stealthy route," he said to himself before dashing out to join Burch and Sallah on the arena floor.

As Kandler reached the pair, Burch growled a greeting at him. "Just like old times," the shifter grinned with a bravado the justicar wished he felt.

Kandler shook his head as he looked up at the titans and said, "I don't remember them being this bad."

The lady knight stood transfixed by the sight of the creatures rumbling toward them. Kandler grabbed Sallah by the arm and turned her to face him. "Ready to fight?" he said.

Sallah stared at him with wide, green eyes. "Those things?" She pulled her arm away as if he was mad.

Kandler jerked his head toward where the warforged now blocked their way back through the tunnel. "I like those odds better," he said.

As the words left his lips, he glanced about and saw identical squads standing at the end of each of the other tunnels. Their best shot was to try for the closest tunnel, right back the way they came.

The three warriors turned together and charged at the warforged standing in the mouth of the tunnel. The defenders stepped out to meet the intruders.

The titans slowed as they reached the brawl, unable to storm in against the strangers without killing their smaller brethren. Instead they stood hovering over the fight, their arms raised high as they waited for a chance to slam down a killing blow.

"Stop them!" a voice rang out from the stands, piercing through the noise of the battle and the roar of the crowd. "Capture them alive!"

"Follow me!" Kandler screamed as he engaged the first of the guards. Having been ordered not to kill, the warforged held back, and Kandler soon had the best of his foe. A shot from Burch's crossbow took out another.

Just as Kandler saw his way clear to the nearest tunnel entrance—only a single warforged still stood in his way— something that looked like an ornate shield slammed down in front of him. Its edge bit deep into the floor as it sliced down through the hapless warforged before him, cutting it in half.

Kandler looked up and saw that the shield was actually the axe-arm of one of the titans. The monstrous creature shambled in front of the tunnel door as it tore its weapon from where it was embedded in the floor.

A scream came from behind Kandler, and he turned to see the other titan knock Sallah aside with its massive hammer. The blow smashed into her chest and sent her flying back and skittering across the arena floor. Her sword sailed away from her grasp and landed several yards beyond.

Kandler started to run toward the fallen knight, but the other titan's hammer slammed down just behind him. The blow missed him, but it shook the floor hard enough to knock him flying.

The justicar rolled with his momentum, tucked himself into a neat somersault, and sprang to his feet, his sword still at the ready.

"Hey, boss!" Burch said. The shifter stood right next to

the justicar, his loaded crossbow in his hands. "We finally out of luck?"

Kandler shook his head. "Not yet."

"You idiots!" the voice from the stands said, even louder this time. "I said I want them *alive!*"

The rest of the voices in the arena fell silent, and the titans froze, their weapon-arms poised to strike at a moment's notice.

Burch grinned at Kandler and said, "Now that's lucky."

"The problem with luck," Kandler said, "is that you can't count on it."

"Archers!" the voice rang out.

A long rank of warforged stood up from the back rows of the stands, raised their bows, and stretched them toward Kandler and Burch. The justicar glanced back to see that one of the titans had blocked the nearest tunnel exit with its foot. It was a long dash to either of the next-nearest exits.

"Surrender, breathers!" the voice said.

Burch nudged Kandler on the shoulder and pointed toward a blue-painted box in the center of the arena stands opposite the side the justicar had come through. It was large enough to hold a score of spectators, each of whom sat in a large chair. These were stacked in tiers to provide their occupants with a perfect view of the entire arena.

A warforged dressed in a crimson cape with a silver hood stood at the front of the box. His silvery armor plates, burnished to a mirror finish, reflected the light of the dozens of torches distributed throughout the arena. In his hand, he held a golden horn that amplified his voice as he spoke.

"Can you hit him from here?" Kandler asked.

"Maybe," the shifter said, "but not all the archers too."

Kandler looked up at the warforged leader in his private box. It galled him to surrender, but he didn't warm to the thought of certain death either. He thought of Esprë and Xalt where he'd left them standing outside the stadium, and he knew the most important thing he could do was buy them time. If he could convince the warforged to hunt down the changeling too, then all the better.

Kandler shook his head and sheathed his sword, and Burch slung his crossbow across his back. They strode across the arena floor to where Sallah lay on the ground. Blood trickled from her nose, and she looked pale, but her eyes were open.

"I can't breathe," the lady knight gasped with a panicked look on her face. "I think my chest is crushed."

Kandler knelt next to her and put his hand on her chest. It was dented horribly, but something was wrong. He couldn't feel her breathing at all, despite the way she panted. "Maybe," he said, lifting the bottom of her shawl to reveal a shiny silver breastplate beneath. He smiled and said to her, "I thought I told you to leave your armor behind."

"All of it?" Sallah said, trying to laugh.

Kandler reached down to Sallah's side and unbuckled her armor, then nodded at Burch to give him a hand. They sat Sallah up, and her dented breastplate fell away. The lady knight sucked in a large breath of air and held it.

"How's that feel?" asked Kandler. He looked around to see that a score or more of well-armed warforged had surrounded the trio. The creatures stood there with their weapons out and ready but did not say a word.

Sallah reached up to feel her ribs. "Painful," she said, "but I'll live." She glanced at Kandler and Burch, "Thanks."

"Don't thank us," the justicar said. "Thank our host. If he hadn't said something, you'd probably be a smear running down the side of that titan's axe right now."

"That's a bit more gratitude than I think I can muster at the moment," Sallah said, seeing the impassive faces of the warforged pressing in around them.

"Bring them to me!" the voice from the stands said.

Many warforged hands reached down and lifted the intruders to their feet. "Keep working at it," Kandler said to Sallah. "You're about to get your chance."

CHAPTER

50

"You are in the presence of a lieutenant of the Lord of Blades," a warforged courtier said as the guards hauled Kandler, Sallah, and Burch through the indigo curtains that separated the leader's box from the rest of the arena's stands.

The warforged leader turned to get a better look at its guests. He stood taller than the other warforged. His epidermal plates of polished adamantine encased him more like a suit of armor than a skin. Long, polished spikes poked from his arms, shoulders, legs, and knees. A crest of smaller spikes ran up from the center of his back. These fanned out and grew longer as they reached his head, like the plumage of a deadly bird. His eyes seemed made of sapphires.

"Bastard, I presume," Kandler said. He stuck out his hand in greeting, but the warforged ignored it.

The guards standing to either side and behind him moved closer until he lowered his hand again.

"My fame precedes me," Bastard said. "As it should."

He gazed at each of his visitors in turn. Sallah fidgeted under the relentless stare, but she kept her tongue and met the creature's eyes.

"I saw the breastplate, and I'd recognize one of those swords anywhere. What has the Lord of Blades done to deserve this honor?" Bastard said, sarcasm dripping from his voice. "Has the Keeper of the Flame heard of our magnificent city and sent you to curry our favor?" The leader turned his sapphire eyes on Kandler and Burch. "Or has King Boranel finally decided that it is time to pay his regards to the Master of the Mournland?"

Kandler shook his head. This sort of talk made him uneasy. He'd gone to live in Mardakine to get away from such nationalism. He appreciated the irony of doing so in a town built on a mission to restore Cyre, but it was the pursuit of such a hopeless mission that set the town outside normal concerns.

"I don't pay much attention to politics," Kandler said.

Bastard nodded. His shoulders creaked as he did, and a servant was there in a moment to oil his plates as he continued to talk. "So it seems. I would not expect an emissary from one of our neighbors' courts to burst into our arena unannounced before our first meeting."

"We were chasing a criminal," Kandler said. "You saw her—a changeling."

Bastard held up a spiked hand. "That may be so," he said. "We saw the person you followed in here fly away. We already have people hunting for her. Even so, that does not excuse this intrusion."

"We only came here looking—" Sallah started, but she winced and stumbled over her words when she saw Kandler's glare. "We were looking for, um . . ."

"Supplies," the justicar said. "We ran low on food and water. Otherwise, we would have waited outside the city for the changeling to leave. If we had not been in such dire straits, we would not have dared to bother you. We hoped to resupply and leave without your notice."

Bastard nodded at the trio, each in turn. "What happened to you before you came here is of little concern to me. I am charged with maintaining this city until the return of the Lord of Blades. Nothing more."

"I understand," said Kandler.

"Because of this," said Bastard, "I am concerned about the innocents you slew here in the arena before my eyes."

Burch snarled at this. "We were defending ourselves."

"You murdered people for whom I am responsible," the warforged leader said. No emotion leaked into his voice—at least as far as Kandler could tell. "The penalty is clear—immediate execution."

"No!" Sallah said. As she moved forward, the warforged guards to either side of her snatched her arms and held her still. "That's not fair!"

"Fair?" Bastard paused a moment before it spoke. "I care not for your knightly concepts of justice and fairness. The Lord of Blades demands retribution for such transgressions."

Kandler extended his open hand toward Bastard. He saw only one chance here, and he needed the warforged at ease enough for it to work. "I understand your situation, and I think you understand ours. Maybe I have another solution."

Bastard shook his head. "The solution I have is fine."

"I'd like to ask for a trial."

Bastard cocked his silvered head at Kandler. "You are a breather. You have no rights here."

"A trial by combat."

Bastard cocked his head the other way, never taking his eyes from Kandler, then he threw back his head and laughed. It sounded like a hammer tapping an iron mug of mead.

"You have strong metal, breather," Bastard said as he brought his head back down again. "But tell me this. Why would one of us risk his life to give you a chance at freedom?"

"Sport," said Burch. All eyes turned to the shifter, who shuffled his feet a bit when he noticed everyone was watching him. "People are bored here. They want action, need distraction."

"Why would you say that?" Bastard asked, his sapphire eyes narrowing at Burch.

Burch squinted out at the arena all around them. "Training grounds don't have stands."

Bastard stared at the shifter for a long, quiet moment then turned to Kandler. "Who would you like to fight?" he asked. "Do you think you could defeat me?" The warforged leader preened, the dim light reflecting off his polished spikes.

"I'll fight anyone you like," the justicar said. Kandler to suppressed a shudder. He had just opened the door for the warforged to do with him as he liked. He was less concerned about Bastard's mercy, though, than in buying Esprë and Xalt more time.

"Yes, you will," said Bastard. "I have made enough concessions today."

Kandler stood like a stone and waited. Sallah shrugged the warforged hands from her arms. Burch gazed out over the arena, and Kandler followed his eyes. No one had left the place since the prisoners had been taken, and none of the spectators spoke as they waited to learn what would happen.

Bastard picked up the golden horn that stood on a small, handsome table next to his chair. He put it to his mouth and spoke to the crowd, the horn amplifying his voice so that those in the arena could hear his every word.

"The breathers we captured petitioned the Lord of Blades for the right to trial by combat! As his lieutenant, I have decided to grant their request!"

The crowd erupted in cheers.

"Should I be worried that they're so happy about this?" Kandler asked Burch.

Bastard looked back at the justicar then continued to speak into the horn. "If their champion wins this fight, they go free."

The crowd booed.

"If our champion wins, they die."

The cheers returned louder than ever.

Bastard turned to the justicar. "How are you called?"

"Kandler?" said Sallah. "Who said that he would be our champion? It should be me."

The justicar glared at the lady knight. "You're a fine knight," he said, "but I'm a better duelist."

Sallah scoffed at that. Bastard ignored her and said to Kandler, "How many people have you killed in a duel?"

Kandler looked at Burch. "What would you say?"

"I lost count a while back. A score? More?"

"More, I think." Kandler looked at Sallah tenderly. "People find out you're something special, they come looking for you."

"You are the breather champion," Bastard said. "Kandler, is it?"

The justicar nodded, avoiding Sallah's frustrated gaze.

Bastard spoke into the golden horn again. "The breather champion shall be Kandler!"

The crowd booed.

"The warforged champion shall be Gorgan!"

The assembled warforged roared so loud that even Bastard covered his ears.

"Who's that?" Kandler asked. "Gorgan?"

Burch jerked his head at the arena. Kandler watched as one of the titans lumbered out into the middle of the floor and raised both of its weapon-hands in the air, soaking up the audience's cheers.

CHAPTER

51

When Te'oma reached the arena, she knew she'd found the kind of trouble she'd been looking for. As she emerged into the arena, the roar of the crowd nearly stunned her senseless, but she managed to keep her wits about her. She reached out with her mind to her cloak, and with each step across the sawdust-covered floor her wings unfurled further.

By the time the changeling reached the center of the arena, the batlike appendages had her aloft. Before anyone in the arena could do something about it, she was soaring over their heads, the beating of her leathery wings pulling her higher into the sky and over the arena's far wall.

As Te'oma banked down over the roofs of the warforged apartments beyond the arena, her mind wandered back to the day her patron had granted her the privilege of being bonded to her bloodwings. At first, the idea of being bonded—physically, mentally, and permanently—to the fibrous, living creature had repulsed her. She had heard tales of others whose bonding had not gone so well. Symbionts of that sort possessed their own animal intelligence, and sometimes their will proved more powerful than that of their hosts. As a psion, Te'oma had trained her mind to be dominant over all of those around her, but being attached to a symbiont potentially meant fighting that battle every hour of every day for the rest of her life.

Fortunately, Te'oma's bloodwings had been young, fresh, and pliable. They had submitted totally to her will, so much so that they were even willing to shrivel up into little shreds concealed beneath her shirt when she so commanded.

Te'oma hung low over Construct, working her wings hard to move slowly. She had seen archers lining the arena's upper bleachers. If she could stay below their line of sight, she would be unassailable.

As she flew, she reached out with her mind, scanning for the thoughts of the one she hunted—Esprë. She knew the justicar wouldn't have abandoned the girl long before entering the arena to rescue his friends, so she guessed that Esprë was nearby. The shifter and knight had been with him, but not the warforged who had burst into the apartment. That meant this warforged was most likely with Esprë.

Thoughts of all sorts flitted through the changeling's head. Nearly all of them came from nearby warforged who were wondering what was happening in the arena. Te'oma discarded these thoughts as she encountered them. She found them uniformly cold and lifeless. Humans, elves, dwarves, gnomes, and especially the halflings were a jumble of thoughts, emotions, desires, all mingling together like a muddied pool. Warforged were more like a stream—just as many particles perhaps, but all separate and flowing in the same direction. She found their single-mindedness disturbing.

After a few minutes, she risked swinging around closer to the stretch of open area that skirted the arena, and she heard a young girl's mind cry out—*Kandler!*

The changeling smiled. She looked down and saw the warforged with the dirty white tabard standing next to the elf-girl as they leaned against an empty merchant's stand. They gazed up at the arena's wall, allowing Te'oma to glide in silently and land on the next street over. As she willed her wings to return to their cloaklike guise, she pulled out a black-bladed knife and listened, then slipped into the merchant's stand via its rear counter.

"I'm sure your stepfather will be all right," the warforged said to Esprë. "We just need to wait here to find out for sure."

"Can't you take me in to watch?" the girl asked.

The warforged opened his mouth to speak, and Te'oma saw her chance to strike. "Such violent places are no place—"

"What is it, Xalt?" Esprë asked. "What—?" She cut herself off as the warforged turned and she saw the black knife in his back.

Te'oma leaped over the merchant's counter and kicked the warforged in the face. He turned, fell flat on his face, and did not move again.

Esprë screamed and whirled to run, but Te'oma was quicker. She reached out and grabbed the girl by her arm. Shrieking, Esprë slapped and clawed and punched. Te'oma caught her other arm and shook her.

"Stop that! Stop it, Esprë! You *know* it has to be this way!"

"You killed him! You killed—!"

"No!" Te'oma gave the girl a good, hard shake. "No, Esprë!"

The fight went out of the girl. She sagged to her knees and burst into tears.

"I just took the fight out of him," Te'oma said. "He'll live. Killing a warforged isn't that easy."

"H-he's not dead?"

Keeping a tight hold on the girl, Te'oma turned to look at the warforged. He wasn't breathing, but that meant nothing. Warforged didn't breathe.

"The knife was just to get his attention," she said, though she had no idea if it was true. It didn't matter, as long as the girl believed it. "I needed him shocked long enough to knock him senseless. He may . . . leak a little, but he'll be fine."

"Where's Kandler?" Esprë asked.

Te'oma smiled as she pulled the knife from the warforged and slipped it back into its sheath. She put an arm around the girl. "Still in the arena," she said. "I expect he'll be dead soon, along with the others.

Esprë tried to break away from Te'oma. The changeling grabbed her by the arm and pulled the girl back in. "I have to help him!" Esprë said.

Te'oma shook her head. "You'll just get yourself killed!"

Esprë glared at the changeling. "What do you plan to do with me now?" she asked.

"We need to find a way off this city," the changeling said. "But that's not enough." She started walking, the girl in tow. "I'm not carrying you all the way to Karrnath. We'll need horses, food, and—" Te'oma stopped in her tracks and stared out toward the horizon. "I'd wondered what had happened to that."

Esprë squinted in the direction of the changeling's line of sight. "Is that the sun breaking through there?" the girl asked.

"The sun never shines in the Mournland," the changeling said with a grin, but then she remembered the light that had cascaded over that old elf wizard's tower. "Almost never anyhow. That's the ring of fire around an airship, and it's coming this way."

Te'oma looked back over her shoulder at the arena. "Yes," she said as she pulled the girl along toward the towering wall. "This might be something worth sticking around for."

CHAPTER

52

Kandler took Sallah's sword in his hand. Silver fire danced along its edges. The flames were weaker and dimmer here in the Mournland compared to bright holy fire he'd seen on display in Mardakine. Whatever foul magics infected the Mournland, even the knights' blades were not immune.

"Take good care of it," Sallah said. "It is sacred."

"I just care if it's sharp," the justicar said as he swung the sword about, testing its balance. He sighted down its edge, looking for any imperfections. "Do you think there's any chance that thing's afraid of fire?"

Burch's words still echoed in Kandler's head—"Wouldn't bet your life on it."

The justicar twisted his head from side to side, cracking his neck and loosening his shoulders as he walked toward the wide black circle painted in the center of the arena's floor. The titan named Gorgan lumbered forth and took its place just within the bounds of the circle, opposite from Kandler's position.

The gigantic creature slammed the arena floor with its weapons, and Kandler had to struggle to keep his feet. In response, the justicar leaped into the air and pounded the ground with Sallah's sword. The warforged in the stands laughed.

"And now," Bastard's voice said through its golden horn, "let the deathmatch begin!"

Kandler stood his ground and raised his sword at the massive creature. Gorgan dragged the blade of its axe-hand across the front of its hammer-hand, sending sparks flying toward the justicar, then the creature threw its arms in the air and rasped out an ear-shattering howl that sounded like a hundred swords being forced against a massive grindstone.

Kandler turned and ran. There was no way he could hope to stand toe to toe with such a creature, and he wasn't about to try. He just needed a bit of time to execute his plan.

The crowd laughed harder than ever. Gorgan stood stunned for a moment, unsure what to do.

Bastard's voice rang out across the arena. "Run the breather down, Gorgan," he said, "then kill it!"

The crowd roared its approval.

Kandler slowed to a trot when he reached the far end of the arena, and the titan started toward him, pounding its hammer rhythmically on the ground as it moved, like an old man leaning on a walking stick. The massive creature covered the ground fast, and Kandler found himself staring up at Gorgan as it bore down on him.

The justicar waved the blazing sword around him like a flag. Weak as the silver flames were, they still shone like a beacon in the dim light of the Mournland. He hoped that this might work like waving a red cape in front of a bull, but he was more concerned about the display he was making than how it affected the titan.

Kandler bounced his head along with the beat of the titan's gait as it charged toward him, the floor shaking with every step. Gorgan raised both of its massive weapon-hands high above its head to smash or slash Kandler to pieces with a single overwhelming attack. As it did, the justicar dashed straight at the titan.

Matching the creature's rhythm in his head, Kandler sprinted toward the creature and dove between its legs. Gorgan stumbled and almost tripped over itself as it struggled to compensate for the justicar's unexpected move. It managed to right itself at the last instant, but by the time it turned around to look for Kandler, he was halfway across the arena again.

The titan charged after Kandler, a low growl building in its barrel-sized throat. This time, the justicar ran over toward Bastard's box and stood before the stands. The crowd booed as the justicar waved his blade at the titan again, goading it toward him faster.

As Gorgan neared, Kandler faked left and then ran right. The titan fell for the feint. When it tried to correct its momentum, it went to its knees right in front of the platform. As it raised its head, it found itself eye to eye with Bastard. The creature was close enough that Bastard eschewed his golden horn as it shouted, "He's making a fool of you, Gorgan! Take your time. Kill him at your leisure."

The titan pulled itself to its feet. Already at the end of the arena, Kandler looked out past the creature as it stood, and he smiled. Panting just a bit from the exertion, he wiped the sweat from his brow. So far, his plan had gone well enough. He just wished he knew what might happen if it worked.

"One more time," Kandler said to himself.

Gorgan lumbered across the arena floor this time, keeping its eyes on Kandler every second. As it neared, the justicar feinted to the left and right, but the giant warforged kept up with him, not giving him a chance to run past. Gorgan waited for the right moment, then struck. Its axe-hand came down with a terrible crash. Kandler managed to sidestep the blow, but the impact knocked him from his feet.

The titan followed up the axe strike with a swing of its hammer-hand. Kandler didn't see a way to outrace it, so he dove next to the creature's axe-hand, which was still where it had landed on the arena floor.

The titan's hammer came down atop its axe. The blow drove the sharp edge of the axe further into the floor, and the axe-blade kept the hammer from smashing Kandler to a pulp.

The justicar scrambled to the other side of the titan's axe. Gorgan tried to raise its axe-hand again so it could attack, but it was stuck.

Kandler lashed out at the titan with his borrowed blade. It bit deep into the creature's arm, and the titan howled with rage. The flames from the sword's edge, meager as they were, caught in the fibrous parts of the titan's axe-arm, and soon the entire limb was ablaze.

Gorgan's hammer-hand fell again. Kandler had hoped it would be impossible for the creature to angle its strike accurately over its stuck arm, but the blow crushed a hole in the arena floor, and the shockwave knocked Kandler to the ground. As the justicar struggled to regain his feet, Gorgan reached back with a leg and kicked Kandler squarely in the chest.

Kandler flew backward, Sallah's sword spinning from his grasp. Spots swam before his eyes, and he fought to refill his lungs with air. One thought struck him—this was not how he wanted to die.

The titan stomped at Kandler again, but the creature's kick had shoved the justicar out of its reach. It rasped with anger at its trapped arm.

Still gasping for air, Kandler scrambled away from the creature and after Sallah's sword. He hefted the blade in his hand. At the moment, the borrowed sword seemed like the best friend he'd ever had.

Kandler turned back to the titan and scanned for a weak joint, some sort of vulnerability he could exploit. He'd seen one of these things on the field of battle before, in a vicious skirmish between Breland and Aundair. That titan had routed an entire platoon of Breland's finest soldiers. When the retreat was finally sounded, Kandler had hoped he would never see such a beast again—especially not this close.

With a spray of splinters and sparks, Gorgan smashed its hammer-hand down into its axe-arm over and over until the limb shattered and it was able to pull the splintered stump free.

Kandler staggered back from the maddened creature, a grin splitting his face as he saw the fiery ring of the airship soaring down out of the sky. His attempt to signal Deothen had worked. The ship was coming in fast.

The justicar sheathed Sallah's sword and ran along the inside wall of the arena, his chest protesting at the way his lungs stretched against the inside of it. His charge took him straight toward the approaching airship.

Kandler's heart leaped as he spied a full set of mooring lines dragging down from the ship—two at her bow and two at her stern. He looked for the rope ladder as well. It was there, but it only hung down half as far as the other lengths of rope. At the angle the airship was coming in, he would never be able to reach it.

Kandler stood at the end of the arena and waved to make sure the pilot saw him. As he looked up, he thought he saw Brendis at the wheel with Deothen leaning out on the bowsprit and shouting orders, but the craft was moving too fast for him to be sure.

As the airship swooped in over the arena, Kandler sprinted back toward the other end where Gorgan stood stunned, watching the airship come in at it. The crackling flames of the airship's elemental roared overhead, echoing off the arena's interior walls and painting everything in an angry orange light.

The warforged in the stands roared. Two of the ballistae squads mounted along the edges of the moving city fired their giant bolts at the incoming ship. One missed, but the other slammed into where Majeeda's spell had exploded against the bow, and it smashed through the planks of the hull and disappeared.

The airship kept soaring along without pause. As she zoomed over his head, Kandler reached up and grabbed one of the mooring lines. After a few steps, he leaped into the air and began climbing the line.

"Stop it!" Bastard shouted through its golden horn. "Stop that ship!"

Gorgan roared with anger and shoved his hammer-arm into the air as the airship buzzed overhead. Kandler grinned when he saw that the ship was too high up for the creature to reach, then his face fell as he realized what the creature was trying to do.

"No!" Kandler shouted to Brendis high above him, although he knew it would be impossible for the young knight to hear his plea. "Pull up! Pull up!"

As the justicar yelled, the ship pulled him farther into the air, and for a moment he allowed himself to hope that the airship might make it.

Gorgan reached up with his splintered arm and stabbed it at the rope ladder as it went by. The ladder's strands caught in the titan's shattered arm and held. As the airship sailed past, Gorgan brought his arm down and pulled.

The airship swung about like a toy boat on a ten-ton anchor. Deothen disappeared from his position on the bow. Kandler winced at the thought of what might have happened to the knight, and he hoped that Brendis had been smart enough to strap himself in behind the wheel.

As the airship spun around, Kandler found himself whipped in the opposite direction and flung into the air. The rope burned his hands as it slipped from his grasp, and he went skipping across the arena floor like a flat stone on a smooth lake.

CHAPTER

53

"Full speed, my son!" Kandler heard Deothen shout. The ring of fire around the airship roared as if the elemental inside it were screaming in protest.

Gorgan dug in its heels, but the airship dragged it along at a snail's pace. It was only a matter of time until something gave. Kandler staggered to his feet and glanced around the arena. All eyes were glued to the conflict between the titan and the airship.

The ship pitched wildly under the strain as if it was a wild horse bucking to break free. Kandler spotted Deothen as the knight tried to make his way along the railing to cut the rope ladder loose, but it was all he could do to avoid being hurled from the ship's deck.

Gorgan lashed out with its hammer-arm, and the weapon smashed right through the arena floor behind it, staking the creature solidly to that surface. The rope bridge snarled in the fragments of its other arm stretched under the extra strain but did not snap. The tension between the ship and her new anchor point lifted the titan off its feet for a moment, but the airship then slipped and dropped Gorgan back to the arena floor with a thunderous boom.

Kandler reeled about to see the other titan bearing down on him from the corner of the arena in which it had sat out the start of the fight. The justicar dashed to the right and dove across the floor at the last moment. He turned as he slid away from the gigantic warforged and saw that the creature had not been chasing him after all.

Instead, the titan reached out and wrapped its axe-arm around one of the mooring lines dangling from the stern of the ship. Once it had a semblance of a grip, it spun, winding the rope around it and winching the ship closer to the ground.

"No," Kandler whispered in horror. If the airship had half a chance to get away from a single titan, that had just slipped away. The entire ship creaked and groaned as she struggled to escape, but the titans anchored the airship as solidly as blocks of granite.

Kandler spotted Deothen making his way back toward the bridge, moving along the ship's railing hand over hand. "Haul back!" the knight commander ordered the young knight at the wheel. "You'll tear the ship apart!"

The airship stopped pulling away so hard, and the two titans fell over onto their backs at the loss of opposition.

"Archers!" Bastard's amplified voice said. "Loose!"

The Mournland sky darkened with arrows as the archers along the top rows of the stadium loosed their bows at the airship. Most of the missiles stuck in the ship's hull. Only a few made it over the railing and onto the pitching deck. None of them found either of the knights.

"Again!" Bastard yelled. "Again! Again!"

Kandler finally saw his chance. Focusing on the mooring line wrapped around the unharmed titan, he drew Sallah's sword and dashed toward the rope, the blade bursting into flames as he ran. But before he could reach his goal, the titan lashed out with its axe-arm and swept the justicar aside.

The flat of the blade smacked Kandler back off his feet and then passed over him. As he scrambled to right himself, he looked up and saw the titan's axe poised above him, ready to cleave him in two. He kicked into a backward dive, and the massive wedge came crushing down only inches from his feet.

"Hold!" Bastard said through its horn. The order reverberated throughout the arena. Every warforged in the arena froze. This included the titans, who ceased trying to haul the airship in closer so they could crush it to splinters.

The airship continued to pull back and forth against the rope ladder and the mooring line that held it fast, jerking about like a fish with a hook in its mouth.

"You, in the airship, stop fighting!" Bastard said. "I have a proposal for you!"

Deothen's arm waved out over the railing he'd fallen behind, and Brendis let the airship come to a rest. She still strained against her bonds, but not so desperately.

Kandler saw the gray-haired knight lean out over the railing nearest to Bastard. He thought he saw blood leaking from the man's nose.

"Speak!" Deothen said as he peered down over the airship's railing. "And be fast about it. I have little patience for tyrants."

On the arena floor below, Kandler edged his way closer to the mooring line he'd targeted before, working his way around so that he was out of the tangled titan's field of view. When he was close enough to strike, he held back and waited for Bastard's gambit to play out.

"I admire your airship," Bastard said. "We could use such a device. I fear that in trying to capture her—and you—we will destroy her."

Deothen clambered his way up to the bridge as the warforged leader spoke. When he reached the narrow stairs, he turned around to reply. "That is a risk you shall have to endure."

Bastard laughed into the horn. "I propose this—If you agree to land your airship here and surrender her to me, I will let you and your people go."

Deothen climbed up the ladder and stood next to Brendis. "Ha!" he said. "So we can die of thirst trying to cross the Mournland?"

Bastard shook his head. "We have food and water. I can even give you horses."

Deothen narrowed his eyes. "I do not negotiate with those who bear evil in their souls. This society—this gang of abominations—you have created here is anathema to me. Had I an army behind me, I would bring your city crashing to the ground and grind you and your fellows to dust."

The warforged in the crowd gasped. Kandler winced at the knight's words. It was just that sort of pervasive attitude that had kept the Last War raging for so long and which threatened to spark it up again. All eyes turned to Bastard.

Kandler readjusted his grip on the sword. He eyed the line carefully. It would take only a single blow to sever it, he hoped. Maybe two. He was sure he wouldn't get the chance to try three.

The warforged leader raised the golden horn to his face again and spoke. "I will not repeat my offer. If you do not accept it, my titans will drag you down to your death. We will hang your remains from the front of our city as a warning to all who would impede our progress. Willingly or not, you will lend us aid."

"You have your answer, fiend," Deothen yelled. "No quarter asked and none given!"

Kandler readied his sword for his swing, then Bastard did something that surprised him. The warforged leader beckoned for the guards to bring Sallah to join him at the front of the leader's box.

"In that spirit," the warforged leader said, "allow me to demonstrate how we treat intruders in our city." He reached out and traced a line along Sallah's jaw with a metallic finger. "Those who come with nothing to trade but their lives."

Kandler's heartbeat pounded in his ears. He realized his hands were sweating, and it wasn't because of the heat from Sallah's sword.

Deothen shouted to the lady knight. "The Silver Flame will embrace you, my daughter. You have been a brave and valiant knight, and it will merge your light with its own."

Bastard drew a massive sword from beside his chair and held it to Sallah's throat. He drew its edge across her porcelain skin until the point rested in the hollow of her neck. Her blood ran red along the length of the blade. She did not make a sound nor shed a tear.

"Would you sacrifice your own child so easily?" the war-forged leader said.

Kandler's face grew ashen. "That's not his daughter!" he shouted. The words surprised him as they leaped from his lips. He grimaced at drawing attention to himself, but he pressed on. "He calls everyone that!"

Bastard looked down at the justicar. "He calls you 'daughter?' " he asked without a trace of irony.

"No!" Kandler said, "He says 'my son' or 'my daughter.' "

"And are you his son?"

Kandler looked up at the bridge of the airship and saw Deothen whispering something to Brendis as he wrapped his hands in a set of the leather straps along the rear rail. "No!"

"So you are not his daughter?" Bastard asked Sallah. As he spoke, he pressed the end of his sword into her throat. The lady knight pressed her lips together until they were white, and she shook her head.

"Do not deny me now, my daughter!" Deothen said. "I want this creature to know who is killing him and why!"

Bastard threw back its head and rasped out a laugh. "You see," he said, pressing his blade against the lady knight's neck again, "I am right."

Kandler shook his head in confusion. This was one thing he'd never suspected.

"Father!" Sallah said. "No!"

"Now!" Deothen shouted at Brendis. "Full speed ahead!"

The airship lurched forward—straight at Bastard's box.

CHAPTER

54

Bastard dropped its sword, and the guards holding Sallah and Burch let their prisoners go and dove for their lives. The airship sped forward, her hull looming larger than a moon before the people on the box's platform. Burch glanced around, desperate for any way to escape.

"Stop!" Bastard said through his golden horn.

The two titans hauled back on the airship's rope ladder and mooring line, and the craft came to a shuddering halt. Deothen pitched forward off the bridge and went skittering along the deck until he came to a stop at the railing across the bow. Still anchored by the two titans, the side of the ship bounced off the arena floor shy of its mark, the ring of fire causing the wooden panels to burst into flames.

"More power!" the senior knight shouted as he scrambled to his feet.

The ship rose back into the air as she strained upward and forward, and Deothen reached out over the railing as if he wished for nothing more than to strangle the gloating warforged below with his bare hands.

Burch took advantage of the distraction to scoop up Kandler's blade where it lay near his feet and vault down onto the arena floor. He turned and beckoned Sallah to follow, but Bastard reached out and snagged the lady knight by her sleeve.

Burch was about to race back into the private box when he heard a roar from behind. He looked back to see Kandler raising the blazing blade he'd borrowed high over his head in a two-handed grip as he dashed the few steps toward the mooring line. The titan next to the justicar spotted him coming and smashed at him with its hammer-hand, but it miscalculated Kandler's intent and the blow went wide.

The vibration in the floor from the falling hammer might have caused Kandler to stumble, but he leaped into the air before the shockwave hit him. Stretched as far as he could go, the justicar slashed down at the mooring line with every ounce of strength in his arms.

The long rope snapped. The titan holding on to the loose end tumbled backward to the hole its hammer blow had just made. It tried to stop its fall, but its hammer-limb disappeared into the hole. There was a terrible crunching sound as the arm was twisted around under the moving city in a direction it was never meant to go.

The mayhem in the stands drowned out that noise. The weight of the titan no longer pulling it back, the airship darted forward and crashed into the stands like a meteor falling from the sky. As the ship came careening in, Sallah tore her arm away from Bastard, leaving him holding an empty sleeve of her shirt. Free from the warforged leader's grasp, she dove out of the box and toward the arena floor.

The airship's bowsprit lanced into Bastard's reserved seats, and Deothen hurtled over the railing. He landed amidst the wreckage of the box. Only his armor saved him from being impaled on the collection of jagged boards on which he landed.

The titan still attached to the rope ladder sailed along after the ship, yanked off its feet by the sudden change in momentum. It crashed into and through the bottom of the airship's hold, its top half wedged in the hole it made. Its legs landed in the airship's ring of fire and were incinerated.

The airship's restraining arches held, although they creaked with the effort. The lower arch broke through the arena floor like a plow cutting through a field. The stands beneath the airship burst into flames as the ring worked to reestablish its natural shape by turning everything in its path to ash. Burch grabbed Sallah's arm and dragged her away from the fiery ring.

The warforged in the stands trampled over each other as they tried to escape the disaster. Some near the top opted to leap over the exterior wall to the platforms far below rather than brave the flames or the stampedes. Some of these crashed through the platforms to the earth moving beneath.

"Hey!" Kandler said, as he dashed up behind Burch and Sallah. "I think you have something of mine." He held up Sallah's sword.

Burch handed Kandler's blade to him, and the justicar returned the sacred sword to Sallah.

"That's a fine blade," the justicar said.

An amplified voice called out from the burning wreckage of the stands. "To me, my people!" It was Bastard. "Kill the intruders! Save me! Save—! No!"

The voice stopped, and Burch led Sallah and Kandler around perimeter of the ring of fire to where they could peer through the smoke engulfing the stands. As they watched, two silvery forms came flashing out of Bastard's private box, their polished surfaces glinting in the angry light of the airship's blazing ring.

"Father!" Sallah screamed.

Deothen landed atop Bastard and pounded the creature's face with the pommel of his sacred sword. The warforged leader snarled and shoved the senior knight off his body.

"Look!" Burch said, pointing at Bastard. "It's stuck." The spikes on the creature's back had pierced the floor onto which the creature had fallen, pinning it there.

As Bastard struggled to break loose, Deothen circled the creature, looking for the perfect opening for his sword. Before he could strike, the warforged twisted its body free. The action wrenched a large part of the flooring behind it away, and it fell through the hole it created.

"You'll not evade me so easily!" Deothen shouted as he leaped through the hole, following Bastard down into the nether region beneath the city's moving platforms.

"No!" Sallah shouted as she watched her father disappear. Before she could race across the arena floor to join him. Burch grabbed her by the shoulder.

"We have a bigger problem," the shifter said.

Sallah turned to see what Burch was talking about. Before her, the titan with a remnant of the airship's mooring line still wrapped about it tore free from its mangled hammer-arm and climbed to its feet.

Burch leaned over to Kandler and said, "What do you suggest we do about that?"

"Only one thing seems to have worked so far," the justicar said, grabbing Sallah and Burch by their arms and shoving them before him. "Run!"

The three raced off across the arena floor. They avoided the hole through which Deothen and Bastard had disappeared and gave the burning section of the stands a wide berth.

When the trio reached the far end of the arena, they looked back to see that the one-armed titan was still lumbering after them. "It's following Bastard's last orders," Sallah said. "It'll run us down until we die or it's destroyed."

"See that?" Burch said. He pointed to one of the ballistae mounted on the low walls on each corner of the arena. The crew that had been stationed at it had abandoned it when the fire began. The weapon stood loaded and ready, pointed outward as part of the city's defenses against invaders. It looked very much like a giant-sized version of Burch's beloved crossbow.

"Bet it turns this way too," the shifter said.

"Get up there," Kandler said to Burch. "I'll keep this moving mountain of armor busy."

Burch slapped the justicar on the back and then raced away, looking for a way to get on top of the wall.

CHAPTER

55

The one-armed titan stomped up to Kandler and Sallah and raised its axe high. The two scrambled away in opposite directions. For a moment, the towering warforged hesitated, unsure which of the pair to attack first, then it swung down at the justicar.

Kandler realized he wasn't going to be able to run away fast enough. Wedged in the corner of the arena as he was, there just wasn't enough room. Instead, he charged the warforged, and the creature's blow smashed down over his head. The swing came close enough that he could feel it brush against his hair, but Kandler rolled forward unharmed.

As the titan's axe landed, Sallah spun around and slashed at the back of its legs with her burning blade. The creature rasped in pain and kicked out to shove the lady knight away. Its foot caught Sallah in the hip and knocked her to the ground. Her sword spun out of her grasp.

Kandler fought the urge to run to her side, knowing that it would only doom them both. His best option was to press the attack, although it was nearly impossible to find a chink the titan's armor.

The titan turned its attention to the lady knight as she

scrambled across the arena floor, reaching for her weapon. As it spun about, Kandler saw a slim chance. It was the only one that had presented itself so far, so he took it. He sheathed his sword and leaped upon the titan, finding a handhold on the many spikes sticking out of the creature's back. He pulled himself up on them, crawling up the titan's metal carapace, scratching himself on the sharp-tipped spikes, until he came to the creature's neck.

The titan drew back its axe-arm to level a blow at Sallah. As it did, Kandler drew his sword, held it high, and threw all of his weight into driving his sword into the back of the creature's neck. The blade jarred in his hands only a few inches into the creature's exposed fibers. Panic shot through Kandler's mind, and pain lanced through his shoulders. He growled and shoved at the blade again. It slid to the left, making its way around whatever iron bands the creature used for a spine.

The monstrous warforged tried to reach back with its missing arm but ended up flailing the shattered stump at Kandler instead. The justicar screwed his sword back and forth in the hole he'd made, sawing through the thick, raw fibers beneath the titan's armor. Dark fluid spurted up from the wound and spattered across Kandler's arms and chest. The quantity surprised him, as did the fact that the crimson liquid was hot.

The titan swung at Kandler with its axe, but its blow glanced off its own armored head instead. The resultant clang set the justicar's ears ringing, but he kept at his horrible task, churning his sword in and out of the creature's savaged neck.

Infuriated, the titan threw itself backward on the arena floor in an effort to crush the justicar with its bulk. Kandler felt the creature start to topple and leaped free, barely clearing the creature's massive body. The spikes on the titan's back and shoulders tore at the justicar, slashing his flesh. Kandler cried out in shock and pain.

The impact on the arena floor knocked the wind from Kandler, and he lay there on his chest for a moment. He hadn't the strength to get back on his feet, and the titan's fall had trapped the justicar in the same corner again. As he heard the titan start to rouse, he willed himself to move.

Kandler rose to his knees and turned. The titan rolled off its back like a gigantic bear. It growled and threw itself back onto its knees where it could raise its axe-hand over its head. It aimed another blow at Kandler, but before it could slam down its weapon, flames erupted along its back.

"Get off him, you monster!" Kandler heard Sallah shout from the creature's other side. The smell of burning fibers filled the air.

Still on its knees, the titan whirled about. The move wrenched Sallah's sword from her fingers but left the blade embedded in the titan's back, its flames devouring the creature from within.

Kandler dashed around in front of the titan as it climbed to its feet. He grabbed Sallah by the arm and led her across the arena floor in a dead sprint.

The titan leaped into the air after the retreating duo and came down hard on all three remaining limbs. The floor beneath Kandler and Sallah bucked like a wave, throwing them from their feet. The titan was on them in an instant. It smashed down at Kandler with the stump left over from the ruin of its hammer-arm and pinned his leg to the ground. Sallah pulled on Kandler's arm, striving to drag him free, but it was like trying to drag an anvil chained to an anchor. There was no escape.

The titan lined up its axe-hand over Kandler's head, like a butcher measuring a cut of meat. The creature raised its arm to deliver the killing blow—

A bolt the size of a lance slammed into the back of the titan's arm, and the axe-hand went spinning into the air. It landed inches from Kandler's face, embedding itself a full foot into the floor.

The titan screeched in frustration. Still pinning Kandler to the floor, it turned its head about to see who had dealt it such a telling blow. Kandler looked over too and saw Burch grinning from behind a ballista as the shifter rushed to reload the device.

The titan swept Kandler and Sallah away with the stump of its hammer-arm. Tangled in each other's limbs, the pair spun across the arena floor, toward the airship still resting in the stands.

The justicar saw the ring of fire rushing at them, and he flung himself between Sallah and the fire. When they spun to a halt, Sallah was clear of the blaze consuming the floor of the arena, but Kandler found himself lying in the flames.

The lady knight pulled Kandler from the edge of the fire, his clothes already burning. She wrapped her arms around him in an attempt to smother the flames, then rolled them around on the sawdust-coated floor until the tongues of flame licking at Kandler vanished.

When the flames were out, Kandler lay on the floor on his face with Sallah lying on top of him. His skin was flushed from the fire, and his eyes were squeezed closed tight.

"Kandler!" he heard her call. "Kandler!"

The justicar peeled open his eyes and looked up at the lady knight. He started to smile at her but coughed instead. "Thanks," he said between hacks. Then where he was and what was happening struck him. He pushed free of Sallah and said, "Burch."

The pair looked back in the direction from which they'd come. The titan had swung out wide so it could get a running start at the shifter, who was still reloading the ballista. He'd gotten the bow winched back and was lifting a bolt into place as the titan lowered its head and charged.

"Burch!" Kandler yelled, his clothes still smoking, as Sallah helped him to his feet.

The shifter slammed the bolt home and brought the weapon about to bear on the titan's new position. Without its arms, the creature couldn't reach up to tear Burch from the wall on which the ballista was perched. Barreling along at its top speed, it seemed determined to bring down the whole wall instead.

Kandler's breath caught in his chest as he watched Burch sight down the bolt's path and point the weapon to where the titan would be in an instant. The justicar didn't see how the shifter had any time left to fire, but Burch calmly waited for the creature's head to fall within his sights and then pulled the ballista's firing lever.

The bow-wire snapped forward, hurling the bolt straight at the titan's head. It slammed into the creature's face and came splintering out the back of its armor-plated skull. Kandler and Sallah cheered, but their joy didn't last long.

The titan's headless form lost little of its forward momentum. It slammed into the wall beneath Burch's position and tore through it like paper. The massive weapon and its shifter handler went down atop the titan's corpse and disappeared in a crush of wood and steel fragments.

CHAPTER

56

W hat's happening?" Esprë said, panic sharpening her voice. "I can't see Kandler!"

"I can't tell," said Te'oma.

The changeling tried to peer through the smoke, but it was too thick. From their vantage point at the top of the stands looking down over Bastard's damaged box, all she could see was the airship, her ring of fire crackling merrily away as it consumed its surroundings. Deothen and Bastard had disappeared over the other side of the ship, and Kandler, Burch, and Sallah had lured the last titan over that way too. The sounds of battle filled the air, but it was impossible to know who was winning the fight.

The airship still stuck out of the stands, the splintered boards of the seats cradling it like an errant child, keeping it from toppling over backward. The bottom of the hull had been bashed in at several spots, but the fires from the blazing floor seemed to leave it untouched.

The changeling looked back at the child. Esprë was being terribly calm, and Te'oma found it unsettling. She peered into the girl's thoughts and read her murderous intent. The changeling realized she was lucky to still be alive.

"Look," Esprë said to the changeling. "You'd think the ship would be burning too."

"The hull must be treated against fire," Te'oma said. "How else would you keep the ring of fire from destroying it?"

"I wonder if Brendis is all right," Esprë said quietly.

The smoke surrounding the bridge was impenetrable. Te'oma gazed out at the ship. She'd hoped to somehow commandeer the thing and escape. Esprë, she knew, was thinking the same thing.

The ship seemed like she might be a lost cause now, but Te'oma still couldn't tear herself away. The idea of hiking to Karrnath on foot held no appeal for her. The changeling stared down at the ship a moment longer and then turned to Esprë and said, "Let's go find out."

The changeling and Esprë picked their way down through the stands until they reached Bastard's box seats. The entire structure had been knocked askew. Parts of it were destroyed, and flames rising from the floor licked the front parts of the box's platform. The warforged who had fled from the fire seemed to be in no hurry to come back. With an enraged titan on the loose amid it all, Te'oma understood why. If it hadn't been for the airship still there, the changeling would have knocked out Esprë and raced off in the other direction.

"There he is!" Esprë said. She pointed up at the bridge, and Te'oma's eyes darted after.

The ship stuck in the stands at an angle. Brendis stood slumped over the wheel on the bridge. The leather strap lashed around his waist kept him from pitching forward into the flames, but the smoke swirling around him was nearly as deadly, the changeling knew. The young knight might already be dead.

"Let's go see if we can help him," Te'oma said. She gathered Esprë into her arms and started down toward the remnants of the airship.

When they reached the point where the ship met the stands, Te'oma stopped and surveyed the damage. She took two steps back and raced forward down through the wreckage of Bastard's box to make a running leap across the splintered boards. Esprë screamed as they left the stands.

Te'oma landed on the tilted deck of the airship and rolled forward on her shoulder with Esprë still in her arms. When they came to a halt, Esprë stopped screaming. The girl flushed, embarrassed with herself for showing fear. They began sliding toward the bow, and she started up again.

The changeling wrapped one arm around the girl even tighter and reached out with her free hand, scrabbling at the deck's surface, trying for a grip but finding nothing. Te'oma rolled over on top of the girl to protect her, and the two slid into the railing at the bow. The changeling shrugged off the impact but the flames licking through the railing's wooden bars scorched her skin. As Te'oma shouted in pain, Esprë stopped screaming again.

The changeling reached over to her left, and made her way along the railing until she could climb the bars like a ladder. She made good time this way, even with the girl in her arms, and the pair soon clambered onto the airship's bridge. The smoke up there wasn't as thick as Te'oma had feared.

"Brendis?" Esprë said as she climbed over to the wheel, a tremor in her voice. Te'oma watched the girl to see what would happen. The young knight didn't respond. The lower half of his face was covered with blood.

Te'oma reached over to examine Brendis. "He's alive," she said. Esprë sighed with relief. "His nose is broken. They always bleed like that."

The changeling removed the leather belt that lashed Brendis to the wheel and lowered the knight's limp form into the angle next to Esprë. She coughed on the smoke curling up into the bridge, and said, "We need to move this ship."

The changeling grabbed a hold of the wheel and tried to turn it, but it didn't move. "How does it work?" she asked.

The girl reached for the wheel and said, "Allow me."

Esprë closed her eyes for a moment, and the ship shuddered. The movement startled her, and her eyes flung open wide. Their rims reddened by the smoke, they looked bluer than ever to Te'oma.

The rear of the airship pulled free of the arena floor, but the front remained lodged in the stands. The ship pitched forward, and Te'oma tumbled against the bridge's console. Brendis's limp form slid toward the edge, and the changeling reached out and grabbed him before he pitched over it.

"Stop!" she shouted until the girl brought the ship's stern back down again.

"We have to pull back first," Te'oma said.

Esprë nodded as she strapped herself to the wheel. "What about Brendis?" she said.

The changeling shoved the young man over and lodged him under the wheel. "Sit on him if you like."

The girl narrowed her eyes at Te'oma for a moment then grabbed the wheel and pushed her feet under the knight's body to keep him tight against the console. When she was ready, the ship started to move again.

Esprë coaxed the airship down and back. The craft slid back a few feet and then caught on something. The ship slid from side to side and then back and forth, trying to work around the catch, but it did no good.

Te'oma watched the girl concentrate harder. She ignored the fire, the man at her feet, and her kidnapper and put her every thought into pulling the ship free. The airship slid back a few more feet and then caught again before starting to shudder like the branches of a tree in a stiff wind.

A massive hammer-arm smashed up through the hatchway from the hold, sending splinters everywhere. Te'oma nearly jumped off the ship. Esprë screamed, and her hands came off the wheel. The ship crashed back to the arena floor, and the titan's hand disappeared.

Te'oma thought the girl would melt to the deck in an utter panic, but instead Esprë displayed a steely resolve. "Too much," she heard the girl mutter to herself. "We've been through too much!"

Esprë grabbed the wheel again, and the airship launched forward into the stands as if it might try to tunnel its way to freedom. A loud crash echoed from the front of the hold. Then the ship switched directions and pulled out of the stands just as hard. With a spectacular splintering of the broken boards surrounding the ship's bow, the airship slid backward without a hitch.

Te'oma smiled as the airship rose into the air. Her good mood was smashed flat as a bug under her boot when the weight in the ship shifted again, and the bow flipped up into the air. Before Esprë could scream this time, the hammer-fist stabbed through the hatchway again.

The hatch was too narrow for the titan to fit more than its arm though. The massive hammer-hand flailed about at random for a moment, hunting blindly for a foe, then it disappeared back through the hatch again.

Te'oma peered over the bridge's console to look down the hatch. As she did, one of the titan's turquoise eyes slammed against the inside of the portal. It withdrew just as quickly.

Te'oma glanced back at Esprë, who had turned white, despite her newfound resolve. Before the changeling could say a word, the hammer-hand stabbed up through the hatchway again. This time, it was aimed toward the bridge. It slammed into the outside of the console, and Te'oma dove aside as Esprë let out a little squeak.

When the changeling looked back, the girl's color had returned. She watched as the girl stuck out her jaw, turned to her, and said, "Hold on."

Te'oma slipped her hands through a set of straps on the bridge's rear railing just in time. Esprë didn't wait for her as she drove the airship forward again at a startling speed, heading straight for the arena's stands again.

At the last moment, Esprë brought the airship to a wrenching halt. The change in momentum nearly pulled Te'oma from her straps. As she prayed to Vol that the battered leather would hold, she heard the titan in the hold let loose a final screech of fury and frustration and felt it slide helplessly toward the hole in the bow through which it had entered the hold. The ship tilted forward steeply as the massive creature slipped out through the holed hull and tumbled through the open air, crashing into the stands below, then the ship snapped back, and Brendis slipped loose from his spot under Esprë and went sliding toward the ship's back rail.

CHAPTER

57

As consciousness slowly returned, so did the pain. The wound in Xalt's back hurt worse than anything in his life. Still, he had patched together enough other warforged in his time to know that the wound would not be fatal, and this helped him to avoid panicking.

Xalt calmly pushed himself up and sat on the platform on which he had been stabbed. He put his hands against his chest opposite of where the knife had entered his back. Recalling his training, he repeated the magical words and rubbed his hands across his skin in the proper pattern. This never worked as well inside the Mournland as it did without, but still, Xalt could feel his fibers knitting back together. They weren't as good as new, but they would do for now.

When Xalt was done, he stood and looked up at the arena. The changeling who had stabbed him and taken Esprë had gone off in that direction. It was time for Xalt to enter the place as well. With no elf-girl in tow, he'd be much less conspicuous.

As he walked toward the nearest tunnel, he saw the airship come screaming in over the arena. The craft stopped in what Xalt could only think was a disastrously fast manner. At first the crowd went wild, but then the assembled warforged fell quiet.

It sounded to Xalt like Bastard was saying something through that horn he liked to wave about so much, but the artificer couldn't make out the words. It felt as if everyone inside the arena was holding their collective breath.

Then Xalt heard the crash. The city's platforms shook with the violence done to the arena, and the voices of hundreds of warforged roared in panic and pain.

Xalt tried to race up the tunnel, but before he got halfway, a flood of warforged came rushing at him, fleeing from whatever disaster had taken place inside. The artificer had to turn back and wait for the great rush of creatures to ebb before he could brave the tunnel once again.

"What happened?" Xalt asked one of the stragglers as the outflow slowed.

"Breather attack!" the warforged said as it kept running. "The stands are on fire!"

Xalt looked down the tunnel through which the straggler had come, then started the long walk into what he thought must be almost certain doom.

When Xalt emerged from the tunnel, he saw an incredible tableau laid out before him. To his left, Kandler, Burch, and Sallah battled a warforged titan bent on tearing them to pieces. In front of him, the airship's stern jutted straight out of Bastard's reserved section of the arena's stands. The floor around the airship burned. To Xalt's right, he spotted Te'oma leading Esprë out of the stands and toward the burning airship.

Now that Xalt got a closer look, he saw that the airship wasn't burning, although everything around it was—including the lower half of a second titan, whose upper half still jutted through a hole in the airship's hull.

Xalt circled around the airship to the right, hoping to get a better look at just what the changeling was doing with Esprë. When he caught sight of them again, Te'oma had gathered up the girl in her arms and was leaping from the splintered stands onto the airship's tilted deck. The pair climbed up the railing toward the bridge. Xalt wondered if he could find a way onto the deck and take Esprë back.

Xalt gauged the distance of the leap he would have to make. The length paralyzed him for a moment, then the decision was torn from him, as the ship started to move. The artificer guessed what the changeling was doing. If she could extract the ship from the stands, she'd be gone before anyone could stop her. Xalt had to move now.

He surveyed the airship, looking for some means of getting aboard other than leaping from the unstable footing of the stands. There was the hole in the bottom of the hull, but the mad, half-dead titan in there closed off that route. The rope ladder was now too high from the ground for Xalt to reach. That left the mooring lines.

The two fore mooring lines lay draped over the shattered remains of Bastard's box. One of the aft lines had been chopped in half, but the other hung down straight from the airship's stern. Xalt decided this was the only option. He stomped toward the line. He could hear the cries of a few injured warforged in the stands, and part of him wanted to stop and help them. It was in its nature to do so, but he did not have time now.

When Xalt reached the mooring line, he grasped it and began the long, arduous climb to the ship's deck. The absence of one of his fingers slowed him, but he was determined and tireless in his task. As he ascended, the ship jerked about like an animal caught in a foot-trap. For a moment, it was all he could do to hang on. When the shaking stopped, he began hauling himself upward again.

Xalt neared the ship's aft rail, and the airship broke free from the stands and started for the sky. But something shook the ship violently, and the craft dove toward the ground. Xalt glanced down at the hold that was now in front of him rather than above. Through the hole, he could see the remains of the half-titan fighting on, and the warforged couldn't help but feel the stirrings of a touch of pride that a creature forged like himself could be so powerful and tenacious.

The ship zoomed forward at top speed, and the titan tumbled into the aft of the hold. A moment later, the ship ground to a halt, and the titan burst out of the front of the ship's hull and fell out. As the titan's bulk left the airship, the craft lurched into the air, and Xalt went with it. For a moment, the artificer feared he would be flung from the rope, but he managed to hang on. Determined to get off the rope and on the ship as quickly as possible, he hauled himself up the line.

Just before Xalt reached the ship's deck, an armored figure slid into the battered rear railing, which gave way. The artificer instinctively reached out to grab the knight who slammed into him.

The warforged's left hand gripped the edge of the damaged decking even as his body went swinging out into space. The remaining finger and thumb of Xalt's right hand ensnared the steel collar of the knight's breastplate. Still unconscious, Brendis dangled limply as the weight dragging on his limbs caused the warforged to howl in pain.

CHAPTER

58

When Deothen plunged through the decking, he had thought he'd be able to make quick work of the coward who had run from him at the first opportunity. Now, he wondered who was the hunter and who was the prey.

The space beneath Bastard's box opened straight down to the ground below. No floorboard separated the platform from the land it moved over at a walking pace. When Deothen dropped to the earth, he found himself standing on crushed gray grass that dozens of the city's walkers had trampled and dozens more would grind underfoot as the city moved along its chosen course.

The platforms here were high enough that Deothen could walk upright, but he could not raise his sword over his head. Compared to the stands above, it was dark and quiet, but the noise level grew as the warforged above stampeded toward safety, trying to escape the blaze started by the airship's ring of fire.

Deothen's silver-flamed sword glared through the gloom beneath the city. He held it up before him and peered into the darkness, looking for some sign of the warforged leader.

All around Deothen, silent sets of legs marched on, each

holding a section of a platform perched atop it. He stood still and let the city move around him for a moment, then he felt something hot and bright behind him. He turned to see the flames from the airship's ring of fire coming down through the floor. As he strode to the side to avoid the oncoming conflagration, he wondered if the warforged leader could have climbed up through the flames to return to the arena above. He decided it didn't matter. If Bastard had gone that way, there was no way he could follow.

Deothen stood to the side and watched the flames as they passed by. As he did, he saw something moving behind them. Bastard. The warforged leader turned to Deothen, and the senior knight saw the light of the fire flickering in the creature's sapphire eyes.

"Without your titans around you, you slither away," Deothen said as he walked toward the warforged. "Like a snake to its hole."

He brought his sword arm back, but before he could swing, Bastard stepped behind a nearby walker. Deothen slashed at the intervening golem, cutting its thin legs in half. The walker fell to the ground, and the platform sagged down where the creature had once held it up.

"You hide behind your tools like a child behind its mother's skirts," Deothen said. "Come out and fight me, coward!"

Bastard laughed as he stepped behind another walker that blindly ignored both its master and the intruder with the blazing blade. "What you call cowardly, I call cunning," the warforged leader said. "I didn't become a lieutenant of the Lord of Blades by charging into battle against every sword-waving idiot who challenged my bravery."

Deothen cut down the walker standing between him and Bastard, but the warforged leader was no longer behind it.

"Face me!" said Deothen, waving his sword about to punctuate his words.

The knight heard something charging up behind him fast, and he turned. He was too late to bring his sword to bear, and the warforged leader slammed into him. He went sprawling across the dirt until he smacked another walker in the back of its legs. It fell away, and the platform sagged down over Deothen's head.

Bastard leaned forward and kicked the downed knight. The spikes on his foot punched through Deothen's armor and punctured his side. The knight cried out in pain, but he slashed up at Bastard at the same time.

The knight's sacred sword bit into Bastard's thigh, cutting deep into the fibers beneath its shining, spiked plates. The warforged leader grunted and leaped back before Deothen could strike again.

The knight struggled to his feet, clutching his chest. Blood seeped through the holes Bastard had kicked there.

"So, this snake can bite," Deothen said through gritted teeth.

He spun about, looking for some hint of Bastard's location. The arena floor above him shuddered as the airship fought to free herself from the stands.

"I answered your taunts once," Bastard called. "I'll not be so foolish again."

Deothen glared into the gloom in the direction of the voice, then he turned to look back the way he'd come. There, in the wan light streaming through the hole the airship had torn in the arena floor, he saw Bastard. The creature's spiked armor seemed to glow in the pool of daylight.

Bastard raised his golden horn and said, "Halt."

The walkers carrying the massive city's platforms on their shoulders slowed their pace to a crawl and then stopped.

"Fire and ashes!" Deothen said. He launched himself at Bastard, but the creature was too far away.

"Down." Bastard's order echoed in Deothen's head. He ignored it and kept racing forward. Nothing was going to stop him from hacking the warforged leader to pieces with his blade.

Deothen grazed his head on the platform over him as he

ran. At first, he thought he must have run up a slight rise in the ground. Then he realized that the walkers all around him were crouching down, each working its way to its knees.

"Down!" Bastard said again.

Deothen bent over and hustled along as fast as he could. Even though the city had stopped moving, Bastard and the hole above him seemed no closer. Soon Deothen could no longer stand at all. He threw himself down and scrambled forward on his hands and knees, his flaming sword still clutched in his fist. Bastard wasn't so far away now—perhaps a score of yards—but it seemed like miles of dark and broken road.

Deothen's hand slipped, and he found himself on his belly. He tried to rise to his knees again, but there wasn't enough room.

All around the knight, the walkers who had been carrying the city above them folded themselves down on the ground. Unlike him, they didn't need to breathe. They had no lungs from which the air would be crushed by the horrible weight above them. They could just lie there in the suffocating dirt for hours, even days, and then rise once again at their master's call.

"Down!" Bastard said one last time.

The heavy platforms came down flush with the ground. Deothen kept worming ahead until his armor wedged stuck between the earth and the platform above. He was almost close enough to strike out at Bastard. He might die here, but he was determined to have one last chance to take the warforged leader with him.

Deothen lashed out with his sword at Bastard's feet, swinging the blade flat and true through the final inches of space left to him as his armor began to give.

"Sallah!" he cried with his final breath.

Bastard stepped backward out of the knight's reach. The platforms came down within bare inches of the ground beneath them. Blood spurted from Deothen's mouth and everything went black.

CHAPTER

59

High above, the airship had stopped bumping around. As Esprë fought to regain control of the ship's wheel, she saw Te'oma slip her hands from the leather safety straps and walk across the bridge to deal with Xalt.

"You're tenacious," the changeling said to the warforged. "I never see most of my victims again."

She reached out with her foot and kicked the artificer's hand that clutched the edge of the ship's deck. Xalt cried out in pain.

"Is it because you're a warforged?" Te'oma asked. "Are your kind harder to kill?"

She ground her boot down on the Xalt's fingers, then stomped down on them again. The warforged shouted in agony.

"You are durable," Te'oma said. As she spoke, she drew her black knife and got on one knee next to where the artificer's battered fingers still clung to the airship's bridge.

"No!" Esprë screamed. She had had enough. She grabbed the airship's wheel and gave the elemental trapped in the ring of fire a nudge. The ship lurched forward.

The changeling howled as she pitched over the aft of the ship. Her black knife tumbled from her hand and spun end-over-end down to the arena floor. Te'oma reached and grabbed at the edge of the shattered railing. The tips of her fingers latched on the last spindle there.

"Don't do this!" Te'oma shouted at Esprë.

"Drop him!" Sallah yelled from below.

Hope leaped in Esprë's chest at the sound of the lady knight's voice. Then, when she heard her stepfather speak, that hope grew tenfold.

"Drop Brendis!" Kandler said. "We'll catch him!"

"I won't let you kill him!" Esprë shouted at Te'oma from the wheel. She didn't want to hurt anyone. Over the past few weeks, she'd seen more than enough death. She couldn't let the changeling hurt anyone else again. She still remembered the look on the warforged's face when the black knife had slipped into his back, and she was ready to do everything she could to stop anything like that from happening again.

The ship bounced just a bit into the air, and Esprë heard something crash to the floor below. Kandler cried out in pain.

"To stop me, you'll have to kill me," the changeling said. "And you're no killer. You're—No!"

The railing from which Te'oma hung cracked and gave way. The changeling cascaded back from the airship, the spindle she'd been clutching still in her hand.

"No!" Esprë screamed as Te'oma fell out of sight. She let go of the airship's wheel, stretching out her hands in a feeble hope of somehow being able to stop it.

The warforged reached up and pulled himself up onto the bridge. Still on his belly, he scrambled across the deck to where Esprë knelt, crying into her hands. He reached out and put a gentle hand on her shoulder.

"Are you all right?" he asked.

"No," Esprë said between sobs. "Did—did you do that? Pull her off the ship?"

The warforged hesitated, then nodded slowly. Esprë felt a terrible mixture of hatred and gratitude toward the warforged. She reached out to hold him and wept into his arms.

"Don't cry for me, little one," Te'oma's voice said from above.

Esprë uncovered her eyes, and she and the warforged looked up to see the changeling hovering over the edge of the bridge on her bat-winged cloak. The girl gasped. The warforged scrambled up and put his arm around her shoulders and their backs to the bridge's console.

The changeling glared at the warforged. "Now," she said, "where were we?"

The warforged stood between Esprë and the changeling. "I will not allow you to harm this child," he said, his raspy voice trembling with emotion.

Te'oma threw back her head and laughed. She executed a sharp loop with her batwinged cloak and came back to where she'd been before. "You silly suit of armor," she said. "She's never been in any danger from me."

The changeling's smile faded from her thin, white lips. Esprë shuddered at the sight.

"You, though . . ." Te'oma said. "What's your name?"

"I am called Xalt."

"Well, Xalt, your time is now."

Xalt reached back to squeeze Esprë's shoulder and then sprinted toward the edge of the bridge. When he reached the damaged railing, he leaped into the air, pushing off hard, and spread his arms wide like a bird of prey soaring down out of the sky at a hapless meal.

Xalt smashed into Te'oma and wrapped his arms around the hovering changeling. Te'oma screeched with frustration and clawed at the warforged's back, but he refused to let go, and the pair plummeted to the arena floor like a meteor from the Mournland's gray sky.

CHAPTER

60

Burch pulled himself out from under the wreckage of the
wall that he'd been standing on when the enraged titan knocked
it down. The titan lay shattered around him. The creature had
pushed though the wall and over the platform beyond to cascade over the city's edge and onto the ground beyond.

As Burch tried to stand, the titan stirred. It raised its head
to look around and spotted the shifter. It tried to reach out and
grab him with its arm, but it only flailed a splintered stump at
him instead.

Burch kicked the titan's head, which hurt his foot more
than the creature. As the shifter stood over the creature and
pondered what he should do, a ballista bolt slammed into the
titan's chest, and the thing fell still.

Burch looked up and saw the ballista crew that had missed
him cursing at each other as they hurried to reload the weapon
again. This close to the arena, most of the stations along the
edge of the city had been abandoned after the stampede away
from the fire, but the warforged staffing this ballista seemed
more determined than most.

Burch retrieved his crossbow from the wreckage and
checked its action. Despite the wild ride and final crash, the

weapon still worked. He slammed a bolt into it and glanced up to see the loaded ballista pointed straight at him. He dove left, and the bolt impaled the spot where he'd stood. He took a deep breath, aimed, and loosed a bolt of his own, and one of the warforged staffing the large weapon keeled over with Burch's missile sticking out of its face.

Burch dashed toward the ballista mount as he reloaded his crossbow. The warforged at the ballista spun the winch and shoved another of the massive bolts into place. They tried to train the weapon on the shifter then, but the bolt went wild above his head.

Stopping long enough to get a good aim, Burch planted another bolt in the chest of the warforged working the weapon's winch, and the two creatures still standing decided to flee. A quick reload, and the shifter shot one of them down as he fled. The fourth keep low as he sprinted away and disappeared around the nearest building before Burch even reached the city's side.

The shifter noticed that the city had stopped moving and seemed to be much lower than before. He reslung his crossbow over his back and pulled himself up into the city, right beneath the empty ballista's mount.

Burch looked up and down the city platforms. In the distance he saw lots of warforged scurrying about. As he watched, another ballista bolt from that area sailed over his head and struck the arena wall far behind him. The shifter ducked behind the nearby ballista mount and tried to think of a plan. As he sat there, he heard a horse whinny in fear. Burch looked over the platform's edge. Not twenty feet away, four horses were tied to a hitching post. Probably mounts for the ballista crew.

The shifter smiled.

✦

Kandler cheered as he saw Xalt tackle Te'oma out of the air and drag her like an anchor to the arena floor. The pair landed hard, but Te'oma managed to twist her way atop the artificier before they struck the ground. The force of the landing tore Xalt's arms from the changeling, setting her free. She rolled off the warforged and staggered to her feet, still stunned from the fall.

Xalt reached out and grabbed one of Te'oma's feet with his good hand. His fingers closed around her ankle like a vise. The changeling snarled and stomped at his hand with her free foot. Once did nothing, so she kept at it. He grunted with each blow but refused to let her go.

"Hey!" Kandler said as he stepped up to the changeling.

Te'oma looked up and Kandler backhanded her. She would have gone flying backward but for Xalt's grasp still anchoring her to the floor. Still, she stumbled, and her hand shot to the sheathe tied around her calf. Too late, she remembered she had dropped her knife off the back of the airship.

Kandler dove down at the changeling and grabbed her wrists. An instant later, a sharp bolt of pain stabbed into his mind. The justicar's head snapped back as he battled the alien thoughts. She laughed as he thrashed about, trying to force her out of his mind.

Kandler fought through the static the changeling forced into his brain. He looked down at her and saw her face grinning up at him, laughing with delight at the pain lancing through his skull. He thought of everything this creature had done to his daughter, how she kept coming back to threaten them again and again. As he did, his rage worked its way out of his heart and into his head. His fury at her focused his mind on a single, burning desire, and he put everything he had left into making that wish come true. Kandler hurled himself forward and smashed his forehead into the bridge of the changeling's nose. Blood spurted from her face, and she fell limp in the justicar's grasp.

CHAPTER

61

As Kandler and Xalt struggled with the changeling, Sallah cradled the unconscious Brendis in her arms.

"You can't go to the Flame yet, my brother," she said as she placed her hands on either side of his head. He was so pale that the blood on his face almost seemed to glow red.

"May the Silver Flame reignite the fire that burns within you," Sallah said, enunciating each word. "May it commend you into the arms of the world so that you may continue to serve its sacred cause." Her hands began to glow with a warm, silvery light. "And may it light your way throughout your life."

The glow ran from Sallah's hands until it covered Brendis from head to toe. It intensified for a moment, growing so bright that Sallah had to close her eyes, then it faded away in a heartbeat's space.

Brendis's eyes opened as he gasped in a chestful of air. He tried to sit up but fell back just as fast, and Sallah caught him in her arms again.

"It's all right," she said as she brushed the hair from his face. "You're alive."

As the words left her mouth, her eyes flicked over to the hole the airship had burned through the floor of the arena.

There in the center, untouched by the flames, stood Bastard.

Sallah lay Brendis down on the arena's floor. As she stood, he tried to rise to join her, but he could barely move.

"Rest," she said. "If I fall, you'll need your strength."

Sallah watched as Bastard leaped over the flames and walked toward her.

"To avenge your death?" Brendis asked the lady knight.

"No," Sallah said. She drew her sword, and the blade burst into silvery flames once again. "To run."

Bastard cackled as Sallah strode toward him, her sword flashing with tongues of silver flame. "The daughter comes to avenge her father," he said. "How very human."

Sallah held her sword before her at the ready. "I'm not here for revenge," she said. "Just for your head."

Bastard raised his golden horn to his lips and started to speak, but Sallah raced forward and slashed at the instrument. The tip of her sword sliced off Bastard's thumb and sent the horn spiraling away through the air.

Bastard took several steps back and glared at her.

"Surrender, and I will spare your life," Sallah said. "I do not wish to fight a weaponless foe."

"I have heard tales of the arrogance of the Knights of the Silver Flame, straight from the lips of the Lord of Blades. I laughed them off. I told my lord that it was impossible for such a feared people to be so foolish." The warforged glared at Sallah. "I should never have doubted the word of my lord."

"You refuse then?" Sallah said, holding her sword before her.

"You smug, little bag of bones," Bastard said. "I don't need a weapon. I *am* a weapon!"

The warforged lowered his shoulder and charged straight at her. He was on her before she could bring her blade to bear. She turned away at the last second, but it was too late. Bastard slammed into Sallah with both of his forearms. The spikes that ran along them punched clear through into her upper arm. She cried out and fell back on the ground.

Sallah scrambled to her feet and away from the warforged, leading him away from the others. Kandler and Xalt were occupied with Te'oma, and Brendis was in no condition to do more than be stomped to death beneath Bastard's spiked feet.

Sallah's blood dripping down the warforged's shoulder, he stalked after her. "You're as much a fool as your father," he said. "You should flee for your life."

Sallah stopped and stood her ground. She flexed her injured shoulder, as much to show the warforged that he hadn't maimed her as to assure herself. She waved her blazing sword in front of her, daring the creature to attempt another attack.

"May the light of the Silver Flame shine on my efforts today," Sallah said. As she said the words, she felt the power of her faith refresh her, and the distracting pain of her wound sloughed away.

"May you rot forever in utter darkness," Bastard said and lunged.

Sallah slashed with her sword, but the warforged parried the blow with its forearm then swung a spiked fist at the lady knight's head. Sallah ducked beneath the attack and spun off to her left, away from the direction of Bastard's momentum. As she did, she reached out with her bare hand, grabbed one of the spikes along the crest of the warforged's back, and stabbed at his back. Bastard twisted to the side, and her blow glanced off his spikes.

The warforged leader swung his arm back at Sallah and hammered at her with a flying punch. The blow landed square in her stomach and doubled her over. She retched as she spun away, splashing the contents of her last meal across the warforged's chest. Bastard recoiled at the vomit and wiped it from itself as best it could.

"I don't think I could describe how revolting this is," the warforged said. "It's disgusting enough that you breathers stuff your faces with once-living things. To have it spilled on my plates—there is no worse insult for my kind."

Sallah wiped the last of the vomit from her mouth and

flicked it at the creature. It landed on his face. "Glad to oblige," she said.

"At least your father died with some dignity," Bastard said as he used his thick fingers to wipe his features clean. His sapphire eyes sparkled with anger. "Being crushed to death beneath the city may be a messy way to go, but at least he was considerate enough to expire away from me."

Sallah's jaw fell open, and she gaped at the creature and then at the arena floor. Her father, who had mentored her as a follower of the Silver Flame her entire life, who had trained her as a knight, who had loved her as no other, lay dead somewhere beneath her feet. She shook her head, wanting to believe it was a lie. Fat, hot tears rolled out of her green eyes and down her flushed cheeks. Bastard threw back his head and laughed.

Righteous fury swelled in her and she charged, raining blow after blow down on Bastard until her arms ached with the effort. The creature fell back before the knight's onslaught, unable to do more than raise his arms to cover his face. Most of the blows glanced off Bastard's spikes. Some made it through to pound against the creature's thick, tight-fitted plates. Few did him any real hurt.

Sallah was panting hard and fast. Striking aside another blow, Bastard reached out with an armored hand and shoved her in the chest. She stumbled backward, tripped over her own tired feet and fell.

Bastard looked past her. "We must finish this game now," he said. "I prefer to fight you breathers one at a time."

Sallah glanced back to see Kandler sprinting in her direction, but she knew he would reach her too late. She needed to do something now.

Bastard stomped toward her and she scuttled away from him on her backside. She was trapped, and she knew it. If she tried to reach her feet, the warforged would kill her. If she stopped to fight him, he would kill her. She thought about throwing her sword, but she knew is would be a pointless gesture.

"You cannot escape," Bastard hissed as he dove at her.

Desperate to take the creature with her, Sallah jammed the pommel of her sword into the floor and pointed the tip upward at Bastard's belly. The blade punched past the creature's armored plates and stabbed clean through his body. For an instant, Sallah was surprised at how soft Bastard's insides seemed to be once the sword punctured his shell, then the warforged fell on her with his full weight, slamming his spiked elbows into her chest. They stabbed through her unprotected flesh, and she felt bone break.

Bastard howled in agony and anger. Dark fluid spurted from his wound soaking them both. As her consciousness began to fall away, Sallah's smelled something coppery and wet. She didn't know if it was Bastard's blood or her own.

CHAPTER

62

Sallah!" Kandler screamed as he charged across the arena floor toward Bastard and the fallen knight. He'd thought his head might explode while Te'oma was probing in it, but now he felt like it might happen on its own. He'd come to respect Sallah over the course of their travels, even if he could never understand her devotion to her deity, and after his daughter he wanted to lose her the least of all. He roared in horror as the warforged stabbed the woman with its spikes again.

"Bastard!"

The warforged leader's head snapped up at the mention of his name. He stopped mutilating the woman beneath him and climbed to his feet, Sallah's burning blade still running through his middle. The flames from the sword scorched the creature's front and back, but its tight-fitted plates of armor kept the fibers beneath from catching fire. Bastard grunted as he pulled at the hilt and tried to remove the length of hot steel from his body, but the warforged's fall onto the blade had wedged it in tight, and it would not budge.

Kandler reached Bastard and leveled a devastating cut at the creature's head. The warforged blocked the blow with his arm, but the justicar's blade bent back a few of its bloodied spikes and bit under the creature's armor. Bastard howled in pain and danced back from Kandler's attack.

"At last," he said, "a worthy foe."

The creature's admiration was little comfort to Kandler as he glanced down at Sallah. She coughed once and rolled on the ground, clutching at her wounds. Kandler prowled away to the right, his sword at the ready before him, drawing Bastard away from the fallen knight.

Bastard growled, then lowered his head and charged. The spikes rising from the creature's head stretched toward the justicar like the horns of a raging bull. The points on these were far sharper.

Kandler dodged to the right, and as Bastard barreled past he tried to gore the justicar with his spikes, but they only tore at the fabric of his shirt. Bastard spun about to face the justicar again, the raging fires glinting off his sharpened and polished tips.

The justicar shook his head and took a deep breath to calm himself. The warforged's anger could work for him here, but not if he was mastered by his own.

Bastard lowered his head and charged again. The justicar spun away at the last second, but this time the creature sliced open a gash along Kandler's left shoulder.

"First blood!" Bastard crowed in delight as he spun back around several yards beyond the justicar.

Kandler cleared his throat and looked down at his blade, which wore the warforged's blood. "Did you forget?" he asked. "Or are you just stupid?"

"I only count the blood I draw," Bastard said, waving an armored hand over his bloodied spikes. "I have plenty of the woman's. Soon I'll have the rest of yours."

Kandler tapped the floor between them with the tip of his sword. At first he dragged it in a semicircle in front of him, then he jabbed the end of the blade into the wood of the arena's floor.

"Come and get it," he said.

Bastard bent down his head, exposing his spikes again, and charged forward, faster than ever. This time, he flung his arms wide. As the warforged came at him, Kandler pushed his own blade aside. Bastard barked out a mirthless laugh and stretched his arms wider. Kandler waited until the last moment then fell on his back and stabbed out his hand to grab the hilt of Sallah's blade, still jutting from the warforged leader's front. The sacred sword firmly in his grasp, he shoved up on the hilt and leveraged it over his head.

Kandler slid underneath the stampeding Bastard, and the creature's momentum carried him somersaulting over Kandler's head. The justicar let loose the hilt of Sallah's sword as Bastard sailed past, then he twisted over on his front to watch the results.

Bastard flipped entirely over Kandler and landed flat on his back. The burning sword jammed through the creature stabbed into and through the floor beneath him. The sword stopped Bastard's forward roll by tearing through the fibers in its chest harder than any human hand ever could. He screamed in agony as the blade tore through his midsection.

Kandler scrambled over to where his own sword lay on the ground and scooped it up. He strode over to where Bastard lay wriggling on the blade that pinned him to the floor, and he hefted his weapon over the warforged leader.

"Do you know where warforged go when they die?" Kandler asked. His voice trembled as he spoke.

The warforged leader hauled on the hilt of Sallah's blade. With more of its fibers exposed by the growing gash, Bastard was starting to burn.

Kandler smacked the warforged across the top of his head as he circled around him, hunting for the perfect spot for a killing blow.

"Do you?" he said.

Bastard glared up at Kandler through its sapphire eyes. "No."

"Well," Kandler said, "you're about to find out."

He reversed his grip on his sword and raised it over his head for a two-handed stab. He threw himself forward, putting all his weight behind the blow and driving the point straight for the warforged leader's exposed neck.

Bastard released his grip on the hilt of Sallah's sword and flung up his arms to protect itself. Kandler's blade caught Bastard square in the forearm, drove through, wedged into the arm's fibers and caught halfway along its steely length, jarring Kandler's shoulders in their sockets.

Bastard roared as he wrenched its arm forward, smashing Kandler in the eye with his own sword's pommel. The justicar fell back, clutching his hands to his face.

Surging with fury, Bastard began to roll back and forth on the arena floor. Each time he did, Sallah's sword cut deeper and deeper. To Kandler, it seemed that the warforged leader was trying to saw himself in half. Perhaps he would have succeeded, but the blazing blade became wedged between two plates of the warforged's armor and stuck.

Kandler stumbled back and fell a safe distance away. He pulled his hands from his face and felt the damage. His eye was still intact, but it was swelling shut so fast he could only see out through a tiny slit between.

Bastard slammed his wounded arm down into the arena floor at an awkward angle, shoving the point of Kandler's blade through the boards. Using this point as leverage, he wrenched against Sallah's sword again, again, and again.

The wet sound of the weapon working its way through Bastard's artificial flesh turned Kandler's stomach. He just wished that the creature would do the right thing and die, that this would all come to an end.

With a snap, Sallah's sacred sword broke in two, and Bastard came tumbling off the blade, his pinned arm twisting at a horrible angle.

Kandler heard the fibers and plates in Bastard's limb crunch and break against each other under the stress. The justicar scrambled back to his feet and watched the warforged through his one good eye.

Bastard pulled his way to his feet, but his arm was still stuck on the floor. He reached down and grabbed the hilt of Sallah's sword protruding from his chest. Its flames had snuffed out when the blade snapped, but the remaining shaft still smoked where it touched the warforged's flesh. Bastard pulled on the hilt, and the sword's shattered length slid free. The warforged snarled at Kandler, who hung back a respectable distance to see what would happen next.

"I may have your sword"—Bastard waved the hilt-shard of Sallah's sword at him, its sacred light extinguished forever—"but you," he said, "you still have something I want."

Kandler stepped backward, ready to run, even though the warforged was still anchored to the floor by its mangled arm.

"What's that?" he said.

Bastard raised the hilt in his hand and brought it chopping down on his pinned arm. The edge of the broken blade sliced through the twisted fibers there, parting him from his maimed limb for good.

Freed from his ruined arm, Bastard stood up to his full height. He held the shard of Sallah's blade and pointed it at Kandler's chest.

"I want your blood."

CHAPTER 63

Esprë stood on the bridge of the airship and watched her stepfather battle the warforged leader. She screamed every time Bastard attacked, and she cheered each time Kandler escaped harm. When he stabbed the creature through the arm, she jumped and squealed.

The girl's joy was cut short, though, when Bastard broke Sallah's blade. Seeing Kandler staring at the creature through his one good eye, without a sword in his hand, Esprë knew she had to do something.

She cast her eyes about. Burch was gone and maybe dead, plowed down with the arena wall. Sallah lay leaking blood from a handful of wounds. Deothen had disappeared under the arena floor and never came back out. Brendis was just this side of the grave. Below the ship, the artificer stood over Te'oma, making sure the changeling didn't get up and start wreaking havoc again.

"Xalt!" Esprë shouted to the warforged below, a spark of hope fanning to a flame in her heart. "You have to help Kandler!"

Xalt looked up from Te'oma and Brendis and waved at the girl. "I would like to help, Esprë," the artificer called, "but . . ."

Esprë's flame of hope began to flicker. She glanced over to see Bastard stand with a fragment of Sallah's sword still jutting from his chest, and the fire in her nearly went out.

From below, Xalt yelled, "The ship! Use the ship!"

"Yes!" Esprë said. "Yes!" She beckoned down at the artificer. "Come up!"

Xalt looked over to where Kandler and Bastard were still circling each other. "There is no time!" he shouted. "You must do it yourself!"

The girl nodded and turned to the steering platform. The wheel stood before her, solid and unmoving, although she could almost feel the elemental beckoning to her through it. She stepped forward and wrapped her long, delicate hands around the wheel.

In the distance, Esprë could see that the warforged who had stampeded from the arena were rallying again. Several squads of warriors were marching her way from the rear of the city. Some were pointing at the ship and shouting orders. She knew she didn't have long.

Two streets over, a lone mounted figure was leading a train of horses to the arena. Esprë squinted down at the rider and realized it was Burch, picking his way along the edge of the city on his way back toward the arena. She laughed at the sight, then a ballista bolt sailed up past her from the ground below. As she searched for the shooter, another bolt struck the ship's hull, shaking the deck.

The attack reminded Esprë how serious her situation was. Kandler was depending on her—everyone was—and she was not going to disappoint them. She stuck out her jaw and looked for her stepfather again. As she did, the ship began to move.

❦

On the arena floor below, Kandler saw the ballista bolt slam into the side of the airship, and dread filled his heart. "Esprë," he said.

"Do not worry about your whelp," Bastard said. "I won't make her suffer long." Then he charged.

Kandler scrambled backward from the warforged leader, turning to run, hoping he could outpace him, but he stopped in midstride. This direct threat to his daughter unleashed a thunderstorm of rage in his head. There was no way he was going to let this beast get near Esprë.

As the warforged reached for him, the justicar pivoted and slammed his fist into the side of Bastard's jaw with everything he had. Bastard dropped to one knee, stunned by the force of the blow. Kandler shook his hand, convinced he had broken knuckles, but he followed the first punch with a flurry of blows to the warforged's face, pounding away at the creature without pause or mercy until his fists bled freely and his arms felt like lead.

Bastard raised an arm to defend itself, and Kandler backed off from the rows of sharp spikes. The warforged used the hilt-shard of Sallah's sword to keep the justicar at bay.

His heart beating like a war drum, Kandler wheezed and huffed as he looked down at the creature to survey the damage he'd done. He felt like he'd been the one given the beating, but the adrenaline pumping through him let him ignore the pain. Bastard's face bore a dozen dents and scratches. One of his sapphire eyes had been knocked from its face, leaving only a dead socket behind. In his left hand, he still held the sword-shard, but his right arm ended in a ragged stump.

"Ready to give up?" Kandler said.

Bastard's jaw dropped. The hinge came down askew to the sound of metal scraping metal. Bastard looked at the justicar through his remaining eye and laughed loud and long.

Kandler turned and ran. While his arms felt like they might fall off, his legs still had some life in them. As he raced across the arena floor, he heard the steady tread of the tireless warforged close behind him. He dared not look back for fear he might stumble, but the footfalls seemed to grow nearer with every second.

Something jabbed into the back of Kandler's thigh, and he tumbled to the ground, clutching his leg. He somersaulted forward several times before he came to a rest. He slammed to a stop on his back and saw that he had the hilt from Sallah's sword in his leg.

Kandler hurled himself to the side, and Bastard's spiked foot came down where he had just been. The warforged leader stomped down again, and once more Kandler rolled out of the way just in time.

Bastard kicked out at the justicar again. Kandler squirmed out of the path of the warforged's foot, grabbed the hilt of Sallah's sword as he came to a stop, and pulled it free. He screamed at the pain and rolled again, just in time. Bastard raised his foot again, Kandler rolled, the foot came down, and Kandler jammed the shard of Sallah's sword straight down through the warforged's foot and into the floor below.

Bastard roared in pain and lashed out with its other foot. His spiked toes caught Kandler in the shoulder and stabbed through to his bone. The justicar spun away, holding his wound and trailing blood as he went. He struggled to his knees and scrambled away as fast as he could.

"You think this toothpick will stop me?" Bastard roared. The justicar hoped so, but he didn't say a word. He kept moving at a shuffle and didn't look back. He could feel his boot filling with blood.

The warforged tried to raise his foot but failed. He snarled down at the hilt stuck through his armored toes. "This ends now!"

The area around Kandler grew dark. For a moment, he wondered if the vision in his unbruised eye was starting to fade too, then the world started to grow light again—lighter than even before, but red and angry. A crackling sound filled the justicar's ears, erupting to a roar. It confused him for a moment until he identified it as the noise of a bonfire roaring straight at him.

Kandler braved a look back and saw Bastard pull the hilt

of Sallah's sword from his damaged foot. What was plummeting down on top of the creature caused the justicar to leap to his feet and put every last bit of energy he had into racing away.

The airship slammed down on top of Bastard and smashed the warforged leader flat. The ship bounced, and the ring of fire caught Bastard like a moth in a flame.

Kandler missed sharing Bastard's fate by a matter of yards. As the ship hit the ground, the arena floor buckled and hurled him forward. He landed on his injured shoulder and had to fight to keep from blacking out at the pain. He rolled several times and ended up on his stomach.

Before he could turn his head, the airship took off again. This time, she shot forward, heading for the far arena wall through which the titan had plowed. The ring of fire brushed past Kandler so close that it singed the hair on the back of his head. Once it passed, Kandler worked his way to his knees and from there to his feet. As he stood, he watched the ship sail just clear the shattered wall. She came close enough to set some of the wreckage ablaze, but the gust of wind in her wake snuffed the flames out.

The ship passed over the wall, and no sooner had it passed than a horse leaped over the lowest part. The rider galloped up to the justicar, leading three more horses behind him.

"How are things, boss?" Burch said as he rode up to where the justicar stood.

Ignoring him, Kandler stared after the airship. "Come on. Turn it around. Turn the ship around."

The ship kept sailing on in a straight line for the horizon.

Covered with blood from his shoulder, leg, and hands, the justicar stood there staring after the ship, willing her to turn around, turn around, please turn around. She didn't even slow.

Burch leaped down from his saddle to put a shoulder under Kandler's arm. He took in all of Kandler's wounds and said, "I'd hate to see the other guy."

Kandler jerked his head over to the pile of charred fibers and blackened metal that was all that was left of Bastard. He never took his eyes off the airship.

Burch let out a low whistle. "Who's on the ship?" the shifter asked.

Kandler's face contorted into a mask of frustration. "Esprë," he whispered.

CHAPTER

64

Kandler reached down and smacked the changeling across the face. "Wake up!" he said.

Te'oma opened her eyes, and the world swam around her. Kandler slapped her again, "Wake up!"

"Boss," Burch said, "we can chase her on horses."

"We can't catch an airship from horseback," Kandler said as he pulled Te'oma to her feet. "We need a way to fly."

The changeling felt the justicar start to remove her cloak, and she fought back. She pushed against him with feeble arms, and he growled at her.

"Just give me that cloak!"

Te'oma shook her head. "Kill me," she said, her voice rough and raw.

"I don't have time for that," the justicar said. "Just show me how this thing comes off!"

"It doesn't!" the changeling said.

He kept shaking her, and her cloak unfurled into a limp pair of massive, batlike wings.

"I'm taking it," the justicar said, "if I have to rip it off you. I'm not letting my daughter go down on a runaway ship!"

"That won't work," Sallah said. Kandler swung his head

around to see the lady knight limping over toward the others. Bloodstains dripped from the many holes in her armor, but she had stopped bleeding. He suspected she'd used her healing powers on herself this time, but they'd barely been enough to get her back on her feet.

"Don't tell me that," the justicar said.

"That isn't a cloak," Sallah said, coughing. "It's a symbiont. A living creature attached to the host in—"

"Spare me the lesson!" Kandler raged. "How do I put it on?"

With every second they stood there talking, Esprë sailed farther and farther away.

Sallah shook her head as she stopped in front of the justicar. "You'd have to kill her to get it off her."

Kandler had no problem with that. He'd wanted to kill the changeling since he first saw her, and now he had every reason to do so. He wrapped his hands around Te'oma's throat and squeezed. The changeling started to turn blue.

"No!" Sallah said. She punched Kandler in his injured shoulder. The justicar cried out as he let loose of the changeling's neck. He fought the impulse to strike back at the Sallah. No matter what kind of feelings he might have for her, no one was going to stand between him and his daughter.

"Would you listen? You'd have to remove the wings carefully and then graft them onto yourself. It takes hours!"

Kandler shoved the changeling into Xalt's arms and snarled at the lady knight. "We don't have that kind of time!"

"You don't think I know that?" Sallah said.

Through his one good eye, Kandler stared off after the airship as she receded toward the east. He felt like his heart might drop straight out of his chest. There had to be something he could do.

Somewhere behind the Mournland's mists, the sun was setting, and the sky was growing dark. The ring of fire stood out against it in stark contrast. It grew smaller with each passing moment.

"Let me go," Te'oma said, struggling in Xalt's arms.

Kandler turned on the changeling. "If I had a sword, I'd cut you down here and now," he said.

"No," Te'oma said. "I mean, I'll save her."

Kandler frowned. "You'll kill her." Despite his fury at the changeling, she held out the only hope he had, and he hated her for it.

"No." The changeling shook her head. "I won't."

"How can I trust—?"

"Let her go," Sallah said quietly. "She won't kill her."

Kandler turned. "How do you know? Huh? After all she's done, how can you say that? *How?*"

"Because," Sallah said. She looked deep into Kandler's eyes. "She wants Esprë alive, remember? She has the mark."

Kandler looked up at the airship as she coasted away into the darkening sky. If he let the changeling go, she would rescue Esprë, but what then? He knew Te'oma wouldn't turn around and bring the girl back. She'd point the ship toward Karrnath and be gone.

"Boss," Burch said. Kandler turned to him. "If Esprë was all right, she'd've turned around by now. She flies that thing better than anyone. Something's wrong."

Kandler knew Burch was right, but he froze. If he let the ship sail off on her own, Esprë might die, but then the Mark of Death would be gone forever. If Te'oma got her hands on Esprë, there was no telling what could happen to the girl. In the end, he didn't really have a choice.

Kandler reached out and took Xalt's hands from the changeling. "Go," he said to her.

Te'oma unfurled her wings, stretching them out to their full span. Their batlike shape made Kandler think of the changeling as if she were some kind of demon, the sort that takes children from their parents in the dead of night.

"She's right," the changeling said to Kandler. "I won't hurt her."

"Just go," Kandler said. "Hurry! And you'd better hope she's in one piece when I finally hunt you down."

"Happy hunting." Te'oma smiled and flapped off into the deepening night.

✦

When Te'oma caught with the airship, she saw Esprë hanging limp in the leather strap that held her to the wheel. Te'oma landed, folded the wings, and rushed to the girl. From the look of her, Esprë had smashed her head into the ship's wheel when the ship put an end to Bastard. Blood trickled from her forehead and down her face.

The changeling undid the strap from around Esprë's waist and laid the girl out gingerly on the bridge. She looked dead.

Te'oma knelt down and put her ear to the girl's chest. The heartbeat brought a smile to Te'oma's lips. As she leaned back, Esprë's eyes fluttered open, and the girl looked up at the changeling.

"It's all right," Te'oma said. She held the injured girl close and stroked her long, blonde hair. "It's going to be all right."

The airship kept sailing toward far-off Karrnath, beyond the Mournland's misty walls, and the changeling did nothing to impede her course.

Glossary

Aerenal: An island nation off the southeastern coast of Khorvaire, Aerenal is known as the homeland of the elves.

Argonth: A floating town designed as a mobile fortress to help defend Breland during the Last War.

ascendant councilor: One of the revered dead of the elves of Aerenal.

Aundair: One of the original Five Nations of Galifar, Aundair houses the seat of the Arcane Congress and the University of Wyrnarn. Currently under the rule of Queen Aurala ir'Wyrnarn.

Aureon: The Sovereign of Law and Lore, the source of order and knowledge. He gives guidance to rulers and those who pass judgment, guides the scribe and the student, and is said to have devised the principles wizards use to work their spells.

Bastard: The warforged lieutenant of the Lod of Blades. He commands Construct.

Blood of Vol: Those who worship the Blood of Vol refuse to bow to the power of death. Drawn from the traditions of an ancient line of elven necromancers, the Blood of Vol seeks to abolish death. They revere vampires and other undead creatures as champions in this struggle. This tradition is especially strong in the nation of Karrnath, and while it is not inherently evil, there are subsects—notably the infamous Order of the Emerald Claw—that have turned the battle against death into a struggle to dominate the living. As a result, throughout most of the Five Nations the common image of a follower of the Blood is that of a crazed necromancer leading an army of zombies as part of some mad scheme. The Church of the Silver Flame takes a particularly hard stand against followers of the Blood, and knights of the Flame may assume the worst when dealing with acolytes of Vol.

bloodwing: A fibrous, living symbiont, possessed of its own intelligence, which can sometimes bond to another creature. When dormant, the bloodwing's fibrous body shrinks to a very small size, but when aroused, the creature expands to large batlike wings, enabling its host the power of flight.

Boranel ir'Wyrnarn: King of Breland.

"breather": A derogatory term used by the warforged to describe non-construct creatures, i.e., elves, humans, dwarves, shifters, etc.

Breland: The largest of the original Five Nations of Galifar, Breland is a center of heavy industry. The current ruler of Breland is King Boranel ir'Wyrnarn.

Brendis: A young Knight of the Silver Flame.

Burch: A shifter and deputy justicar of Mardakine.

Cintila: Burch's horse.

Changeling: Members of the changeling race possess a limited ability to change face and form, allowing a changeling to disguise itself as a member of another race or to impersonate an individual. Changelings are said to be the offspring of humans and doppelgangers. They are relatively few in number and have no lands or culture of their own but are scattered across Khorvaire.

clawfoots: A human-sized predator of the Talenta Plains, this dinosaur is often used as a war-mount by the Halfling nomadic tribes. (A velociraptor.)

cold fire: Magical flame that produces no heat and does not burn. Cold fire is used to provide light in most cities of Khorvaire.

Construct: A mobile city of the warforged in the Mournland.

Council of Cardinals: Along with the Keeper of the Flame, the ruling council of the Church of the Silver Flame.

Cyre: One of the original Five Nations of Galifar, known for its fine arts and crafts. The governor of Cyre was traditionally raised to the throne of Galifar, but in 894 YK, Kaius of Karrnath, Wroann of Breland, and Thalin of Thrane rebelled against Mishann of Cyre. During the war, Cyre lost significant amounts of territory to elf and goblin mercenaries, creating the nations of Valenar and Darguun. In 994 YK, Cyre was devastated by a disaster of unknown origin that transformed the nation into a hostile wasteland populated by deadly monsters. Breland offered sanctuary to the survivors of the Mourning, and most of the Cyran refugees have taken advantage of this amnesty.

Dargent: Kandler's horse.

Darguul: Common name for someone or something from Darguun.

Darguun: A nation of goblinoids, founded in 969 YK when a hobgoblin leader named Haruuc formed an alliance among the goblinoid mercenaries and annexed a section of southern Cyre. Breland recognized this new nation in exchange for a peaceful border and an ally against Cyre. Few people trust the people of Darguun, but their soldiers remain a force to be reckoned with.

Dark Six, the: The six malevolent deities of the Sovereign Host, whose true names are not known.

Day of Mourning, the: A disaster that occurred on Olarune 20, 994 YK. The origin and precise nature of the Mourning are unknown. On Ollarune 20, gray mists spread across Cyre, and anything caught within the mists was transformed or destroyed. See *the Mournland*.

Deothen: A senior Knight of the Silver Flame.

Devourer, the: One of the Dark Six, who represents the destructive power of nature. He is strongly tied to the sea and the mystery of the deep waters, but earthquakes, avalanches, and tornadoes are all his children.

Dol Arrah: The Sovereign of Sun and Sacrifice. She is a patron of war, but she fights her battles with words and cunning strategy as well as steel. She is a god of light and honor, and her holy paladins seek to bring her sunlight to the darkest places of the world.

Dol Dorn: The Sovereign of Strength and Steel. He is the lord of war and patron to all who raise their arms in battle. He is the patron of physical arts, and the greatest sporting events of the year are held to mark his holy days. His followers are not held to the same standards of nobility and sacrifice as those of his sister, Dol Arrah, but he still encourages honorable conduct.

Dolurrh: The plane of the dead. When mortals die, their spirits are said to travel to Dolurrh and then slowly fade away, passing to whatever final fate awaits the dead.

dragonmark: 1) A mystical mark that appears on the surface of the skin and grants mystical powers to its bearer. 2) A slang term for the bearer of a dragonmark.

dragonmarked houses: One of the thirteen families whose bloodlines carry the potential to manifest a dragonmark. Many of the dragonmarked houses existed before the kingdom of Galifar, and they have used their mystical powers to gain considerable political and economic influence.

Droaam: A nation on the west coast of Khorvaire. Once claimed by Breland, this region was never settled by humans and was known as a wild land filled with all manner of monsters and creatures who had been pushed back by the spreading power of Galifar. In 986 YK there was a movement to organize the creatures of Droaam into a coherent nation. While this has met with some success, the new nation has yet to be recognized by any other country.

Eberron: 1) The world. 2) A mythical dragon said to have formed the world from her body in primordial times and to have given birth to natural life. Also known as "The Dragon Between."

Entiss: A veteran of the Last War currently living in Mardakine.

Eternal Fire: See cold fire.

Esprë: Kandler's elven step-daughter.

Esprina: Kandler's elven wife, now deceased.

Everbright Lantern: A lantern infused with cold fire, creating a permanent light source. These items are used to provide illumination in most of the cities and larger communities of Khorvaire. An everbright lantern usually has a shutter allowing the light to be sealed off when darkness is desirable.

Fairhaven: The capital of Aundair.

Five Nations: The five provinces of the Kingdom of Galifar—Aundair, Breland, Cyre, Karrnath, and Thrane.

Flamekeep: The capital of Thrane.

'forged: A slang term for the warforged.

Fradelko: A resident of Mardakine.

Galifar: 1) A cunning warrior and skilled diplomat who forged five nations into a single kingdom that came to dominate the continent of Khorvaire. 2) The kingdom of Galifar I, which came to an end in 894 YK with the start of the Last War. 3) A golden coin minted by the kingdom, bearing the image of the first king. The golden galifar is still in use today and is worth ten sovereigns. See page @@.

Glass Plateau: A highland plateau in the Mournland that is made up entirely of sharp, glasslike formation.

Gorgonhorn: A Darguul fort near the border of the Mournland.

Gurn: The local baker in Mardakine.

Gweir: A young Knight of the Silver Flame.

hammertails: A herbivorous dinosaur native to the Talenta Plains. (An anklyosaurus.)

House Cannith: The Dragonmarked House that carries the Mark of Making. The artificers and magewrights of House Cannith are responsible for most of the magical innovations of the past millennia. The house made tremendous profits during the Last War through sales of arms and armor, including warforged soldiers.

Howling Peaks: A mountain range on the southeastern border of Breland.

Jaela Daran: The young Keeper of the Flame, head of the Church of the Silver Flame.

justicar: An official chosen to enforce the law and keep the peace. Justicars have little legal authority beyond their local jurisdiction.

Kandler: Justicar of Mardakine.

Karrnath: One of the original Five Nations of Galifar. Karrnath is a cold, grim land whose people are renowned for their martial prowess. The current ruler of Karrnath is King Kaius ir'Wyrnarn III.

Keeper, the: One of the Dark Six, the embodiment of greed, decay, and hunger so great that it lets all else fall to rot and ruin. While he amasses gold and jewels, the Keeper covets the souls of the living. He seeks to snatch the spirits of the dead as they pass to Dolurrh, hoarding these souls and gloating over his treasures.

Keeper of the Flame, the: The head of the Church of the Silver Flame. See Jaela Daran.

Kennrun: A fort on the Breland border.

Khorvaire: One of the continents of Eberron.

Khyber: 1) The underworld. 2) A mythical dragon, also

known as "The Dragon Below." After killing Siberys, Khyber was imprisoned by Eberron and transformed into the underworld. Khyber is said to have given birth to a host of demons and other unnatural creatures. See *Eberron, Siberys.*

Last War, the: This conflict began in 894 YK with the death of King Jarot ir'Wyrnarn, the last king of Galifar. Following Jarot's death, three of his five children refused to follow the ancient traditions of succession, and the kingdom split. The war lasted over a hundred years, and it took the utter destruction of Cyre to bring the other nations to the negotiating table. No one has admitted defeat, but no one wants to risk being the next victim of the Mourning. The chronicles call the conflict "the Last War," hoping that the bloodshed might have finally slaked humanity's thirst for battle. Only time will tell if this hope is in vain.

"Leth!": Elven for "Now!"

Levritt: A young Knight of the Silver Flame.

lightning rail: A means of transportation by which a coach propelled by an air elemental travels along a rail system of conductor stones, which hold the craft aloft.

Llesh Haruuc: A Darguul hobgoblin leader in the Last War.

Lord of Blades: A warforged leader reputed to be gathering a substantial following of other warforged somewhere in the Mournland.

lupallo: A breed of horse noted for its distinctive russet-colored, shaggy coat.

Majeeda: An ancient elf wizard.

Mardak: The founder and mayor of Mardakine.

Mardakine: A small settlement on the border between Breland and the Mournland.

Mark of Shadow: The dragonmark that holds powers of illusion, deception, and scrying.

Mourning, the: A disaster that occurred on Olarune 20, 994 YK. The origin and precise nature of the Mourning are unknown. On Ollarune 20, gray mists spread across Cyre, and anything caught within the mists was transformed or destroyed. See *the Mournland*.

Mournland, The: A common name for the wasteland left behind in the wake of *the Mourning*. A wall of dead-gray mist surrounds the borders of the land that once was Cyre. Behind this mist, the land has been transformed into something dark and twisted. Most creatures that weren't killed were transformed into horrific monsters. Stories speak of storms of blood, corpses that do not decompose, ghostly soldiers fighting endless battles, and far worse things.

Mror Holds, the: A nation of dwarves and gnomes located in the Ironroot Mountains.

New Cyre: A large town in Breland that began as a refugee settlement but has since grown into a sizeable community.

Norra: A resident of Mardakine and friend of Kandler. She often watches Esprë when Kandler is out.

Nortok: A resident of Mardakine.

Oargev ir'Wynarn: The last surviving son of Cyre's ruling family, who has since become the unofficial leader of the Cyran refugees scattered throughout Khorvaire.

Patelko: A resident of Mardakine.

Point Mountain: The northernmost peak of the Seawall Mountains.

Pradak: A young resident of Mardakine. He is Mardak and Priscinta's son.

Priscinta: A resident of Mardakine. She is Mardak's wife.

Rings of Siberys: A ring of dragonshards that encircles the world high above Eberron's equator.

Rislinto: Mardakine's resident blacksmith.

Rissa: A resident of Mardakine.

Sallah: A Knight of the Silver Flame.

Seawall Mountains: A mountain chain in southern Breland. The Seawall separates Darguun and Zilargo, and many kobolds and goblinoids still lurk in its shadows.

Sharn: Also known as the City of Towers, Sharn is the largest city in Khorvaire.

Shawda: A resident of Mardakine.

Shifter: A humanoid race said to be descended from humans and lycanthropes. Shifters have a feral, bestial appearance and can briefly call on their lycanthropic heritage to draw animalistic characteristics to the fore. While they are most comfortable in natural environs, shifters can be found in most of the major cities of Khorvaire.

Siberys: 1) The ring of stones that circle the world. 2) A mythical dragon, also called "the Dragon Above." Siberys is said to have been destroyed by Khyber. Some believe that the ring of Siberys is the source of all magic.

Silver Flame, the: A powerful spiritual force dedicated to cleansing evil influences from the world. Over the last five hundred years, a powerful church has been established around the Silver Flame.

Sovereign: 1) A silver coin depicting a current or recent monarch. A sovereign is worth ten crowns. 2) One of the deities of the Sovereign Host.

Sovereign Host, the: A pantheistic religion with a strong following across Khorvaire.

Talenta Plains: A vast stretch of grassland to the east of Khorvaire, the Talenta Plains are home to a proud halfling culture. The people of the Talenta Plains live a nomadic lifestyle that has remained more or less unchanged for thousands of years, though over the centuries a number of tribes have left the grasslands to settle in the Five Nations. A wide variety of large reptiles are found in the Talenta Plains, and the halfling warriors are known for their fearsome clawfoot mounts.

Tan Du: A vampire.

Temmah: A dwarf resident of Mardakine, currently serving as one of the deputy justicars.

Te'oma: A changeling.

Thrane: One of the original Five Nations of Galifar, Thrane is the seat of power for the Church of the Silver Flame. During the Last War, the people of Thrane chose to give the church power above that of the throne. Queen Diani ir'Wyrnarn serves as a figurehead, but true power rests in the hands of the church, which is governed by the council of cardinals and Jaela Daeran, the young Keeper of the Flame.

Thunder Sea: The large sea separating Khorvaire from the continent of Xen'drik.

Tira Miron: Founder of the Church of the Silver Flame.

Treaty of Thronehold: The treaty that ended the Last War.

Valenar: A realm of southeastern Khorvaire populated primarily by elves who came to Khorvaire to fight in the Last War and later founded their own nation.

Vathirond: A town in Breland on the border with Thrane, it serves as a watchpost and trading center.

Vol: The Lich Queen, founder of the Blood of Vol.

warforged: A race of humanoid constructs crafted from wood, leather, metal, and stone, and given life and sentience through magic. The warforged were created by House

Cannith, which sought to produce tireless, expendable soldiers capable of adapting to any tactical situation. Cannith developed a wide range of military automatons, but the spark of true sentience eluded them until 965 YK, when Aaren d'Cannith perfected the first of the modern warforged. A warforged soldier is roughly the same shape as an adult male human, though typically slightly taller and heavier. There are many different styles of warforged, each crafted for a specific military function—heavily-armored infantry troops, faster scouts and skirmishers, and many more. While warforged are brought into existence with the knowledge required to fulfill their function, they have the capacity to learn, and with the war coming to a close, many are searching their souls—and questioning whether they have souls—and wondering what place they might have in a world at peace.

Xalt: A warforged artificer.

Zilargo: Located on the southern coast of Khorvaire, Zilargo is the homeland of the gnomes. Known for its vast universities and libraries, Zilargo also possesses considerable mineral wealth in the form of gemstones and Khyber dragonshards. The gnomes themselves are masterful diplomats, shipwrights, and alchemists, renowned for their cunning and inquisitive nature.

FORGOTTEN REALMS®

R.A. Salvatore's
War of the Spider Queen

THE EPIC SAGA OF THE DARK ELVES CONTINUES.

EXTINCTION
Book IV
Lisa Smedman

For even a small group of drow, trust is the rarest commodity of all. When the expedition prepares for a return to the Abyss, what little trust there is crumbles under a rival goddess's hand.

ANNIHILATION
Book V
Philip Athans

Old alliances have been broken, and new bonds have been formed. While some finally embark for the Abyss itself, others stay behind to serve a new mistress—a goddess with plans of her own.

RESURRECTION
Book VI

The Spider Queen has been asleep for a long time, leaving the Underdark to suffer war and ruin. But if she finally returns, will things get better... or worse?

April 2005

The New York Times *best-seller now in paperback!*

CONDEMNATION
Book III
Richard Baker

The search for answers to Lolth's silence uncovers only more complex questions, allowing doubt and frustration to test the boundaries of already tenuous relationships. Sensing the holes in the armor of Menzoberranzan, a new, dangerous threat steps in to test the resolve of the Jewel of the Underdark, and finds it lacking.

Now in paperback!
DISSOLUTION, BOOK I
INSURRECTION, BOOK II